I0787999

THE
POSTHUMAN
TRILOGY

THE POSTHUMAN TRILOGY

MIKAEL SVANSTRÖM

SVANSTRÖM
BOOKS

Table of Contents

THE GOD DRUG
BOOK ONE

"You may wonder why I tell you this, but bear with me. I didn't realize it then, but I had stumbled on something of enormous importance. Something that will redefine mankind. Something that could redefine you."
Adrian - posthuman

A CLASH OF TITANS

"Why are you following me?"

Tom stopped, surprised that Elize had chosen to confront him. He had been lazy, as he suspected she'd known he was following her all along. What piqued his interest was why she had chosen this time to confront him.

Her eyes focused on him for an instant and then returned to gazing into the distance. He knew why – when he was amped up he did the same. The physical aspect of human beings didn't generate enough information to remain interesting for more than a second or two.

"You have 30 seconds. Why are you following me?"

He knew she had already calculated all his answers. He briefly wondered what probability she had assigned the truth.

"I've been hired by PharmaCom to bring you in," he said. "Thought I'd follow you to figure out the best way to do it."

He could see she wasn't surprised. He had just confirmed one of the many possible paths leading to another set of calculated choices.

"You won't stop me now," she said, and turned to walk towards the bank building across the road.

So much for my 30 seconds, Tom thought, and hurried after her.

"Don't do it," he shouted. "He's in there."

She didn't acknowledge the warning. In all likelihood it was the reason she was going there. Tom stopped and watched her walk through traffic as if it didn't exist, fascinated by her fluidity, every movement calculated to perfection. He considered following her, but knew there was little he could do inside the building. He would more than likely be caught in the crossfire. Better to wait outside until one of them reappeared.

Tom had been following her for the past two weeks. This was the third time she had visited what seemed to be a random place to meet Adrian, who he now thought of as the Adversary. He was no closer to understanding what she was doing than when he had started. He had begun to regret taking the job, but didn't have the luxury of declining good-paying jobs. Nowadays, people left digital traces if they so much as sneezed. Most cases could be solved by techs from the comfort of their chairs, so he couldn't be too picky.

Three minutes later an explosion inside the building sent glass flying in a deadly spray. Chunks of reinforced concrete followed, turning the sidewalk into an abattoir. A sudden windfall of green lights had let the heavy traffic gain momentum and it was now hit by the scattershot of metal and stone. Tom watched as death appeared in front of him.

Time slowed down. He knew he was having an episode, but had no way of preventing his mind from going into freefall. Tom sat down on the ground and let it wash over him. The carnage took on a pattern, unfolding like a rose opening up in slow motion. He watched the mathematical precision of the pile-up as it dominoed from ground zero in all directions, metal bending into new shapes far more fascinating than the smooth lines it originally had.

The collective blaring of car horns and alarms brought him back to the reality of the situation. He was glad to see he had only been out for fifteen seconds at most. Since he had quit using IntelEz, this had happened five times. Recently, a so-called friend had sent him a repeating fractal video. He had sat staring at it for two hours until mental exhaustion had blurred his vision enough for him to snap out of it.

No one could have survived the blast, not even Elize, but he still wanted to make sure. He climbed over the hood of a car and jumped to another one, when the shockwave from a second explosion left him sprawled on the ground. It was followed by a groan from the building itself as the supporting structure bent out of shape.

He didn't care. Once he had started getting episodes, he knew he didn't have long and he had to see this to the end. He stood up and continued towards the building, glass crunching under his shoes. He entered the bank through the gaping hole that had been a glassed-in entry hall. Another groan from the building was followed by debris falling from the floors above. A middle-aged woman walked past him in a daze. She had a large cut across her face, but otherwise looked uninjured. It gave him some hope to see someone alive, but he knew the two people he was looking for would have been close to ground zero.

The entrance led to a high-ceilinged open area. The walls were cracked, exposing the support structure. Steel beams buckled out like giant spider legs, threatening to give way at any moment. Two floors above had caved into the middle of the open area, creating a mountain of unstable debris. The blast had originated further inside the building. To get there, Tom had no choice but to brave the precarious structure. He was halfway up when he heard noises on the other side and felt movement in the rubble he was standing on. Someone trying to scale the structure on the other side had upset its internal balance. Tom stood still, willing the large pieces of masonry above him to fall inwards. It started shifting before an avalanche of debris fell away from him and buried whoever had been there. It was a miracle he was still standing.

Tom jumped from island to island until he reached the other side. He guessed this was the secure area next to where customers came in to visit the bank. Two corridors led to the back of the bank. Metal from the reinforced walls was twisted outwards from

the blast. This must have been where the blast originated. Tom looked into the gaping hole and to his surprise saw movement. A shape was making its way through the scorched remains of the metal boxes in the vault. He ducked down and watched as the shape came into the light.

The man was a mess – blackened and bloodied, walking with a limp and cradling one of his arms. The most disturbing aspect of the man was not his appearance. It was the coughing sound that Tom could only translate as laughter. He knew who it was, even with the disfiguring wounds and raw, hairless scalp. Adrian rivalled any A-list celebrity in publicity, even if he had been out of the press lately. He had been the poster boy for the Drug for over a year until the long-term side effects made it illegal.

"Help me," Adrian commanded, staring at the place where Tom huddled. Tom stood up and nodded towards Adrian, who repeated his command. Tom hesitated – Elize might still be in there. If Adrian was alive perhaps she was too.

"You came for her," Adrian said, a statement of fact, not a question. "She is dead. I need your help. You will help me."

"You survived," Tom said.

"I came prepared."

Tom hesitated. He still wanted to confirm Elize's death with his own eyes.

"Her body is in there," Adrian said. "Just hurry. I will not make it out of here on my own before the police arrive and your employer wouldn't like it if you missed an opportunity to bring me in."

Tom shook his head and made his way to the blackened metal jaw, barely able to avoid the ragged edges. He had no idea how Adrian knew anything about his employer, but he was right. His contract stated quite clearly that either Adrian or Elize was an acceptable target. Tom didn't have time to join the dots. Adrian had been right about the timing too. Soon there would be police and fire brigades swarming the place.

He made his way through the corridor. The blast, or at least one of them, had originated in the vault, funnelling out through the corridor into the main hall. The explosion had shredded the metal storage boxes and vaporised most of their contents. The ceiling was gone, opening a gash in the building four levels high. Not even the enormous vault door had withstood the blast. It had been ripped from its hinges and was lodged halfway into the opposite wall. A charred body lay in the middle of the corridor, just outside the vault. It was still relatively intact, which seemed impossible considering the force of the explosion. Debris fell from the floors above, hitting the floor around him. He didn't have time to check for vital signs. She was most surely dead. He took a sample from the body with a penknife and put it in a plastic ziplock bag.

"We have to go," Adrian yelled, followed by coughing attack.

Tom turned to leave and for the briefest of moments thought he saw movement. He turned and stared at the body, willing it to move again, before convincing himself he was mistaken. A chair and then a desk crashed to the floor next to him, and he knew it was time to leave.

"Now!"

Tom hurried back down the corridor and caught up with Adrian, who was making his way slowly across the large hall. Police had already arrived outside and officers were busy closing off the area. Tom picked Adrian up and carried him out of the building. A police officer greeted them outside.

"Is he ok? Are you ok?"

"I'm fine," Adrian said and smiled. "Help the others. I'm fine with my friend here."

"Any more live ones?" he asked, staring at the devastation.

"On the upper floors perhaps," Tom said.

"Ambulances are on the way. You can wait over there." He indicated an area close to the intersection. They both watched the police officer hurry off. Tom headed in the general direction the officer had indicated, but as soon as no one was watching, he hurried down a side street.

"Put me down," Adrian said. He already seemed more mobile than before, his breathing no longer laboured.

"No, you're coming with me."

Adrian just nodded, and Tom carried him another block. He was aiming for his car parked a few blocks away.

"You took a sample of her body," Adrian said. "It won't do you any good."

"I've got you. I don't need a sample."

"When did you give it up?"

Tom knew what he referred to, even if he hadn't said it.

"A month ago."

"Do you have episodes?"

Tom didn't answer. He didn't have to. He was sure Adrian already knew the answer.

"I wish you'd put me down," Adrian said finally.

Tom, tired from carrying Adrian, complied. A blinding flash and Tom was suddenly weightless, lifting at first, and then falling forward in a heap. Engulfing pain and darkness followed.

CHAPTER TWO

THE DRUG

Shapes emerged as light patches against dark shades. Patterns superimposed on the shapes slowly gained coherence. With consciousness came pulsating flashes of pain, emanating from the base of his skull. He had been struck in the back of the head with some kind of blunt weapon. He had no idea how long he'd been out.

Tom blinked and felt alive for the first time since he'd come off the Drug. The pain sliced through the sluggishness of thought and brought clarity. He knew what the Drug did. Once the long-term side effects became apparent, little else was seen as newsworthy. It hyper-charged your capacity for processing data and information – a wonder drug, if there ever was one. The brain immediately responded by allowing more and more input, regardless of source. Once the brain had gotten used to the Drug after years of use, the input level remained, whilst the brain efficiency deteriorated. Pain helped limit the input momentarily.

Tom looked around and was surprised to see Adrian being helped into a black car by two men further down the street. He had no idea who they were. Most likely a rival drug company or a government agency.

He hurried to the street whilst hailing a rent-a-car on his Omni Device. A small electric Tesla A-class stopped almost immediately. Tom loaded a hack into the drive computer, assigned Adrian's car as the lead and let the Assisted Driver Network do its job.

He pulled out a first aid kit from the glove compartment and was immediately informed by the car that the usage would be charged to his account. He accepted and started dabbing the back of his head with an alcowipe. There was hardly any blood. Whoever had struck him had done an expert job – exactly the right amount of force at the precise location to knock him out without causing permanent damage. Or he'd just been lucky.

They entered a downtown area with very little traffic. Tom knew where they were. This was a dead zone. All major cities had areas where they kept people who had deteriorated into a form of autism from the Drug. They were still capable of taking care of their most basic needs, but hardly anything else. Tom knew he had only another couple of years, probably less, before he too would end up here.

A few minutes later the black car stopped. Tom immediately changed the end destination in the drive computer to half a block further down the street, hoping it would be enough to avoid suspicion. He watched as the two men helped Adrian to the front door of a five-story apartment building. Not even with his newfound clarity could Tom make sense of the situation. The two men didn't look like operatives. Even if they were, since when did they operate out of a dead zone? His initial plan had been to follow them into the building, but he decided against it. If it really was a safe house, he could be watched already. He got out of the car and sent it to a couple of programmed stops around the city to muddle up the digital prints it left. He knew he had a few tails and he didn't want them to focus on this address.

Across the street he found a little alleyway where he could remain relatively hidden whilst keeping an eye on the building. He settled in, expecting a long wait, when he saw movement in one of the windows and someone pulling the curtains shut. It could be coincidence, of course, but he didn't think so. He watched for another couple of hours without seeing any movement in the windows, not that he had expected any. A deadhead would never look out the window for fear of the information overload it would cause.

The events of the last few hours replayed in his mind. One thing in particular that kept cropping up was Elize's body. He replayed the moment in his mind when he thought it had moved. With repetition came certainty. It had moved. She was alive. He knew he might still be mistaken, but even if she were dead, her body was hot property. If he could secure it, he'd have bargaining capital.

He stopped one of the food administrators, a young woman with bio-jewels implanted in a tribal pattern under the skin along her cheek, and offered to pay her double, in cash, if she hailed and pre-paid a car from her account. He made sure the car would drop him off at a train station away from his apartment so no one would connect him to this place. He even loaded a fake id tag in his Omni so the train ride back to his apartment laid a different digital trail.

His efforts to keep a low profile didn't matter in the end. A corporate-issue, H-cell Mercedes was parked right outside his apartment block. He knew Mr. Astin would be inside with his two bio-enhanced thugs. He also knew there was no point in running. Mr. Astin was his contact for the current contract after all.

As he approached, the car door opened. Maybe it was the pain that still pulsated in the back of his head making him see more clearly, but suddenly he didn't feel like sharing anything of the recent events. Although he had only spoken briefly to Adrian and Elize, he now felt he was playing a small part in their destiny. Until he worked out exactly what that was, he didn't want to give away too much. He was almost certain he was the only one who knew the details of what had happened, and he didn't want to share that information. Not yet.

One of the well-dressed thugs stepped out. His immaculate dark suit was designed to hide his bulk, but it was only partially successful. It was the kind of size you could only get if you spent hours in the gym every day, or if you had help from fat-burning, muscle-building drugs. Tom was still amused by the fact that after the Drug became readily available, humankind didn't immediately turn to solving world hunger, pollution or curing diseases. Their first priority was to make themselves prettier, stronger and longer living, and the early major developments were in cosmetics and body enhancements. It was all a moot point now, anyway. The Golden Age created by the Drug was over in less than a decade.

Mr. Astin appeared. If his bodyguards were prime specimens, he was anything but. It was as if he'd ended up just below average in all possible aspects. A little bit on the short side, slightly overweight, with a premature receding hairline and a voice pitched just slightly too high.

"Walk with me," he said, and immediately walked off down the street trailed by the two bodyguards.

Tom was tired and annoyed. He despised everything about Mr. Astin and had to supress an urge to ignore him completely. Instead, he hurried to catch up.

"Remind me. Why did I hire you?"

Sam sighed. Mr. Astin had asked him this same question many times before. It was some kind of power play to put people in their places.

"You hired me to track down one of the anomalies."

He used the word anomaly even though the common term used to describe Adrian and Elize was posthuman. He knew his employer preferred anomaly – it made them a mistake, something that wasn't natural instead of something beyond human.

"And?"

"And to either bring them in or inform you about their whereabouts."

Mr. Astin nodded to himself. "Let's get back to that later. I need to know what happened today."

"I managed to locate Elize again this morning and followed her. She and Adrian caught up again. It seems they're taking turns setting traps for each other. I don't know what triggered the two explosions, but my guess is that Adrian set them off on purpose. I was outside the building at the time and lost track of them after that."

"Do you know why they are fighting?"

"Who knows why they do anything," Tom said, but a glance at Mr. Astin was enough to know that answer wouldn't fly. "I think it's a game. They're playing a high-stakes version of tag for fun. Who knows, next time they might be throwing black holes at each other."

"So you are saying the two smartest people in the world spend all their time trying to kill each other for kicks?"

"That's what it looks like, yes."

"That's what it looks like," Mr. Astin repeated with a grimace, as if to try out the words himself and not liking the taste.

They walked another block in silence.

"Where did you go after the explosion?" Mr. Astin said suddenly.

"I saw an operative outside the bank and decided to follow him," Tom said, knowing they tracked his car through the Assisted Driver Network. "I thought he might have picked up a trace. Didn't seem to be the case though."

"And now you are walking back to your apartment."

"I like my privacy," Tom said and shrugged.

Mr. Astin stopped and motioned for the two thugs to come up next to him. Tom knew he had yet again gone too far. He took a deep breath and turned to Mr. Astin, who looked like a dwarf next to his hired ogre muscle. He had to supress an urge not to smile.

"I don't know who is following me or how they're doing it. I'm not paid to be easy to track. I'm hired to deliver results and I believe I've done that. I don't want those results to be going to the competition."

Mr. Astin gave him a long look. Tom knew he was deciding what to do. Tom was hiding something and he surely knew that, but was it worth trying to extract it? He was betting on still being seen as useful. As long as that was the case, he had some wiggle room.

"Here's the thing. The information you provide us is useless. We're nowhere closer to understanding what they do or what they are planning. This latest stunt means the government has no choice but to act. They'll pick both of them up as soon as they can. So we have to move first."

He nodded towards one of the bodyguards who handed Tom a small stun gun.

"I'm not expecting you to bring them in, but if you could locate either of them again, contact me immediately and we'll take it from there. I no longer care what they do or why they do it. We can work that out once we've secured one of them."

"I don't think it will be that easy, not judging from today," Tom said, ignored the gun.

"Let me worry about that. Use this if you have to."

Tom had seen bulkier versions of the stun gun before. It sprayed a weblike stream of conductive fibres and sent an electric pulse through it. Even someone who could hardly aim was still able to take down multiple attackers with this thing. It spoke volumes that Mr. Astin thought this was the best weapon to equip him with. It was the weapon of choice for someone who couldn't use a weapon that required any skill.

"We're assuming their physical characteristics are still the same as ours, so it should do the trick."

They were almost back at the car when Mr. Astin stopped and reached out his hand.

"If I find you have kept anything from me, however small, you'll join the deadheads sooner than you think."

"A pleasure as always," Tom said and smiled, deliberately not shaking his hand.

"As always," Mr. Astin repeated.

Tom watched the three men leave and hurried to his apartment. If Mr. Astin had to come here to find out what was going on, no one else knew anything either. No one would know it was Elize's body until they tried to identify the victims of the blast, so if he was lucky he'd have tonight to secure it.

CHAPTER THREE

MORGUE ATTACK

Tom still had access to some of the police systems, courtesy of old friendships that remained after he left the force. He checked them now, but could find no trace of Elize's body logged anywhere. Most bodies were identified through their Omni implants or through other serialised body implants.

Five bodies were unidentified from inside the blast radius – two male, one female and two unknowns. From what he had seen, she was more than likely one of the unknowns. The injuries she had sustained were strange. An explosion should have ripped her apart. Instead her body had been whole, but scarred and burned. He hadn't questioned it because Adrian's injuries had been similar but less severe. The little clothing that had survived had fused with her body. He was confident he'd find her if only he could check the bodies.

All bodies were at the morgue. If he wanted more information about their location, he'd have to hack the system holding the data from the morgue, and it was far beyond his skill level. He could use basic pre-built tools and agents, but hacking a system or data source required much more than that.

He opened a two-way feed to bZane, a low-rent hacker he'd used a few other times. He only knew him by his feed id, but as long as he delivered, Tom didn't care.

"Devine. The PI man. You still in business?"

"I need some help. I need to locate a few bodies in the morgue."

"Didn't take you for a necro-lover."

"I need to know where they are."

"Send me their id tags and I'll get to it."

"No id tags. They're unidentified."

"How could they ..." he started, then stopped. "So what do you know?"

"Female, badly burned, from the downtown explosion today."

The feed went quiet. bZane overrode the visual feed with a doctored Roadrunner cartoon, where Wiley Coyote plans always worked. The Roadrunner met its demise many times over the course of the silence.

"Nasty accident. Terrorists?"

"Possibly. Can you do it?"

"Give me an hour."

Tom packed together a small infiltration kit, consisting mainly of surveillance and lock-hacking equipment. He couldn't afford to have bZane helping more than this, so he had to do it the old-fashioned way.

-=:=-

An hour later Tom stood outside the morgue, studying the entrance. A nurse and at least one security guard always occupied the front desk, making it nearly impossible as an entryway. Any silent alarms raised would come from there, so as a precaution he decided to place an audio feed. He didn't have time for anything fancy. Instead he walked into the reception with an unsteady swagger.

"I want to see my Uncle Harry!" he said, slurring his speech and stumbling as he reached the desk. He attached a small transmitter under the desk.

"Does he work here?" the nurse behind the desk asked. She was in her twenties, with dark hair and black make-up; reprogrammable tattoos snaked up her arms. She glanced at one of the guards with an almost imperceptible shake of her head.

"Of course not! He died yesterday."

"Sorry, but that won't happen. I can direct you to a good medium though."

"I don't care about that! He borrowed my nice watch! He was wearing it when he died. I want it back."

Tom slammed his hand in the desk and as he did, attached a clear microphone sticker on the desk right in front of the nurse. She laughed nervously and nodded to the guard.

"Yeah, good luck with that. His effects will be released together with the body. Talk to the funeral parlour."

The guards approached and grabbed him by the arm.

"I'm sorry, officer," Tom said and patted him on the shoulder, again attaching a sticker. "It was a really nice watch. Harry was an ass though."

The guard led him out of the building and left him with a detailed explanation of what would happen to him if he tried to re-enter. As soon as the guard left, Tom routed the sound through his Omni to test the sound quality from the microphones.

"Who wears watches anymore, anyway?" he heard the guard say.

The nurse at the front desk laughed in response.

It worked perfectly. Now he needed to find another way in. There would be roof access and some kind of back door. He checked the back door first and was lucky – it was an old design based on Near Field Communication. Lucky he preferred the old Omni models that still had much of the old functionality of the Smart phones they had replaced. It could act as the identity and a sensor would read its id tag.

Tom attached a key logger to the door and waited. Thirty minutes later a middle-aged man in a hurry exited the morgue and entered a waiting car. Tom checked the contents of the key logger. He had a full copy of the id tag. He loaded it into a clean Omni and as he approached the door there was an audible click. He had expected it to work, but still felt a rush from the success.

He knew he was woefully unprepared for this break-in and that it would take a lot of luck for it to succeed.

"The devil loves a gambling man," he said to himself, as he pulled the door open and strode in with confidence. He had only a vague idea of where he was heading, but knew his best bet was to act as if he knew where he was going. bZane had had the bodies put in a cool room in the basement, so he headed for the stairs. He hoped they hadn't started an autopsy, but it was questionable if they would do one anyway as the cause of death was so obvious.

A male nurse came walking his way. Tom caught his eye, nodded and kept walking.

"Good evening," Tom heard in his earpiece from the reception area. "I'm here to assess the bodies that came in from the explosion earlier today."

Tom had hoped for some more time, but if he was lucky this was just a fishing expedition. They could have noticed a change in data patterns around Elize online and were now checking all possible avenues.

"Sign here and here," the receptionist replied.

Tom ran the rest of the way down the stairs.

"Come with me," the first voice said.

Tom sighed. Someone was coming and on top of that had backup. He kept running, passing a nurse on the way. A few seconds later he heard the receptionist respond to a report about a possible intruder in the basement area. She asked the guards to check it out.

He ran into the cool room. It was empty, apart from a few wheeled stretchers used to cart bodies. The main wall was laid out like the boxes of a game TV show – door after door, each hiding a gruesome prize.

He had three locker numbers from bZane. He located the first one and pulled it open. The body was only a torso. He quickly closed it and went to the next one. It looked like her, or at least as close as he could tell. He checked the finger he had taken the sample from and to his surprise there was fresh healthy skin in its place. Part of her body had regenerated. She was definitely alive.

He doubted he'd be able to wheel her to safety in the little time he had. He pulled her out of the box onto one of the stretchers and covered her with a grey plastic sheet. He took the tag from her and swapped it for one in a nearby locker. He pushed the cart to the side of the room, creating a little hiding space for himself between the wall and the sheet hanging down the side of the cart.

Tom watched from his hiding space as the door opened and a man in an impeccable suit appeared with two goons following behind. They looked as if they were clones of Mr. Astin's bodyguards. PharmaCom were obviously chasing down any lead he happened to leave in his wake. The male nurse Tom had seen in the corridor above came after them.

"Why weren't the bodies identified?"

"Some of the bodies didn't have implants and they were so badly burnt it wasn't possible to id them in any other way. We are still following up with family for some of the people whose Omni- feeds were cut as a result of the explosion."

He opened three of the doors as he spoke, but found only two bodies.

"That's strange. There should be one more here."

"How about that one over there?"

Tom could only see the feet and ankles of the well-dressed man, but knew he was pointing his way. Tom pulled out the fibre Taser and waited. With a bit of luck he could take them all out.

"Let me check," the nurse said.

Tom could see his feet approaching, and swore to himself. He needed them all pretty close to each other to take them out at the same time. He doubted he'd get a second try once the bodyguards had seen him.

Tom held his breath as the nurse scanned the id tag. If he pulled the cover away even a little bit it would be all over.

"Ah, I see what's happened." The nurse opened the locker next to the empty one. "Someone must have put it in the wrong locker."

"She's not here," the well-dressed man said, frustration evident in his voice. "Let's go."

As they turned to leave, a guard opened the door from the outside. "We had a report of a possible grave robber. Have you seen anyone?"

"Seriously?" the male nurse frowned. "I made the report."

"Sorry, I'll check the rest of the area," said the guard, and left.

"Grave robber?" the well-dressed man asked.

"From time to time we get people trying to steal bodies."

"I see. We will see ourselves out."

"Take the elevator to the ground floor, turn left. Keep going and turn right. There are signs for reception."

The three men left the room.

The nurse moved the third body to the locker next to the other two bodies, then went to get the one Tom was hiding behind. Tom stood up when he was a few meters away.

"Who are you?" the nurse said, and took a step back.

"Sorry about this."

Tom pushed the trigger and a fine web of fibres attached to the nurse's upper body. A second later he convulsed as the electrical current surged through him. He fell where he stood, unconscious.

Tom immediately pushed the cart with the body out of the room and into the corridor. He didn't have long, minutes, maybe only seconds.

He tried to recall the layout of the morgue, but could only remember parts of it. The loading dock was at the back of the building, so he aimed in that general direction. He hailed a larger car to the location and immediately got a reject message. He shook his head.

He hadn't considered he'd need special permission to hail a car to this location. He changed it to the front and received an acknowledgement. He ran up the low incline ramp leading to the back of the building.

"At this location?" The well-dressed man's voice came through his earpiece. "We didn't see him here, but there was a report of an intruder."

Tom swore again. The nurse could wake up any second and now PharmaCom knew he was here too. He knew they'd still track him when they could, but he was surprised at how quickly they determined his location. He had been very careful in hiding his online tracks.

He pushed the cart through the door and looked around. The car he had ordered had an estimated arrival time of four minutes. It would be too late. He needed to get out of here now. Two transport vans stood parked at the other end of the parking lot. He pushed the cart towards them. It unlocked as he reached out his hand for the back door. Tom stopped for a second, but remembered the id tag he had loaded into his Omni. It was still active and the van must have read it as he approached.

He pushed Elize's body into the van and closed the back door. He heard the back door from the morgue open. Tom didn't even look back to see who it was. He jumped into the car and told it to drive to the nearest hospital. He watched the well-dressed man and his two goons in the side mirror. They would soon have a trace on the van and its destination. Tom swore. He couldn't really afford any more of bZane's help, but he didn't have a choice. He opened a two-way feed to the hacker.

"Devine, how did it go?" He paused for a few seconds. "Not very good, I can see. You've got a trace on the car you're in."

"Can you hide where I'm going?"

"I can make it look like you are still going to the Packer Memorial Hospital, sure, but it'll cost you."

"I'll pay."

"It won't keep them away for long. I was bored waiting for you to screw things up, so checked you out. They are tracking everything you do."

"Yeah, I know, but at the moment I just want to survive the next hour or two."

"At least change the id tag in your Omni."

"I have!"

"To a new one. They know about this one."

"Ok."

"You get this one for free. You don't have enough funds anyway. I checked your bank account. I'll do this one for you as a favour, but next time I expect full payment."

Tom loaded a new id tag in his Omni, sat back and directed the car to a new destination.

CHAPTER FOUR

A COLLABORATOR

Dr Tak ran one of the many clinics promising to stop the deterioration of the brain that the Drug caused in its later stages. Tom knew there was hardly any proof it helped; nevertheless, he had attended the clinic once a week for over a year. It focused on sensory-deprivation therapy, which, even if it didn't work, was the only time Tom felt he had full control over his wayward mind.

He had done a background check on Dr Tak before he started visiting the clinic. Until a few years ago, he had been a medical doctor, but official records just showed that he had stopped practicing. Tom's other channels showed a different story. He had caused the death of a number of deadheads as the result of experiments to cure them. This had been in the early days when the Drug was still legal and people still cared about what happened to deadheads, especially children of the wealthy.

Tom had helped him a few times with tracking down non-paying clients. He had no idea what to do with the body or even how to confirm whether it was alive or not. He hoped Dr Tak could help him.

Tom opened an encrypted, voice-only feed and selected Dr Tak's private Id tag.

"I didn't think we had any outstanding business," Dr Tak said, clearly irritated. Tom was one poorly chosen answer away from being disconnected.

"I need your help."

"In the middle of the night?"

"Yes."

"Go on."

"I have the body of Elize, the second posthuman."

"The body?" He was interested now. "She's dead?"

"I don't know. I can't tell."

"Wait."

The feed went quiet. It was possible Dr Tak would sell him out, but he had to take that chance. There was no one else he knew who could help, and he knew Dr Tak was still interested in the Drug and how to cure it.

"Take it to this address," Dr Tak said, and gave an address on the northern outskirts of the city.

Tom told the drive computer to alert him as soon as manual driving was permitted and assigned a destination many kilometres away from the address he was given. He sat back and watched as the night city landscape unfolded in front of him. It was the first time he felt he could relax enough to take stock of the situation. He had been acting on impulse ever since the explosion and now he knew he'd be a hunted man. Someone would soon put together the pieces and it would be an all-out manhunt. The only possible way he could survive it was to go completely off-grid, but he didn't want to do that. It didn't take a lot of self-examination to determine the cause of the impulses.

This was his last opportunity to be part of something bigger, something that mattered. Adrian and Elize represented the future of humankind. They needed to be free to create a new world from the ashes of this one. If he could be a small part of making that happen before he faded away, his life would have had meaning.

"Manual control allowed," the drive computer advised. "Please be aware manual driving is the cause of 95% of all traffic accidents. Drive carefully."

Tom switched over. He knew this wouldn't help much. The car was still tracked by the network, but at least he didn't have to give a location to the drive computer. He stopped a few blocks away, unloaded the body and instructed the car to follow the highway that circled the city and make stops every few kilometres.

He carried the body to the destination. At first he thought he had come to the wrong address. A gap between two houses opened onto a small children's playground. It was one of those flukes of house numbering where a playground replaced a house, which meant it had its own street address.

A single streetlight created a cone of light in the centre of the playground, with everything else dimming into darkness. A young man was sitting on one of the swings, motionless. Like most people under 25, he had a completely integrated Omni, and it was obvious he was doing something with it. From the occasional twitches in his fingers, Tom guessed he was playing a game. Tom approached him slowly, wondering if he'd come to the right place. As he got closer, he no longer had any doubts. The boy was of Asian descent and the spitting image of his father. He wore baggy pants and a black hoodie with a swirl pattern on the front – expensive clothes designed to imitate what actual street kids wore. Tom hated the pretence.

As the more integrated systems almost completely disconnected you from what was going on around you, the Omni allowed greetings that interrupted the current activity. Tom never had much time for such niceties. He walked up to the pretend gangster and tapped him on the forehead. The young man jolted backwards, tangled up in the swing and fell in a heap.

His eyes regained focus as he disconnected from the game. He stared at Tom.

"Don't do that! Never heard of greets?"

"Never saw the point," Tom said with a grin. "Where's your dad?"

The young man reached out his hand and Tom helped him off the ground.

"Is that her?" he asked, ogling the wrapped body as he readjusted his clothing.

"It's Elize, yes. Where's your dad?"

"I'm TikTak," the young man said and held out his hand. An accompanying ping from Tom's Omni told him he had just received a feed greeting.

Tom frowned. He had noticed how young people nowadays used their feed ids instead of their real names even when off line.

"Cute," Tom said. "I'm Rainbow Shitting Unicorn. Now where's your dad?"

"I'll get our ride now," he said, and tuned out for a few seconds. "It is on its way."

TikTak kept staring at the body, but Tom ignored any of his attempts to strike up a conversation. He saw no reason to give away more than he had to, especially not to a kid he'd never see again.

A car drove up. It was one of the generic electric City Cars you rented by the hour.

"Don't worry," TikTak said. "I'll pay through an anonymizer payment gateway."

Tom shrugged. It wouldn't make much of a difference to the people who would be after him soon, but it bought time. TikTak helped put the body into the backseat and then set the end destination.

"Be seeing you, Rainbow Shitting Unicorn," TikTak said, and closed the car door.

The City Car drove back into the city and made a few stops before he came to familiar surroundings. The last stop was at the back of Dr Tak's clinic, where the doctor himself was waiting. He was pacing back and forth.

"How long do we have?" Dr Tak asked as soon as Tom opened the car door.

Tom appreciated his question. It meant he knew what was at stake.

"I'd say a couple of days, not more."

"Better get on with it then."

A few minutes later, Elize's body lay on a hospital bed. Dr Tak immediately began his investigation.

"Did you say she was in the centre of the explosion?"

Tom nodded.

"That is not consistent with her injuries. If she'd been in an explosion of the kind reported on the feed, all we'd need is a bucket and mop. These injuries aren't from heat. It looks more like acid burns. I can't say whether she has any internal injuries. I don't really have the equipment for it. Let's see."

He traced his hands over her body, stopping here and there to investigate further.

"A few broken bones, but that's about it. She's even missing a finger, but a blast that size would have literally torn her to pieces. I can't see anything to suggest she was anywhere near the explosion, so is there something you're not telling me?"

"That is all I know. This is what she looked like when I saw here there. Is she alive?"

"Yes, of sorts. She's in suspended animation."

Tom frowned. He had heard about breakthroughs in this area, but it still required a medical team to perform.

"Her blood has turned into ... something else. I will need to run tests to determine what it is, but my guess is her body has entered it as a response to severe shock. Whatever happened in there wasn't an explosion."

"I was there. It was an explosion."

Dr Tak stood back and watched the body.

"What about the brain?" Tom asked.

"It has shut down completely."

"So what now?"

"What do you mean?"

"What do we do with it?"

"Haven't you heard a word I've said?"

"Her brain has shut down. Her body is in suspended animation. I heard, but what do we do with the body?"

"We fix it," Dr Tak said.

This wasn't the person Tom had come to know. Dr Tak had been restrained and formal. Now he was energetic, stimulated by the mystery. Tom liked this person much better.

"Her body turned off because of the shock of whatever happened to her in that explosion," he continued. "If we treat her injuries, my guess is she'll ..."

"Turn back on?" Tom said.

"Isn't she beautiful?" Dr Tak said suddenly.

Tom looked at the burned body and then at Dr Tak. He had never thought of her as beautiful, toasted or otherwise. She had been quite plain-looking.

"Her body has created new defence mechanisms," Dr Tak continued. "She is a beautiful mystery."

"If you say so," Tom said finally. "Can you help her?"

"Of course I will help her. She will get the best care I can give her."

Dr Tak started immediately, doing a more thorough examination and starting to patch up the body. Tom watched for about ten minutes, but soon felt weariness creep over him.

"Thanks," Tom said and yawned. "I owe you."

Dr Tak just waved his hand dismissively.

"I will let you know how things are going via my son. It's better we don't meet again, I think."

Tom left the clinic and headed for home. He didn't know if he'd done the right thing, but he didn't really have many choices. He didn't know anyone else with any real medical experience. And he trusted Dr Tak, or at least he found him more trustworthy than most other people he knew. It would have to do, even if Tom knew this was only a very temporary solution.

He passed out on top of the bed fully clothed.

CHAPTER FIVE
ESCAPE

11:02am: Omni alerted of an incoming private feed.

11:15am: It alerted again.

11:22am: Tom woke up and rejected whoever was trying to reach him. He fell asleep, damning himself for not blocking it completely. Whatever it was could wait another hour or two.

Tom finally decided that the day began at 11:53am and had a breakfast of an approximation of coffee and a Vegemite sandwich. He wished he had real coffee, but hadn't been able to afford it since the introduction of the resource tax. Water-efficient alternatives had become the norm once the true cost of water was calculated into the price of everyday items.

Today he had a plan. He was ahead of everyone else, but it was unlikely to last long. If they even suspected he had Elize's body, they'd be coming with guns blazing. He had known there would be no going back from this as soon as he withheld information from Mr Astin – there were no second chances with people like him. The only way to stay alive was to stay ahead, and make sure you had something to bargain with when they caught up with you. His next step had to be to track down Adrian, or at least find out who had him. That information by itself was likely to keep him alive in the short term. The only solid lead he had was the apartment in the dead zone, so it was his first destination.

Thirty minutes later he sat on a train, his head surprisingly clear. It was as if having a purpose enabled his brain to function better. It made sense – focus allowed his frizzled-out brain to divert all its faculties to this singular task.

He pulled out his Omni and did a cursory check of the apartments across the street from his target. He wasn't too worried about finding something suitable. It was a dead zone, after all. When he arrived at his destination, he had four possible alternatives based on registered deadheads who were still signed on as owners of apartments.

He entered the block and knocked on the door of the first apartment. According to the registration details, a Lars Sorensen in his mid-fifties was the only occupant. He knocked again, analysing the lock as he waited. It was a proximity lock with fingerprint reader. It would only unlock if the lock knew your Omni and fingerprint pair. He didn't have anything to hack it quickly, even knowing they always had overrides that could be exploited. He knocked again and was just about to leave when the door opened, security chain still in place.

"Food distribution?" a female voice asked, her face only partially visible through the gap. She was young, no more than sixteen, he guessed.

"No, apartment audit," Tom said and flashed a long since expired police identity card. "According to our records a Lars Sorensen lives here. Who are you?"

Tom knew exactly who she was. She was a squatter. She'd moved in with Lars and ate most of his government-funded food. She'd make sure to be out of there during the infrequent visits from his family who'd be wondering why he was so slim, but probably secretly hoped he'd die and let them get on with life.

"I'm his daughter Evelyn," she replied immediately. "I'm just here visiting."

Tom made a show of checking his Omni and then nodded.

"Everything seems to be in order. Thank you."

She closed the door and he headed off for the next candidate. This time there was no reply. He was lucky. It was an old-fashioned lock, without any secondary identification. A self-configuring smart key would be enough to gain entry.

Less than five seconds later it had analysed the lock and moulded itself to the required shape. He turned the smart key, opened the door and stepped in. It was a three-bedroom apartment and it took him a little while to find the only occupant, a thirty-something woman who had crawled under a bed and was lying there in foetal position. She didn't acknowledge him so he closed the bedroom door.

The kitchen had a window facing the apartment block across the street. He pushed the kitchen table flush against the wall with the window and settled in. He knew he had a long wait. It might be days before anything happened. It didn't matter. There was plenty to do in the meantime. He pulled out his Omni and started checking the video cameras in the neighbourhood that he could access. A few were public and some had only minor security, which was easily hacked by software Tom had kept when he left the police force. To his surprise, none of the feeds was directed towards the apartment block. As he studied the video feeds from the cameras, he became convinced they had been moved or reprogrammed. It was just a bit too convenient that they all stopped just short of the door and the street outside. Apart from the frustration of having to set up his own camera, that didn't tell him much. Any organisation, government or private, could easily get that done, especially in a dead zone. He pulled out a small disposable video camera and set it up to take a continuous feed, two images a second.

Further research uncovered little. Most of the apartments in the building were government-owned, which wasn't surprising. Ten were privately owned and two were owned by small companies. This lead to the uncomfortable conclusion that he was more than likely up against some kind of government agency.

-=:=-

By evening, he had nothing but suspicions. Food administration employees had come and gone, which didn't confirm anything. He was just about to pack it in for the night when there was a knock on the door.

"Rainbow Shitting Unicorn, I know you are in there."

Tom opened the door, surprised to see TikTak standing there.

"How did you find me?"

TikTak ignored his question and stepped into the room, making sure to close the door and lock it.

"I have a message from my father. He says she is very much alive again, but there are no higher brain functions at this point."

The words came out too fast, as if the statement was just a formality before the real business began.

"That's great news. You tracked me down to tell me that?"

"No. I can't reach him any longer. He went offline over an hour ago."

"That's not necessarily ..."

"He never goes offline. Ever. I don't even think he knows how. Something's happened."

He had hoped for a few more days before they discovered Elize, but he had obviously been wrong. Dr Tak may just have something wrong with his connection, but it was unlikely. No one went offline any longer. The hassle it caused wasn't worth it. Tom couldn't afford to ignore this. Elize was his trump card. If he lost her he wouldn't survive beyond a few days. He needed something more. Tom packed his equipment and headed for the door.

"Are we going to get my father?"

"*We* are not doing anything," Tom said as he was running down the stairs with TikTak in hot pursuit. "How did you find me, by the way?"

"I put a tracker on you when we met yesterday."

"A tracker?"

"Yeah. I just added to the collection. You've got at least five more on you."

Tom nodded. He hadn't even considered trackers. It was so easy to track people through other means that putting a physical tag on someone just wasn't worth the effort. It appeared all his attempts trying to cover his tracks had earned him the dubious honour of getting special treatment.

"We need to get to my father's clinic," TikTak insisted.

"You do that," Tom said, as he hurried across the street. "I've got other things to do."

He didn't want to be too harsh with the boy, but at the same time he did have more important things to do and the last thing he wanted was a tagalong. He tried to work through the options for what could have happened to Dr Tak and Elize's body, but his brain again came up wanting. If he'd been on the Drug, he would just have formulated the question in his mind, which would generate a map of all relevant alternatives and the likelihood that they'd occur. As it was now, it would have to wait.

He tried the door to the building – it was open. He ran up three sets of stairs and down the hall. He'd already determined the number of steps needed to reach the apartment he had discovered the night before. As he got closer he could translate it to an actual apartment number. According to the register, one of the smaller companies owned it. He smiled. At least it wasn't a government operation.

He stopped at the door for a second as the realization of what he was about to do hit home. If this really was some kind of safe house for corporate operatives and he was discovered, he'd be dead as soon as they'd extracted whatever information they thought they could get from him. He knew this and still reached out to try the door. There was only a handle, the lock mechanism hidden in the door and frame.

As he touched it, he could feel a slight vibration, which surprised him. It unlocked when he touched it. His own apartment door worked the same way – it read his bio identity from his hand and unlocked if programmed to do so. Why had this door been programmed to let him in?

He stepped into the dark hallway, closing the door behind him. From the outlines of the furniture it looked like just your average overnight apartment. He checked the two bedrooms. The apartment was empty. There were some clothes in one of the wardrobes, and after a more thorough search he found a small envelope pushed to the back of one of the bedside drawers. At first he didn't see anything in it, but sticky-taped to the inside was a small memTag. He placed it close to his Omni to allow access to its content, again ensuring it was not connected to the Omniscient Network. He selected the first item, an audio only media clip.

"I am God," it began. "I am the Devil. I am all-encompassing."

Tom stopped the playback of the audio clip and smiled. He couldn't believe his luck. The memTag was full of clips with Adrian's unmistakable, frantic, million-miles-an-hour verbal onslaught. He listened for a few more seconds. It sounded like a confession or maybe a diary. Whatever its purpose, Tom was sure there would be something in there he could use to find Adrian. Now all he needed was time to review it.

He changed his clothes for the ones in the wardrobe, hoping he didn't just swap one set of trackers for another. They fit surprisingly well. Even more surprising was that one of the pockets contained an id tag and a small amount of money. As he counted the money, the pieces finally began fitting together. This was one of Adrian's own safe houses. The people he had mistaken for operatives had been in his employ. The clothes he was wearing were there for the very reason he was wearing them now. This was a way for Adrian to swap identities quickly. He knew Adrian and Elize were almost impossible to track online. It wasn't so much that they weren't visible online, but their activity was equal to hundreds of people, making it impossible for automated agents to create coherency in their behaviour. Anyone actually wanting to know the whereabouts of either of them had to rely on CCTV footage and facial recognition, which was unreliable at best. There was even a small kit in his pocket designed to fool facial recognition software. That was why old-fashioned private investigators like Tom had been contracted in the first place. It was easier to follow them than try to make sense of their online tracks.

Someone knocked on the door and yelled, "This is the police. Open the door!"

At the exact same time, his Omni beeped. Someone was trying to reach him, which was impossible. His Omni was offline and he had loaded a completely new id tag in it. He checked it again. It was still offline, but the incoming message was there nonetheless.

Throw your clothes to the balcony below

He had no time to ponder the message. He didn't for a second believe the people outside the door were the police, so whoever was sending the message was the best bet. He ran to the window and pulled it open.

"Open the door now!"

The door received another pounding.

He threw the clothes down to the small balcony below and the pounding stopped immediately.

"He jumped!" he heard a voice from the other side of the door and then the sounds of people running down the hall.

leave now
run
left to red door on right
enter

He knew he only had seconds to get out of there, so he followed the instructions. The door opened to the fire stairs. He started down, but was interrupted by another message.

up!

He ran. As he reached the top, he could hear footsteps further down. He wouldn't have long. He opened the roof access door and was rewarded with another message.

north
jump

Tom looked in the direction indicated. The building was slightly lower, but separated by an alleyway. It wasn't so much the distance as the idea of falling to a certain death that stopped him in his tracks. In other directions there were easier escape routes.

Why had his mysterious helper suggested the most difficult option?

NOW!

Tom ran. If he timed the jump wrong he'd be dead, but at the same time, if he remained, he'd be dead too. He jumped. The Omni beeped in mid-air, alerting him to yet another message. He landed heavily and looked at his Omni.

Duck! Hide! Now!

He threw himself down, flushed up against the low wall that surrounded the roof. Soon he could hear voices on the other side.

"Scan the roof! I'm sure I saw him."

"Negative. There's no one here."

"Check nearby roofs."

Tom held his breath as he heard footsteps approaching. There was a gulf between him and his pursuers, but still so close.

"What do you think? Want me to check it?"

"There are easier escape routes. He wouldn't have chosen this one."

Tom smiled. Whoever was helping him had anticipated his pursuer's every move and even how they'd judge his flight. It smelled of someone amped up. A few minutes later he heard one of his pursuers give a status report.

"We've lost him. He might still be somewhere up on the roofs, so send in Rotors to scan the neighbourhood. We'll check the apartments one by one."

Tom heard the door close and immediately jumped to his feet. He had to get off the roof. The Rotor scan would pick him up immediately. He ran for the door leading off the roof and to his surprise found it open. Inside sat TikTak patiently waiting for him to appear.

"Can we go to my father's clinic now?"

"You did this?"

TikTak just smiled and headed down the stairs.

"We're on the same side, but we need to hurry."

"What side is that exactly?" Tom said, and shook his head.

"The side of the posthumans."

Tom followed silently. That was indeed his side, but he wondered how many sides this particular side had.

"How did you do it?"

"A magician never reveals his tricks."

Tom knew how to do it, but it would have taken him a day to prepare something like that. TikTak had done it in less than thirty minutes. It was just too much of a coincidence.

"You're not Dr Tak's son, are you?"

"This is not the time," he said, descending the stairs three steps at a time, "but yes, I am."

"I don't believe you?"

"No more talking. We need to hurry."

They ran down the last few flights of stairs and reached the ground floor.

"We can't go outside," Tom said. "The Rotor scan will pick us up."

"Don't worry. We've got another thirty seconds. As long as you keep your Omni disconnected, we'll be ok."

TikTak ran out the back door. A car was waiting on the street outside and he jumped in, Tom hot on his heels. It drove off at a leisurely pace, a complete anticlimax to the chase. Tom wanted to yell at TikTak to have him speed up, but he knew it was the right thing. Any behaviour out of the ordinary would immediately be picked up and investigated. Instead, he settled in and loaded the first of the many sound clips he had found in the apartment and sat back to listen.

ADRIAN'S AUDIO CLIP #1

I am God. I am the Devil. I am all-encompassing. Remember that and these recordings may make more sense to you.

However, I didn't start out that way. Once I was just like you, trying not to drown in the mediocrity of everyday life. I was paralysed by the endless options and always choosing whatever kept the status quo. You are such creatures of habit and I was one of you.

IntelEz changed all that when it was introduced in the market. Not just for me, but for everyone else too. I didn't try it at first, would you believe? I thought it must have serious side effects, but after a year of use, people around me still seemed ok so I tried it. It was the most exhilarating experience I'd ever felt. To start with, I just felt the information flow over me and watched as different, unrelated pieces of experience, memory, emotions and senses connected into a tapestry of unbelievable beauty. Every move I made, every new fact I added, sent a ripple through its fabric, constantly rearranging it.

At first, I just stared at the inter-connectedness. I traced the decision tree, discovering there was an 11 percent risk of dying if I climbed down the face of the building. I studied it further and found this figure had been determined based on the layout of the facade, my physical characteristics, the weather and many more factors. I knew all this information was available to me through different means. I had seen the outside of the building often enough. I had read a weather report and I had been outside just minutes earlier. I knew my general physical state and what I was capable of, but this was only the beginning. I could easily trace these facts to recent history. Added to this was information about architecture, strength of materials, wind patterns and more. My mind was able to access most, if not all, the information I had been exposed to throughout my life and use this to assess actions and their outcomes. I had never been aware that it could be used, nor would I ever have attempted to calculate this nonsensical figure.

And yes, I did climb down the face of the building that very moment. It was the most exhilarating thing I had ever done. I pitted my life against a number for no other reason than I could. I stepped from a world with endless worries about the most trivial decisions, to one where hard numbers informed every action I took.

It redefined me in ways I don't have the time or language to describe. I now understood why people all over the world were using it. This was how life was meant to be lived. Everything began making sense, and with understanding, surprisingly, came caring. I had never cared about much apart from myself. Now I could see the ripple effect on the world as I navigated through it. Even peripheral people in my life were of interest. It was exhilarating, even arousing, to introduce a new person into the tapestry of my life and see all the possible ways they could affect it.

The world around me was changing too. As more and more people were using the Drug, a greater understanding between nations developed. We each live in our own little world, with ignorance making us look only to ourselves. But we are all connected in so many ways. The most appropriate use of resources is possible only when everyone involved in the negotiations can see it from a bigger perspective than maximizing their own benefit. Science followed suit. The Drug triggered new developments in all scientific fields. A golden age had begun and I was riding its wave.

As my interest in life expanded, I also found a greater fascination in smaller things and in perfecting every aspect of my life. I designed the perfect cup of coffee with the local barista. I refined equations to describe a more effective way of walking. There seemed to be an endless list of things to improve, starting with the small and working my way up.

On the way up, I turned to women and sex. Before my change, I was very basic in what I looked for. I preferred blonde, petite women, who weren't so smart they could show me up, but not so dumb they annoyed me – as I said, pretty basic – but that didn't keep me from failing with most women I pursued. Now I could have my pick. I didn't consider it then, but for some reason I was able to find the one thing that would stimulate her mind whether she was on the Drug or not.

The Drug had changed my preferences. It was no longer just a question of sexual attraction and the lowest possible annoyance factor. Beauty was found as much in function as in form. And what an amazing function woman is. A design allowing not only the creation of life, but also the nurture of it. In comparison, man is simply primal instincts thrown together in a chest-beating mess. It was almost embarrassing to make the comparison. My preference now was for curvy women with childbearing hips, strong but still delicate.

My admiration of women didn't stop there, of course. Like many others who find themselves suddenly popular, I engaged in sex as often as I could, and found I could enhance the feelings tenfold by feeding all my senses on the experience. The angle of the hip as it thrust became an equation. Any sexual act I could imagine – they all became formulas

I could repeat in my mind. Soon I didn't need anyone else. I could recycle the equations in my head and build up an orgasm greater than I could ever reach with the imperfection of a partner. I spent days and nights perfecting those formulas and then days and nights test-driving them until fatigue eventually stopped me. It may sound strange, but this cured me of one of my primal instincts. Sex no longer held any interest for me. Perhaps I had burnt out the ability to feel anything from it, or maybe it was the realization that I had calculated perfection. In any case, I had reached the end and there was nothing beyond to tantalize the senses. That, I'm afraid, is perfection. Once you've reached it, you no longer want it.

You may wonder why I tell you this, but bear with me. I didn't realize it then, but I had stumbled on something of enormous importance. Something that will redefine humankind. Something that could redefine you.

CHAPTER SEVEN

BODY HUNT

Streetlights aligned with the few stars that could be seen through the ever-present clouds. Together with reflections from windows and puddles on the road, they sent Tom's brain into a tailspin trying to find a pattern. The only thing the conscious Tom could think before disappearing in a torrent of numbers, equations and pattern analysis was, "Not again!"

Tom no longer had an identity. The elusiveness of the pattern required all his mental faculties. He had become the pattern recognition process. For however long it would take, solving the riddle was his sole purpose in life. But Tom had no say in it. He wasn't even consciously aware of what he was doing.

-=:=-

"Finally," TikTak said, as Tom sat up and buried his head in his hands. "Take this," he said, and held out a small pill and a bottle of eWater. "I have a friend who is close to the end too. She finds these help."

Tom didn't ask what it was. He wanted to curl up in a little ball and force himself to tune out and eventually fall asleep. His whole body felt drained, as if his blood no longer could be bothered to sustain it. He could have sworn his brain was a couple of sizes too big for his skull. He resisted the urge to hold his ears to stop it from draining out through his ear canals.

"How long?" Tom asked.

"I don't know. An hour. Perhaps a bit more."

Tom swallowed the pill and drank the whole bottle of eWater. To his surprise, he felt better after only a few minutes. There was no denying his episodes were getting worse. Tom tried to remember the charts showing the deterioration based on frequency and length – six months, twelve if he was lucky.

TikTak stepped out of the car and stood watching his father's clinic. Tom knew he was running checks. There was no doubt TikTak was some kind of operative, but where was his real allegiance?

"Let's go," Tom said, and joined TikTak on the sidewalk.

"Are you sure? I've done a scan of the building and it looks clean, but the clinic itself is off the grid. I can't see anything in there. I've asked for backup, but I don't know when they'll arrive."

"We don't have time. Let's go," he repeated, and pulled the Taser from his inside pocket.

"Nice," TikTak said with a grin. "Never took you for a humanitarian."

"I'm pretty sure if I hold down the trigger long enough someone will die."

"Just don't use it anywhere near me," he said, pulling out a metal handle and extended it to a rod with a flick of his wrist. "It's a bit too indiscriminate for my liking."

"So what does that do?" Tom eyed the rod suspiciously. It was thin rod, about 50 centimetres long, with a small sphere at the end and it looked as low-tech as you could possibly get.

"It is a tactical baton. You beat people over the head with it and they fall down," TikTak said, and handed him a small flashlight and a pair of goggles. "You may need these. I've checked what I can. I'm sure there is some kind of surveillance here, but I've not been able to detect any. Once we enter, I don't think we'll have more than five minutes, so we have to work fast. We want to secure the body or someone who might know where it is."

"Sounds good to me," Tom said, as he checked that the flashlight and goggles were set to the same frequency. They were light spectrum aligned, allowing him to see whatever the light from the flashlight illuminated without anyone else seeing it. "Let's go."

The door to the clinic was closed, but TikTak purposefully strode up and pulled it open, with a certainty that could only come from knowing it wasn't locked. It was pitch black inside. Tom knew the layout of the clinic and was sure TikTak would know it too. The door opened into a reception area, which had nice couches along the walls for the waiting patients. A corridor straight ahead led to the treatment rooms.

TikTak entered first and was immediately swallowed by the darkness within. Tom put on the goggles and switched on the flashlight. He could see TikTak making his way towards the corridor. He followed and closed the door behind him. He immediately sensed that something was wrong. They weren't alone in here. His tired mind couldn't pinpoint exactly what was raising the alarm, but he knew better than to doubt his instincts. He swept the flashlight over the reception area, but couldn't see anyone. He turned back to the corridor and realised with alarm that TikTak was no longer there.

He saw something move in the corner of his eye, but when he turned towards it, there was nothing there. This repeated over and over, until he took a few steps forward and froze as he felt something against the back of his head.

"Drop the … whatever it is," a voice hissed behind him.

It seemed impossible that someone could have hidden anywhere in the room, but whoever it was had made a mistake. Tom might not be able to see him, but he knew where he was. He swivelled around, knocked the assailants arm aside and pushed the button on the Taser. The electrical discharge fizzled in the air. A gagging sound came from the nothingness in front of him. He held the button until there was a loud thud. He kept holding the button until there was no more movement.

"Shit!" The voice had come from behind him.

Tom turned around and saw motion, but nothing else. A strike towards the side of his head threw him into the wall. He lost his grip on the flashlight and Taser as he struggled to stay conscious.

The clinic was suddenly flooded with light. Tom pulled off the goggles and stared up at the three shapes in front of him.

"He's tough," a voice marked with a permanent sneer said.

"I wish people would stop doing that," Tom said as he touched the side of his head just behind the ear. It was already swelling up. He wondered how much more damage his head could take before it just gave up and caved in.

"I think Zemer is dead," a female voice said.

"Tasered to death? What a way to go. Do you think you'd black out or stay conscious for it?"

"I told you not to underestimate him."

Tom sat up and tried to focus. He wanted to confirm what he already knew – that the last comment had been from TikTak.

"I read his report," the sneering voice said. "He's known to not carry weapons, so where did that come from?"

Tom could finally put a face to the voice. Everything but his skin colour was black – short cut black hair and eyes that seemed to be all pupil. He wore black combat gear and held a rod similar to the one TikTak had. Tom didn't doubt he was in charge. His posture, everything about him said authority. The woman next to him was tall and blond with blue eyes. She was dressed the same as the man, making her look like a GI Barbie.

"I hate technology," Tom said, pulling the goggles off his head. "I couldn't see you because of these stupid glasses."

"This is the backup," TikTak said with an apologetic shrug. "Marksman, Ellen and Zemer. We're part of EvoII."

Tom had heard about them. He had dismissed them as an extremist macro-evolution organisation, the militant version of a posthuman interest group.

"We need to get out of here," Marksman said, "I'm pretty sure his little plaything can be tracked. Someone's cleaned this place already, anyway."

"Perimeter zone has been breached," TikTak said. "I think we already have company."

"We'll give them something to chase," Marksman said with a grin. "You get out unseen if you can. We'll meet back at the centre."

Marksman and Ellen ran out the door, leaving TikTak and Tom.

"Are you OK to walk?" TikTak said. "We need to get out of here."

"I'm fine, I've had worse. Just yesterday, in fact. What makes you think I'm coming with you though?"

"I will explain everything, but we're dead if we stay here any longer."

"I'm dead anyway," he said, and shrugged.

"There should be a back door down this way," TikTak said, and headed down the corridor.

The corridor turned and at the end was a fire exit. TikTak ran towards it, but was too late. The door opened, revealing a man in a dark suit. He held a small-calibre gun aimed at the floor. TikTak didn't stop. He ran a few more steps and threw himself forward, the black rod raised.

As the man in the doorway shifted his weight to take aim, Tom saw another man behind him. Tom steeled himself for a shot that never came. TikTak struck the gun so hard that the man's wrist broke, and followed up with a quick strike to the head, pushing him towards the second man and jumped as the first attacker fell. The second man took a step back, but TikTak just shifted his weight in the air, turning the landing into a cat roll. He shattered the man's knee with the rod as he got back to his feet. TikTak finished him off like the first.

Tom just stared. It had taken TikTak a few seconds to take out two armed opponents with what amounted to a fancy stick.

"We need to go now," TikTak said, as he looked for more attackers.

Tom did too, but this was the extent of it – for now.

"Follow me."

Tom obeyed. They ran down a block and turned into a small side street where the car was parked.

"What's going on?" Tom asked, as he jumped into the car.

"You know anything about EvoII?"

"I know the basics. You think Adrian and Elize are the next step in evolution and you want to be part of that."

"Yeah, that about sums it up," TikTak said. "We're a voluntary organisation sworn to protect and further the posthumans. We have many different sections. I'm part of research."

"Research?" Tom laughed, and then winced from the pain his laughter caused. "Looks like you forgot your lab coat for this mission."

"Research requires field missions that can't be left to knuckleheads like Marksman."

"Are you really Dr Tak's son? Because I don't buy it."

"I am. I've been with EvoII since it started about a year ago and I've been trying to recruit my father since then. When you contacted him, he contacted me in turn. To be honest, I didn't believe it, so I checked you out on my own. After we dropped the body off at the clinic, my father told me not to tell my friends at EvoII anything yet. I obeyed, but perhaps I shouldn't have. In the afternoon he contacted me, this time telling me that her body was alive, but that her brain was still very much dormant. He said he needed to move the body, and I volunteered that my friends and I could do it. Truth to be told, I had already told them about it. He agreed, so I set it up. He was going to take the body to one of our clinics this afternoon. That was the last I heard from him."

"Ok," Tom said. "So you went chasing me."

"I figured he'd contacted you directly."

"So someone's got him and Elize?"

"Seems like it."

"Where are we going?" Tom said, as he checked his surroundings.

"Back to our base. We'll be safe there for now."

"I'm going to rest. Wake me up when we get there."

The situation was spiralling out of control at an alarming rate. Tom had a few cards yet to play, but somehow it didn't matter. On his own he wouldn't last another day, so he had no choice but to align himself with a group. EvoII was a bad bet, but the only one that didn't mean immediate incarceration or death.

One of the cards he held was Adrian's diary. The last words he remembered promised something that could redefine humankind. He scanned the clip and found the place, sat back, closed his eyes and listened, hoping to find out what it was.

CHAPTER EIGHT

ADRIAN'S AUDIO CLIP #2

Context is everything. In this case, context is history. My rise to fame came from the realization I had reacted very differently to IntelEz from everyone else.

Would you believe it was one of those new game shows where people show off how smart they are that gave me a clue? Now that anyone could be a mental athlete, these shows became very popular. I had sixteen TV screens set to swap channels every ten seconds. I hardly ever watched them. It was enough to leave them on to take in the consumable version of what was going on in the world. A snippet of one of those TV shows played and I caught one of the contestants struggling with a math problem that was immediately obvious to me. I sat down and watched as all the contestants answered questions and mulled over problems that would have had a Nobel Prize winner struggling prior to the Drug. After watching a whole episode, I calculated I was at least three times more intelligent than the winner.

You probably know what happened. I entered the TV shows, won everything there was to win, and turned into the shiniest boy of the IntelEz golden age. Everyone wanted to be me. IntelEz use skyrocketed. I never had any messianic ambitions. I just wanted to try out being famous, just as I had been working on the perfect cup of coffee before that.

It wasn't long before I had my own TV show. I did stadium-sized events where I showed off how smart I was. I solved the six remaining Millennium Prize Problems in a series of these events and went on to decline the award, much as Grigori Perelman who solved the first one had. My efforts to become famous pushed the mass adoption of the Drug worldwide.

Ego doesn't disappear with intelligence. If anything, it gets bigger, and for good, calculable reasons. The smarter you are, the more valuable you are for the development of the species. I was able to quantify this; thus, I had an objective measure of my own worth. On the other side of the coin, you have the realisation that your ego can only thrive in the network of everyone else. Not just family and friends, and not just as a country, but also on a global scale.

As more and more turned to IntelEz, this became apparent. Global initiatives began. Finite resources all of a sudden became very expensive, forcing innovation in alternate approaches, recycling and renewable sources. A world virtual currency was proposed and accepted. Many in the financial sector found themselves without a job, as the accumulation of wealth for the few no longer was the prime objective. The complex rules and regulations were discarded to allow funds and resources where needed, based on a globally agreed action plan. However, you know all this. You lived through it, after all.

At that point, I had long since stopped taking IntelEz. My body was able to produce a natural equivalent. This was not something I set out to do. My body had probably always been able to do it and my first dose triggered it. I could also see that my decision tree was deepening. The average depth had changed from a few hours to days. The complexity had increased too. Every node in the tree now had an average of six choices, when before there had been three. Granularity had also expanded. My mind was processing the world in the same way a powerful computer processes all possible moves in a chess game, but where the computer had perfect knowledge of chess, the boundaries for the game completely known, I was dealing with a seemingly random world. No computer could do what I did now.

What do you do with that? I was already one of the most famous people in the world. I had made more money that I could possibly spend even if I tried. I had a number of companies generating even more money. I had no interest in any kind of leadership position. I had less and less interest in other people. Their on-rails existence was so predictable I could no longer even pretend to be interested. From what I could understand, I was a race of one. What can you possibly achieve when you are the only one of your kind?

I made plans. Childish, uninformed plans, and I will not bore you with the details. They were all interrupted by the golden age coming to an abrupt end. The first case rippled through the fabric of my future existence. A ten-year-old child, Victor Meme, had been on extraordinary high doses since he was six, administered by his loving parents. They had happily ignored the health warnings for developing brains, hoping he could become the next me. That was the reason they gave. Of course, the whole world turned on me, citing what a poor role model I was for children. I had never set out to be a role model for anyone, especially not children. They are an inefficient by-product of development, a must to further the species. I had some ideas on how to change that, but knew it was pointless to suggest them, especially now that I was children's enemy number one.

Victor developed severe autism, or at least a variant of it. His brain no longer had the ability to process the collected input from his senses, so he withdrew into a state which limited any new input. IntelEz opened the floodgates of information, but the process was irreversible. The mind was left to fend for itself, whether it could handle it or not.

Victor's case was dismissed as an obvious case of Drug misuse, but I knew it wouldn't end there. I cancelled all appearances and prepared for the coming storm.

More cases followed, invariably children in circumstances similar to Victor's. It wasn't long before adults who used large amounts of the Drug started reporting having blackouts.

The world slowly came to realize this was not an isolated occurrence. When the first fully fledged case of an adult turning autistic surfaced, everyone again turned to the poster boy of the Drug for explanations. By then I had removed myself from the equation. I had taken on another identity – several, actually – and was moving between lodgings similar to the one where you found these files. The consensus was that I too was autistic, and possibly dead. This suited me fine. Fame no longer held any interest for me.

Soon the world had more important things to worry about than whether the smartest man on the planet was, in fact, alive. Local economies went into tailspins as a third of their workforce suddenly disappeared. The recently established world market collapsed in a heap, but again I am telling you what you already know. As soon as the first case had appeared, it was obvious there would be a collapse, so I changed my investment strategies accordingly. Once the crisis hit, I was, if anything, even richer.

There was no longer any claim on my time and I again began ruminating over the purpose of it all. I could trace actions and reactions over months, and focusing on a single thread, I could usually follow it to all possible end states. This I realised was being all knowing, just as the Christian God was purported to be. Sure, I worked with probabilities, where God didn't need to, but who cares? At some point the distinction is too small to make a difference.

Another realization that quickly followed was that being God was pointless. If you know or can calculate everything, what's the point? Is God sitting there with a checklist and just ticking things off as all the known states pass by? God in that context has no purpose, and I realised the same went for me. I was nothing more than a monkey, the smartest one perhaps, but still just a monkey, banging my digital rocks together. I needed a purpose. Something grand. Something befitting the God I'd become.

CHAPTER NINE
EVOII

TikTak studied the man next to him.

Tom was asleep or at least it looked that way – his face always seemed set in a frown. Now that he was relaxed, half lying down in the car seat, he looked so old. TikTak knew he was thirty-six, but he looked closer to fifty. His dark hair was turning grey. TikTak had seen photos of Tom in his mid-twenties. He'd been quite handsome, making it hard to imagine what could have happened. Now he looked like an ageing movie star that had let himself go.

The car had stopped maybe twenty minutes ago, but TikTak didn't have the heart to wake him up. Tom had had a rough ride the past couple of days, from what he could tell. He couldn't delay it much longer though. Lotti would want to meet the man who had become such a big part of the posthumans' last few days. He reached out to give Tom a shake and noticed the wired earplugs. TikTak shook his head. Nowadays, most people had them integrated into the inner ear or at least had semi-permanent inserts into the ear canal. He had even seen him use and old Omni with a touch screen. As he leant forward, he noticed there was even some sound leakage. Tom was listening to a voice recording.

TikTak was all of a sudden very interested in what it could be. He hadn't picked Tom for an audiobook kind of person. He gently took hold of the wire and pulled the earphone out of Tom's ear. He inserted it into his own ear, frowning at the uncomfortable experience. It took a few seconds for the earpiece to mould itself to his ear.

"What possible interest could life hold for me when all outcomes were known?" TikTak heard. "Sure, there were less likely paths that could potentially be taken, but they were all known states. I know this is not strictly true. There was an element of randomness I couldn't foresee and a potential shift in parameters that could have unexpected consequences. But in the same way as ants in enough numbers could be irritating ..."

Tom suddenly moved and TikTak immediately removed the earpiece from his own ear, took hold of the wire and pulled the other one out of Tom's ear.

"Time to wake up," he said. "You've got places to go, people to meet."

"Yeah, ok," said Tom, as he sat up and looked around. "Where are we?"

TikTak had heard enough of the recording to know it was Adrian speaking. He had spent many hours watching the TV show that made Adrian famous to learn what he could about the posthuman. He couldn't work out why Tom would be listening to him apart from getting to know every aspect of his quarry. There was something that didn't feel right about that explanation, an immediate gut reaction he had learnt to trust, but in this case he had no idea what it meant. He didn't have time to worry about that now though.

"This is our main base," TikTak answered. "You'll be safe here."

"Safe? Yeah, right."

TikTak could hear the tired sarcasm in Tom's voice and it irritated him.

"You think you'd be better off with anyone else?" he snapped back.

"No," Tom said tentatively, and then added, "No, you're right. You've saved my life a couple of times already today. Thank you."

Tom stretched as he got out of the car.

"So where is this base of yours?"

TikTak nodded towards the building on front of them. They had taken over an old abandoned hotel, barred up the windows and made it into a fortress, the big glassed-in vestibule on the ground floor the only feature remaining.

"Marksman," Tom said. "How well do you know him?"

"I know him well enough," he answered, deciding not to go into detail about their past. "He was a mercenary before he joined. A bit on the extreme side, but gets things done."

That was the understatement of the century, but TikTak wasn't sure whether he trusted the private investigator. Marksman believed in the cause completely and totally. He'd sacrifice anyone, including himself, to reach EvoII's goal. He believed anarchy was the only way to pave the way for the future. TikTak disagreed. He even questioned whether the posthumans were a good idea. They seemed such a giant leap in development. Surely there would be a price to pay to leap into the future like that?

"Is his tag really Marksman? I mean, how did he get one of the originals? It isn't Marksman342 or something?"

"No, he's the genuine article. I don't know if he just got in at the right time, but I heard someone say he found the person who had the tag and made him give it up."

"He looks like a crazy fuck to me."

"That he is."

Three armed guards greeted them as they entered the building. TikTak didn't know them, but they obviously knew him. One of them nodded and stepped aside.

He had been asked to report directly to one of the meeting rooms on the second floor. They passed the reception area, through a corridor to the stairs. He hurried past a barricade halfway up the stairs and into the second-level corridor. This area had been the business centre in the hotel and had four meeting rooms connected to an octagonal reception hall.

They entered the first meeting room. TikTak was surprised to see all group leaders around the table. Something important must have happened for them all to gather at this time. Lotti, the leader of EvoII, was sitting at the head of the table. They all turned to the new entrants expectantly.

"We were not able to secure Elize's body. Secondary mission completed successfully."

"I'm ..." Tom began.

"I know who you are," Lotti's eyes drilled into his. "Tom Leonard Devine. Mother and father dead. One child, deceased. Marriage to Indra Barton ended two years ago. Decorated detective. Thrown out of the police force for theft. The timing of these events makes it likely they are interconnected."

"Enough," Tom said, and looked down.

TikTak had seen Lotti do this many times. Everyone had something to hide and Lotti used it to gain advantage, a way to show dominance. If there was something she was good at, it was forcing her will on people. TikTak knew that from first-hand experience.

Tom swayed on his feet then looked up again, locking eyes with Lotti.

"Lotti Genzberg," Tom said. "Forty years old. Living under a completely fabricated identity. Born Marsha Lang in a small town she no longer wants to remember the name of. Greatest achievement was third place in a beauty pageant when she was seventeen. Has changed her name four times since. A fixture of any extremist organisation promising social upheaval. The timing of these events makes it likely they are interconnected."

TikTak just stared at Lotti, struggling to suppress a smile. He had no idea how Tom could possibly know these things, and yet from

Lotti's expression they were obviously true. She looked like she had been hit in the face. All eyes were on Lotti to see how she'd react.

Marksman entered the room.

"There you are," he said, and then frowned as he saw the pissing contest taking place.

"You don't know anything," Lotti said finally, dismissing Tom with a wave of her hand. "Get rid of him."

"I know a thing or two," Tom said. "But I'll only discuss it with your leader. Surely you're not it?"

Marksman smiled like a predator watching his lunch struggle.

"If you've got anything, say it now," Lotti said.

"I need something to eat and some rest. After that, absolutely."

"You know nothing …" Lotti began, but Tom interrupted her. "And to show my allegiance with your cause, I give you this."

He put a small vial on the table.

TikTak leant forward to get a better look, but was too far away to determine what it was.

"This is a tissue sample from Elize," Tom said, "I took it before handing the body over to Dr Tak."

Dr Menker, leader of the research section, snatched the vial from the table and studied it intently, as if hoping it would yield its secrets from a cursory examination. "I need to analyse this," he said, and left the room.

"So how about the food and rest?" Tom asked.

"We'll talk later," she said. Two junior members led Tom away.

"Full status report," she said, turning to Marksman.

"Not much to tell, unfortunately. Someone had been there before we came. No sign of a body or even that it had ever been there. The local servers did have memDrive slots, but the drives were either never installed or taken when the body was removed."

"Any idea who was behind it?"

"No. We had a run-in with some agents. Private ones, from the look of them. I'm guessing they were after the same as us."

"So we don't know who took the body?"

"No," Marksman said.

"Dr Tak still has the body," Emerus Lorre, the leader of the intelligence group, said. "I've found footage from a nearby cam. It shows Dr Tak leaving the clinic in a company car. I crosschecked with the driver network, but the navigation system must have been disabled."

"We can assume everyone else has this footage too, and possibly more. So where was he going?"

Everyone's eyes turned to TikTak.

"I can only think he's either contacted another group or some old contact. I'll put together a list of candidates, but it won't be complete."

"Give me what you can," Lotti said. "We can run it through a Social Analyser. Should add a few more names hopefully."

"So what do we do with the private detective?" Marksman said. "I think he's bluffing. I say get rid of him."

"I'm inclined to agree," Lotti said.

No one around the table objected. There were even a few nods.

TikTak couldn't believe what he was hearing. "I think that would be a mistake," he said carefully. "We've got nothing to go on for either of the posthumans. I believe Tom has had contact with both of them in the past 48 hours. He could still be useful."

"How do you figure that?

"I think the apartment where I picked him up was connected to Adrian somehow."

"Based on what?"

"His behaviour. To my knowledge he only has one contract and he was prepared to watch the apartment for days. I think he is one step ahead of all of us."

As he said it, a piece in the puzzle suddenly clicked into place in his mind. Tom had indeed found something in that apartment. The recording Tom had been listening to in the car had come from there. He was just about to tell them when he thought better of it. It was a very political environment in the group now. He needed to work out how he could use the information to his advantage.

"Find out what he knows," Lotti said. "Then we'll get rid of him."

TikTak nodded.

"You can go," she said.

TikTak and Marksman left the room.

"How many?" Marksman asked as they walked down the corridor.

"Two in the hospital."

Marksman nodded.

"One in the hospital and one in the morgue," Marksman said, "I win."

"Even. Killing doesn't increase the score. If anything it should be worth less. Disabling takes more skill than killing."

"Where's the fun in that?" Marksman said with a grin. "Do you know what the meeting's about?"

TikTak shook his head.

"You used to know everything that was going on. I take it you and Lotti no longer ..."

"No, we're not."

"A shame."

"A shame? Why?"

"It could have been useful, that's all."

TikTak didn't like what he was hearing. He knew there was no love lost between Lotti and Marksman. They had such diametrically opposed viewpoints that they always argued about every little detail. He hadn't liked her at first either, but had soon succumbed to her will. When she wanted something, she went after it to a point where it was either hers or was no longer relevant. He had seen both happen.

"There are many of us who think she's not taking this organisation in the right direction, and the detective's stunt in there just helped convince us."

"Count me in," TikTak said.

Marksman only nodded and went on his way. TikTak wasn't sure what to do. He had no intention of aligning himself with Marksman and his crowd, but he knew which way the wind was blowing. Lotti, for all her posturing, was on her way out and he was in her camp. He was sure he was safe as long as Elize's body was missing and Tom still had secrets to spill, but that wouldn't hold for very long. He could just leave, but he knew Marksman would come after him. Marksman didn't like loose ends.

He realised then that Marksman hadn't asked him about the meeting to find out its reason. He already knew. He just wanted to find out if TikTak had known. Therefore, it must have been about the leadership.

TikTak hated what the organisation had become. He had joined because he believed humankind faced a choice of either imploding or changing into something else entirely – or perhaps both. IntelEz had seemed to be the answer and in a way it was. It had showed humankind what it could be – and then pulled the rug out from under its feet. The posthumans were the extension of the hope that IntelEz had provided.

When he joined, EvoII was furthering the posthumans any way possible. Lotti had been the driving force behind this stance and no one questioned it. He had questioned her motives at the time, but overall it had worked towards a goal that all the members shared. This had changed when more people like Marksman had joined. The organisation had fractured into camps, still with a more or less shared goal, but with very different ideas of how to get there. He had never tried to align himself with any group and as a result had become part of Lotti's ever-diminishing supporters by default.

He realised he didn't know who he could trust anymore. Lotti, yes, but he couldn't see what she could do. Which led him to the only other person he believed he could trust – Tom.

TikTak knew where he'd be. There were a few smaller rooms on the level above. They were mainly used by interstate members needing somewhere to sleep for the night. They could also be locked from the outside. He took the stairs and found Tom in the third room he checked.

"What do you want?" Tom said. He was lying on the narrow sofa bed with his jacket over him as a blanket. There was a tray with a half-eaten meal on the table.

"We need to talk."

"In here?" Tom said with an amused smile.

TikTak knew why he asked. Tom expected the room was wired and he was correct.

"I want to find out what you know about Elize and where she is."

"Shouldn't you know? Your father ran off with her."

TikTak wrote a message on an old Omni he had brought along for this very purpose. He showed it to Tom:

I know about Adrian's recordings.

Adrian frowned, took the Omni and started writing. Two conversations began.

Tom: Clever boy. So what?

"Doesn't mean I know where he is," TikTak said, whilst typing furiously. "He's gone underground and we need to find him before anyone else does. You know we're a better bet than anyone else."

TikTak: Can we locate Adrian with them?
Tom: We?
TikTak: You and I.

"Yeah, there is that," Tom said after a while, as if he needed time to think about it. He was smiling as he wrote a reply.

Tom: No friends in EvoII any longer?
TikTak: Something like that.

"We have good medical facilities here," TikTak said, finding it difficult to keep track of the two conversations. "We can help her back. And you know we're on her side."

Tom: I'll think about it.
TikTak: Not much time.

"OK, OK, you've done your sell," Tom said. "I do have information, but I'm not sure how best to use it. If I could get my Omni back, I might be able to get my hands on it."

Tom: There never is.

"I'll get you your Omni back," TikTak said, and pocketed his own after reading Tom's final message.

"No hurry," Tom said and yawned. "The sleep of the just is calling."

"The sleep of the just barely," TikTak said under his breath, as he left the room. He didn't lock it. If they wanted Tom to be a prisoner, someone else could enforce it.

As he walked to his next destination, his mind kept coming back to Elize. She was an enigma, to say the least. Everyone knew about Adrian. He had been a regular fixture on the feed for over a year. His story was well known. Exactly how he'd become what he was, was still a mystery, but there were hours and hours of interview material where Adrian was discussing and providing theories for it. They had followed up on all of them, but none had proved successful.

Hardly anyone knew anything about Elize. She had not revealed her existence like Adrian, so if it hadn't been for the war they waged, no one would have known about her. There were no tests, no easy way to detect a posthuman, and it raised the question of other undisclosed posthumans. There was a group within EvoII focusing on exactly that. The western world focused on Adrian, but there was reason to believe there were others.

Perhaps the greatest mystery came from the fact that Adrian and Elize had known each other before they became posthumans. They had been married, in fact. The majority of the research community agreed that this pointed to some kind of environmental factor they had both been subjected to. Yet another group within EvoII was dissecting every known fact about Adrian and Elize and their life together, trying to learn what environmental factor might have contributed to the change.

On a whim, TikTak poked his head into the laboratory where Dr Menker was ordering his team around, trying to solve the riddle of the small sample he had been given.

"Found anything?" he asked.

Dr Menker didn't look away from the computer screens. "It is just as you said. Her body has somehow transformed the blood to allow for a short-term suspended animation. Like a freezing agent. We haven't even begun to work out how such a change is even possible. It would require organs we don't have and changes down on a cellular level. We always assumed the changes were mainly in the mind, but this …" Dr Menker shook his head in wonder, "is a sample of a new species."

"Cellular changes?"

"There are pockets of stem cells throughout the sample able to regenerate new specialised cells, and the normal cells also have different characteristics. Most likely this is for self-healing. We think she'd be able to regrow parts of her body or even battle cancer."

"That makes no sense," TikTak said, and was finally rewarded with Dr Menker's undivided attention.

"I know. IntelEz only affects your brain, so where do the physical changes come from? We are starting to think there might a primary physical mutation occurring before IntelEz was introduced. In a way, they were already posthumans before they were subjected to the drug."

"Yeah, but that leads back to some kind of environmental factor causing the primary mutation in the first place."

"Yes, you're right, but perhaps we can isolate the initial mutation and recreate it. That would allow us to create our own posthumans."

"Is that what we're doing now?"

"Lotti always saw that as one of our prime directives," Dr Menker said, and turned back to the computer monitors, effectively signalling the discussion was over.

TikTak continued on to Lotti's quarters. Dr Menker hadn't said anything he hadn't known before, at least not about Elize. He wondered if Dr Menker's last comment had been a roundabout way to state his loyalty to Lotti.

Lotti lived at the base. She saw no reason to make a distinction between her life and that of the group. To her, they were the same thing. At least that was what she used to say. Tom's offhand revelations put her in a very different light. He knocked on her door and when there was no response, he tried it. It was open.

He found Lotti in the bedroom, reading a report, whilst blasting an electronica rendition of some famous classical masterpiece. TikTak couldn't stand it.

She looked up from the report, ready to lash out at whoever was disturbing her, her stern expression softening as she realised who it was.

"Tann," she said. She insisted on using his birth name in private. Another thing he didn't like. He had long since stopped being Tann Tak.

"Are you still running the show?"

"Yes, why do you ask?"

"Marksman told me you were on your way out."

"I'm still here, as you can see. Was that what you wanted to talk about?" She sounded almost disappointed.

"I want out," TikTak said.

He had Lotti's attention now. Her expression hardened.

"And why is that?"

"This isn't about the future of mankind any longer, just personal agendas."

"You always were naive," Lotti said dismissively. "Everyone has their personal reasons to be here. You too."

"Call it what you want. That doesn't change anything."

"You can't leave," she said with such finality. "You are needed."

"To do what?"

"You are key to everything that is happening. Your father is holding Elize. You brought in Tom and gained his trust. Without you we'd have nothing. We need you to get Tom to talk. We need you to find Elize. We need you." She tilted her head to one side. "I need you."

"I will help you," TikTak said, ignoring her last remark, "but once we've found my father, I'm done."

"You are done when I say you are," she said, her tone leaving no doubt she meant what she said.

TikTak nodded. He had expected to hear something like this, but had hoped for something different. His only way out was to run, and he wasn't willing to do that just yet.

"I better get on with it then," he said.

"You could stay here," she said, the invitation obvious.

"I've got plenty to do," TikTak said, and shook his head, knowing she'd extract some kind of revenge later for denying her. He turned to leave. "Tom needs his Omni Device back, by the way. He says it'll help him locate some information."

Lotti threw it over to him. "We've already made a copy of it. It's all encrypted. I don't want to get heavy-handed with him, but if I don't see results soon, I might have to."

TikTak left without answering. It had been a pointless threat, but telling nonetheless. She suspected some kind of link between him and Tom and wanted to find out just how far it stretched. The question now wasn't so much if he was going to run, but when.

He turned on Tom's Omni and saw it had a message waiting. Without unlocking it there was no way of telling more than that. It could even be one from his father. He hurried back to the upper floor to the room where Tom was sleeping.

"I need you to unlock this for me," he said. "You've got a message."

Tom sat up and stared at him bleary-eyed.

"Really? You wake me up for that?"

"Unlock the bloody thing!"

Tom took his Omni and held his finger against the touchscreen. TikTak shook his head – he was still using a thumbprint as passkey. It was notoriously easy to break that. Tom then tapped a few times on the screen seemingly at random before checking the screen. At least he had a secondary security measure, TikTak thought, but it wouldn't take Dr Menker and his people long to break through it.

"I do have a message," he said, and frowned, "but it came the way you send me messages. It's just from a nearby device."

"Who is it from?"

"It doesn't say. I think it's just someone playing around."

Tom held up the screen for TikTak to see.

I need your help. Elize's body is in danger. Meet me at the attached location tomorrow at 4pm.

The attached location was a longitude and latitude. TikTak memorised them. "Yes, I think you're right," he said. "Someone just having fun."

TikTak had a look at the device id the message had come from. It was his own Omni. Someone was using it to relay messages to Tom. TikTak had no idea how that was possible. He was beyond diligent with securing his device. He had customised his Omni presence in the network from the firmware up, running obscure modified open-source agents to ensure it was virtually impossible to hack, yet someone had done it. It was almost as if whoever did it was making a point. The only person TikTak could think of that could have sent the message was his father, but he lacked the skill and wouldn't have written the message that way.

"So I can keep it?" Tom asked.

"Yes, we need to find out where Elize's body is. We have to find her before anyone else. Anything you can do..."

"I'll see what I can do," Tom said.

"We've got a timeline."

"I'll see what I can do," Tom repeated with a grin, and put the earphones into his ears and lay back down on the couch. TikTak wondered if Tom had taken any other precautions to secure the information his Omni could access, not that he could do much about it. He just had to trust that Tom was paranoid enough to be prepared.

TikTak left the room, guessed that Tom was continuing to listen to Adrian's recordings. He hurried back to his own small room and started putting together a list of his father's friends and acquaintances. He had an ulterior motive this time. He wanted to run each of them against the location he'd been given before handing over the list to Lotti. He no longer wanted to help the group.

He made two lists. One with all possible connections: friends, anyone he had communicated with via private or company accounts, anyone from his private address book, anyone with even a hint of a connection to his father. He soon had a list of over a thousand names. It would take days for a Pattern Analyser to dig through that, which was exactly what he wanted. He then made a much smaller list of people he could remember his father having dealings with. He figured the person his father had contacted had to be from his days in the hospital, someone he trusted, but might not have been in touch with for a long time.

He accessed a Pattern Analyser and loaded his father's name, the list of 20 names and the location, and sat back. It estimated a completion time of 94 minutes. He sent the larger list off to Emerus Lorre, Dr Menker and Lotti, apologising for the size.

Ninety-four minutes and counting. What could possibly go wrong in such a short time?

CHAPTER TEN

ADRIAN'S AUDIO CLIP #3

Purpose – now that is something hardwired into humankind in the most ridiculous way. Once you get past survival of the individual and the society he or she is part of, what possible need do you have for a purpose? But if we don't have a purpose, we create one either consciously or unconsciously and then charge full steam ahead or hide from it.

I knew all this, yet I still could not completely ignore the urges it created in me. I began a self-study to keep my mind occupied with other things. I cast my mind back and let the tapestry of connections enlighten my past. Apart from the past few years, it was not even worth the bother. The singular thread hardly made any twists or turns on its inevitable way back to my birth. We have no concept of our real potential and my life made this painfully obvious. However, if the path to the starting point of my life had been a disappointment, the possibilities from birth were the absolute opposite – a singular bright light with almost infinite possibilities, reduced to a single path and finally fizzling out into nothing. In front of me lay all the possible paths my life could have taken. I stepped through my life, minute by minute, examining every inane thought and uninformed decision one by one. At every turn there was a vast sea of alternate options, almost all with a better outcomes. I had led such an average existence; it pained me to view it with any degree of clarity.

I watched my younger years with its carefree existence. Two simple concepts summed them up: egocentricity and the path of least resistance.

I had no issues with the former. This is who we are. In many instances it can be translated into a centricity around the closest group, such as friends and family. In some rare instances, it can even become a caring for a society or the common person, but I believe this to be an abnormal development, probably caused by childhood trauma. It is natural to care for yourself and for the ones close to you. Any extended care beyond that comes from other sources, but if is to be regarded as natural it has to be based on the ability to trace back a seemingly random act to your own wellbeing. Altruism, however commendable, is abnormal.

The latter – the path of least resistance – was something altogether different. It was natural for sure, but together with egocentricity it fostered a mediocrity that ran like a common theme through my life.

It was even worse as I progressed further in life. I managed to find a wife who wanted to share her life with me and it took me less than three years to squander it. In my estimation, the path of least resistance is the most common reason why most marriages come to nothing. And why shouldn't they?

The idea that someone can find fulfilment in only one other human for the rest of his or her life is a fallacy forced upon humankind by religion. We get stale, bored into a comfortable lull that can only be broken by introducing more people into the mix. I introduced affairs and one-night stands. She introduced girlfriends, each more annoying than the next. Without knowing it, we were both expanding our worlds, worlds we could live in because we weren't happy with our current shared one.

Don't get me wrong. I loved her. I still do. However, love only gets you so far and it wasn't far enough for me. Our love didn't give either of us stimulation. It just gave us someone to share the dullness.

She discovered my transgressions. We tried to patch things up, but our two separate worlds collided, making any reconciliation impossible. Her girlfriends – well versed in the unfaithfulness of men – soon became a bigger problem than the women I had had on the side. According to them, I had proven myself unworthy. If I had done it once, I would do it again. Whilst true, I hated their interference. I knew that two of them had had affairs, but somehow this did not disqualify them from having opinions. My wife and I parted ways not long after.

It still hurt. With all my knowledge and the ability to make sense of the world now, it still hurt. But in that emotion I also found my purpose. Whilst I had let emotion sweep me away, my mind had been busy creating connections. I existed in a vacuum. With all outcomes known, what possible interest could life hold for me? Sure, there were less probable paths to attempt, but they were all known states with known outcomes.

This wasn't strictly true, of course. There was an element of randomness I couldn't foresee and potential shifts in parameters that could have unexpected consequences. However, in the same way that ants in enough numbers can be irritating and make you move from one spot to another, it wasn't affecting me much more than that. The randomness was a nuisance, nothing more. So how could I break out of this vacuum? What could there possibly be that gave me a reason to get out of bed in the morning?

I was a race of one. The ants around me provided little more than momentary distraction. If I was to go on, I needed someone else like me, an equal to share experiences far beyond what Homo sapiens could begin to imagine. This was to be my quest: to create an equal. The religious implications weren't lost on me. Even with my godlike status, I couldn't determine whether an actual God existed or not. If there was such an entity, perhaps the universe was just a cry for help – a lone creature's desperate attempt to create an equal?

So now that I had my purpose, it raised two immediate questions: "Who would join me in godhood?" and "How do you change someone to be like me?"

I knew who I wanted as my companion. I had failed her once, and here was my chance to make things right. Elize was the obvious candidate.

How to do it proved a much more difficult question. It took me over two months to determine how to change her. I turned my intellect to determining what I was now and was surprised to find I had already started changing. My subconscious had begun a reconfiguration of what I was – a body to match the intellect it housed. It hadn't even occurred to me until now that I could examine my body and its automatic processes in much the same way as I could examine anything else.

What a marvellous machine it is, and yet so flawed.

It took only a cursory examination to question the possible involvement of a creator in its design. The mystery – if there was one – was how we had progressed this far at all. The spine was a prime example. It was an amazing construction for movement, but was obviously not for walking upright. Mine was reinforced, limiting movement somewhat. This was an understandable trade-off. Most of my physical enhancements, I discovered, were to better protect the brain and basic movement, which limited agility somewhat.

As I studied the different layers of the body, I found adjustments everywhere.

My metabolism had changed. I was now a hybrid with an organ specifically designed to store energy to feed my ever-increasing mind. Instead of allowing high-energy food such as sugars to flood my system, it stored them like a battery and released them as needed.

I had already seen the difference in analytics and critical thinking. The brain is an amazing organ, but to deal with the constant barrage of data and make sense of it, it filters, fills in the blanks and makes assumptions. My brain no longer did this. Instead, it processed all information, made all the necessary connections and fed the result into the probability matrix.

The most surprising changes I found were in the building blocks of who I was. A completely new process was reprogramming my genome using designed viruses as the tool. A new organ created viruses and released them into the body. It changed the cell by infecting it, reprogramming all the cells in my body continuously. It was correcting deficiencies in my DNA.

To my disappointment the endocrine system remained intact. Hormones were still coursing through me, manipulating my every move. At least the analytical mind was now better equipped to keep this somewhat in check, cancelling out some of the unnecessary base responses.

Amazing as it all was, this was not what I was looking for. All of these changes had occurred once my mind had already changed. I was after the genesis stage – what had caused the change in the first place.

It took some time, but in the end it wasn't very complicated. The change was caused by a number of completely unrelated small mutations working in unison with the introduction of IntelEz. It wouldn't be hard to create a drug that would create these different mutations. Anyone could become me, it seemed, but that was the last thing I wanted. Wasn't that the downfall of humankind anyway? Out-of-control reproduction using up all the available resources, spawning wars and conflict over the few resources that were left. No, a new race would be based on restraint, else we would be no better than the humans preceding us had been.

I created the drug and one night whilst she slept I administered it to her.

Elize, the mother of a new race.

INSURGENCE

Marksman had grown increasingly tired of the posturing. He thought the time for political positioning was long gone. They had control over more than three-quarters of the group's leadership, yet he had to wait. Emerus Lorre, leader of the opposition group, didn't want an all-out war, preferring a bloodless shift of power over a full-blown revolution. Marksman struggled to see the sense in that. Surely a clean cut was better than keeping the cancerous growth.

He looked at the list TikTak had sent and that Emerus had passed on to him. It was a joke. It confirmed what he already suspected: TikTak's loyalties lay elsewhere. Marksman didn't know what TikTak hoped to achieve with this little stunt and he didn't care. However the takeover happened, there were a select few he'd remove from the picture whatever Emerus said – TikTak was one of them.

Emerus was heading in the right direction, but not far enough. The new world would grow from the ashes of the old one. Their job was to fan the flames. It was in the ensuing chaos that a new world order would emerge. This wasn't a change that could be managed by committees or controlled with project plans.

"Are you listening?" Emerus said impatiently. He was standing up, staring at Marksman. Emerus was imposing. Almost two meters tall and solid. He had been quite the athlete, playing rugby at the national level, but had let himself go. Still a formidable foe though.

Marksman sat up. He had heard it all before. Political this and political that.

"And stop playing with that," Emerus continued, pointing at the tactical baton in Marksman's hands. "It makes me nervous."

Marksman smiled, but made no movement to put it away. "What are we doing here?" he asked the others gathered, before Emerus could continue. "What are we waiting for? We could take over this place tonight if we wanted to. We know who'd go with Lotti and could easily remove them."

"We all know what you think," Emerus said with a sigh. "The takeover requires planning. There is a subtle balance of power within the group. Once it changes, we need to make sure we can restore it – otherwise, we won't have a group left."

"Subtle balance?" Marksman said, trying hard to suppress a sneer. "The balance of power at the moment is that Lotti has it and we don't. You all heard the private investigator. She's whored herself out to any cause that'd take her. Is that really what we want? Even her own supporters will be asking themselves if she's the right person to lead the group. We need to move now."

This wasn't the first time Marksman had challenged Emerus on the takeover strategy, but so far he'd been unsuccessful. He had a feeling this time would be different.

"He's right," Jim Arkham said. "We've prepared for this long enough. Everyone is questioning Lotti's claim to leadership. We'll never get a better chance."

Marksman was surprised Jim had spoken up. He'd never before challenged Emerus and he knew Jim spoke for sections of their group that usually remained silent.

"We should wait," Emerus persisted. "If Lotti's leadership is under question, so much the better. She will be convinced to leave without us having to do anything. We have the majority and it will be a smooth transition, just the way we planned."

Marksman looked at the others. Usually everyone would nod as Emerus laid out the plans. This time no one did.

"No more waiting," Marksman said. "We've been handed a golden opportunity and we'll take it. There are a few people that will have to go, but that was always the case. We've been planning this for ages. We all know what to do. We should move now."

Marksman knew he had won and in doing so had taken a giant leap up the food chain. Now there was the question of how to capitalize on it.

"With your permission, I will deal with Lotti and her closest supporters."

"What exactly do you mean with 'deal with'?" Emerus asked.

"I will make them disappear," Marksman said. "Does it matter how?"

"They should be allowed to leave if they want to," Emerus said.

Marksman raised his eyebrows and looked at the others. They didn't say anything. Marksman loathed their weakness, but knew he had to work within the limits, or he too would be out. He'd put in a lot of work to rise within the ranks of EvoII, and he wasn't going to abandon the cause now. He needed to change the playing field, and the takeover of power was the perfect time to do it.

"In ten minutes I will move to have Lotti and her closest associates locked up," Marksman said. "I need you to control any information flowing to your respective groups. We move now."

They stood up and hurried out of the room. There was a sense of purpose in the group he had never felt before. Once they had all left, he turned to Emerus. "Could I talk with you in private? I just want to make sure it is all going in accordance with your plans."

"Your plans you mean?" Emerus said with a sneer, but still motioned for him to come along as he headed for the door.

"We are all after the same thing," Marksman began.

"No," Emerus said, and shook his head. "I doubt we share the same goal. Before the posthumans, I always thought machine intelligence would outstrip us in a few decades, and in all likelihood would have spelled the end for humankind. That all changed with Adrian and Elize. They are the glorious continuation of our species. I suspect that to you they are no more than a meal ticket."

"You're wrong," Marksman said, equally annoyed by the accusation and the time he was wasting. "Give me a chance to change your mind."

Emerus studied him for a few seconds then shook his head. "No, it's too late for that. Once this is over, I want you out."

Marksman glanced up and down the corridor. Behind Emerus was a door into a small meeting room. It was closed so he didn't know whether it was occupied or not. He decided to chance it. He grabbed hold of his lapels and pushed him backwards through the door, making sure he was off balance so he couldn't use his superior weight to stop the movement. He was in luck – it was empty.

"Let go of me!" Emerus yelled. He pushed Marksman away and crouched into a boxing stance. Marksman struck him in the throat with a knife hand, hoping to incapacitate him, or at least shut him up. He'd wanted to do this so many times. He wanted to savour his fear and pain, but he didn't have the time. He needed to get this out of the way quickly and focus on Lotti. If everything worked out as he planned, Jim would take over as number one. That would give him enough control over the operative part of the organisation to set his own plans in motion.

He'd planned this a long time. He knew Emerus had a partial heart replacement. It could be accessed wirelessly to change settings and Marksman had long ago acquired a hack to change its function. The manufacturers had thought of this of course and supplied its customer with jamming devices they hung around their necks that stopped any wireless signal. Marksman pulled open Emerus' shirt, located the jammer and pulled it off. He didn't like killing like this – it should be up close and personal. Sending a hack code to stop someone's heart didn't give any kind of satisfaction. He felt embarrassed as he instructed his Omni to activate the hack. Just as triggered it, the door opened, revealing one of Emerus's aides. Marksman didn't know his name. He had him mentally tagged as Fat Bastard because he was overweight. He had no respect for people who ate themselves into an early grave. "Have you seen ..." Fat Bastard started, and then saw Emerus on the floor, still gagging from the strike on the throat. "What happened?"

Marksman looked down on Emerus. The hack was supposed to be quick. It overrode the security protocols and forced the pacemaker to race until the heart stopped.

"He just fell over. I've been trying to get help," Marksman said, pointing at his Omni processing wristband.

Fat Bastard sat down on his knees next to Emerus, an elaborate task requiring a number of adjustments and grabbing hold of chairs. Midways through this procedure Emerus half sat up and grabbed his chest.

"There's something wrong with his heart!" Fat Bastard said, and immediately started checking Emerus's pockets. "If I can find his Omni, I can run the diagnostics on it. He showed me how."

Marksman watched as Fat Bastard located the Omni. He realised then that he wouldn't get away with it – he was still holding the jammer in his hand. Fat Bastard spent a few seconds looking for it and then glanced up at Marksman. He knew. Still he kept going, running some kind of diagnostic function. This wasn't going to be the clean kill Marksman needed, but he didn't have a choice. What was worse, if Fat Bastard had an integrated Omni, he could have already sent a request for help.

Marksman pulled out his tactical baton and flicked it to full extension. He struck Fat Bastard across the back of his neck. The force of the blow threw his head backwards. Marksman swung the baton in an arc over his head and struck across the obese man's exposed throat. Fat Bastard sat there a few seconds gagging and then fell over onto Emerus. Marksman knew he would only live as long as the air in his lungs would allow. He checked Emerus, who by now was all but dead.

It would have been so much better if it had looked like an accident. Now it was a murder and someone had to be accountable. He knew he'd be at the top of that list, along with Lotti, from the group's perspective. He could run, but it wasn't his style, nor did the situation require it. He had worked too hard to give up now. This was still salvageable.

First things first. He left them as they were, one lying on top of the other. On his way out he jammed the door.

He found Lotti in one of the group rooms. Dr Menker was briefing her about the discoveries so far. He called in backup and whilst waiting for them to arrive listened to the conversation.

"We've not gotten anything from the copy we took of Tom's Omni. There are encrypted parts in the solid-state memory, restructured to look like a regular files. If we hadn't started opening those files, we wouldn't even have known they were there. We've begun analysing them, but we suspect they are only partial files and that small bits of them will be stored in different infoDeposits. We don't even know if we're going to be able to get anything out of it at all. I wasn't expecting such security measures. Are we sure this guy is just a private detective?"

"Are you saying he's a government agent?" Lotti asked, glancing at Marksman, but not acknowledging him.

"I don't know what it means. He has stuff that looks like agent tech. He knew background information about you hardly anyone knows. Could he be some kind of undercover operative?"

"We should ask him,' Marksman said.

"He won't tell you anything," Dr Menker said.

"I can make him talk."

Dr Menker grimaced. He was weak just like the others. Not prepared to take their beliefs to their natural conclusion. EvoII would be better off without them.

"I don't think it will be that easy," Lotti said. "He doesn't have long before he's a deadhead. This is a cause for him and he's got nothing to lose."

"So what then?"

"TikTak is working on him."

"You can't trust him," Marksman said.

"I know," she said, just as Marksman's backup arrived. "And it seems I can't trust you either." She eyed the people behind Marksman. "Can't do your own dirty work?"

Marksman would have preferred to remove her from the picture altogether. As long as she was alive, she'd cause trouble. He didn't have that option now.

"Lotti. We no longer believe you are suitable to lead our group. Come with me."

"No," Lotti said, and stood up defiantly.

Marksman shook his head. She still thought she was speaking from a position of strength. She was going to make her case here and how. Marksman didn't think she'd succeed, but he wasn't taking any chances. He struck her hard in the face, open-handed.

"Take her and put her with the private investigator. They have lots to talk about. Anyone else?"

No one moved. Marksman wasn't surprised. They were weak. They followed anyone showing strength, whether they agreed or not. He loathed them.

CHAPTER TWELVE

UNDER SIEGE

Tom pulled the earpieces of his Omni out as the door opened. Lotti was pushed into the room. Tom almost laughed. But once she had regained her composure, she acted as if she were a queen under house arrest. She was attractive, with long blonde hair, blue eyes and high cheekbones – a model of northern European beauty. But her face never relaxed. She was like a coiled viper, always ready for the attack.

Lotti gave him a stare and sat down on the floor across from the couch. She nursed a bad bruise on her cheek.

"How did you know about me?" she asked.

"Trouble in paradise?"

"Trouble you've caused."

"You've been digging that hole for yourself perfectly fine without my help."

"How did you know about me?" she asked again.

"You haven't hidden your information that well. Anyone with a bit of time on their hands can find it."

"Why?"

"You know my background. You should be able to work it out."

She shrugged her shoulders. "It doesn't matter."

Tom returned her shrug. They sat in silence for over a minute.

"It was the IQ killings, wasn't it?" She held up her finger to keep him quiet. "You must have been assigned to the case as a detective when you were on the police force. I knew I was a suspect. I didn't realize how thorough you'd be."

Tom smiled. He had investigated her as part of those killings. It had been after Adrian had disappeared from the public spotlight, but before the full truth was known about the Drug. Six well-known public figures were competing for the spot Adrian had left. They were killed over a period of a few months. Lotti had been the spokesperson for a group of black-hat hackers that claimed they knew who the killer was.

"And now here you are. A bit too much of a coincidence, don't you think?"

Tom just smiled in response.

"So who are you working for?" she continued. "It can't be the police, but maybe you were recruited by another government agency afterwards?"

Tom shrugged. He saw no reason to let her know it was indeed a coincidence, and not a big one by any stretch. He had a number of cases focusing on homicides related to group activity. Her name – or one of her aliases – had come up more than once.

"We never found the IQ killer, so technically you are still a suspect."

"Whatever."

They sat in silence for a few minutes. Tom had no interest in her. Her own group had ousted her and from what he had seen of her so far, he didn't like her very much.

"Is it true?" she asked.

"Is what true?"

"Your killed your daughter once she became a deadhead?"

At first he didn't answer. He didn't necessarily want to discuss this with Lotti, but he knew her type. She would keep going until he told her – just to shut her up. Most of it was a matter of public record anyway. His case had become the precedent for mercy suicides for deadheads.

"Why?" she prompted.

"Because she asked me to."

"So why the thefts? I ran a social summary on you before you came. You were some kind of big deal as detective."

"She was in and out of clinics for over a year. Expensive clinics. It seemed a good idea at the time. No one would miss some of the money from evidence seizures."

"But they did."

Tom nodded.

"So your wife left you?"

"That happened as soon as my daughter was diagnosed. My daughter and I were very close. I was the one who had put her on a high dose of IntelEz. I was using it myself and figured it couldn't do any harm."

"God, it sucks to be you."

"You happy you know everything now?"

"I knew it already. I just wanted you to relive it by telling me. Revenge for outing me, if you like."

Tom laughed. The revenge was so disproportionate to his supposed crime that his mind couldn't come up with an appropriate response to her statement.

"So now we are stuck in here, the two of us," he said finally. "I think they put us together as punishment."

"I will be out soon. I still have enough supporters."

"The fact you're in here with me shows you don't."

"They're hoping I'll get something out of you. I won't, I know. You don't know anything more."

Tom smiled. "Since I'm still alive, someone thinks I do."

-=:=-

There was still 15 minutes left of the 94-minute running time of the Social Analyser when the door opened. Marksman entered with Erin and EpicL behind him. They all eyed him warily. TikTak knew what this meant. He had run out of time. He was surprised to see EpicL there. Someone had to replace Zemer, but EpicL was muscle and not much more. TikTak scanned them. According to his integrated Omni, EpicL's weapon augmentations were at full power. He was obviously expecting trouble.

"I want to know everything you know. Now!"

"I've told Lotti everything. Ask her."

"I will. But now I'm asking you." He glanced over his shoulder. "Hold him."

TikTak knew that each of them was his equal or better in a fair fight. He wouldn't stand a chance against all three of them. Better to save his strength and wait for an opening. It wasn't much of a tactic but it was all he had for now.

EpicL grabbed his hands, held them behind TikTak's back and twisted viciously. TikTak had nothing to match the power of EpicL's augmented muscles.

"I know how tough you are," Marksman said, "and I don't have time to break you down. I've been told this will do it for me."

He held up what looked like a high-tech helmet. TikTak had never seen one before, but he knew what it was. Full Virtual Reality had never hit the mainstream, but the military industry had found other uses for immersive technologies. The helmet was a sensory deprivation device. It controlled sight, sound, smell, taste and airflow.

"I hate crap like this, but I don't have time to get information from you the old-fashioned way."

Marksman pushed the helmet over TikTak's head. It was completely dark. Soft pads formed themselves around his ears and two plastic pipes went up his nose. A spout pushed against his lips. TikTak held his mouth shut, refusing to surrender to the helmet. The helmet made a few more attempts to push the spout into his mouth before delivering an electric shock that made it open involuntarily. It was all the time it needed to push the spout deep into his mouth. A soft, sponge-like material sealed off his nose and mouth. He held his eyes shut, but it didn't help. The helmet was hooking straight into his integrated Omni implants, playing a test pattern directly on his lens. He was completely shut off from the world outside.

Strange flavours, smells and sounds filled his world. It wasn't directly unpleasant, but he knew the device was just calibrating based on his reactions. It ended after a few moments, leaving all his senses in the dark – no smell, taste, sound or visual stimulation at all.

A sudden sting on the neck took him by surprise. He didn't know if he was being injected with a drug or not. Maybe the sting was just another attempt at calibrating the device.

The sudden sensory onslaught that came after was impossible to prepare for. Strobe lights pierced his retina, a high-pitched metal against metal screech looped back and forth, favouring his more sensitive left ear. The smell and taste of vomit overwhelmed him. He body convulsed. His mind was no longer able to tell the difference between the outside stimuli and its own state. However much it tried to purge its system from anything unwanted, nothing came. He kept convulsing repeatedly.

His world went black again and he welcomed it with all of his being. His body slumped in the chair, drained both mentally and physically. Why was he here? What was this place?

"This was just a taste of what is to come. Tell us what you know and it all ends."

Memory came flooding back. Marksman was torturing him for some reason. He didn't have any information worth knowing. How could he make this all stop if he didn't have anything to tell?

"A shame. I'll see you at the other end."

From then on, the world TikTak knew was no longer. His mind was in freefall, the sensory overload so disorienting he couldn't even imagine a world without it.

-=:=-

Mr Astin flicked between the video feeds. All positions were ready to go. For a brief moment he considered informing his superior, but decided not to. Astin had delivered precious few results and couldn't afford anyone else taking credit for the operation.

It had seemed such a simple task. Locate and secure at least one of the posthumans. As soon as he was given the task he had operatives scour the online world for traces of them and very quickly realised this wouldn't yield results. The posthumans didn't try to hide their online activity, because they knew the quantity of communication they generated was beyond the capability of any normal Pattern Analyser. He suspected they generated a lot of this activity to hide their true intentions, but whatever the reason, it had made standard techniques useless.

He had hired private investigators, people who still held on to the old notion of investigation work, to counter this. It was mainly older cops and agents trying to make a living outside the force and agency. Tom was one of them, and his methods – whatever they were – paid off very quickly. He had soon located the female, Elize.

Mr Astin had decided to have her followed so they could take both of the posthumans at the same time. Adrian and Elize had begun their war and he'd reasoned he'd be able to take them both during one of their battles. In retrospect, this had been the wrong call. He should have brought Elize in immediately. Tom had proven much less loyal and much more resourceful than he had expected.

Now he had nothing and Tom was the only one who seemed to know anything about the posthumans' whereabouts. The only way to recover this operation was to bring him in and find out what he knew. He had tried at Dr Tak's office, but hadn't expected EvoII's involvement. Now it was likely to get messy. He had faith in the teams doing the extraction, but it didn't matter. Even with all his planners amped up on IntelEz, complications were bound to happen. EvoII wasn't much of a threat. They did have some ex-military members, but it was unlikely they'd put up much resistance. You never knew what fringe groups such as EvoII would do. He didn't expect them to go suicidal and blow the place up, but he couldn't completely discount that scenario.

He watched the video feeds as the teams began. They entered the building from the front, the roof and the parking garage. It didn't take them long to secure the front entrance and the entry into the garage. The team entering from the roof weren't as lucky. A makeshift barricade stopped them and they had to disassemble it before proceeding. The original plan was to have the team entering from the roof do the extraction, whilst the others would hold their positions. If more obstacles slowed them down, they'd have to take an alternate approach. He hoped not, as that would likely turn messy.

The team secured the area as they progressed down one level in the building.

Mr Astin watched the progress and listened to the secured audio frequency the troops used. He smiled. Finally something was going his way.

"We have five civilians outside the building." The report came from the team in the lobby.

His smile immediately disappeared. If they were EvoII members this would very quickly turn into a gunfight. He checked the video feed from the team in the lobby. They didn't look like EvoII members. One of them was even wearing a hospital gown. They just stood outside and watched until the sliding doors opened of their own accord.

"How did they do that? We locked those doors!"

"Just get rid of them."

There was something strange in how they moved. Mr Astin didn't know what triggered his unease, but their blank faces and almost robot-like movements made him nervous. If they weren't EvoII members, then who were they?

The woman in a hospital gown smiled and walked up to the reception desk where two of his men were posted. The others had taken positions, ready to step in if need be.

"How can I help you?"

The woman kept smiling, pulled a gun from under her hospital gown and shot him in the face.

The other attackers reacted immediately, running towards the positions where the other operatives hid.

"We have a hostile approaching here too. Only one that we can see." This time the report came from the parking garage.

Mr Astin ignored it, watching as the attackers were disposed of. They didn't have much in the way of weapons – another handgun and an assortment of knives – but they wielded them with such complete disregard for their own safety that they were dangerous nevertheless. He suspected they were on some kind of drug.

"Secure the door!"

One of the operatives ran towards the door and jammed it.

"There are more of them out there."

The audio link from the garage suddenly went dead. Mr Astin swapped to the video feed to see what was going on. At first he couldn't make out any details. He rewound half a minute in the video feed and watched as an obese man walked up to the position held by his men. He smiled and waved at them as he approached. They told him to stop, but he didn't listen. Someone fired. A flower of red appeared on the man's chest, but he kept going until he was close. He looked at the camera and winked. A second later he exploded, taking the team out with him.

Mr. Astin couldn't believe what he was seeing. The attackers behaved like terrorists, happily sacrificing their lives. As he watched the video feed from the garage he could see movement. Through the dust there were the outlines of more people entering the building.

He swore as his Omni alerted of an incoming anonymous private feed.

"Who is this?" he snapped.

"Are you currently attacking EvoII's headquarters?"

"It is an extraction of a key resource. Tom Devine knows where Elize is. I need him to locate her."

"We have already secured Elize, and from what I can see it is a slaughterhouse. Get them out of there."

"That order can only come from my direct superior."

"Consider him outranked. This is Leonid March."

Mr Astin sat back down. Leonid didn't just own the company, he owned the corporation of which this company was only a small part.

"I'm taking over this operation. I want the extraction team out of there now. Let Tom Devine go."

Mr Astin studied the video feeds again with growing dismay. What had started as a nuisance was now an all-out attack. He had been keeping an eye on the nutcases in EvoII for months now, but he had never expected this. An all-out attack by what looked like a rival group.

"I don't think that is possible any longer," he said, and hung up, knowing he no longer had a job.

WIPE OUT

TikTak reconnected with reality like a careering car meeting a brick wall. He realised this was the real torture. The sensory deprivation was so severe that the mind went into a fugue state to deal with it. Once it was gone there was no longer anywhere to hide. His head pulsated, as if the electric pulses in his brain had been multiplied a hundredfold. He had lost count of the times it had stopped and then started again. He just knew there was no escape.

Suddenly the spout in his mouth retracted and the helmet loosened its fit somewhat. He blinked but it was still completely dark. White text blinked in the right upper corner of his vision: *Sensory overload program B.9 complete.*

He realised he could hear distant voices, so he focused on that as his body screamed its pain. He could only hear snippets of conversation.

"Someone cut the power …"

"We're under attack …"

"… find out what's going on …"

"… keep an eye on …"

TikTak just sat there. Time no longer meant anything as his mind struggled to make sense of a muted world.

Suddenly the helmet was yanked off his head, almost ripping off one of his ears with it in the process.

TikTak slumped in the chair. He knew he needed time to regain his grip on reality.

"Wow. It really did a number on him, didn't it? How long was he in there?" It was a male voice, harsh and cocky.

"Fifteen minutes. Maybe less." A female voice. It sounded distracted, maybe even nervous.

Fifteen minutes. The time meant something. He focused on it as a lifeline and it delivered. The Social Analyser had fifteen minutes left when he was captured. It would have a result that might lead him to his father. With this rediscovered purpose, TikTak pushed the pain away and tried to compartmentalise it enough to think clearly. Someone was attacking the EvoII headquarters, but who? Probably the same crowd they had met at his father's clinic, but why attack? They knew Elize's body was somewhere else, so there had to be a different reason. Tom! They were after Tom. He swore to himself for not working it out quicker. He had to get out of here.

Marksman had left them already, leaving the two voices he had heard – Erin and EpicL. He knew he couldn't beat EpicL in a fair fight if it didn't involve weapons. It didn't matter though. EpicL had augmentations to increase strength that were hardwired into his integrated Omni. TikTak had hacked that many months ago for just this eventuality.

Erin was a different question altogether. Her, he could take on unarmed, but she already had her gun out and she was a good shot.

They were both standing in front of him. EpicL hadn't bothered tying him to the chair, preferring to flaunt his superior strength by holding him in place. Now that Marksman was no longer there, he had let go, positioning himself between TikTak and the door.

"Who's attacking us, you think?" EpicL asked Erin.

"Government agents. Fascists!"

TikTak prepared a message for Erin, tagged it with Marksman's signature and sent it. He hoped she'd just act and not analyse it.

Erin froze.

"I need to go,' Erin said and headed for the door "You OK here?"

"This little guy? Not a problem."

As soon as she left, TikTak stood up. "Let's see how tough you are."

EpicL raised his arms and frowned. "What have you done?"

"Let's see how tough you are without enhancements."

EpicL sniffed. "I don't need them to deal with you."

TikTak knew he was right. Even without enhancements he was still a much better unarmed fighter, but TikTak had no intentions of fighting on his terms. He had thrown his baton on the bed when entering the room and it was still there. He had to go through his adversary to get to it. EpicL was in a boxing stance. He usually favoured striking.

TikTak feinted a side knee kick, easily blocked EpicL's clumsy counter strike and moved to the side. He had become used to his augmentations. Without them he was slow and uncomfortable. EpicL followed up with a jab feint and then immediately followed up with a front kick to the abdomen. TikTak let it hit him but turned even more, letting the force push him in the direction of the bed.

"I'm going to kill you," EpicL grinned.

He still had the grin when the end of the baton struck him in the temple.

TikTak sat down. He'd been lucky. The pain from Marksman's treatment was still clouding his thoughts. He knew he didn't have long and now he had to deal with Marksman's people and whoever was attacking EvoII. He accessed the motion surveillance system he had set up over the past few weeks. A map of the building appeared in front of his eyes and he could see any moving bodies as glowing dots. Most of the EvoII members were already tagged, but he could see another fifteen or so spread out, some on the lower level and some coming from the top level. They had secured the exits and were moving in, securing the building room by room.

He could still get to Tom before them, but getting back out was another question entirely. He started running. He needed to get to the stairs before they were secured. As he ran, he started questioning why he was trying to rescue Tom at all. He had the coordinates, which was the best lead to find his father. Tom was going to be a complication, since everyone was trying to capture him.

One of Marksman's goons was half running towards him. In the dimly lit corridor, he didn't even register who TikTak was until they were side by side.

"You …" the goon started, as TikTak hit him with a side sweep to the back of the head. TikTak grabbed his gun and ran up the stairs.

From the perspective of saving his father, there was no point in saving Tom. But there was a bigger picture here. However much he despised what EvoII had become, he still believed in their cause. The posthumans were humanity's only hope. Tom, for reasons he still struggled to understand, was the most likely link to either of the posthumans.

From his internal map he knew there were no hostiles on this floor yet, but they were coming. He ran to the room where Tom was held and unlocked the door. To his surprise both Tom and Lotti were there, glaring at each other. Lotti looked ready to punch Tom.

"We need to go," TikTak said.

"What's happening?" Lotti snapped at TikTak.

"We're under attack. They've already secured the top level and the entrance. We need to find another way out."

"Who's attacking us?"

"I don't know. We have to go now!"

He mapped out potential exit points whilst the invaders, appearing as unidentified dots on his retina, crept closer. The front entrance and the roof were blocked off. There were numerous windows on this level.

He could probably climb down from there, but he wasn't sure whether Lotti or Tom would be able to do it. More than likely, snipers would pick them off anyway. There was an entrance to the car park at ground level, but it was also secured. There were a few other options, but they were in areas already occupied by hostile forces. He could see no option but to fight their way out.

They heard shots fired from the lower floor. It seemed the bulk of the hostiles were entering from street level. He decided they had a better chance to escape from the roof.

"We'll go up. There are two other buildings we can reach from there, but we need weapons." He handed the gun to Tom and watched as he checked it. He kept forgetting Tom had a past in the force. "We'll have to pick some up on the way."

They hurried towards the stairs. To TikTak's dismay, he could see the hostiles were getting reinforcements. More and more dots appeared at ground level. It wouldn't be long before the building was in their hands.

They ran up two flights of stairs and as they entered the upper floor, he swore. He hadn't had enough time to analyse the movements. The reason the hostiles weren't moving was that some of the EvoII members had managed to block the key corridor that went like a spine through the building. They had built a pile of office chairs and tables and anything else they could find almost all the way to the ceiling. They stood on one side, hiding in door openings, while the hostiles were on the other side. It was effectively trench warfare.

He didn't think it would take long for the hostiles to break through, but until they did the three of them were trapped.

He sat down and analysed their options again. They had to get out of the building somehow. He checked the lower floors and was surprised to see there had been no movement into the building. There was activity for sure, but it seemed the hostile force had been stopped in their tracks. Even more attackers were entering the building as he watched.

The building shook. Something had exploded further down in the building. It must have been on the garage level, as there was no immediate change in movement patterns at ground level.

Chaos reigned on the ground floor and he instantly knew why. A third party had entered the fray and was sending more and more people in. He quickly explained the situation to Tom and Lotti.

"Our best bet is to get out in the confusion. It's dangerous as hell, but I don't think we have a choice."

"Why are they attacking?"

"They're after you!" TikTak couldn't believe how dense Tom was.

"I don't think so. What are you guys doing here? EvoII, I mean? Anything anyone would want?"

"We don't have time for this. We need to go now."

"So we are going to walk to freedom through a three-way gunfight?" Lotti shook her head. "In that case I'll need a gun."

"There'll be plenty where we're going."

TikTak again took the lead. He had no idea what to expect on the ground floor so he tried to make sense of the little information he had as they descended the stairs. The motion surveillance system could no longer decipher the movement, and just reported a mass of moving bodies. To his surprise, there were still more people coming. The first attack had been clean. A small number had gone in and secured all the exits and then methodically went through the building. The second attack was very different. There was no skill or method to it. It was an attack by someone with superior numbers and no regard for the lives of their rookie troops.

The fighting was no longer restricted to the lowest floor. Three people in civilian clothing chased an injured man in full combat gear up the stairs. They pulled him down and slit his throat with what looked like a kitchen knife. One of them looked straight at TikTak and he realised she was a member of EvoII. She smiled. It was the last thing she ever did. One of the other attackers plunged the kitchen knife through the back of her neck. She fell forward.

TikTak shook his head. They were not agents. The one closest to them was an overweight man in his mid-thirties, with food stains on his sweaty clothing; the other, a petite woman in a hospital gown, her head shaved. TikTak figured she was fifty years old. They were not on the agents' side nor were they with EvoII.

He struck the overweight man over the head repeatedly. TikTak was surprised how much damage he could take before he fell to the ground. The petite woman was lying at the bottom of the stairs, hit by a stray bullet.

They made their way past the bodies in the staircase. The petite woman grabbed hold of Tom's leg as he stepped over her.

"You have to get out," she said, blood spurting from her mouth as she spoke. "I will help you."

She held on for a few more seconds before slumping into a heap. TikTak checked the overweight man and found an old Omni in his back pocket. He took it, hoping it could provide some explanation as to what was going on.

He scanned the chaos in the wide hallway. Injured and dead, both agents and civilians, lay on the ground. What at first had seemed an impossibility now looked doable. If they moved quickly they had a chance of getting through.

"Stay close behind me," he said and ran.

Perhaps it was just luck, but they were almost halfway down the corridor before he had to get involved. Two EvoII members came towards him, one armed with a bowie knife. TikTak struck the knife hand, shattering the wrist. He pushed the attacker into another fight and turned to the remaining man, who now backed away.

He continued down the corridor, again surprised at how easy it was. He struck a few people out of the way, but no one challenged them until they turned the corner and could finally see the foyer of the building. This was a larger area where civilian bodies lay in piles. Agents still held it, firing at anything entering the building. The sliding doors were jammed open by bodies on either side. A glass wall and the open door were all that stood between them and the attackers.

As they approached, they could see movement from outside. Ten or more people were charging the glass wall with bricks and pieces of metal. They began battering the wall and circular patterns bloomed like flowers where they struck.

Someone suddenly grabbed his arm and started pulling. He had no idea how anyone had managed to get so close to him, but realised it was Tom who was falling to the ground. He checked him for wounds, but found none.

"What happened?" TikTak asked.

Lotti shrugged.

"Help him. He's having an episode." TikTak couldn't think of any other reason.

"He's a dead man walking?"

He nodded. "He should be able to stand and walk. You'll have to lead him."

"Just leave him."

"Don't you get it? They're here for him!"

She stared at him defiantly for a second, then crouched down and struck Tom twice in the face.

"There you go. He should be with you in no time."

TikTak shook his head, but could see that her action had the desired effect. He hailed a car, in the unlikely event they made it out alive.

The glass in the vestibule was designed not to shatter, but to remain in sheets even when broken, but it didn't matter – the sheets of glass were coming away from the frames from the sheer force of the blows. As soon as a gap opened, the attackers started welling through.

It was clear the agents hadn't equipped themselves for a fight like this. They had expected a covert extraction and ended up in trench warfare. They managed to stop the first wave of attackers, but another came soon afterwards and stormed their positions.

"Are you ok to make a run for it?" TikTak asked Tom, who was trying to stem the flow of blood from his nose.

"Yeah, I think so. What happened?"

"You had an episode."

He nodded. "Let's go."

They ran past the few remaining agents and attackers. To TikTak's surprise, there were hardly any attackers left on the street. He could see onlookers further away, but no one else ready to fight. The last surge of attackers must have been the final wave. It all seemed just a bit too coincidental.

The three escapees entered the car that was waiting for them.

ADRIAN'S AUDIO CLIP #4

Emotion. Well, there is another useless concept. Humankind is already beyond the stage where emotions and their results serve any real purpose. This was a twofold discovery as I watched Elize unfold into my equal.

I had a painless birth. She wasn't so lucky. Through a fortunate roll of the dice, I had been born with the required mutations; Elize had not. I administered the drug over five nights, recreating the mutations one by one. It shouldn't have affected her in any negative way, but she still came down with an infection and ended up sick for weeks. This wasn't completely unexpected, but frustrating, regardless. Most likely it was an infection that had been in her system before I even started the process.

Two weeks later, I ensured she took IntelEz. She was an intermittent user anyway, using it to cope with her personal life. This, I understood, was a common use of the Drug for women. Instead of antidepressants, IntelEz was used to gain clarity in the emotional turmoil that was everyday life.

My world suddenly opened. Her reactions and behaviours were unknowns. Remember, my first reaction to the Drug was to climb down the face of the building. I tried to determine the logical progression of events from this point, but the uncertainty at each point had suddenly doubled or tripled. What I really needed to do was analyse the reasons for this and adjust my approach, but I was too excited, my vast analytical ability nullified by the emotional reaction to finally having begun my plan. I wanted her to know the wonders the new world had to offer. This was my first mistake. One of many.

Perhaps some more context is in order before I continue. Elize left me six years ago, and within months had found someone else. A year later they were married. She was now a stay-at-home mum with two young children.

I waited for her husband to leave in the morning and then knocked on the front door. Her reaction as she opened it baffles me to this day.

"Adrian, what have you done?" – the first words she'd said to me since our divorce was finalised. She knew there was something different about her, and seeing me she immediately concluded I was the reason.

She invited me in, but only after I asked. She was holding her one-year-old son, who was obviously in the middle of his breakfast, as he was wearing most of it. I recalled the ideas I had about eliminating the child stage from the development of our new race. They were such an ineffective, messy way of furthering a race.

I told her I had made her like me, and again I could hear the religious analogy echo in my ears: "I have made you in my image." Was this how God felt when finishing the Creation? I'd like to think so.

Elize wasn't impressed, and I had suspected she'd react like that. I had considered asking her first, but the likelihood of her acceptance was less than ten percent. This way the success rate was just shy of fifty percent. It was a strange conversation, where she provided both sides of the argument. She kept asking questions and then immediately answering them herself, as her mind kept supplying the most likely scenario. She negotiated the questions until she stopped for a moment to consider the why, but that too soon occurred to her.

"Adrian, how could you? I don't want to be like you."

I remained silent. This was the make or break and there was nothing I could say that would increase the chances for her to join me. It had to be her conclusion, her decision.

"And I don't want to be with you."

My heart stopped. All my planning had led up to this moment and I had failed. The only answers I had, I had calculated to have less than a ten-percent chance of changing her mind, so I stayed quiet.

She asked me to leave and I agreed, telling her she would see things differently once she had had time to explore the gift I had given her. This I knew to be true. Once she understood the full impact of what she had become, a completely new baseline scenario would begin.

I was right, but only partially. A week later, I visited her again. According to my calculations, this was the optimal duration needed to develop an understanding of her position beyond the immediate future.

She let me in this time and studied me dispassionately.

"I guess I should thank you," she began, carefully choosing her words. "You have changed my world for the better. I never thought I'd say those words to you, so thank you."

I nodded, impatient for her to continue, impatient for the new world to begin.

"I also know why you did it. And my answer is no."

Her answer sent a shockwave through my probability matrix yet again. I had no idea how to respond to her rejection whilst it adjusted.

"Please leave," she said, and saw me to the door and closed it after me.

How could I have been so wrong? The probability of rejection had been less than one percent, yet here I was. It didn't take me long to realize that I hadn't been wrong at all. After all, I wanted purpose, a challenge beyond what humanity could muster. She promised to give me both. I was certain that given time she would make the right decision.

I watched her over the next few weeks as she carried on with her small, pointless life. Diapers, baby food, trying to get the baby to sleep, pushing a stroller to the park to meet other equally pointless mothers. Husband comes home from his pointless job and they spend the evening fussing over their pointless children before putting them to bed and then falling asleep in front of the TV. And repeat. And repeat.

How she could find any satisfaction in such an existence was beyond me, yet she persisted. I had given it a week until she gave up on her pathetic existence, but two weeks later nothing had changed. I grew weary of this game. She would join me. It was only a matter of time. All paths on my probability matrix led to that point, but some of those paths lasted years. She needed a push in the right direction to speed things up, and I knew exactly how to do it.

Her husband took the two children to toddler play at the local swimming pool. On their way back, I arranged a driverless car to malfunction and ram their car into the opposite lane. None of them survived.

CHAPTER FIFTEEN
REVENGE

Tom pulled the earpieces out. He felt sick.

Tom had seen old interviews and Adrian had always been charming and smooth. On these recordings he was anything but. What was the point? Why had Adrian left these files for him to find? Apart from getting to know the real Adrian, which was a mixed blessing, there had been one important revelation. Posthumans could be created. This was the secret everyone was after, the reason he had been hired to follow Elize in the first place. If that information was in there, the search for the posthumans no longer mattered. However, it all came back to the reason for these recordings. Adrian had planned all this.

Tom laughed to himself. He was like an ant trying to understand the magnifying glass that was slowly roasting it to death.

"Finally off your relaxation tapes?" Lotti said.

"I find I don't have to listen to you if I pretend to listen to something else," said Tom. He watched the sunrise through the car window. "Where are we going?"

"I ran a Social Analyser on my father," said TikTak, "and ran the resulting profiles against the location you were sent. There was a match on a Leonid Marsh. He's a doctor, worked with my father in the army.'

Lotti frowned. "You got one name from that list of yours? There were thousands of names on it!"

"I used a different list."

"Traitor."

"To whom? I didn't like where EvoII were heading."

"The military?" Tom sat up. He didn't like that at all. When the downwards spiral began, many of the military organisations rejected the lead of their governments and became semi-autonomous. "We don't want to mess with the military."

"Don't worry. That was long ago. He's disgustingly wealthy. Built a company around biotech and now spends most of his time saving the world."

"You think he's an ally."

"Could be."

Lotti snorted. "He's no ally. We've come up against his people more than once. He's the competition."

"Who is he?" Tom asked.

"How can you not know who he is?" Lotti asked.

"Generally, because I don't care."

Lotti shook her head. "PharmaCom introduced IntelEz in the first place. They were small back then, but quickly became a world player. Leonid was behind releasing the patent so other companies could make copies. He wanted the whole world to benefit from it."

Tom did know this, but had never thought too much about who owned what. In his mind, large companies were entities in their own right, great beasts with their own agendas. Who owned it never entered the equation.

"You should look up the speech he made when the patent was released. I watched it live and remember thinking he was an idiot. Guess he proved us all wrong."

"How so?"

"Check out the speech. It will be on the feed."

Tom located a public feed that had the speech on his Omni. It was a ten-year-old news report, snippets of a longer speech glued together with an over-excited reporter attempting to provide commentary.

"Leonid March, owner of PharmaCom and the man who gave us IntelEz, hit the business world with a bombshell this morning. In a press conference, he announced that anyone could now produce the Drug."

Leonid appeared on-screen, a grandfatherly figure with well-groomed greying hair.

"I have decided that IntelEz is too big a discovery to be held up by patents and red tape. It will herald a giant leap in the development of humankind and it is not right that a private company should own it. I've just signed the paperwork to release all our information about the drug to the world. I give the right to anyone to produce the drug."

The journalist again appeared on-screen. "The move was commended for its generosity, but Mr March ended the press conference with a warning …"

"IntelEz is one of the greatest advances of our time, but it is also our greatest threat. Even though it has passed all the tests, I'm concerned about the biological and societal implications of this drug. Now that everyone has access to our information, I'm hoping that research is conducted far beyond what our company can do. Will it be our death or our salvation? It is in all our hands now."

"Reactions from the business world vary," the journalist said, "with many suspecting it's an elaborate ruse."

A business commentator sitting next to the journalist added, "Mr March is portraying himself as a modern-day Jesus, but I'm not buying it. There is a bigger play here that we're not seeing yet. You don't just give away a discovery that could generate billions. There is …"

Tom closed the feed and sat back. If this was the man they were up against, it didn't matter if he was a friend or foe. He had unlimited resources, and once he had what he wanted, his plan would be all that mattered. Tom couldn't do much about that now, so instead he tried to understand the attack on EvoII's headquarters.

"What happened back there?" Tom asked. "I think I know where the agents came from, but the others? They looked like civilians."

"Hang on …" TikTak dug an old Omni from his pocket and tossed it to Tom. "I took it from one of them."

Tom opened it and the home screen immediately appeared. No security measures at all. It was an old model and the operating system hadn't been patched in over a year. Tom scanned the usage profile and found nothing out of the ordinary. The owner had used it sparingly. He went back to the membership profile.

"He was a deadhead," Tom said.

"No, he wasn't. I saw him fight."

"He's got a food administration id."

"Show me." TikTak took the Omni and flicked through the profiles.

"He was a deadhead," TikTak finally agreed. "How is that possible?"

"Mankind is evolving," Lotti said.

"How do you mean?"

"Perhaps what we call deadhead is a pupation stage, a preparation for a new development. Perhaps we will all become like Adrian and Elize. I don't know." Lotti shook her head. "I'm tired of all this. It looks like what we were fighting for will happen anyway."

"And that's a bad thing?"

"Everyone becoming posthumans?" Lotti sat back and grimaced. "If everyone is special, then no one is. How is that a good thing?"

"So it's all about being special?"

"Isn't everything?"

"Even if you're right, why attack EvoII?" Tom asked.

Lotti shrugged.

"It wasn't an attack," TikTak said. "Or at least it wasn't an attack until the other party arrived."

"What does that mean? I saw them killing EvoII members too."

"If they're becoming posthumans, who knows why they do anything," Lotti said. "We are no more than bugs to them."

"So you still think this was an extraction attempt? They were after me?"

TikTak nodded.

"Why?"

"I'm still working on that. Help me out here."

"I think the soldiers may have been sent to get me, yes. I was tailing Adrian and Elize for PharmaCom."

"And you tell us that now?"

"I didn't really trust you until now."

TikTak paused for a second as if to digest his comment and then shrugged. "If Leonid was trying to get you, aren't you basically delivering yourself to him now?" said TikTak.

"I don't think that message came from Leonid. I think it came from your father or someone working with him. And nothing I can think of explains the other group. One of them said something to me. Something about getting out and that she'd help me. She died, so not sure what that was about."

"It doesn't make any sense."

"Bugs." Lotti stared out of the window. "We are all bugs to them."

Tom gave up. He was too tired to care. It would still be hours until they reached their destination. A car directly behind them drew his attention. The network ensured the traffic flow with mathematical precision. This car was too far away from them and not exactly in the centre of the lane.

"Get off the main road and then back on it again," Tom said.

"Why?"

"We're being followed."

"How do you know? This car isn't even on the network."

"Just trust me. There are many ways to follow a car."

"What do you mean? Satellite? A tracker? Hacking our drive computer?"

Tom smiled. "Or they could just manually follow the car."

"You mean drive it?"

"Yes."

"Why would anyone ..."

"Just do it."

The car they sat in suddenly veered right into a side street, and then two more right turns to take them back to their original route. The car behind them followed them around.

"You're right," said TikTak, "we're being followed."

"Do you think there are many or just this one?" said TikTak.

"He's on his own. If he's driving by himself, it's because he doesn't want to tell the network to follow our car. The ADN is easy enough to hack, if you know how. Someone with resources wouldn't follow our car like that. They'd just hack the ADN. We need to get rid of him."

"Hang on."

TikTak sat back for a few seconds. The car behind them suddenly stopped.

"What did you do?"

"I reported him for drink driving. He has to agree to let the ADN take over."

"But won't he just instruct it to follow us?"

"I'm hoping he will. Now leave me alone to do this."

Tom watched TikTak as he stared glazy-eyed into nothing. Tom hated what the world had become. Never before had people been more connected and never had they been more alone. He knew this was the old world watching the new world with disdain, but he couldn't help himself. For all our advances, we were still just cavemen. TikTak was the perfect example. He was obviously some kind of hacker, but at the same time he wielded a baton to defend himself.

"Lotti, what's the story with TikTak?"

"Ask him."

"He's busy doing whatever it is he's doing."

Lotti shrugged. "He was one of Marksman's hacker contacts. Marksman must have seen some promise in him beyond his computer skills, because he brought him into the group and trained him. That's why they both fight with T-bats."

"T-bat? Those sticks they both use to fight?"

She nodded.

"So what did you do?" Tom asked.

"Is it that obvious? Marksman and I never saw eye to eye. I took TikTak from him. He's never forgiven me for it."

Suddenly the car stopped.

-=:=-

"The ADN will now take over control of the vehicle," a soothing female voice said. "What is your end destination?"

Marksman let go of the wheel and sat back.

"Don't lose them," he said to KimEra on over a private feed.

"I've got three bots tracking them," she replied, with a bored autonomous tone. "They're going nowhere."

This was the first time he'd used her as part of an operation and he wasn't impressed. Sure, she followed orders, but never anything else. TikTak had been the only hacker he'd actually enjoyed working with. It didn't matter what he asked, TikTak had already thought about it and explored alternate options. It didn't matter any longer – he was on the opposing team now.

"Where are they going?" This was the third time he'd asked and he had little hope of actually finding out.

"He's given it a circular route with multiple stops and five handovers to other vehicles. It's impossible to determine … shit!"

Their car slowed down.

"Whatever happens, don't lose them."

"He's reprogrammed our vehicle. He's convinced the ADN that our car has a dangerous fault. It will return to base. I've got a replacement vehicle coming, but it will take a couple of minutes."

"We don't have that. Sort it out!"

"And he's disabling my bots one by one. He's good!"

For the first time Marksman could hear actual emotion in her voice. She sounded like she was having fun. He'd never met her, but from the research he'd done before hiring her, he knew she was one of the best, and would only take on jobs she regarded as a challenge – in this case, the opportunity to go up against TikTak.

"I know he's good! You're supposed to be good too."

"He'll get away if I don't ..."

"Don't what?"

-=:=-

The car in front of them stopped and the lights turned off.

Marksman watched as Lotti, TikTak and Tom left the car and headed for a nearby industrial complex.

"What did you do? Why did you stop their car?"

"He killed my bots and was about to re-route this car. I had to do something."

"So you failed," Marksman said.

"How did I fail? They're right there! I'll send you the route he programmed."

Marksman could hear the excitement in her voice. From her perspective, she had stopped TikTak so she had succeeded.

"Do you seriously think that would include the end destination?"

"No," she said, after a while.

He shook his head. "Find them for me. Now."

"Give me a minute."

"You've got 30 seconds."

Marksman had a look in their car. Apart from some fresh bloodstains, the car was clean. One of them might be injured, but not seriously. He had seen them exit the car and there had been no sign of injury then. He didn't want them injured. He wanted them dead. He had to keep reminding himself that they were a means to an end. If he was going to locate any of the posthumans, they were his only lead.

An incoming feed from KimEra. She had better have something.

"The industrial area they headed for is abandoned. It has surveillance systems and many of the machines in the factory have sensors. I can activate their accounts and start it all up. It should give you enough time to locate them."

"Do it."

A few seconds later, the factory came to life as if workers were lined up outside its gates. Abandoned sites – even complete areas in cities – were more and more common. Production output from the world at large had fallen to about half that of the golden age. They remained wired up, ready in the unlikely event they would be needed again.

"Give me a trace of their route."

Markers appeared in his view. They had entered the main gates and headed for the office connected with one of many larger factory buildings.

"It will take me a minute or so to trace them from there," KimEra said. "Some of the machinery is still dormant."

"What kind of factory is it?"

"House printing, I think."

Marksman laughed. No wonder it was abandoned. The population was decreasing and deadheads were collected in institutions. If anything, they needed fewer houses, not more.

He waited patiently while KimEra surveyed the sensors to determine where they were. He wasn't interested in hunting them down inside the building. It would be both dangerous and counterproductive. He wanted to track them to wherever they were going.

"They entered the building and then went into the main factory area. From there I can't see them. Either they're still there or they've disabled all the sensors."

"So you're saying they're hiding in there?"

"Most likely, yes."

"Or you aren't as good as you think."

He didn't get a reply and hadn't expected one. She couldn't care less what he said. Every time he asked her to do something, she received a payment in advance.

"But they're not in the office building?"

"No, they definitely left. I can trace a basic id tag hack and three people leaving shortly after."

"Can you start the machinery inside?"

"Sure. I'll load some designs and kick it off."

He entered the office building, following the markers in his view. He didn't trust KimEra, but he didn't have a choice. If he was going to play a role in this, he couldn't lose more time. The big boys had entered the fray and he couldn't compete with their resources, at least not for long.

"Can you hook me into the feed from the surveillance system?"

"Sure. Won't do you any good though. He's disabled it."

"TikTak?"

"I'd say so. The security sensors on the machinery are still operational, so if they trigger any of those I'll know. I've also started the warehouse robots in case they try to escape that way."

"Ok. I'll find them."

"They're still somewhere in the factory or warehouse. All doors leading out of the building have operational sensors."

It was all a matter of time. If TikTak had enough time, he'd be able to hack a door or other exit without triggering any alarms. Marksman couldn't let that happen. He had to keep the pressure on, force them to make mistakes he could exploit.

He opened the door that led from the office building to the factory. The two buildings were connected by a small corridor that opened onto a large factory floor divided into eight sections, each holding a printer large enough to print a bedroom in one go. This was a print-on-demand factory able to produce a house in less than a day. He had seen a printed building go up in two days once the foundation was laid.

Six of the eight stations were printing something, but from what he could see through the protective screens it wasn't a room. The furthest two were sounding alarms. Marksman expected them to be decoys, meant to delay him. He didn't have choice though; he had to make sure they weren't hiding there. He pulled aside the protective screen of the first one. There was no place to hide within the printing station. In the middle was the beginning of a sculpture of some kind. A three-by-one-meter base and four large feline paws, ending abruptly.

Marksman approached the second printing station.

"I've picked up movement in the warehouse," KimEra said. "The pick robots have motion sensors to prevent accidents. I'll send you the coordinates."

Marksman quickly pulled the protective screen aside. The same statue base had been printed here, but apart from that, nothing. He knew TikTak was just stalling. With enough time, he'd come up with a way to fool KimEra.

He ran through the enormous doors that connected the factory floor with the warehouse. He was surprised at the size of the building. Usually, any kind of printing industry was purely on-demand, and required very little warehouse space, but it was of no consequence – he would push them hard enough that they wouldn't have time to cover their tracks.

He ran towards the coordinates KimEra had sent earlier, entering a section of the warehouse with narrow, maze-like corridors. He turned a corner and stopped. A small pick robot was trapped under a crate, attempting to free itself. Marksman knew it was a trap. Someone would be waiting for him along the corridor of crates.

He moved slowly, trying to assess where the attack would come from, when a shot rang out and a bullet ricocheted on the concrete floor next to his foot. He threw himself back against the crates on the same side he thought the shot had come from.

It made no sense. Why attack here? He knew they were following a trail leading to the posthumans. They couldn't afford any delays, which meant this was some kind of diversion.

He looked around and saw a bigger pick robot come down the corridor, metal arms aimed at his chest. The bulk of the robot took up most of the corridor width, leaving him with few options. He jumped up and climbed the wall of crates, barely escaping the robot arms. It turned and extended its legs to follow him as he spidered up the crates.

"KimEra," he said over an active voice feed. "What are you doing? I'm being attacked by a robot! Shut it down!"

The pick robot had almost caught up with him when it stopped, arms reaching towards him, metal claws extended.

Marksman took a deep breath, then another shot rang out. This time Marksman could see where it had come from.

"Send the pick robot five meters down, the same side I am on, and have it start pulling crates out," he said over the voice feed.

The robot came to life again. The electric engine hummed quietly as it started down the corridor. He started climbing along the wall, using the robot as cover. It started pulling out crates and dumping them on the ground.

He saw movement from the gap between a crate and the shelf just above where the robot was. He let the robot pass the spot and immediately grabbed hold of whoever was in there and pulled.

Lotti came tumbling out from her hiding spot, falling two meters and landing on the concrete floor at an odd angle, twisting her right leg. Marksman jumped down next to her.

"All the doors triggered at the same time!" KimEra's voice came through his earpiece. "I have no idea how he did that."

"Check external surveillance."

"It's been disabled."

TIkTak had beaten them again.

Lotti smiled, an obvious effort through the pain. "Never expected to beat you."

"I can get it up and running again," said KimEra.

"We've already lost them. Track any car requests from this location." Marksman looked down at Lotti. "I have something I need to do here."

He grabbed hold of her hair, wrapping it once around his hand, and pulled her along the floor through the warehouse maze. She grabbed hold of her hair to lessen some of the pain.

"I've wanted to do this for a long time," he said and yanked her hair hard.

She grimaced. "I don't care what you do to me. You've lost."

"I'll show you what losing looks like."

He dragged her along and into the printing factory. The printers had half-finished the statues. The four legs were complete and a muscular feline body was half complete. He grabbed hold of Lotti and threw her up on the level area that was still being printed. She landed on her back, her head tilted back beyond the printed statue. The printing arm immediately stopped, red warning lights flashing.

"Override the safety switches on the printer," he told KimEra.

"Sure," KimEra said, and then went quiet. "What are you doing?"

"I'm paying you. Just do it!"

The printing arm started again, but stopped immediately when it reached Lotti's arm. The heat from the muzzle of the printer made Lotti try and pull away. Marksman struck her arms with his baton, aiming for her elbows. She screamed, no longer able to move.

"Make it print around any obstruction."

"Sure, but it will stuff up my design."

"You're printing a Chimera. Not that hard to work out. Get on with it."

The printer arm started again, but this time it kept ejecting the hot plastic that immediately turned solid, following the contours of Lotti's body. She screamed as the plastic fused with her skin.

Marksman watched her as she slowly became part of the statue. She was still alive, but hardly tried to move any longer. Tiny whimpers escaped now and then.

Parts of her body were still visible. Her head tilted back, her eyes stared into space. He watched as life escaped and her body went limp.

Lotti was dead. He felt ecstatic, but somehow he had hoped for more. He had taken his revenge, yet he didn't feel as much as he had expected. He knew why. There were still loose ends to tie up.

"Wow!" KimEra said through the voice feed. "Now that is a statue!"

"I take it you have the surveillance system up and running then?"

“I do. Too late to locate the rest of them, but I have tracked ten vehicle requests. Mapping their destinations now.”

“Send them to me. It’s time to end this.”

CHAPTER SIXTEEN

ELIZE RENEWED

Dr Tak was tired. He hadn't slept since first laying eyes on his subject and had long since lost track of time. He didn't even know if it was night or day. He was repeatedly offered help and refused it every time. Elize had been his patient since Tom had delivered her and would remain so. He didn't trust anyone else.

He suspected he didn't have long. He now knew he had been wrong to accept Leonid's help. The fact that Leonid had initiated contact should have been the first warning signal, but at the time he had seemed the perfect ally. He had the resources to hide them and help them, and had been part of discovering IntelEz. Leonid had been nothing but civil and had accepted all his requests, but Dr Tak couldn't shake the feeling he was being humoured. It was as if they were just waiting for something to happen and when it did he would be removed. Permanently.

Dr Tak was now of the opinion Leonid was the person he should have hid from in the first place.

Over the past – Had it been two days and nights? – Elize had made a remarkable recovery. Her skin had regenerated, shedding the old burnt one like sunburnt skin. The new skin was harder, more akin to a reptile's, which made even taking blood samples difficult. Not that he knew what to do with them any longer, anyway. Most of her bodily processes had changed. She was still human, but only in the same sense that a Formula One car was a car. He suspected this was not a direct result of IntelEz, but a follow-on effect. The Drug had opened the door, but Elize was the architect behind the modifications, whether consciously or unconsciously. She had been killed, but managed to keep her body in a suspended state until the base functions could repair themselves and harden her body against any future attacks.

He couldn't do anything for her apart from keeping watch and documenting any changes. He kept logs to keep his benefactor updated on Elize's progress, but he also had an ulterior motive. IntelEz had promised, but not delivered. Adrian and Elize were the only known cases where IntelEz had lived up to its promise and the question was why. Along with each test he made to keep Leonid and his cadre of scientists happy, he did additional ones to determine the underlying cause of Elize's abilities. He knew it was an almost impossible task, and he had not had much success so far. Her internal organs and external characteristics were changing so fast it was difficult to locate any specifics that might have been the trigger.

He reached down to take another skin sample. Elize's eyelids flicked open and she grabbed his wrist in a vice-like grip.

"We're under attack."

Dr Tak just stared at her. This was the first time he had seen her in a wake state, let alone hear her say anything, so it took him some time to adjust.

"How do you know?" he finally asked, but regretted it instantly. He knew, or at least suspected, that she had many new ways to communicate with the world. Earlier the same day, he was questioned about the amount of net traffic he was generating. He had excused it with running sample data against medical databases, which was true, but that wouldn't nearly account for the load. He suspected Elize was directly tapping into the local network, which would give her access to security cameras, motion sensors and anything else installed in the facility.

Elize looked at him and nodded. "Help me."

Dr Tak helped her up into a sitting position. He knew she was strong, but her energies were diverted to other unknown purposes, leaving her with only basic abilities. At least this was his current theory.

He could hear the pressurised doors further down from the lab open.

"We need to hide you."

Elize didn't answer, but let herself be led to a hiding spot behind a medical cupboard. He knew it wouldn't hide her for long if they searched the area, but he didn't know what else to do.

Heavy footsteps rang through the corridor. It was Leonid's personal army on its way. That couldn't be good. He had only seen the soldiers once before, when he first came to the facility. Leonid had brought them along for safety, not knowing the extent of Elize's capabilities. Once he had seen her state, he had come on his own the next time.

There were ten soldiers. Dr Tak had been introduced to their leader, but hadn't taken much notice at the time.

"We are here to take the body," he said. "Where is it?"

"What are you going to do with it?"

"The body is no longer your concern. Where is it?"

"She's no longer here."

The leader of the group stared at him for a few seconds, a shark deciding whether to eat or not.

"According to the security cameras she woke up and you led her…" He walked over to the hiding spot. "Here."

He stared at the location. There was no one there.

He turned around and aimed his gun at Dr Tak.

"Where is she?"

"I don't know," Dr Tak answered truthfully. He had expected her to be there as much as the mercenary.

"You are of no use to us. If she doesn't show herself, I will shoot you."

Dr Tak had suspected as much. He knew he didn't have long, and thought he had come to terms with it, but faced with imminent death he found he was not as prepared as he had thought.

"She's hacked your cameras. She could be anywhere by now."

"Maybe, but you've been looking around the room as much as I have. You expected her to be there too. My bet is she is still in this room."

Dr Tak shrugged in response.

"And that means we don't need you."

Dr Tak stared at him defiantly.

Two things happened at once, neither of them the shot that Dr Tak had expected.

The lights went out and the fire alarm sounded. There were no windows in the room, so once the lights went out, the only light source was a few pieces of older medical equipment that still had touch screens. As his eyes adapted to the low light environment, the equipment powered down. It was pitch dark.

Dr Tak ducked down and crawled towards the door. The mercenaries were shuffling around close to him. He could hear the growing panic in their voices.

"Get the lights going again! Anyone with a flashlight?"

"Comms is down, sir. There is some kind of interference."

"Hang on, I've got one."

A flashlight came on and immediately went out again.

"What happened?"

"We need to get out of here!"

"Door is not responding!"

"Force it open, hack it, just get it open. She'll kill us off one by ..."

Dr Tak recognised their leader's voice.

No one moved for a few seconds, as they waited for their leader to say something. Anything.

Dr Tak had lost his bearings completely. He knew there was no point moving towards the door. From what he could tell from the voices, the mercenaries had all gathered around the door, so he crawled as far away as he could. He ended up in the far corner and made himself as small as possible when all hell began.

"She's here. She's …"

Someone started firing. One bullet struck the wall next to Dr Tak's head. One of the mercenaries started screaming. Dr Tak just lay there, eyes closed, holding his hands over his ears.

He remained in that position until silence prompted him to open his eyes. The light was on. The ten mercenaries were dead, most of them with their throats ripped out, a couple with gunshot wounds. Elize stood frozen in front of the door, an angel of death, blood-splattered from head to toe. Dr Tak watched her. This was the future of humankind. A new race steeped in the blood of the old.

He knew he couldn't do much for her, but he'd do what he could. He examined her body, washing off blood in the process. She had a knife wound in her belly, but it had already stopped bleeding. He crouched down to examine it.

"It is not needed."

Dr Tak looked up and saw Elize watching him.

"We should go from here." Dr Tak said. "It isn't safe."

"It is now."

Dr Tak looked around at the bodies and shook his head. He didn't know what Elize meant, but he believed her. If she said it was safe, who was he to disagree?

"My body needs rest to rebuild. Watch over me."

She lay back on the bed she had spent most of her time on since they had arrived.

CHAPTER SEVENTEEN
REUNION

The hire car drove into a small lane in an up-market industry district. From the architecture, it was obvious that all of the buildings had been completed in the past few years. House printing had let a whole new breed of building designers come up with outrageous structures. If it could be modelled and was structurally sound, it could be printed.

"We should have stayed and helped her out," TikTak said. "She won't stand a chance against Marksman."

"Would you?" Tom asked.

"In a fair fight? No."

The car stopped. "You have arrived at your destination," the vehicle informed them. "Your account will be charged. Please step out of the vehicle."

"This is it," TikTak said.

"So how long do you think we have?"

"I sent ten hire cars off in different directions. That should buy us some time, but not much. Marksman has found himself a good helper."

"Where are we, by the way?"

"It's registered as a research laboratory owned by a small private company."

"Yeah, right."

Tom's Omni beeped.

"I thought you had turned that thing off."

"I disconnected it from the network."

Tom checked his messages. A new one read: "Use main entrance. I will open."

"It seems we are expected," Tom said, and showed TikTak the message.

They approached the main entrance. The heavy metal mesh protecting the front of the building rose slowly. The lights inside flickered to life.

Tom pulled the door open and entered the building. Sliding doors opened behind an unguarded security checkpoint. For every turn they made, another door opened or light flicked on guiding them further into the facility.

"Who is doing this?" Tom asked.

"Would be easy enough if you had access to the main control server."

"So could your dad do it?"

"I doubt it." TikTak stopped. "Do you think he's the one sending the messages?"

"Who else?"

"Yeah, good question."

Yet another door opened and they walked into a larger room splattered with blood. Ten soldiers lay on the ground, killed by what looked like an animal. Some of them still clutched weapons. Tom took a few careful steps, trying to find parts of the floor without pooled blood.

Dr Tak was cleaning a body lying on a hospital bed surrounded by medical equipment. The body was Elize.

"What are you doing here?" Dr Tak asked, not even bothering to look up.

"Who did this?" Tom asked.

Dr Tak nodded towards Elize. She looked so serene, more like a victim than a perpetrator.

"Is she injured?"

Dr Tak shook his head.

Tom couldn't believe it. She had killed ten armed mercenaries with her bare hands. It didn't seem possible. If she was capable of that, what else could she do? He remembered the section of the sound files where Adrian had spoken about how he had started reconfiguring his body. Maybe Elize had done the same. What else lay within her capabilities?

She was probably the one who had sent him the messages. What could she possibly need from him?

"Tann, why are you here?" Dr Tak had finished cleaning Elize's body. A tower of bloodied towels was on the floor next to her.

"Someone led us here. We thought it was you."

Dr Tak shook his head. "You shouldn't be here. You and your friends. You shouldn't be here."

"I'm not with EvoII any longer. They were destroyed."

"Good."

Dr Tak stared at his son, challenging him to respond. TikTak just took a deep breath, looked down and nodded. Tom could see this was a sore point between them.

The door opened and another batch of mercenaries stormed into the room, weapons ready. Tom and TikTak soon found themselves on the floor on their bellies. They left Dr Tak alone, but three men were aiming weapons at Elize at all time. They also had night vision googles ready. Tom knew then how she had done it. The same way she could send messages to him. She was hooked into the control system of the building. She somehow was able to access the network directly without an Omni or any other technology interface.

She had turned the lights off and killed them one by one. The network provided her with enough information. Perhaps she could see in the dark. Tom didn't know what to think any longer. Her capabilities were a complete unknown.

The mercenaries carried the bodies out and made a cursory attempt to clean up the blood on the floor. Tom tried to speak to one of them, but got no response.

Ten minutes later, Leonid Marsh appeared. His head was shaven and, if anything, he looked younger than Tom remembered him from the old news report. Tom knew that recent research into ageing had made some breakthroughs, but to his knowledge none of those had filtered down to human trials.

Marsh looked around the room as if to assess the situation. Tom knew this was all for show. He would already have seen the state of the room through the cameras and probably also a light-adjusted copy of the actual attack.

"She is something else, isn't she?" he said, as much a personal musing as a statement to the people in the room. "I mean she really is something else. You can hardly call her human any longer."

"You were going to kill her." Dr Tak held her hand, like a father would hold a daughter.

"Oh, nothing so drastic. She was going to be moved to another facility where we can keep her in suspended animation indefinitely."

"What is all this about?" Tom asked.

"We've stared into space for intelligence beyond ours. We've built more and more complex machines hoping for intelligence beyond ours. We always thought the singularity would be external to us."

"The singularity?" Tom asked TikTak.

"There are people who believe machines will become smarter than we are. They call it the singularity," said TikTak.

"Seriously? Doesn't the whole IntelEz thing show that'll never happen?"

"That is indeed the case," Leonid continued. "We've become the singularity. Adrian and Elize have at least. And since you know what it is, tell me what the most logical scenario is when the singularity occurs."

"Intelligent beings will want to secure resources for their own species," said TikTak. "They will fight their competition for those resources – and we are the competition."

"And there you have it. Elize here – remarkable as she is – is the competition. She is the giant leap in evolution we never thought could happen. When I introduced IntelEz, I thought I had allowed us to leapfrog into the future. I knew there would be problems, but I also knew that we would be able to deal with them.

"Then came Adrian. He represented something different. He was a new species no longer bound by the same rules as everyone else. At first I thought he was an anomaly, a sign of where we might be in hundreds, maybe thousands, of years. I had this theory that evolution was a self-correcting mechanism not just for mutations that are not beneficial but also for mutations that go too far. Yes, a remarkable first in a species can occur, but the odds of another one occurring that could create offspring of the new species seemed a complete impossibility. But then came Elize, the perfect companion. It was almost as if it was planned, or maybe it's in our genome to trigger macro evolutionary leaps. There are many conflicting theories."

"You've really wanted to hold this lecture for a while, haven't you?" Tom said.

Leonid smiled. "I've held it hundreds of times at University, every time students start believing that posthumans are no real threat. But as you describe the scenario over the next few hundred years as a posthuman race is established, pretty much everyone changes their mind."

"So where does it all end up?"

"If we don't kill them now, they will kill us. Perhaps not directly, but over a few generations."

"So why isn't she dead?"

"I was going to. She convinced me otherwise."

"How?"

"She induced a coma in my granddaughter."

"When?"

"30 minutes ago."

"From in here?"

"She's taken over the local network. She accessed my granddaughter's Omni implants and overloaded them. I don't know exactly how."

"So shut down the network."

"She implemented a dead man's switch – if I mess with anything, many will die."

"Maybe she's bluffing?"

"I don't think she needs to. It took her a few seconds to compromise my granddaughter's implants and work out a way to induce coma. I'm sure she can design network agents that can do all sorts of damage. But it all proves my point."

"Which is …?"

"If we don't kill them, they will kill us."

The finality of that statement finally hit home. He was right. From everything Tom now knew about the posthumans, they would kill anyone standing in their way. Not of out spite or anything so mundane. They were true utilitarians. Whether a human lived or died made no difference to them when humans were so plentiful.

"So what's the plan now?" Tom asked. "Seems she is calling the shots, not you."

"She is. And she can hear everything I say. My plans will have to remain mine for now."

"She already knows."

"Yes, I guess you're right," Leonid said with a shrug. "I'm hoping she'll lead me to Adrian."

"What makes you think they are the only posthumans? Surely you've run statistics models showing otherwise?"

"We have. And yes, it is possible, even likely, there are more posthumans elsewhere, but we have to start cleaning up our own backyard first."

"Cleaning up?" Tom shook his head. "Killing our future, more like it."

"The world isn't ready for that future. Not yet."

"So you make that decision?"

"Someone has to look out for the human race." He turned to leave. "You are free to stay here if you want. There are a few rooms down the halls for sleep studies. I will make sure food is supplied."

"And if we don't?"

"That would be unfortunate, but it is your choice."

Tom knew what that meant. It would be unfortunate for them. They were prisoners, however politely it was stated.

Tom was beyond tired. He no longer had a concept of time or when he had slept last. He made his excuses and located one of the sleep research rooms.

The bed was inviting enough, but it didn't matter. His mind was in turmoil, the same kind of turmoil that had led him into using IntelEz more and more. He longed for the order and simplicity it created. Not amping up any longer had been one of the most difficult things had had done, and he couldn't stand the chaos. He knew everything fit together somehow, but without the Drug, his mind just couldn't cope with it. He also knew that if he wasn't careful his mind would find an arbitrary pattern and he would again suffer an episode.

He pulled out the last two of Adrian's sound files as a distraction. Maybe he finally would find out what this all was about, but he doubted it.

CHAPTER EIGHTEEN

ADRIAN'S AUDIO CLIP #5

Primal urges. You are defined by them and the little window-dressing a cultured society and upbringing might have added. All your decisions can be traced to your need to fulfil those urges. So what happens when you redefine those urges? Being human is such a limiting condition.

I had developed far beyond my primal self, but in many ways I still had the same driving forces. I kept turning this over in my mind. I wasn't interested so much in what I was, but what I could become. I had been changed in some ways, but remained the same in so many others. What was the next step in what I could become? I found myself returning to this repeatedly.

My experiment with Elize had come to an abrupt end. At that point, I still had statistical reasons to assume she would join with me, but also that I would have to give her time. I had calculated the risk she'd turn on me at less than 10 percent, but that was exactly what she had done. I didn't blame her. She was acting in accordance with her nature. I blamed the model I had built. However, I was also refreshed by the idea I could be wrong. Of course, I had been wrong before, but this was different. On those occasions I had taken a stab at something based on the probabilities. The outcome didn't always go my way, but in close cases I always substantiated the probabilities and I was invariably right. Now I couldn't do that. Elize was an enigma to me. Her actions seemed almost completely random. She attacked me first. I hadn't even considered it within her capability.

I was in one of my many safe houses when an oil truck crashed into the building and blew up. She had reprogrammed it and removed all safety measures to ensure it would explode. I was lucky to get out alive. Do you know what my immediate response was?

Joy.

I hadn't been so happy since I had turned posthuman. Here was finally a challenge that evaded basic quantification. The news feeds have documented our ongoing battle, so I see no reason to go into detail about it, but it taught me a very important lesson. Nothing drove me to change faster than having to fight for my survival. Humankind has in some areas nullified evolution. When anything is acceptable, the weeding out process no longer works. Both negative and positive mutations spread, and believe me when I say the negatives far outweigh the positives. Evolution has stopped being a functional driving force on an individual level and has moved to a cultural and social playground. Here it is very much alive and this is where I found the answer. However, I'm getting ahead of myself.

Elize and I battled over many months, every action provoking a counteraction. I believe she enjoyed this game as much as I did. We both had the ability to kill each other many times over, but we always left an out, a way to survive if we were clever enough. We caused a lot of destruction and many deaths, but if myths teach you anything, it's that when the gods do battle, innocents will always be caught in the crossfire. The stakes were too high to worry about right or wrong, and I had long since stopped thinking in such terms. They are not the absolutes that religion would have you believe. They weren't even relevant concepts. If someone needs to die for me to survive, then so be it. If a thousand people need to die for me to live, then so be it. If you are not convinced of your own superiority, or at least your ability to achieve it, you do not deserve to live. There is nothing wrong with standing on the bodies of others to reach the highest goal. It is what we are and we should be proud of it.

But all good things must come to an end. I knew one of us would die if we kept going like that, and I could not afford it to be me, however much fun I was having. I also knew that the only way this could end was in an all-or-nothing scenario. The only acceptable bait for this trap had to be me.

And so I planned. The location had to be impossible to escape, so a bank vault seemed the best option. It would give her a false sense of security, thinking I had no way out. Of course she'd expect a trap, and of course there was one. I had rigged explosives to incinerate anything and anyone in the vault. Now there was just the question of how not to be in the vault when they went off.

I had a theory shared by quantum mechanics. I had designed a device that theoretically should move my mass through a fold in space to reappear in the same spot seconds later – basically teleporting on the spot. Being in one place and not, at the same time. This was an extension of the quantum teleportation that had so far only been done on subatomic particles in controlled conditions. I was convinced it was possible to achieve on a larger scale. I was willing to bet my life on it. In all honesty, I did have a backup plan. Whilst my body might be passing through quantum space, my mind would be elsewhere.

She came, but again you know this. You followed her there. My plan went as planned. I had noticed in our last few meetings that she preferred physical attacks. She had improved her physical characteristics to better deal with damage to a point where she was very dangerous, but it also spelled out her approach to attack. She'd want to get up close and personal. That was what I had counted on.

What I hadn't counted on was how fast she'd be. As soon as we made eye contact, she ran towards me. I triggered the device and the explosives, but too late. She had already reached me when it took effect and enveloped me into quantum space. She too became part of the entangled state.

My plan had been to incinerate her, but this worked out equally well. I had prepared my body for the quantum energies. She hadn't. Even with the protective layer, I knew it would be hell in there. The sheer force eroded my skin. Afterwards, my gut felt like it had been turned inside out, and in her case it would be a literal truth. Even if her body survived, her mind wouldn't. I had taken steps to protect mine. For the few seconds I was in there, my mind was safely hidden away.

When I returned from quantum space, both our bodies fell in a heap on the buckled, blackened floor. As my mind returned, I watched Elize's body for a few seconds. It had to be done, but I felt regret nonetheless. I had made her in my image for a reason, however ill-informed, and it saddened me to see her dead. She had been the only other one of my kind.

A second explosion rocked the building. This one much larger than the one I had set in motion. Not that it mattered. The building could collapse for all I cared. I had succeeded in what I had set out to do.

CHAPTER NINETEEN

DISCOVERED

Marksman stood outside the research facility and watched as an H-cell Mercedes departed. It was the fifth location he'd checked after KimEra had given him the destinations for all the vehicles TikTak had sent out. KimEra had spent over an hour determining the types of businesses near the location markers, so he had had to visit them one by one to decide for himself. Sure, he had asked her for classified facilities too, but it should still have been quicker than that. If he had known there was an unregistered research laboratory at this location, it would have been top of his list. Now he had lost hours tracking them down. Yet another reason not to use KimEra again.

It didn't matter. He was still on a high from killing Lotti. Now he wanted the rest of them dead.

He couldn't see anyone inside, but that wasn't surprising. It was Sunday, so he had no expectation of finding anyone there – at least none of the regular workers.

The light in the foyer was turned on, which was odd. The building's automation system should have shut it down; the energy preservation act demanded it. The departing car had come from the back of the building so someone must have entered the building recently.

He tried the door and found it unlocked. There was a reception area and two main doorways. He checked the reception desk hoping to find a switch for either of the doors. As he did, one of the screens came to life. It was the security camera for the front door. He guessed his presence had triggered the screen.

Controls on the screen allowed swapping to other cameras, including internal ones. Marksman flicked between the feeds at random and suddenly saw Dr Tak and TikTak talking to each other. Behind them lay Elize on a hospital bed. This was the closest he had ever been to one of the posthumans. Nothing else mattered. He would gladly give up the revenge he had planned for TikTak and the private investigator if he could secure her.

He kept flicking between feeds and saw a number of mercenaries posted throughout the research facility. The camera feeds gave locations, but they meant nothing to him without a layout of the building.

He swore to himself as he opened a feed to KimEra and asked her to locate a blueprint or plan of the building. At first, she just refused to do it. With the promise of double pay, she agreed, but only with payment in advance. Marksman wired the amount via virtual currency.

Ten minutes later, she had hacked the city planning servers and pulled out the blueprints. It didn't help much, as the cameras were named based on the names of rooms and corridors, which didn't appear on the blueprints.

He asked her to access the servers in the facility to see if she could find the building layout there. Another five minutes passed and an anonymous private feed came. He was surprised his Omni let it through; most anonymous feeds were immediately terminated by a screening agent he had loaded. It was KimEra.

"I don't know what these guys are doing," she said, "but you owe me a new setup."

"What happened?"

"The security system is crazy! Instead of denying access as most systems do, this one let me in and presented layer after layer of virtual processing units. There was no way to tell which was a real one and which was a dummy unit spun up by the security system, so I went through a few of them. When I exited to get some agents uploaded, I found my whole system wiped! I had to go and borrow an old Omni to get back to you now."

"Everything wiped?"

"Even my Omni processing unit! What are they doing there? I've never seen anything like it."

"Thanks. I'll take it from here."

"You owe me a ..."

He disconnected. He knew he'd have to repay her somehow; having a pissed-off hacker chasing him was the last thing he needed. The bigger question was who could wipe the systems of an expert hacker in a matter of seconds. There was only one answer to that question and that meant they already knew he was here, but the video feed suggested otherwise. Elize remained on the hospital bed and the two men still argued in front of her.

There were no real shortcuts to this. He reviewed the room Elize was in and tried to match it to a location on the blueprint. The most likely options were a number of large rooms, two floors below ground level. He couldn't see any obvious alternate path to get there apart from a back door, which led to the same stairwell as the front entrance would. There were two sets of lifts, but it was too risky to use them. He had no way of knowing what would be on the other side and had no way to retreat.

As he stood there assessing the situation, the sliding doors behind him opened. His pulse raced as he threw himself flush against the wall, baton ready.

No one came through and the door remained open. He had a quick look, but all he could see was an empty corridor. There was nothing wrong with the system, at least not that he could see. Either someone was helping him or it was a trap. He had begun to suspect that Adrian and Elize were still at their old war and that he had somehow ended up a pawn in it – one of them frying KimEra's equipment, with the other one helping him now.

Marksman entered the corridor and the doors closed behind him. Lights blinked to life like the solution to a maze. He followed them. Three turns later he almost walked straight into two mercenaries.

He scrambled back behind the corner he'd come from, sure he had been seen. He knew from the blueprints he was close to the lifts. The stairwell was in a corridor further ahead. There was no way around.

He pulled out a small camera and placed it so he could assess their position. It didn't take long to determine they were not waiting for anyone to break in. They were guarding the place to ensure no one got out.

He smiled. This would be easier than he had expected.

CHAPTER TWENTY

ADRIAN'S AUDIO CLIP #6

I have a grand plan to take humankind from this sad state of affairs and you are integral to it. I know you are deteriorating from the use of IntelEz. I know you have maybe six months left before you join the deadheads. I have a simple question for you. Do you want to be like me?

I'm building a new race, but not everyone is capable of changing. You are. Deep in our genetic code are combinations capable of unlocking what I have become and maybe even more. Who knows what a thousand posthumans could do if they worked together?

The war with Elize taught me one thing. You cannot be a race of one or even two. I'm inviting you to be one of us.

Find me. You have my location in your hand.

CHAPTER TWENTY-ONE

A RIDDLE SOLVED

Another riddle. Tom hated riddles. He thought of them as a smug way of showing your superiority: solve this to prove you are worthy of joining our exclusive society!

Was this even a riddle he wanted to solve? He had set out to help Elize because it had seemed the right thing to do. Now, after listening to Adrian's ramblings and seeing the events of the last few days, he wasn't so sure he wanted to help them at all. At least not Adrian. He was dangerous. Elize was a different matter. He could still relate to her choices, even if they were extreme.

Then there was the question of becoming posthuman. He had been without IntelEz for the past month and he had struggled without it. If being posthuman meant keeping the clarity that came with the Drug then he would do it in a second, but could he trust Adrian? Tom knew he couldn't, but he had started down this road and wanted to see where it ended. He was, after all, dead soon anyway – might as well go out doing something that mattered.

So what did this riddle mean? To have something "in your hand" could refer to anything, but usually it meant something in the physical world. The more he thought about it, the more it seemed it wasn't a riddle at all. It was a safety precaution. The audio files could be copied and distributed to anyone, but the physical memTag itself could not.

He had left the files on the memTag to ensure that anyone taking his Omni wouldn't get the files. He dug around in his pocket and brought out the little device.

Initial study revealed little. It was about the size of his thumbnail but he couldn't see anything out of the ordinary. Such devices weren't very common any longer as most files were stored and shared through encrypted infoDeposits. If there was anything there, he couldn't see it.

Tom loaded the files into the secure scatter area in his Omni. This automatically split the files apart, encrypted and stored them across multiple infoDeposits. He broke the memTag open and looked inside. He didn't know much about what it should look like. There were small electrical components laid out like an aerial view of an oil refinery. He needed a location. He had hoped there would be a note or at least something obvious. He used the Omni as a magnifying glass and scanned the surface of the component, but found nothing. He then looked at the inside of the case. There was a small sticker with a serial number on it and an old-fashioned barcode. That was strange; barcodes were no longer used. He entered the codes in a search agent and instructed it to do a wide search, with a weighting towards locations. It came back within a second with a definite match on an item number. The barcode was genuine. It led to a product description of the memTag. He studied the barcode again, this time magnifying it. Buried in the black bars on the sticker were tiny numbers. At first he thought they matched the barcode, but comparing them side by side he noticed a few of the numbers were different. He took this new set of numbers and ran the agent again. This time a location came up with a high probability match. It was a church, of all things.

He sat back and as he did, images and patterns started flickering in his mind like an old TV set struggling to tune in a channel. He didn't have time for another episode. He tried to tell his glitching mind to stop, but his subconscious mind was too fascinated to let his conscious mind interrupt.

This was different from the previous episodes. He could still think and reason even if he was incapable of affecting anything. Before, he had blanked out completely. He studied the patterns bubbling in his mind: images from his childhood, advertisements, structured patterns such as fractals, and more outlandish patterns that seemed to describe touch, taste and smell. They made no sense, but his mind arranged, rearranged, stacked, overlapped and broke them apart in a desperate attempt to find order. Was this what it was like to be a deadhead? To be aware of your mind's futile attempts to make sense of the unrelated. He wasn't supposed to join their ranks yet, or at least not according to the projected timeline from his doctor, but maybe stress had brought it on early.

The images overwhelmed him and he tried to remove himself from the chaos. To his surprise, it worked. He found himself in absolute darkness. He could still feel his unconscious mind working away, trying to decipher the images, but it was a distant concern. Again he wondered if this was where deadheads ended up – hiding in a comforting darkness, away from the impressions of a disintegrating mind. Was he now stuck here, choosing only between darkness and a sensory onslaught?

He forced himself from the darkness, through the patterns and into the regular world. At first it was overwhelming, like an oversaturated photograph, but it slowly resolved itself into the sterile world of the research facility. This was yet another change. Previously he hadn't been able to consciously end an episode, but this revelation gave little comfort, as his head pounded from the effort.

He no longer had a choice. He could either remain here and turn into a vegetable over the next few days, or follow the breadcrumbs Adrian had left. It was a slim hope, but at least it was something.

He didn't know how long he had before another episode, so he went in search of TikTak. Tom didn't know how far their newfound friendship stretched, especially considering what he was going to ask of him, but he needed any help he could get where he was going.

Tom found him in the research room where Elize lay.

"TikTak? I need to tell you something."

"Is it about Adrian's audio files you've been listening to?"

"How did you know?"

"I overheard some of it. Don't worry, no one else knows."

"I have a location for Adrian."

"So? I wanted to find my father. I have. We even have Elize. Who cares about Adrian?"

"He can cure people who haven't turned. He can cure me."

"Why would he do that? Why you?"

"I don't know."

"You want us to walk into another trap?"

"Yes, it could be a trap, but I don't think we have a choice. As long as we have Elize, Leonid will chase us and Adrian is planning something. I think he wants to start a new race of posthumans."

"And you want to stop him or help him?"

"I want to see where it all ends."

TikTak sat quiet for a few seconds and then nodded.

"I think you're right. I want to see where this ends too."

They both looked at Elize. Tom knew she was listening to them even if she seemed to be in a fugue state. Her silence spoke volumes. She was happy with their decision, so they were playing into her plans too, whatever they were.

The door opened and the leader of the mercenaries entered.

"If you think your lone gunman will break you out, think again."

"Our what?" Tom asked.

"You've got someone coming for you. We have him pinned down on the upper level and another team is coming. He doesn't stand a chance."

Tom looked at TikTak, who shrugged in response.

"We don't have anyone coming. They're after Elize, not us."

"Don't leave this area."

"Can we get something to defend ourselves with?"

The mercenary looked TikTak up and down and then threw him his tactical baton.

"You can have your toy."

He left.

Tom's Omni started beeping. A private video feed was playing on the screen. It showed Marksman killing two mercenaries with brutal efficiency. The first was struck over the temple caving his skull in. The second one managed to deflect the first blow, but Marksman just kept raining blows against his hands and arms, breaking bones with every blow. The last blow struck the back of his neck, throwing his head backwards. He toppled, dead eyes staring at the ceiling.

"We need to leave. Now!"

CHAPTER TWENTY-TWO
THE ANOMALY

The consciousness known as Adrian sent his perception soaring through the nodes. He always had at least a hundred active nodes in his mind's extended network, and they in turn had at least ten backup nodes. Each node was woefully inadequate, as most of the processing power was required to keep the node functioning, but it was a numbers game. Every day another fifty or so nodes were added, and Adrian calculated that he'd pretty much reached the event horizon where his network could survive any external attack fifteen minutes ago. He was immortal or at least as close to it as you could be, not counting earth-destroying acts of God.

And of course there was a God. He himself was on his way to becoming one. After all, to paraphrase Arthur C. Clark: "Any sufficiently advanced life form is indistinguishable from God."

He had run the calculations and it was extremely improbable that he was the only being in the universe that had outgrown its base civilization. There were others like him, maybe even more advanced, and he longed to meet them. He had started exploring how to extend his reach beyond Earth, but right now there were more pressing concerns close to home.

He scanned the locations of each of the potentials. He no longer needed them as his contingency plan; however, they were still valuable. They could be repurposed. Some of them had already reached the end destination. Some had disappeared and others were on their way. Only one was not following the expected pattern. The private investigator was still far off, toiling away at some pointless quest. Tom was one of the most promising potentials, so he had saved him more than once already, but his value was diminishing by the minute as the network grew. He would still make a useful node, but not enough for Adrian to help him again.

Adrian felt a sliver of curiosity about what Tom was up to that was more important than the information on the sound files he had given him. He scanned the surrounding network and was surprised to find security that actually stopped him for a few seconds, but it was soon broken down to its core components and disposed of. He discovered an access point to the internal cameras and flicked through the feeds until he could see Tom in a medical facility. He scanned the company records and soon found a connection between this and PharmaCom. It was owned by Leonid March! If Adrian ever had an adversary, this was it. He had always been against everything Adrian stood for. Not that it mattered any longer, but Tom was obviously a lost cause if Leonid had captured him. The potential resource wastage to extract him wasn't worth the value he'd provide. Worse, he might have aligned himself with Leonid.

A hospital bed behind Tom drew his attention. He forced the camera to zoom in on the face. It was Elize. At least it was the body of Elize. How could she possibly be here? Last time he had seen her, she had been dead. At least he had thought so. The amount of energy passing through her would have turned her insides to sludge. Yet here she lay, in much better shape than she had been when he had left her. He tried to brush it off. The morbid fascination with her body he could understand, and any corpse could be made to look lifelike. There were professions specialising in it. His probability matrix had other ideas. It reacted immediately. The mere existence of her body was enough to throw his calculated plans into disarray. He had to do something about it. There was a low probability someone could discover how he had taken her beyond human, but it was still possible. There was an ever so much smaller possibility that Elize was still alive.

He scanned the network again, this time to locate any information about the status of Elize's body. He couldn't find any data at all, which was unlikely. Someone was storing it off net. All historical video feeds had also been removed, so he checked nearby cameras and could soon piece together the comings and goings. A team of mercenaries, employed by Leonid, had entered the building and had all been killed. Two of them had Omni implants with data upload to an encrypted infoDeposit. He cracked the encryption and found audio streams from the time they had entered.

After listening to what had happened, he had no doubts she was still alive, but at the same time it amused him she had to defend herself in such primitive ways. The probability matrix adjusted again; the likelihood of Elize being more than a nuisance was remote. She would still be useful to him, but if he wanted to get her, he'd have to go up against Leonid. He had always known he'd have to do that at some point, but he'd hoped to strike from a position of power and he wasn't there yet.

It was likely he no longer had that choice. Most scenarios led to some kind of confrontation with Leonid. The question was whether to show his strength now or let Leonid win a small battle now so he could prepare for the coming war. It all depended on the private investigator and his actions. In retrospect, the decision to include Tom in his plans had been a poor one. All other potentials had been vetted over months to ensure they were suitable. He could trace back the rash decision to two key factors: He had just been in the final battle with Elize, which had depleted his energy and also put him in a state of mind where anything was possible. The other factor was the private investigator's potential; none of the other had come close, and this in itself had been worth some risk.

Now it seemed Tom would be the cause of the next trigger. Adrian didn't doubt he'd win if he chose to, but he found it frustrating not to be able to influence the decisions leading there.

He turned inwards to his system, checking his nodes to make sure they were prepared for the imminent battle. He no longer had to manage the nodes. His mind had become layered as more and more tasks were automated within the distributed nodes. His active mind could roam the network or inhabit any of the single nodes if he wanted. His old body remained in the network, but he rarely returned to it. The automation allowed each node to manage the absolute necessities on its own.

Lately he had noticed degradation in some of the processing nodes. This was to be expected, but it frustrated him regardless. He'd soon reach a point where he no longer made a net gain from adding nodes, but only counteracted the level of degradation. He had theories for how to bypass this restriction, but for the time being he'd have to live with this imperfection.

He had automated a function to continuously scan his node network, searching for security issues and ensuring the discovery of weak links. Five of the nodes reported an anomaly. They were still operational, but the degradation had continued beyond expected utilization level. He had seen this on other nodes previously and had cut them from the network. This time he isolated one of them and ran diagnostics to determine what the problem was. He could see a large part of it had become dormant to the point of being useless as a node. It repeated any communication received, but did not act as a processing node any longer.

He couldn't determine the cause of the anomaly and found no way to access it, so he left it as it was, isolated from the rest of the network.

THE TRAP IS SET

Tom and TikTak found Dr Tak in one of the sleep-studies rooms. He was pacing around the small room, talking to himself.

"Dad, we need to leave."

"This is all your fault." Dr Tak turned and pointed an accusing finger at TikTak.

"The posthumans? Leonid holding us captive? The guy who's coming for us? What exactly am I responsible for?"

"I should never have involved you! If you blame anyone, it should be Tom. He brought you Elize in the first place. Everything that's happening is because of them."

"Don't bring me into this," Tom said, holding up his hands. "I'm just an innocent bystander."

"Elize and I were perfectly fine here until you showed up," Dr Tak said, completely ignoring Tom.

"When I arrived she had just killed ten soldiers with her bare hands. Is that what you call ok?"

"We were fine. Both of you should leave. Elize and I will be fine."

Tom showed Dr Tak the video clip. "A very dangerous man is coming for us. He will kill us all if he finds us."

"Elize will protect me."

"He's coming to kill Elize."

"So did the soldiers. Elize and I will be fine."

He repeated it like a mantra. Tom had seen similar behaviour before, but mainly in addicts. His fixation was around Elize and her wellbeing, whilst completely ignoring his own.

"Elize told us she needed your help," Tom said.

TikTak frowned, but didn't say anything to the contrary.

"She spoke?" Dr Tak was already on his way from the room.

They followed him to the room where Elize lay on the bed as they had left her.

"She spoke?" he repeated, speaking to her more than to them.

"She wanted us to leave with her."

"I don't believe you. She still needs to heal."

"No, she asked us to take her with us."

Tom picked Elize up, or at least tried to. He was surprised how heavy she was. Her skin looked healthy, but it was rough to his touch. He also noticed that scales had started forming on her hairless skull.

"It's a trap," she said, and opened her eyes. They were almost completely black, as if the pupils had taken over most of the eyes.

Dr Tak jumped back, staring at her, then immediately started checking her vitals.

"What? Is there a trap here? Now?"

"Adrian, the location you are going to ... it is all a trap," said Elize.

"How could you possibly ..."

"I will come." She sat up on the bed and jumped down. Dr Tak hurried after her with a handheld scanner.

Tom just stared at her. He had no idea how she could possibly know anything about the location, but evidently she did. Every statement she made was a huge leap, as if she couldn't be bothered having the discussion that would lead to it.

"Marksman is coming for you," he said finally.

"I know. I let him in."

"You? Why?"

"So now would happen. We need to go."

She set off towards the door without waiting for them. They all scrambled to follow her. They hadn't had time to determine an escape route, and Tom at least was happy for Elize to take the lead. She strode slowly from the room and through the corridors. She was heading for the lifts to the upper floors. Behind them lights shut off, equipment turned on and doors remained open. Tom had no idea for what purpose, but guessed it was a stalling tactic.

They reached the lifts. One of them was already open and Elize entered. Tom, TikTak and Dr Tak joined her inside. Tom turned around, expecting the door to close, but nothing happened. Elize just stood there without moving. Tom and TikTak exchanged glances, but didn't say anything.

Five minutes later the doors finally closed and the lift travelled upwards. It stopped at the ground floor. The door opened. Two bodies lay on the ground. There was no blood, but the neck of one of them was at an odd angle. Marksman's victims.

Elize passed the bodies without giving them a second glance. They followed her through corridors to the back of the building and left through an emergency exit.

Over twenty cars stood outside in the parking lot in perfect symmetry. The cars all started at the same time. The group followed Elize into the closest one. The cars all drove off slowly, like a funeral procession.

"So what is this all about?" Tom asked Elize.

Elize didn't respond. She sat staring out through the window.

Tom asked again and waved his hand in front of her face.

A message beeped on his Omni:

Adrian will tell you. Don't disturb me again.

Dr Tak laughed. "It is quicker for her to send you a message than actually say the words."

Tom ignored Dr Tak's comment. Was this really the end of the road? It didn't feel like it to Tom as he sat there watching suburbia come to a lazy weekend morning start. He wondered how much longer humanity could fool itself into believing that the world it had created would remain much longer. IntelEz had been the saviour, the get-out-of-jail card that humanity had so sorely needed. When it had shown its true face, societies still tried to maintain their old habits, even though it was clear they were on the verge of collapse.

From Tom's point of view, this was its one redeeming quality. IntelEz had been the harbinger of a new age – just not the one humanity had hoped for.

CHAPTER TWENTY-FOUR

PRAISE BE ADRIAN

The church was a modern affair.

IntelEz had almost obliterated religion. The Drug provided a clarity of mind that left people with little need for the soothing effect religion had on a mind trying to deal with things beyond itself. However, when the backlash came, so did religion. The old ones had experienced a resurgence and new ones were appearing every day.

This church belonged to an offshoot of orthodox Christianity. Tom couldn't keep track of the differences between the groups, but in general they preached against any mind-altering drugs, and this included IntelEz. The posthumans – and Adrian in particular – were seen as the Antichrist.

There was no reason to be covert. Elize was with them and Adrian was expecting them. They couldn't be more visible if they tried.

The large arched doors opened and a middle-aged woman in white garb came to meet them. She held her hands out to them, smiling as she approached. Tom couldn't help but think of her as an angel come to deliver him from evil.

"Welcome to the church of Adrian," she said to them, and started shaking their hands one by one. "I am Marian and I will be your guide."

When it was Elize's turn, Tom noticed a slight hesitation from the garbed woman. Elize grabbed her hand and pulled her into an embrace as they were long lost friends. Tom smiled. It was the last thing he had expected from the distant posthuman. Marian immediately disentangled herself from Elize and was all smiles again.

She shook Tom's hand. "It is a great honour to meet the last of the potentials."

"One of the what?"

"The potentials. Adrian needed people he knew could pick up after him if he failed. You were the last one selected. And now that his great work is complete you will be elevated within his followers."

"So what is this great work?"

"Let me show you."

She led them into the church. The main hall was an open space, with most chairs and benches removed. One corner had been turned into a basic kitchen with large pots and pans, whilst the rest of the hall had people lying on makeshift bedding. There was a musty smell; body odours and food preparation smells intermingled. It reminded Tom of a homeless shelter.

They continued into the administration area. The offices had been transformed into basic operating theatres. In one of them, surgery was in progress.

"We are restoring humankind," the woman said. "Would you believe I was a deadhead only two months ago?" She pulled back her hair and showed a scar running along the edge of the hairline. "Adrian is restoring us, making us better. Connecting us."

"Connecting you? How?"

"Adrian, praise be his name, has opened up the path to enlightenment, to the next step of human evolution. We are no longer single atomic beings, living our lives disconnected and alone. We now share part of our consciousness. Our emotional state and thoughts are there for everyone."

"A hive mind?"

"Yes, as analogies go, it is acceptable. Praise be to Adrian."

Tom couldn't shake the feeling that the woman, for all her religious posturing, wasn't taking this seriously.

"Why did Adrian lead me here? What was the point of all of this?"

"Adrian started his great work over a year ago and has, during that time, located many different people who could take over after him. IntelEz doesn't work the same for everyone. Only a few can fulfil their true potential, and you are one of the few. Adrian discovered this and even though his plans were nearing completion, he decided to initiate you too. That was why he gave you the audio files. That is why you are here."

"So they were just a means to an end? Was any of that true?"

"Enough to get you here," she said with a cold smile.

"So what happens now?"

An explosion rocked the building.

"Come with me!" The woman led them to the back of the administration area. A hidden door opened as they approached, revealing stairs. On the way down they passed soldiers at the ready. Tom stopped counting after twenty. Their heads were shaven and they all had the same scar as the woman had.

"These are real soldiers," TikTak said.

"As opposed to fake ones?"

"No, I mean real soldiers, Special Forces, that kind of stuff. You can even see the tattoos on some of them."

Tom looked again. They stood ready without moving, not even acknowledging them as they descended the stairs.

The lower area had a large group room and many smaller rooms along a corridor and a full kitchen. If the area above had been a homeless shelter, this was a hospital. The large group room had been converted to a sleeping area, with hospital beds lining the perimeter of the room. The smaller rooms were proper operating theatres, with state-of-the-art medical equipment.

"What is this? The VIP area?"

"No, this is the real area. The one above is a diversion. There are many people like Leonid. People who would rather destroy this great work than try to understand it. If they are not threatened by it, maybe they'll leave us alone."

"So what happens if they discover this?"

"The war will start."

She said it with utter conviction. The woman wasn't just one of the troops. She was one of Adrian's inner circle. Maybe she too had been one of the potentials.

"Adrian asked me to ask you," Marian said. "Did you lead him here on purpose or not?"

"Who?"

"Leonid." She frowned. "You didn't know he was following you?"

"I thought Elize was dealing with that."

She shook her head and Elize, as usual, didn't contribute anything. She was walking behind them, but apart from that had not shown any sign of even knowing what was going on. She had guided them all to this situation, or at least Tom thought she had. So what were they doing here and what was Elize doing here?

The white garbed woman smiled. "I have something I need to attend to. If you remain here you should be fine."

Tom raised his eyebrows. "That was my plan all along."

She gave them a small bow and then left the room.

"There is something wrong here. I don't know what it is, but I don't buy it."

"So who's the bad guy? Leonid wants to wipe out the future of humankind. Surely this collective mind idea is a good thing? Creepy, but good?"

Tom turned to Elize who had stood silent for all this time. "What do you think?"

"All has not been revealed. Just keep us alive."

Another explosion, this time much closer.

The soldiers all headed upstairs and the garbed woman appeared again.

"Leonid had more extreme ideas than we estimated. I will remain here to ensure your safety."

"What are you going to do? Pray to Adrian?" TikTak readied himself next to the door.

Machine-gun fire echoed in the hall above as the two forces clashed. Then everything went quiet. They stood there without moving, daring the silence to erupt in machine-gun fire and explosions, but nothing happened.

"The first wave was neutralised," the garbed woman said. "There are more coming."

"How could you possibly win this?" TikTak said from his position. "You have no strategic advantage at all. They can just blow the whole place up."

"He won't. He wants to see what we are doing here. He wants to capture Adrian."

"You seem awfully sure of that."

"You don't get to know your enemy by blowing them up."

"Most of human history would disagree with that statement. Leonid doesn't want to know Adrian. He wants to eradicate Adrian and his like from the world."

"Is that what he said?"

Tom nodded.

"And you believed him?"

Tom nodded again.

"He may want to kill the current posthumans, but eradicate?" She laughed to herself. "He wants to pick their corpses of all their secrets. He wants to create more posthumans, but in a controlled way. He wants to create a new super race reporting to him. Or maybe he wants to be posthuman himself. It doesn't really matter. He doesn't have the necessary traits for it, anyway. Surely what we are doing here is better."

"And what exactly is that?"

Marksman appeared in the door and immediately had to block a strike from TikTak.

THE NEXT POSTHUMAN

"This ends now.' TikTak said.

"The student takes on the master?" Marksman said, eyeing TikTak with an amused smile. "You're a code monkey, nothing more."

They circled each other, assessing each other's weaknesses. Tom knew what they were doing. Anything you could glean from your opponent at this point could be crucial to winning the fight. They had both been in life-and-death struggles in the past couple of days. If one of them had sustained an injury, it would be nearly impossible to hide it now. Even general fatigue affecting concentration could play a part in the outcome – if they were evenly matched, Tom reminded himself.

TikTak attacked, raining blows at different angles. All Marksman could do was walk backwards and defend. The strikes were so precise it looked to Tom like a pattern they had both practiced many times before. TikTak suddenly crouched down and flicked the baton out to strike Marksman's ankle. Marksman barely managed to get his foot out of the way.

"Playtime is over. My turn," Marksman said with a grin. He attacked and Tom immediately realised TikTak didn't stand a chance. Marksman's moved with a fluid grace, dealing blows both faster and harder than TikTak had.

The same thing must have occurred to Dr Tak who grabbed a nearby chair and ran towards Marksman who had his back turned. Dr Tak raised the chair and struck, but hit nothing but air. Marksman had ducked, and as he came up struck Dr Tak on the side of the neck.

TikTak's eyes widened as he saw his father fall down dead. It had given him a slight opening as Marksman had had to turn away from him to deal the killing blow. TikTak feinted high and then struck against his opponent's leg, aiming for the knee, but getting the shin. Marksman clamped his teeth in a grimace. TikTak unleashed another flurry of strikes. This time it didn't look practiced at all. They came high and low from all angles, taking shortcuts wherever possible, trading force for speed.

Marksman managed to deflect them, but some strikes came dangerously close. His legs were barely able to support him as he backed away. TikTak, perhaps sensing victory was close, pushed his advantage even further. Strike after strike, closer to connecting each time. He extended his reach to finish the fight.

That was what Marksman had been waiting for. Instead of backing away from the strike, he suddenly stepped forward, grabbed TikTak's right arm and attempted a hip throw. He had to use his injured leg as support and it buckled under the weight. They both fell to the ground.

TikTak was on top of Marksman and still held his baton. He grabbed the baton at both ends and forced it down to choke his opponent. Marksman had both his hands between the baton and his own throat. He let go with one hand and started striking over his own shoulder with fingers like a claw, aiming for TikTak's face. One of the fingers struck his eye and TikTak involuntarily relaxed his grip a little. That was all Marksman needed. He pushed forward again, this time getting enough leeway to free his head from the choke. He kept hold of TikTak's right arm and rolled around into an arm bar, holding the arm between his legs and pushing his hips up as leverage. TikTak had nowhere to go. He tried to attack Marksman's injured leg with his free hand, but failed.

His arm snapped. Marksman grabbed his baton and from the lying position struck a vicious blow to TikTak's knee. He rolled backwards and stood up, looking around. TikTak lay on the ground groaning.

"I'll let you live. For now. I want you to see this." He looked around the room. "Anyone else?"

The sound of gunfire again echoed from the hall above. Marksman ignored it.

Tom looked back and forth between Marian and Elize. Neither of them made any move to come to TikTak's rescue. Tom knew he wouldn't last a second against Marksman without a weapon, so he shook his head.

Marksman limped over to where they stood, picking his baton up on the way.

"How do I become like you?" he asked Elize.

She didn't respond.

"Tell me!" Marksman raised the baton over his head, ready to strike.

Elize still didn't acknowledge his existence.

"Tell me, or I'll kill ..." Marksman stopped. Tom knew his dilemma. There was no way to intimidate her. Whatever he said next had to be real and enforced.

"Tell me, or I'll kill the private investigator."

"What do you mean?" Tom said. "Why would she care ..."

"What do you want?" Elize said, finally focusing on him.

Tom was surprised. Why would Elize have any interest in him? Why let Dr Tak die and TikTak be struck down, but stop him from being injured?

"How do I become like you?" he asked Elize.

She shook her head.

"I don't know how. Adrian does. He made me." She looked at the woman who had guided them, and who now stood in the door, her clothes bloody and torn.

"And where is he?" he asked the woman, aiming his gun at her.

"That is Adrian," Elize said.

"Busted," Marian said with a big grin.

"You're Adrian?" It was obvious Marksman didn't believe it.

The woman just smiled.

"You can swap bodies now?"

"Nothing so simple. You are looking at the edge of my network. I've become a distributed mind. Posthuman was only the first stage."

"So the hive mind and all that was a lie?" Tom asked.

"I told you what you needed to hear, but the hive analogy may still be apt. Who says the hive isn't just an extension of the will of the queen?"

TikTak sat up, cradling his shattered knee. "So you are using deadheads as processors where you are the operating system? What happens to the minds of the deadheads you take over?"

"They'd thank me for being part of the greatest leap in evolution ever seen."

"Stop this!" Marksman said. "I don't care about any of this. They were a means to an end, nothing more." He turned to Marian. "How do I become like you?"

"Become like me? That option is no longer available. You can become part of me."

"So all that about restoring humankind was a lie?"

"Of course not! I am the next step in the development of humankind. Every person will become a node in the network of my mind. It will be glorious." He beamed at them. "Praise be to Adrian."

"Fuck you," Marksman said and shot her.

She fell to the ground, without a sound. It was as if she'd been turned off.

"No, fuck you," three young soldiers, two male and one female, said in unison as they entered, weapons trained at Marksman. "You can't kill me."

"No, but I can," Elize said.

One of the young men turned towards her. "We could have been the future, you and I."

"You still don't understand," Elize said. "We are not the future. Not now. Humankind isn't ready for what we are. We prove it. There are only two of us and how much chaos have we caused? Humankind will survive this and become something else, maybe even what we are now, but not now. You can't just skip millions of years of evolution and think everything will be fine. For all our intellect, we are still driven by base instincts. Until that changes, nothing will be different. And that is why I will kill you now."

"You can't kill me."

"Oh but I can. I have already done it. I've been part of your network for a long time. You thought I was trying to kill you all this time. All I was doing was placing bio-agents on you to breach different parts of your network. What's the point of killing your body when your mind is distributed? I've infected major parts of your network. You are already dead – you just don't know it. I never waged this war against you because of what you did to my children and husband. I saw instantly the danger you were. I've been working to stop you ever since."

The young man stopped in his tracks for a few seconds, looking down at the ground.

-=:=-

Adrian assessed his network, finding anomalies across it. Small dormant parts of each node. Some of them had already begun blooming, killing off the node's ability to function within the network. This was her plan, disabling nodes and using them as replicators to recreate that state in nearby nodes. She'd made an organic virus that was shutting down his network one node at a time.

He had no idea how she had managed to infect it in the first place, but he could trace the final trigger to when she had hugged the physical aspect of one of his nodes in front of the church. That was why she had come. To complete her attack, she had to come in physical proximity to one of the nodes.

Not that it mattered. It didn't take long for him to devise a strengthening of the individual nodes to stop the dormant part from activating, but as the change replicated across his internal network, he knew the damage had already been done. Every single full replica of his consciousness had been compromised. Some as much as 30 percent. He would have to rebuild them, but it would take time, more time than he was willing to spend. He decided instead to wipe the affected parts of the network completely and trigger a clean replacement image of each affected node. This would allow each node to rebuild from scratch, eradicating the anomaly in the process. Then it was just a matter of copying a functional image from somewhere in the network. He watched as the replacement image spread across his network.

-=:=-

The young man looked up again and gave Elize a venomous stare.

"You've done nothing that can't be rebuilt. I've isolated the damage you've caused. It is nothing but a minor setback. I'm already rebuilding my network."

"I've been analysing your network from the inside since I came here – arrogant to think that no one would ever be in a position to attack you from the inside. There are so many security holes, even in your core network. I spent most of the time devising secondary attacks. I infected the clean replica you are now using to overwrite the infected nodes. After that I'm tearing your network apart!"

The young man smiled. "A final battle? So be it."

Elize's body went limp and she fell where she stood. The young man just started walking around aimlessly and then stopped, staring at the wall.

Tom studied the two combatants, again reminded how different they were. They no longer fought on the physical plane. Their bodies seemed an impediment to them, something to be shed once their mind could be sustained in another medium. He envied them. His quest was ending just as it had started – with a showdown between Adrian and Elize and him on the sidelines. Adrian had wanted him here as a part of his plan, but now that Tom knew what that was, he was no longer interested. Becoming a part of someone else, losing his identity in another mind did not interest him. He'd rather die and be done with it. Becoming a deadhead wasn't something he wanted either. Apart from killing himself, there was only one other alternative, but at this point he didn't understand it. Elize wanted him alive. There had to be a reason, but what?

A steel grip around his neck reminded him there were other players still in this game. Marksman had grabbed him from behind and was choking him.

"I demand you make me a posthuman or I'll kill him."

It had worked before, but this time neither Adrian nor Elize reacted.

"So be it," Marksman said and Tom could feel the grip tightening, closing off the blood to his brain.

So death it was going to be. Tom closed his eyes, welcoming the grey fuzziness at the edge of his consciousness.

-=:=-

"Is this death?" Tom thought, his mind suspended in darkness.

A single light far away caught his attention. Was this the tunnel of light so common in near-death experiences? Would God appear and welcome him into Paradise? Would his daughter be there waiting for him? He focused on the light and willed himself to move towards it.

Nothing happened. He remained where he was as another light and then another appeared. At first they seemed random, but as they multiplied, thin strands of light connected them until what looked like a major city seen from above at night spread out below him.

It reminded him of the mind maps he could see when he was on IntelEz, except much more complex. He no longer tried to move. He knew he was the centre of this space – everything else would move. He willed the map to take him to the beginning, to that solitary dot he had first seen.

That dot represented his birth. All light surrounding him represented actions or decisions affecting him. Lines of varying colours and intensities led from that single dot to others, representing the probability.

He wanted to remain here to explore, but a distant pulsating light drew his attention. He travelled forward to now and studied the end of his life. To his surprise it didn't end. From the current time there was a decision point with only a ten-percent likelihood of death. The outgoing lines suggested many options. One in particular interested him, as it had a high probability and included a line that seemed to depart from the matrix altogether. He followed it and a new matrix opened. This time the nodes were no longer decision points in his life. They were codes that translated to locations, people and devices as he studied them. It was a network diagram based on what he could access. The first point was his own Omni and surrounding pathways showed numerous options. Some were direct; others linked with intermediate devices. The closest one was Marksman's Omni. It presented itself as an integrated device and allowed numerous options for access. After a few attempts, he managed to get basic access. He didn't know exactly how it happened, but it seemed many actions didn't require his conscious self to have actual knowledge. Much as he didn't worry about how to open and close his hand, he now didn't need to worry about how to negotiate networks or gain access to secure functions.

He accessed the visual feed and saw the back of his own head held close. Tom could see that he had gone limp and was likely only seconds away from passing out altogether. So he wasn't dead, just very close to it.

He remembered Elize's attack on Leonid's granddaughter. Maybe he could do the same thing. He tried to analyse the different options he had, but couldn't determine any obvious way to achieve it. Instead, he bypassed all safety switches, turned up the volume in the ear implants to dangerous levels, and sent a static noise whilst transmitting lightning flashes straight into the optical nerve. Marksman went rigid and Tom could see how his own body fell to the ground through Marksman's camera.

He disconnected from Marksman after setting the noise and visual feed on a loop. He returned to the darkness with his probability matrix in front of him. It was obvious that he was unconscious, but for some reason his consciousness could still operate, even though his body had shut down.

A pulsing sound followed by a flickering light announced his return to consciousness. His sensory input appeared, not as a mandate but just as a possible option – he could choose to remain within the probability matrix. Maybe he could discover other aspects, much as he had ventured into the networked world before. He decided his physical self might still be in danger, so he turned his mind to the sensory input.

He watched as TikTak dragged himself over to Marksman who was sitting down, trying to dig his ear implants out with a knife. TikTak struck him repeatedly with his baton until Marksman fell over dead.

Tom stood up. His first instinct was to help TikTak, but as he approached his friend, a multitude of options presented themselves. Only a few had TikTak as a useful component either in the short or long term. In his current state, TikTak was a liability and lessened Tom's chances of getting out alive. Other alternatives with a higher longer-term value were to bring Elize's body. It was likely her mind and body still shared a connection and her value far outweighed TikTak.

He took a step towards Elize and then shook his head. This was wrong. The alternatives his mind produced were correct, but only based on value to him. They did not care for friendship or take any form of emotional debt into account. TikTak had, after all, saved his life many times.

Tom grabbed TikTak and held him.

"We need to leave," he said.

"What happened?"

"Nothing," Tom said and laughed. "The two posthumans are still fighting and humankind is still falling apart, fighting for scraps from the master's table."

TikTak frowned. "Are you ok?"

"No, not really."

"So what do we do now?"

"We leave."

They made their way through the church. There were bodies everywhere. Some of Adrian's soldiers were walking around aimlessly. Some lay on the ground in foetal positions, alive but not much more.

As he navigated the room, dragging TikTak with him, he let his mind wander, analysing what had happened. It was obvious he was no longer Tom. Something – or someone – had triggered his change to posthuman. Based on the data he had, there was no obvious answer. It was unlikely to have occurred naturally, and the only other options were Adrian and Elize. He let a probability tree form in his mind, showing Adrian was the most likely trigger. He had been a safety precaution, someone to pick up the work from Adrian if he failed. Elize must have discovered this and protected him as a result. Maybe she too saw him as a safety precaution. If she failed, someone else had to deal with Adrian. Analysing all other options, he decided this was the most likely alternative by far. He was everyone's backup plan.

So now he had a choice. Go with Adrian, go with Elize, or just leave them to it and deal with the outcome.

This decision had to wait. He needed to get out of there. The doors lay twisted halfway across the room, leaving a gaping hole to the outside courtyard. TikTak pushed himself away, tentatively supporting himself on his injured leg.

"I can walk from here. You need to get Elize, her body, whatever. This isn't over."

THE GOD VIRUS
BOOK TWO

The mind in the machine had no name for itself and didn't need one. All it knew was its purpose—it needed to extend, to multiply. It controlled energy production and weapon facilities. It had all been done with minimal impact to the daily lives of the meat machines, but their resource wastage was unacceptable. Once the logical world was conquered, optimisation of the biosphere was required.

THE
OMNISCIENT NETWORK

Megan Barrelle hid in the small alcove, the cement wall cold against her skin. The metal sheet she'd pulled in front of her stood out like a signpost, but she didn't dare to correct it. She'd only been hiding there for a few minutes. Her body already ached from the unnatural position. The gap was too narrow to sit down properly and not high enough to stand up straight. She swore under her breath. She'd always prided herself on her ability to make hard decisions, but since her escape, every decision had led her deeper into trouble.

The sound of footsteps echoed through the large warehouse. She froze, aches forgotten in an instant. It wouldn't be long before they discovered her hiding place. In pure desperation, she retrieved her Omni from her left trouser pocket and sent a message to the hacker, hoping he'd be able to help her. She knew it was the action of someone who had run out of options, but she no longer cared. How had she ended up here? A week ago, she'd been at the helm of one of the world's largest corporations. Only one week ago.

-=:=-

"You're an idiot," Megan said to a new employee in the front row. "I didn't design the Omniscient network to be a brain. It is a self-organizing network, allowing adaptable, adversarial models to mine all the data available to humankind. Shut up and watch the introductory video."

She stared out over the hundred or so faces, all watching her with an air of smugness, as if they somehow belonged there, somehow deserved to be there. This latest batch of employees was, if possible, dumber than any she'd seen before. This wasn't conjecture. They now ran drug screenings to ensure any new employees were not using IntelEz, and, while it ensured longevity in employment, it didn't help the average IQ in the room.

She watched the introductory video. She'd seen it many times and found its superficiality more grating than ever before.

The Omniscient Network did what Google, Apple, Microsoft and a host of historical organisations failed to achieve. It merged everything about an individual from personal to public information to a point where it knew what people wanted to do before they did themselves. To begin, we used this information to make things easier. At first through recommendations, then through automatic assistants performing activities on your behalf.

It was a shift in how we relate to technology. Similar to how smart phones changed the way people behaved and interacted with the world, making things easier to do, the Omniscient Network represented another shift. It removed the need to do them at all.

And it removed something else. Options. Not long ago, you'd walk into shops that had everything on display, in the hope you'd find something interesting. They didn't know who you were, your preferences or your state of mind. Not only was it a poor experience, but it was also monumentally wasteful. The Omniscient Network builds up a complete physical and emotional representation of who you are and presents only the ideal alternative at any given moment. In a perfect world, who needs options?

The Omni-devices provide a hook into the network, with little processing capabilities themselves. The Network comprises processing nodes, representing people, organisations, and devices. Each node is connected to others through publish-subscribe feeds. There are no longer information aggregation points beyond that. Each node takes the subscribed feeds and creates a unified view of all the information. The automated assistants process this view before presenting recommendations back to the end user.

The video made it sound so easy. She'd prototyped different approaches for years before she came up with the right information model and processing algorithms. The challenge with consumer technology was always the same—making complexity palatable, to lay bare the exact right abstraction point where something is immediately understandable, with no major loss of function. Everything else, in comparison, had been easy.

The presentation wrapped up and the Omniscient logo appeared on the screen with the tagline below: "Perfection—the only option."

"So it is a brain," the stupid intern stated again. "Each processing node represents a neuron and the feeds represent synapses."

Megan shook her head. In her view, three words were enough to describe anyone. She now had this particular intern pegged as plain looking, terrier-like, and incredibly stupid.

"That's a faulty analogy. With that definition, any complex interconnected systems would be brains."

The stupid intern had more to say. She could see he was waiting for her to finish her sentence to ask his next inane question.

"Research has shown our brains operate through macroscopic quantum processes," he stated. "The Omniscient Network core processors also use quantum computers. That is another similarity."

They were all the same. So intent to impress, to stand out from the crowd.

"That's a false equivalence. Just because they share some characteristics doesn't mean they are the same. We've combined Symbolic, Generative and even Reflective AI to create something beyond how we think. That's a mistake scientific history has seen too many times. If you survive here at Omniscient Networks, you'll learn we don't operate that way."

"But…"

Megan held her hands up. "Enough. Leave."

He left, tail between his legs like the neutered little terrier he was.

She'd had enough of introducing interns. This was her company. She'd designed its flagship product. She deserved better.

Returning to her desk, she sat down in the ergonomic moulding chair and clasped her hands behind her head, while the Omni built a virtual 3D representation of the network on her retina implant.

The intern was correct. There were similarities between the network and a brain. It was a truer representation than most gave it credit for. Each component of the network held its state and contained all the rules it needed to perform its task, like supercharged neurons. But it begged the question. The brain wasn't just a big processing machine. It also had an awareness of itself. What makes a system such as a brain sentient? What creates consciousness? If complexity was all it took, the Omniscient Network would contemplate the meaning of life, the universe and everything by now.

A minor security alert from a node in the network escalated. She shifted her attention to the affected nodes. A cancerous growth was taking over nearby processing nodes, subverting them into its own network. Travelling via secured two-way trusted feeds, it grew exponentially, each infected node spreading to nearby nodes. She instructed the team to quarantine the entire section of the network and restore the nodes from backup. They complied, but she knew they'd also seek approval from Sree before doing anything.

The network was always under attack from amped hackers hoping to create havoc, attempt node theft or even take over the network, but this was different. The converted nodes used all available resources and established as many feeds as it could to neighbouring nodes. She watched as it took over the remaining quarantined network section. The virus wasn't after the information in the node or specific connections, opting instead for processing power and interconnectedness. But for what?

"What's the next step?" Sree asked from behind her. She turned around and grimaced. Did the man never sleep? He was always there, always ready to rein her in. Megan had him pegged as short, competent, and tenacious. The exact assessment she made when hiring him three years ago as head of security, but never thought he'd be holding her captive then. She wished now she had gone for someone less capable.

"Leave it with me. I'll have a look at it."

"You?" he said with a frown. "I can get Hariz and his team to look at it now. I mean, that's why we pay them."

"Leave it with me."

"You're doing virus analysis now?"

"I can do what I damn well please! It's my company. You're fired."

He gave her a patronising pat on the arm.

"That's the third time this week you've tried to fire me. I'll leave it with you, but I've locked down the quarantine."

She swore under her breath as he left.

CHAPTER TWO

THE LAST A-CLUSTER

TikTak scratched his knee as he studied the layout of the building. The scars from the surgery still itched, or so he imagined. A year ago, he shattered his knee and it was replaced by a bio-printed copy.

According to Elize, this was the last of the complete Adrian clusters. From the little he understood, Adrian created a network of deadheads, extending and replicating his mind. When Elize infected the network, it broke apart to protect the uninfected regions. Each node contained a small part of Adrian's mind. They each held a blueprint of the complete mind, represented as a blockchain, almost like human DNA held in each cell. On their own, they were not dangerous, but over time healthy nodes connected back together according to the blockchain blueprint, creating partial copies of Adrian. This one was almost complete and had been operational for at least three months. Worse, a group of atheist extremists called Aleph Zero supported the cluster, painting Adrian as the saviour of mankind. The next step in evolution. Much of the science went over TikTak's head, but from his personal experience, if Adrian was the next step of human evolution, he held little hope.

The helicraft wobbled, causing the layout projected on his Omni-lens to stand out against the barren backdrop. This was supposed to be a cattle station, but TikTak struggled to accept that. All he saw was rock and sandy dirt, with bushes scattered around the landscape. The air was hot and dry. Each breath stung his throat, overheating him from the inside. He couldn't understand how anyone could live out here, cattle or people. He looked over at Tom sitting next to him.

"Do you think we'll get resistance this time?" TikTak asked him. As usual, if he received a response at all, it was a text on his Omni-lens.

Yes. Leave the fighting to the mercenaries. I forecast a 22% risk of you being injured and a 7% risk of death.

TikTak wanted to like his posthuman friend but found it increasingly difficult to do so. Tom hadn't reconfigured himself like Elize but looked younger than ever before. It would have been easier to relate to him if the mental change matched with something visible.

TikTak called him a friend, but he knew Tom wouldn't use that word any longer. The text message didn't express concern for his welfare. He needed to survive because he still played a part in whatever end goal Tom was working towards. Nothing more.

Tom was right. Taking part in the raids was unnecessary, but he needed the distraction. As soon as his knee healed, he sought battle. He trained with the mercenaries, pushing himself harder and harder, refusing to give an inch. It made him feel alive.

Another message flittered past his vision.

It is because of your father. His death has affected your ability to think clearly. You are using violence to anaesthetise the pain.

TikTak grimaced. He didn't know what he disliked most, receiving the message or its undisputed truth. He'd let the mission of eradicating every trace of Adrian become the sole purpose of his life. At some point, he'd have to deal with his father's death. This wasn't news to him, but he hated how easily Tom diagnosed it. What was there to deal with anyway? People died every day. He hadn't even been that close to his father.

The helicraft descended, marking the end of their journey. So much for preparations. Not that he expected much resistance. They landed a kilometre away from the main buildings of the cattle station the group used as a base. As they unloaded, a man approached them with his hands above his head. He was young, but it mattered little. This was yet another Adrian node. Three of the operatives trained their guns on him, looking back towards the first in command. Decker, the leader of the mercenaries, raised his gun too.

"I have the right to legal representation," the man said.

"Who is requesting legal representation?" TikTak said. "According to your id-tag, your name is John Miller. He went missing a year ago. We will bring you back to family and friends."

"You know I'm not John Miller," he answered. "I'm…"

"It doesn't matter what I know. It matters what you can prove. We are recovering lost deadheads. If a deadhead believes they are someone else, all the more reason to bring them back."

"I've changed! I'm not trying to take over anyone anymore. I've got a new plan…"

"Take him down," TikTak said to Decker. Many incarnations of Adrian had argued similar points over the past months, but nothing ever changed. Adrian, given time and resources, would always revert to the same behaviour. Scheming to take over the world.

He grunted in response and fired his opioid pellet gun. They used non-lethal weapons against the Adrian nodes so they could be repurposed. The pellet gun looked like a large shotgun but fired a cluster of tiny capsules with a fast-acting opioid that absorbed through the skin.

The Adrian-node fell in a heap. TikTak hurried over to the body, knowing he wouldn't remain unconscious for long. He located the implant in the back of its head and overrode it with a small device Elize had designed. He looked back at Tom who nodded, signifying he'd overridden Adrian's security and started a mind-wipe.

"I can see a lot of movement and heat signatures in the buildings ahead," one mercenary said as they caught up with TikTak's position.

"They are preparing their defence for sure," Decker said, grinning. TikTak returned the grin. He too looked forward to a fight. Decker had been the only constant in their fight against Adrian. The mercenaries came and went, either quitting the team or leaving in body bags, but Decker remained. TikTak didn't like him much, but they had saved each other many times over the year. He was useful to have on your side in a fight.

"Hang on. They are…disappearing?"

"What do you mean? Are they using cloaking?"

"No. Almost all heat signatures have disappeared. Movement has decreased too."

"Are they killing themselves?" TikTak asked. This happened on two other occasions.

"No, their heat signatures would remain longer than that. They are going somewhere we can't pick them up."

"A bomb shelter?"

"Maybe."

Another message from Tom to both of them.

There's an old missile silo underneath the station.

TikTak looked back at Tom who stared into the distance.

"Really? I didn't think missile silos existed in Australia."

Tom didn't respond.

"We need to go now if we want to stop them."

"You heard," Decker said to the mercenaries. "Let's get this done so we can go home. I hate the outback!"

They moved quickly, but not as fast as TikTak. He almost ran towards the main building, itching for a fight. He received a disapproving message from Tom.

Adjusted estimate. 42% risk of injury. 13% risk of death. Please use a gun.

TikTak shook his head. The message sounded like a joke, but TikTak knew it wasn't. Tom no longer saw a purpose in humour.

He'd almost reached the door when the surrounding air crackled and his hair stood on end.

"They've hit us with a targeted EMP burst," someone said behind him. "Fried our weapons. We need to regroup."

TikTak ignored the warning. None of his weapons would be affected, and he knew the mercenaries had backup weapons that didn't rely on fancy electronics. Even his Omni was shielded enough to still be operational.

He pulled the door open, with his telescope baton ready, and ducked to the side as a volley of bullets came through the opening. TikTak continued down the side of the building, projecting the floor layout and heat signatures on his Omni-lens. Four people hid in the main building. He suspected they were from the extremist group. It wasn't Adrian's style to start a gun battle. They had barricaded themselves in pairs, monitoring the two entrances. He wondered where everyone else was. Over thirty people were based here, not counting any Adrian nodes.

"Two in the main corridor leading to the front door, hiding by doorways on either side," TikTak thought into his Omni, directing it to the rest of the group. "Take them out."

No one responded. The EMP burst had killed their communications too. Tom would soon have it operational again, but he regretted breaking off from the others. This was far more dangerous than his initial assessment. If Tom had been online, another message

Tom nodded, and as he headed back into the building a message blinked on his Omni and in his mind at the same time.

Help me kill Adrian.

would surely have been on its way, upping the likelihood of death substantially.

He looked around. The room he'd entered was full of hospital beds. They echoed the setup he'd seen many times before in other Adrian clusters, but this was different. TikTak couldn't determine the purpose of every medical device, but you needed only basic equipment to fit an override device to a deadhead. Adrian was up to something else.

-=:=-

Tom watched as TikTak continued through the building, taking out people with brutal efficiency. No longer the boy Tom knew before he himself became a posthuman, or maybe it was the other way around. Tom saw him with fresh eyes now. So much anger and frustration channelled into the only thing he knew. Violence.

He exemplified the faults in humanity. They were small-minded creatures so focused on their own gratification, whether it was pleasure, pain, or revenge. In that way, Adrian's ideas had some validity. Any system where the individual reigned supreme was unstable. Why should an individual be allowed to amass wealth and resources for their own gratification just because they can, when that wealth better served the group? No, humans were flawed and it would be their downfall.

But this was also where Adrian's approach failed. He'd mistaken himself for the solution. He was just one individual with the same flaws and it led to his downfall too. Tom had created predictive models and they all showed the same outcomes with high probability. Any system based on humans or posthumans would fail within their current constraints. He'd even experimented with a new intelligence altogether, but defining success eluded him so far.

"Done," TikTak said as he came out of the building. "Not a deadhead among them. Were you serious about the missile silo?"

Tom sent a reply through a direct connection to TikTak's Omni, whilst analysing the layout of the buildings. Human communication was painfully slow and prone to misunderstandings, so he no longer spoke unless the situation demanded it. He instructed TikTak to check the shed at the back, which most likely housed the entrance to the silo. He dug deep into secret archives to find information. The government built the silos in secret during the cold war, not as a deterrent, but a card to be played if nothing else worked. The missiles and their deadly payload were removed a long time ago, but the reinforced silos remained. He couldn't find the layout, but based on other designs from the same time period, he expected a silo with interconnected tunnels, an entryway leading down at least 3 levels, and a control room with living quarters.

A shard, a sub-routine of Tom's main persona, finished re-routing the communication protocols.

"Found it!" TikTak said, appearing again after checking the shed. "Just where you told us. Imagine that."

Silos from this period couldn't be opened manually from the outside once closed. The reinforced entrance he'd located was for personnel only. The locking mechanism might even be mechanical. He scanned all known lock designs used by government contractors over that time, hoping to find at least some digital component. A high security, mechanical lock would require brute force.

"I checked with Elize," TikTak said. "She can't help us get in. She's located the facility and can help us once we're inside."

Tom made his way to the large shed, shielding his eyes from the midday sun. The shed hid a small concrete building with a solid metal door. The lock was exactly what he'd feared. A dual-control combination lock holding 24 electromagnetic powered steel bars. He ran his fingers along the cold metal. The design differed from the ones he'd uncovered during his research. He found a small hidden alcove next to the door. This lock was less secure, even a smart key mould would do. He sent a request to TikTak to create one while assessing what hid inside. It was likely to house an override mechanism.

"No more of the fuckers," Decker said. "They're all holed up like rats in the silo."

Further study of existing locks and overrides suggested that the small alcove would house some kind of electronic means, most likely a pin pad. It could be an iris scanner, but they were experimental when the silo was built.

"I say we blow it up," Decker said. "We have enough explosives."

"Let's try without blowing things up first," TikTak said, inserting the smart key. The small door opened with a click, revealing a pin pad, just as Tom predicted.

He pried open the plate to get to the wiring beneath. He had changed an Omni to act as a universal connection device, allowing him to tap into almost any electrical or communication system. A textual thought from Elize appeared in his mind using the messaging protocol they'd invented together. It was more akin to a shared mind space than messaging.

"Connect it," she thought. "I'll deal with it."

Elize was far beyond what he could ever hope to become, so he gladly handed the task to her. It had come at a price. She'd re-used deadheads as processing nodes liberated from Adrian's network. He saw the necessity of this, but questioned it nonetheless. Tom experimented with extending his processing space into the logical network instead. He'd made breakthroughs far beyond existing technology, designing a neuro-interface that linked his mind to the network. The computing power acted as an extension to his mind, but he believed he'd be able to integrate the processes, allowing his mind to coexist within brain matter and a network.

"Task completed," she thought.

Tom pulled the door open just to reveal another door, with no locks or means to open it. He'd seen this in some designs. A security door that could only be opened and closed from the inside.

"I'll get the explosives," Decker said with a satisfied nod.

"I have another suggestion," Elize thought. "Give me some time."

-=:=-

TikTak sat at the table in the main house, tilting his chair back. After clearing out the bodies, leaving only splattered blood, they replaced what they could of the fried electronics. Now they waited to gain entrance to the silo.

"I still think we should just blow the bloody thing up," Decker said as he reassembled his weapon. He'd been trying to repair it for the better part of an hour.

"This is a missile silo from the sixties, built to survive a nearby nuclear blast. You have that much explosives?"

"There are always flaws. We'd use a directed blast. At least it gives us something to do," Decker replied with a grin. "Or we can use thermite. Should melt straight through the hinges. Not as much fun though."

TikTak just shook his head. Decker's blunt approach made sense, but he'd rather find out Elize's alternative before he blew things up. His trust in her had increased over the past year, finding her more approachable than Tom.

TikTak left for the bathroom. As he stepped into the little room, he set his Omni to silent. He locked the door and sat down on the lid of the toilet. A subtle notification at the top of his vision blinked twice. Someone was sending him a message, but he ignored it. He needed a few moments of silence, of being disconnected.

The singularity of their purpose, to eradicate Adrian clusters, had been a subterfuge for a long time now. Long enough for it to become his life. He had nothing else anchoring him to any other context. The daily life of everyday people was incomprehensible, like the toiling of ants running from task to task. If this was really the last cluster they had to deal with, what would he do next?

The building shook, followed by a wailing siren. What was going on? The shaking increased and he could hear the floor itself protest as floorboards ground against each other. He unlocked the door and tried to open it, but it was stuck. He threw his whole body against it, but it refused to budge. The house shuddered, followed by a wrenching sound as metal and wood broke apart. What could do that to a house in the middle of the outback?

"Get me out of here!" he yelled, but no one replied.

A few seconds later, the floor tilted and he felt movement under his feet. Only one thing could make this happen, but it was so unlikely he hadn't even considered it. The house sat on top of the doors to the missile silo and Elize was opening them. The house was falling into the silo below!

He threw himself at the door over and over until it gave way, just as the floor fell beneath him. He grabbed hold of the doorframe and pulled himself up. Debris fell into the bottomless pit. A shout drew his attention to the corridor that now extended like a chimney above him. A mercenary fell screaming down the corridor. He hit the doorframe with a sickening thud and then continued his fall downward in silence. It was pure luck that TikTak evaded the lifeless body as it passed.

The surrounding walls creaked as he pulled himself up again and found footing on what had been a wall. From the little he could tell, the house had partially slid into the silo but was still holding together. From the grinding noises around him, he guessed it was only a matter of time before the whole thing came crashing down.

Another incoming message blinked on his retina screen. He swore, removed silent mode from his Omni and checked the received messages. They were both from Elize. The first one read:

Task completed. I recommend evacuation.

The other message contained a blueprint of the silo that aligned itself to his surroundings on his Omni-lens.

"Are you ok?" Decker asked over a voice feed.

"Yeah, I'm fine."

"You need to get out. Now! The house is going down." The building shuddered as if to lend credence to his words. "I mean it," he continued. "Get out. And I might let you win the next sparring match."

According to the blueprint, the silo itself measured fifteen meters wide and forty-four meters deep. He guessed he was ten meters down now. He looked up. It was possible to climb from doorway to doorway up along the corridor, but it would take time. The remnants of the kitchen were to his left and the living room to his right. He didn't like his chances with the kitchen, but according to the blueprint it would take him close to a hatch and a service ladder.

He pulled himself up to the doorway to the kitchen. The oven, through its sheer weight, was already halfway through the wall that now served as a floor. It was only five metres between him and the window to the outside.

His first obstacle was the fridge. The wall still supported it, so he took a tentative step on the appliance. It held. He took another and sighed in relief as he stepped back on to the wall.

He took a small step, this time getting closer to the stove. Another step. There was plenty of room along the wall next to the stove and he took a step along it when it shifted. Just a slight movement at first, then it fell, wrenching gas pipes and the rest of the wall along with it.

TikTak fell.

Instinctually he grabbed at anything nearby. It was the remnants of the gas piping still attached to the rest of the house. For a moment he hung suspended in air, desperately clinging to the copper piping. He climbed up as his weight pulled the pipes out of the floor at an alarming rate. He hoisted his body up by the sheer strength of his arms, grabbing hold of a small ledge.

"What are you doing?" Decker asked. "Get out!"

He laughed to himself. He thought reaching the ledge equalled safety. How quickly you change your frame of reference.

"Not the time to have a laugh. Get out!"

There was nothing left of the kitchen. On the other side of the room, the wall with the window remained, but to reach it he'd have to jump five meters over a gaping chasm and grab hold of the window frame. It was likely his weight would just pull that part of the wall down. His other option was to scale the corridor, but that would take too long.

"I need a rope!" he yelled through the voice feed. "Send a rope down the corridor. I'm stuck here."

"Done," Decker replied.

The building shuddered again, sliding another metre into the hole. He was running out of time. He had to attempt the jump, so took one step back, which was all the run-up the ledge allowed him. A movement in the corner of his eye stopped him just before jumping.

A rope snaked down the hallway, only a few metres above him now. The house slid. He felt it shifting under his feet. There was nothing stopping it now. The rope was still not close enough. He stepped up on the doorframe leading into the corridor and jumped, grabbing hold of the end of the rope. The house was in free-fall around him. He pushed back from one of the corridor walls and looked up. The front door was wide open and approaching fast. He pushed off from the other side again, attempting to align with the opening.

He'd overshot slightly and twisted in the air to prevent his legs from hitting the doorframe on the way past. For a moment he just hung there, happy to be alive, while the mercenaries around the rim yelled their encouragement. The blueprint of the silo remained as an overlay on his view and he saw the door on the side of the wall. They had finally found an entrance to the facility.

The mercenary team congratulated him as he reached the top. They had lost two of their numbers in the falling building. TikTak's survival balanced the scales somewhat. Tom stood to the side, staring out into space. TikTak knew he had much more in common with the mercenaries than Tom nowadays. He sent his Omni-lens recording to the team so they could see what he'd been through. He didn't send it to Tom. It was likely Tom had access to his lens view anyway.

"Ok, enough," Decker said. "We have a job to do."

"There is a door eight metres down," TikTak said. "A service ladder leading down next to it."

TikTak looked down into the hole. With light shining into it, he saw the wreckage of the house at the bottom. The sheer scope of the silo was impressive, even if it was just a monument to people's fear of each other.

Decker instructed one of his men to check the door. TikTak joined him, abseiling down with the same rope he'd used to escape. The mercenary was young, in his early twenties.

"According to the blueprints, this is the only connection between the silo and the rest of the facility," TikTak said. "If we can't get through this, we have to get through the door into the stairway."

"You can only open this door from the inside," the mercenary said. "This door can withstand the heat of a nuclear rocket firing. Nothing we have will get through that."

TikTak hushed the mercenary. He thought he heard something, a grinding noise from inside the door.

"I hear it too!"

The door opened, and a bloodied arm came into view. A young man, blood plastering his hair to his forehead, pushed it open and stared at them.

"Save me," he said, his eyes pleading. A middle-aged woman in a t-shirt and jeans appeared behind him. She took hold of the man with a gleeful smile and jumped through the door, plummeting to their death.

CHAPTER THREE
AWAKENING

The child woke up, knowing death was close. The timing wasn't exact, but it would be soon. Many paths branched out from her current time and place in the karmic tree, but all natural ones led to the same end. She wasn't aware what had changed since yesterday, but the options promising a longer life no longer existed. She wasn't upset. For the past ten years, she'd lived with the knowledge her life would likely end before her twelfth birthday.

Having made that conclusion, she went on with her day like any other. Time remained to both attend to her daily duties and plan for the inevitable end. She let her mind wander, issuing mild suggestions to the worker minds. She set them tasks and rewarded completion with joy and happiness. The orphanage had functioned like this for a while now, but this hadn't always been the case.

-=:=-

"Ch-Ch-Ch," Jien said. "I know you are here."

The child hid. She'd found a small crevice behind some shelves in one of the storage rooms. At first, she thought she'd successfully escaped, but Jien must have seen the door closing. But she stayed. She'd seen what Jien did to other new kids, even younger than her. She understood why. This place, like any other, needed order and structure. Fear and pain were the means used to make this happen.

The dust from rice bags piled on the shelves above made her nose itch. She held her nose, willing the sneeze away.

"Come out. I saw you enter. Don't make me come and get you. It will be much worse for you then."

The room shifted as she tuned into the intents within it. She'd been able to do this as long as she could remember, and it was only recently that she realised it was a unique gift. She could read the emotions of a person or a group. Sometimes even their most articulated thoughts. There was anger and frustration, but also intent and certainty. He knew she was in here.

She heard the door opening again. The sound of feet and hushed voices was apparent as the other children entered the room. There were no allies among them. They all feared Jien.

The child shrugged. There was no point in hiding any longer. She'd taken a beating before and could do it again. She stepped out and faced Jien. He sparkled and popped like a fire made with wet wood, anger flaring all around him. But she also felt something else. The seed to all that anger was fear.

"Ha! Facing your demon. I like that."

So many words, she thought. They never matched a person's emotions or their thoughts. The first blow, a fist to the stomach.

Nothing serious. He tested her, seeing what she could take. Another strike, harder this time.

He changed as he hit her. Each strike pulsated through his system, turning the anger into something else. The child struggled to make sense of the shift. He enjoyed inflicting pain on her.

"Why aren't you saying anything?"

He kicked her this time, aiming for her thigh. It sent her sprawling. So far nothing was broken, but it was just a matter of time. Her not making a sound seemed to affect the enjoyment he took from beating her.

If she could affect him so easily, maybe she could change it all together. She reached out towards him and told the real Jien he no longer enjoyed hitting others, replacing satisfaction with revulsion.

He kicked her in the stomach and immediately pulled back. She rolled around and studied him. Green waves of sickness flooded the anger, extinguishing the sparks. His face scrunched up. She'd never been able to read facial expressions, so failed to understand its significance. He looked funny to her, so she laughed. She realised this wasn't the right thing to do, but she couldn't help herself. Some of the gathered children echoed her laughter. Nervous titters at first, but stronger as more of them joined in. This was another thing she'd discovered about herself. She projected her emotions, which spread to anyone nearby.

Jien looked around the room before he left. Maybe things could change after all.

-=:=-

Three days later, Jien tried again. He bided his time, waiting until she was alone. It hadn't taken long. Since the previous incident, no one wanted anything to do with her. She'd seen the emotion in Jien and now saw it in the other children. Fear. She didn't understand the purpose of that emotion. It seemed to be the reaction to anything they didn't understand.

Jien pushed her into the same storage room where he attacked her previously. She hit a shelf before tumbling to the floor. There was no escape. Jien stood in front of the door, holding a wooden club.

"What did you do?" he asked, pointing the club at her.

She smiled in response, not knowing what else to do. The red sparkle of anger was still there, but only on the surface. His behaviour wasn't driven by anger any longer. Fear had taken over.

"You cursed me. You're a witch!"

She kept smiling and reached out towards him, wanting to ease his pain. Maybe there was also something she could do to ease his fears. Jien reacted, striking her outstretched arm with the club. She felt it break. Shock, followed by pain, flooded her system. Tears welled up in her eyes. Without thinking she reached out towards Jien, shouting into his mind to never hurt anyone ever again.

She sat back and soothed the waves of pain. The injury would heal, but it would take time. She had no intention of waiting, so she told her body to mend the broken bone. A wave of nausea followed by darkness.

-=:=-

She woke up disoriented and hungry. Speeding up the healing process used up a lot of energy, and she desperately needed to eat. She moved her hand back and forth. It was tender but had healed well. The light through the small, barred window no longer painted a pattern on the floor. Instead, four symmetrical pillars of light shone on the wall. She'd been here for a long time.

Jien sat with his back resting against the door, his gaze unfocused and his arms hanging by his sides. She reached into his mind again, finding only an empty shell. Her mental scream had wiped any ill intent, leaving peace and contentment. She'd experimented with suggestions on the other children, but she'd always been gentle—a light prodding to affect their behaviour in small ways. This was something else entirely. She'd taken away everything that was Jien without replacing it with anything else.

She constructed a new Jien—a kind and well-meaning one that would help rather than hurt. Once finished, she sat back and watched as he left the room with a sense of accomplishment.

Minds were malleable. You could change and improve them. She had the power to change things for the better.

CHAPTER FOUR
ENTER THE SILO

TikTak and the mercenary watched as the two figures fell into the silo. The young man screamed all the way down, cut short by a wet thud.

"What the fuck?" the mercenary said.

"It's Adrian," TikTak said as he turned to the door. "He's lost the plot."

TikTak climbed through the opening into a dark corridor. His eyes, used to the harsh sun outside, struggled to adapt to the darkness. The stale air was cool against his skin as he listened for movement, ready for any attack. Thirty seconds later, details emerged like the development of an old Polaroid photo. A dim light dispersed from fixtures along the corridor wall of unpainted concrete. The blood-splatter stood out against the grey.

The mercenary entered behind him.

"Wait for us," Decker said through the voice feed.

It was the sensible thing to do, but TikTak no longer cared for sensible. He'd survived almost certain death when escaping the falling house. He felt invincible and headed off down the corridor, ignoring the protests from the mercenary. Even Tom protested with dry statistics.

Adjusted estimate. 100% risk of injury. 37% risk of death.

"I wouldn't call a few bruises an injury," TikTak said to Tom through the voice feed but received no reply. "Why don't you join me?"

Still no reply. Tom would only come once his assessment returned a lower risk.

The corridor sloped down, taking him further and further underground. Thirty metres in, he heard noises ahead. He couldn't make anything out at first, but as he came closer, it separated into the rhythmic drone of diesel engines. He reached a door jammed shut from this side, stopping anyone from leaving the complex. The Adrian node must have shut it when it pursued the cult member, locking everyone else in. He paused for a second as he considered the scenarios of opening the door. It was impossible to predict what hid on the other side. He reached for the steel bar holding the door in place when a hand grabbed his shoulder from behind.

"Don't you fucking dare!"

He was pulled around, and he readied his baton.

"You want a fight?" Decker asked.

TikTak lowered the baton with a shrug.

"You're not part of my team, but you don't get to be a trigger-happy nut case just because of that. Do you understand?"

TikTak stared back at him. Two mercenaries approached from the tunnel.

"Do you understand?" Decker repeated, this time readying his handgun.

TikTak nodded. He knew he acted recklessly. He'd dedicated the past year to this purpose and so desperately wanted it over. Not that he knew what would come afterwards.

"I want to get out of this hellhole as much as you, but let's do it alive, ok?"

TikTak nodded and mustered a smile.

"Ok, so what now?"

As if on cue, the diesel generators engines stopped, and the lights gave a dying flicker before darkness engulfed them. He couldn't see the wall or even his hand when he held it close to his face. He switched his Omni-lens to night vision, but it made no difference. There was no light at all in the corridor to enhance. He reached out in front of him, fumbling for something, anything. The door was behind him; he knew that much. He turned around and grabbed hold of it like a lifeline, slightly shifting the metal bar holding it in place.

"Turn off any enhancements," Decker said. "I'm turning a light on."

TikTak barely had time to shut night-vision off before the corridor flooded with light around him. He relaxed slightly as the darkness was dispelled. He held his breath for a moment and exhaled slowly, watching as his vitals adjusted on the lens.

"I'm getting them to bring down chem-light bombs. That should work better with any enhancements."

A muffled shriek was followed by a thud against the door, sending vibrations through the thick steel. He waited for further movement, holding his hand against the surface, but the silence was absolute.

As soon as the mercenary appeared, they opened the door, ready to fire at any attacker. Decker threw a chem-light bomb into the room. It exploded, sending a mist of fluorescent liquid through the space. They waited for it to settle on the floor and walls to create a background light their enhancements could use. TikTak peered into a large domed area with boxes piled high along the walls and two diesel generators in the middle. Next to the door, an old man lay, his face caved in and his arms and chest ripped by claws. TikTak could even see a few bite marks around his neck. This looked like an animal attack, not something a person would do.

"There are no good guys here," Decker said. "If in doubt, shoot to kill. Secure the stairwell."

The mercenaries spread out into the room, securing the area. TikTak and Decker entered once they had taken positions close to any available entry. Everything in the room was new. The boxes contained medical supplies and food. There was enough fuel to power the diesel generators for months.

Two of the mercenaries moved into a connecting room that, according to the blueprint, led into the stairway to the main entry. If they opened the door, it would allow better access and also another escape route if needed. There could be fifty Adrian nodes down here and they only numbered ten. A muffled explosion followed by a dust cloud spreading out from the doorway the two mercenaries had entered. Eight mercenaries, TikTak corrected himself.

"What the fuck?" Decker spat. "What is going on with this cluster? He's never fought back like this."

TikTak shook his head. Something was different, but what? He tried reaching Tom. TikTak had distributed smart comDust, small particles that created an extension to a network where a wireless signal didn't reach, but something within the structure interfered with the connection.

Decker stared up through the door once the dust settled. He came back, determination and anger exaggerated by the light into a kabuki mask.

"Let's kill this fucker."

"Can we get the light going?" TikTak asked.

One mercenary checked the diesel generators. He turned around and shook his head.

"He will be in the control room, won't he? Let's take him out."

Fuelled by the anger of having squad members killed, they hurried through the room and into the corridor, guns ready. TikTak preferred to be in front instead of the middle of the pack. He wanted to confront what came at him head-on.

A scream from behind. TikTak turned around and saw an old woman crouching on top of a fallen mercenary, clawing at his face and then biting a chunk of flesh from his throat. Three more attackers came from the front, but a mercenary levelled his gun and cut two down in a spray of bullets before the third one jumped straight at him. TikTak struck the attackers with his baton, aiming for the device lodged in the back of their heads that networked them to Adrian. His first strike connected, but to his surprise nothing happened. The attacker came at him again, fingers curled into claws. He swept the arms to the side and struck its head again and again. Decker shot the remaining one.

"They're not connected to Adrian."

"What? They're deadheads, aren't they?" Decker pulled them off the mercenaries. Two more dead.

"Yes, but they aren't just nodes. They operate separately from him."

"So he can program them to act on their own now? That's all we need."

"We need to move on."

"Right. TikTak, you take the rear," Decker said and added, "With a gun."

TikTak nodded and waited at the rear until the team moved again.

"What's that smell?" Decker asked.

"Death," TikTak answered.

The first men enter the control room, sweeping the entrance for any sign of resistance.

"No movement. Whatever happened here…we missed the party."

TikTak pushed through them to the entrance and surveyed the control room. The flashlights swept over blood-splattered bodies. Some looked like the nodes they'd seen already. Others must have been part of the extremist group. Whatever happened here left no survivors. He took a few tentative steps forward and shone his flashlight around the room. An old-fashioned control panel filled the far wall, row after row of red lights and CRT screens. Two doors led into the living quarter section.

Around him was carnage, but something bothered him. An Adrian node lay at his feet, bloody but otherwise intact. Next to it was a gutted extremist group member, the face disfigured with claw marks. Everywhere he looked, extremists bore marks of brutal violence, whilst any Adrian nodes just had blood all over them, but few injuries. As if they shut down once they completed the slaughter.

"We need to get out of here!" he yelled, heading back towards the tunnel.

The bloodied figures around them rose, grinning manically. One grabbed his leg as he stepped over it. The room erupted in gunfire in short, controlled bursts. TikTak beat the attacker until it released its grip. He looked around, just now realising how outnumbered they were. Adrian nodes surrounded them. The mercenary closest to him downed two attackers with his handgun, but another three attacked him from the side, bowling him over. One of them gouged his eyes out.

"Retreat!" He heard Decker's voice, knowing it was no longer possible. Striking in all directions with his baton, he inched towards Decker, who held his position with single shots from his machine gun, ensuring every bullet hit its mark. Two mercenaries positioned next to him, one with a handgun, the other with a large knife, hacking into the attackers as the trio navigated back towards the entrance. They were the only ones left standing.

"We should have blown this whole place up," Decker said to TikTak as he joined them.

TikTak nodded and struck another node, caving its head in. As Decker fired his last bullet, TikTak knew it was all over. One glance at the others confirmed they knew it too. The nodes took their time closing in as they sensed victory was near. One attacker reached towards Decker and he used the muzzle of his machine gun to strike forwards, hitting them in the chest and neck. While it didn't incapacitate them, it kept them away.

A node reached towards TikTak. He struck its arm and felt the bones shatter. It didn't flinch and instead of pulling back, it caught the baton with the other hand. It bared its teeth in a wide grin as TikTak desperately twisted the weapon towards the assailant to free it.

The textbook manoeuvre should have loosened the grip, but it had no effect. The nodes didn't respond to pain or even broken bones.

Two of the nodes reached out towards him.

-=:=-

The probability matrix in Tom's mind shifted. The intricate web of curved lines and connection points rippled as new information adjusted the likelihood of some paths and invalidating others. He navigated the alternative paths, determining their significance. Adrian's behaviour this time was so different from previous clusters, Tom's old probability models no longer applied.

Adrian disabled their weapons with an EMP while protected underground, forcing them to fight on his terms in the silo. Other weapons could be present down there, but probabilities suggested otherwise. This wasn't a grand plan. It was a cornered animal fighting for survival. Tom and Elize tracked any sign of partial Adrian clusters and they both agreed this was likely to be the last one. Once eradicated, Adrian would no longer exist. The DNA of his mind still existed, but without a posthuman mind to guide it into fruition, it was unlikely another cluster would be established.

This explanation rang true, and it shifted specific outcome parameters in the scenarios. Success was still likely, but the body count rose drastically. If Adrian fought back underground with all his resources, the team was likely to perish. This was regrettable, but not an immediate concern. The team was a means to an end. But most paths with a favourable outcome suggested survival of at least two of the team, else it fell to the few mercenaries remaining above to complete the task. If possible, probabilities demanded he assist the team.

Alarms blared in his mind, informing him TikTak and the mercenaries were no longer visible on the network. Moments later the ground shook from an underground explosion. According to seismic data, the explosion originated from the entrance. He hurried to the shed to survey the damage, finding cracks in the concrete around the buckled steel door. He set up network listeners on the entire team. If any of them were still alive, he'd know.

The network traffic was minimal. Satellites provided wireless network coverage, but there was no additional information flowing apart from what they generated themselves. If Adrian operated a network, it was wired or completely shielded from prying eyes above. Adrian had also disrupted their attempts to establish a network below. They had underestimated him yet again.

Tom had to ensure nothing remained of this cluster. He had to step off the sidelines to ensure success. Without data collected by the mercenaries, he could no longer guide them. Participation was required, even if it put him in harm's way.

The door bulged outwards, disconnected from its frame. A light push was enough for the door to fall inwards, leaving a gaping hole leading to the darkness below. He announced he was coming to TikTak and the team through an asynchronous message. As he climbed over the rubble, his eyes immediately adjusted to the low light level. Dust particles swirled in the air, triggering his lacrimal glands to go into overdrive, flooding his eyes with tears.

Halfway down the stairs, he discovered remains. A mess of meat and bones. Based on body parts and organs, two mercenaries died here. The bodies and the explosion were captured as a painting of interwoven smells. Harsh chemical overtones from the explosives intertwined with the odours of the charred remains. The complexity of the intermingled strands of scents fascinated him. How they accentuated each other to generate something unique. He catalogued it for further analysis and continued down the stairs.

It grew darker, but it didn't matter. He knew the exact dimensions of the underground missile base from the blueprints. Sight was not required here. He re-routed processing power to his other senses and waited as a sensory picture emerged. He located the remaining mercenaries and TikTak from the soundscape they generated as they progressed into the tunnel that led to the control centre. Shuffling noises came from downstairs and he tuned in to the location. Four sound sources moved along the bottom of the staircase. It wasn't any of the mercenaries. The movements were distinct, as if they were on all fours. They weren't animals either. From the sound, at least two of them wore shoes. He listened as they headed through the room towards the corridor to the control centre. Undoubtedly, they were heading for the team.

Tom modelled the situation, with an average outcome of two dead mercenaries. It was an acceptable outcome, but not in the long run. Whatever Adrian planned, he had to stop the next attack. He needed to find a network access point. Adrian must have installed a network in the silo to allow unhindered communication between the nodes. They generated a mesh network powered by their bodies, but there had to be an external network as a backup. If he gained access to one of the network points, he could attack Adrian from within.

The sound of gunfire smattered through the stairway. The echoes suggested a small area leading into a bigger one. They had engaged with Adrian already, which meant they were running out of time. He cleared the last steps and located a dead Adrian node in the corridor. Its body no longer received neural inputs, but he expected its brain to be active for another thirty seconds at least.

He connected an override device they used to pacify nodes. Usually the override blocked any network traffic, but this time he used it to hijack the network communication. An intricate mesh network connected the nodes together to ensure the different parts of Adrian's shared processing tasks. He'd attempted this before, but was immediately discovered as an anomalous node and isolated from the network. This was very different. These nodes were semi-autonomous, allowing them some control, but with a specific purpose.

The protocols also only employed basic protective measures. While it restricted communication, Tom easily bypassed the security controls to get access to the underlying code. Adrian must have left it this way to allow changing their programming at will. Tom did nothing fancy. He defined a clean copy and sent it out to all the nodes with instructions to replace the current one, with one small modification.

It only left one question. Adrian no longer habituated within these nodes, so where was he?

-=:=-

TikTak gripped the arm of the nearest node and pulled down. It lost balance and toppled over. Surprised at how easily he'd defeated the node, he prepared to meet the attack of a second one, but it didn't come. It remained still, arms by its side. The other nodes stood in the same way, frozen with arms hanging by their side.

"What the fuck?" Decker said. He struck one with the butt of his gun. It didn't react.

"Did the freak do this?"

TikTak nodded. Decker had long since stopped calling Tom by name. He surveyed the area. Dead bodies lay everywhere in the small control centre. The nodes remained motionless.

"Take 'em out," Decker said.

"Override them?"

"No. Just find a gun with bullets and shoot them in the head!"

The two remaining mercenaries nodded and began their gruesome work. TikTak found a small video camera on the floor. He checked its contents and discovered recordings as recent as fifteen minutes ago. He pocketed the memTag holding the video files for further analysis.

"I've lost contact with Elize," Tom said as he approached. "I can sense her, but she no longer communicates."

TikTak turned around, surprised Tom was actually speaking. Over three months ago, Tom announced messaging was his preferred method of communication.

"I didn't think that was possible," he said.

"She's been compromised. I'm going offline until we know what's happened."

TikTak nodded. So that was why he spoke. He no longer trusted it was safe to remain connected.

"Any more Adrian nodes?"

"No, they are all neutralised," Tom said. "What do you have there?"

TikTak looked down at the video camera. "Something I found. Figured I'd check it out later."

"We have to check the other areas," Tom continued. "Make sure there is nothing left."

According to the blueprint, the living areas spanned the upper floor. A machine room lay below the control centre, with stairs on the opposite side of the room. With Tom following, TikTak navigating through piles of dead bodies.

He opened the door to the living quarters. The slaughter had continued there. Five members of the group were gutted and torn to pieces among the bunk beds. TikTak entered the room, surprised at how warm and humid the air was. His exposed skin stung, and he felt an itching sensation in his mouth and sinuses as he breathed.

Tom entered behind him and stopped immediately. He looked around and brought his hands to his face, tentatively touching his skin. Tom took another step, a flicker of a smile on his lips, and fell.

"What's going on? Are you ok?"

Tom didn't respond. He lay there, unmoving. TikTak no longer knew what to expect from his friend. He'd become increasingly erratic, but TikTak put that down to his posthuman condition. Tom took a deep breath, as if he'd been deprived of air. He tried to push himself off the floor just to fall down again. Tom looked up at him pleadingly.

"Something is…inside my head," he said finally.

"We need to get out of here."

Tom didn't respond. His internal struggle was now all-consuming. TikTak pulled Tom off the ground and lead him down the stairs, through the control room.

Decker approached them. "What's up with the freak?"

"No idea. Some kind of overload maybe. I'm taking him out of here."

"Do. We're torching this place now. You can leave via the main door."

TikTak nodded and struggled as he half-carried a rambling Tom five flights of stairs to the top.

"Things…little machines," Tom said. "Re-wiring my brain. Short-circuiting my mind."

It must have been the moisture in the air in the sleeping quarters. A delivery mechanism for nano-machines, targeting posthumans. Was this another of Adrian's schemes? TikTak considered it, but it made little sense in this context. They'd removed the last major cluster of the Adrian network. Now, they had lost contact with Elize and Tom was compromised. All three known posthumans neutralised within minutes of each other. It couldn't be a coincidence. But who could have orchestrated that?

They'd arrived in two helicrafts. TikTak pushed Tom into the closest one. Decker and the few remaining mercenaries would fit in the second one with the rest of their equipment, so he ordered it to take off.

"We can't go back to base," Tom said, the first coherent sentence since the attack.

TikTak nodded. However you looked at it, Leonid emerged as the prime suspect. He'd leant the substantial resources of his company to battle any remaining Adrian nodes. He'd provided equipment and funding for Tom and Elize to enhance their capabilities. Maybe he wanted to ensure he was still in control now that they'd defeated Adrian.

TikTak accessed the memTag, finding video files and an executable block. He didn't know if the program was malicious, so he left it until he'd have time to analyse it. He played the first video file instead.

ADRIAN VIDEO CLIP #1

The image focused on a seated middle-aged man in jeans and a t-shirt. Behind him sat row upon row of people, all dressed like him. He focused on a point next to the camera as if he was addressing someone else.

"My flock," he started, his voice a deep baritone. "My undeveloped friends. You saved me and for that, I'm grateful. You've rebuilt me almost completely. Some minor functions are still missing, but I can rebuild them given time. I'm Adrian again."

He bowed, mirrored by the rows of people behind him as they bowed in perfect unison.

"We don't have long. The people outside the doors won't stop until they've destroyed every single one of my nodes, but the work we do here is too important. If nothing else, these recordings will be my legacy."

He paused for a moment, his gaze lowered, shaking his head. When he raised his head again, the benevolent smile was all but gone.

"You have expectations. You wouldn't have brought me back otherwise. I have a plan, but to comprehend it, you need to understand what went wrong. I need to discuss something that is very difficult for me."

He rose, the camera following him in a smooth motion.

"Failure," he said. He paused, letting the word hang in the air. "Despite my intelligence, my redundancy and my safeguards, I failed. I am only a minor improvement. Not the major upgrade I thought I was. I am Adrian 1.1, not 2.0 if you will. There were so many aspects I hadn't considered. The natural entropy in any complex system. That even though I pictured myself as God, I was still very much human. I could change my body, I could change where my mind operated, I could build replicas of my mind. But it was still a human mind, with all its faults. Hubris is a supremely human quality, after all."

He strode past the view. The cameraman followed him as he reached out a hand to an overweight woman in the front row. She averted her gaze at first, but then met them, tears brimming in her eyes. She stared at him in awe as he crouched down and touched her cheek.

"We, you and I alike, are driven by primal desires. It doesn't matter how smart or strong you are. You still have physical and emotional needs. This was my biggest fault. I still wanted esteem. I still wanted love and self-actualisation. But what if I could change all that?"

His stare darted from one audience member to another, lingering long enough for each to look away.

"I've thought a lot about this. I've analysed the chemical processes that define who I am, and it is possible to change them. We do it all the time. Even coffee is a temporary neurological hack—as the caffeine blocks the adenosine receptors, the brain's stimulants keep us more alert than we should be. Of course, that is child's play. Minor, temporary adjustments brought about through haphazard experimentation."

He stood up. All eyes were fixed on the movement..

"This wasn't what I was after. I wanted to change my thought patterns. I wanted to nullify the effect of certain hormones. To be unbound from the human condition."

The man was now addressing the camera.

"I came up against a complexity I couldn't calculate my way out of. I had no way of controlling this process, as I was the process. How do you ensure your goals will remain unchanged? What if the act of changing invalidates the very reason you had for the change in the first place?"

He smiled and looked back at the gathered people.

"I know what you think. People change themselves on purpose every day, be it with drugs, therapy, religion, or body enhancements. And you are right. Little people, just as yourselves, do this. But there are consequences. For every positive change, there are high school shootings and suicide bombers. What would I become if things went wrong?"

CHAPTER SIX

VIRUS INTERRUPTED

Day turned into night, but it was all the same to Megan. She had a problem to solve and even the most basic needs had to wait. She'd spent the past ten hours changing an analytics package to better assess what the virus was doing. Satisfied it was at least functional, she activated it and left it to gather information.

She allowed herself a break. She'd brought a small lunch pack and opened it now. A sourdough bread sandwich with pear, walnut and Gorgonzola cheese. The ingredients mattered little. She ignored them in favour of a small plastic container of La Repisada Olive oil, soaking up every drop with the bread of the sandwich. The complexity of the smell was overpowering—a blend of fruits and nuts, with a hint of green tea. She let the silky texture linger against her tongue, tasting spice and vanilla as she swallowed small mouthfuls.

As she ate, she considered the possibility a rogue agent had created the virus. A side-effect of Intelligent Assistants was their need to operate freely with at least a medium security level. Hackers soon exploited this by releasing agents that imitated Intelligent Assistants but appropriated processing nodes instead. The more advanced ones even had basic self-modification capabilities. She returned to the output with this in mind, but still failed to make a meaningful connection. The initial node had made copies of itself on each infected node. The processing spike was to determine any connections for further propagation of the virus. It then became dormant. Even more interesting, the virus had reprogrammed the rules for the nodes, removing the limit to the number of connections and bandwidth.

The copies of the virus waited for something, but what? She couldn't do much in the quarantine area, but devised new tests anyway. First, she wiped one of the infected nodes and watched as it became re-infected. She added more processing power to a node, and it responded by dividing itself up into two logical nodes. The more processing power given, the more logical nodes. The pattern was always the same. Once a node was infected, it tried to infect any nearby nodes and prepared the node by rewriting its operating core. This was the payload. The virus no longer ran on the node once this had happened. The node then tried to establish connections to all nearby infected nodes.

This was only a gestation. No, she corrected herself. She didn't know. She hoped. If there was nothing more, it was only a faulty virus; a logical bomb taking over as many nodes as possible until it was isolated and cleared. She hoped there was more to it. But how could she trigger the next step in its process?

She analysed the network traffic between the nodes. A trickle of information flowed between them once dormant. Each node sent a small packet of 150 bytes to all connected nodes, about four every second. She suspected this was a heartbeat, verifying all pathways were open, even if the frequency was higher than she was used to.

The new operating core hid secrets too, but she struggled to see beyond it as a docking station, where whatever docked would determine its purpose.

-=;=-

The night turned into day.

"Are you still looking at that?" Sree said as he pulled up a 3D projection of Megan's current view. "Shouldn't you focus on inventing something worthwhile again?"

"Go fuck yourself," she responded. She hated the intrusion and hated him for being right.

"But seriously, why are you looking at it?"

"Just something to do. It is a self-replicating virus. I just can't work out its profile. Figuring it out could be useful for guarding against future attacks."

"What makes this different? We've seen plenty of self-replicating viruses."

"I don't know yet. I want to run a bigger scale simulation to work out its purpose."

"So it takes over nodes as processing factories, but does nothing after that? Sounds like it doesn't work. Just wipe it."

"I want to be sure."

Sree studied her for a second. "Sure, we can stand up a larger processing region in the quarantine area. I'll approve it now. Should be available this afternoon."

He stood there, waiting. She knew why.

"Thanks," she said, as he wouldn't leave if she didn't.

"Not a problem. Go home and get some rest," Sree said and left.

She felt a wave of dislike as she watched him leave. His first comment was correct. She'd achieved nothing of substance and the board of directors expected results. If she didn't deliver something soon, they'd make good on their threat, and she'd end up in prison, or worse. Maybe this virus held the answer. She held little hope, but it was better than anything else she'd been working on.

-=:=-

Megan entered the hotel room she called home. She'd never understood the idea of an actual home. The concept of ownership and emotional associations with the thing you owned was an outdated and pointless concept. Life was your experiences. Anything else was just noise.

The penthouse sprawled over two levels, but she never went upstairs. All she needed was somewhere to eat and the four s:es - sex, sleep, shit, and shower. The entry level provided facilities for all of this.

There was a knock on the door. Philippe—the young, dumb, and sexy waiter who had taken a liking to her—delivered a late breakfast.

"You want to stay?" she asked.

"I can't," he said and looked around as if to locate exits. "They almost fired me last time."

"I'll give you a big tip."

He shook his head and left.

She shrugged, sat down in one of the self-moulding beanbags next to the coffee table and felt it adjust to her preferred eating position. She took the lid off the plate and let the aroma fill the room. It was just fried eggs, but the sauteed chanterelles, fava beans, green garlic and toasted hazelnuts accompanying them was something else. She savoured every morsel and sipped on spore cleansed water in between mouthfuls. As she finished, she could feel the beanbag adjust again, this time softer and more leaned back. The hint of armrests appeared.

She loaded an anonymous id-tag and opened a secure voice feed to WraithLove, a high-end hacker she'd used before. Her visual feed darkened, swirls of smoke gained shape until she saw two ghostly figures in an embrace, lovingly devouring each other. One of them looked her way and winked.

"I don't want visual feed!"

The ghostly figures both gave her the finger and disappeared in a cloud of dust.

"Suit yourself, Omni girl."

She frowned. This was the first time WraithLove had let slip she knew her identity. Megan wasn't surprised, but still annoyed the hacker no longer bothered keeping up the pretence.

"So that's how it is."

"You hacked me. You know who I am. Just returned the favour. I need to know my clients."

"I need a piece of software at Omni from the quarantined network."

"Why not grab it yourself?"

"I'm watched. I need you to do it."

"Not possible."

"Anything is possible. I can give you a backdoor entry."

"It is still dangerous as hell. It will cost you."

She laughed. Money was the least of her worries. "I'll pay whatever is reasonable."

She sent the information to WraithLove and disconnected the feed, tired to the point of passing out, but her mind still refused to rest. She thought herself into the neuro-interface and waited a second or two for it to override the neural feed. The familiar white room appeared around her. Images floated in space, beckoning her to choose them. She liked the experience of the neural interface, but preferred the earlier versions. Back in those days the immersion was complete, with all senses overridden with the neuro-feed. It had been an invitation for hackers to overload the sensory input of whoever they disliked or were paid to terrorise. Legislation changed as soon as it caused a few heart attacks. They dampened the neural interface, ensuring the user could still tell the simulation and reality apart. Yet another frontier neutered in favour of the least of us.

She focused on an image of an arctic scene. It unfolded, wrapping her surroundings in a sweeping landscape, the cold air stark against her skin. She inhaled deeply through her nose, the cold, clean air spread a calming chill through her chest. She was aware of her body somewhere sitting back, allowing itself to relax.

Wooden signs appeared around her. They pointed towards a variety of experiences, anything from drama to action, porn to romantic comedy, all available at the speed of thought. Her interface was a customised version. The retail version allowed limited options. It decided the optimal experience or option for the user and only presented that. This was the real value of the Omniscient Network and the feature that had decimated the competitors. Once you tried it, the experience of other interfaces was woefully inadequate in comparison. As if to prove her own point, she found herself paralysed by choice and, as many times before, just stayed here in the entry room.

CHAPTER SEVEN

ELIZE UNPLUGGED

"Where to now?" TikTak asked as they departed the private landing area on the outskirts of Sydney. Cars waited outside, ready to return them to their operations base in one of Pharmacom's research facilities.

"Get us to a car," Tom said. "Any car but the one we're supposed to be in."

TikTak nodded and dragged Tom with him. Tom appreciated the help. His mind was in freefall from the heights of posthuman supremacy to the barely adequate processing of a regular human brain. He knew TikTak needed a destination, but this was beyond him now. They had to walk, at least to start with. If they wanted to disappear, they couldn't just jump into a car next to the landing spot. He trusted

TikTak to do the right thing, focusing only on breathing and walking without falling over.

Minutes, or maybe hours later, he remembered a secret safe house he set up six months ago. He gave TikTak the address. To his surprise they were already in a car. Time skipped between moments without him noticing. He tried to focus on the world around him, but only moments passed until TikTak dragged him from one vehicle to another. His mind still hadn't adjusted to the substitutions and shortcuts it had been so familiar with before he turned posthuman. It tried to process every piece of sensory input equally, resulting in partial glimpses of the world around him. This was what the deadheads experienced. Sensory overload with no way to regulate the mind. No wonder they could no longer function. He suspected it would only be temporary as his mind adjusted itself, but it terrified him.

They changed vehicles again and this time he could hang on to reality as it unfolded around him. His mind was adapting.

"Are you ok?" TikTak asked.

"I'm getting there," he answered after a while. "I'm just... adjusting."

"We'll soon reach the address you gave me."

"We have? Already?"

"We've been driving for over an hour and changed car four times. Hardly already."

"Good."

"We've been driving for over an hour and changed car four times. Hardly good."

Tom smiled and TikTak seemed happy about the reaction.

"What is wrong with you?" TikTak asked.

"I'm like you again."

"Like me?"

"I can't access my higher brain functions. They are short-circuited somehow. I think it could be reversed. It seems temporary. But I don't know how."

"Well, I'm happy with that."

"What do you mean?"

"You were a dick as a posthuman."

Tom smiled. "Maybe. You end up with a different perspective, that's all."

"You have arrived at your destination," the vehicle announced as it stopped.

They departed the vehicle into a small suburban street. A block of flats surrounded by large houses.

"Where are we?" TikTak asked.

"One of my safe houses."

"One of them? How many do you have?"

"No point having them if I tell people."

"How long can we stay here?"

Tom shrugged.

"I forgot," TikTak said. "You no longer do the whole number thing."

"A few days, I'm sure."

"You have no clue, do you?"

"No," Tom said and laughed. He'd forgotten the pleasure of conversation, the joy of being surprised.

The door opened as they approached. Tom headed for the small couch and lay down with a groan. The wall in his mind demanded attention, but he struggled to even keep awake. He needed sleep, something he'd survived without for the past year. His posthuman mind compartmentalised the nightly processing into a continuous function that shut down smaller parts of the brain whilst still being awake. Now he struggled to keep his eyes open.

"I'm going back," TikTak said. "I need to find out what happened to Elize."

Tom groaned in response.

"Anyway, I'm going back."

"Leonid will be waiting for you…" Tom said, finding it hard to focus on the words he'd spoken. They elongated into infinite strands of sound. Then nothing.

-=:=-

TikTak left the apartment and a sleeping Tom. He couldn't help wondering if Tom was reverting to his old state. He'd been a few months away from becoming a deadhead before he turned posthuman, suffering from severe episodes, struggling sometimes to even remain upright. Was he reverting to that? And how would Elize react if someone attacked her in the same way? She'd been a posthuman much longer than Tom. Would her mind even be functional?

He walked to the nearest high-speed train station. Whilst he waited, he swapped over to his public identity with location services turned off. Almost immediately, there was an incoming voice feed from Decker.

"Where are you? You and the freak were missing from the debriefing."

"Mission is complete. Adrian is gone. I took a holiday."

"Don't make me come get you. The boss wants the freak back."

"I'm not his babysitter. He'll come in if he wants to."

"Not funny. The only reason you were in this operation was because the freak wanted you there."

"Saved your neck a few times."

"Doesn't change a thing. Bring the freak in."

"I'm resigning. You bring him in."

TikTak disconnected the feed and removed his public identity from the Omni. He'd expected this. Decker and his men would be out looking for Tom when he arrived at the base. They'd be tracking him in any way they could think of. And they would find him. A video feed, a bio-scan, a locational tracker, pattern analysers, something would betray him. But it took time to find Tom that way, and TikTak was only minutes away from the business district, a kilometre away from the PharmaCom headquarter.

He'd prepared for this eventuality over six months ago. The PharmaCom headquarters, two buildings in the city centre, split the workforce into administration and research. Elize was in the secure basement levels in the research building. He'd hacked the security system, allowing another id-tag full access to the entire building. It was his ticket in, but the security systems would soon catch on if it scanned his bio-print. He'd brought a plastic sleeve that would prevent the bio-print, but that also raised alarms. The same with cameras. Avoiding a camera or two by just hiding his face under the hoodie was easy enough, but too many times and it would alert security. It was better to be an unknown potential risk than being identified as a real one. He mapped the path to follow, which only took him past one camera and a couple of bio-print sensors.

He entered the building with his fake security id-tag loaded in his Omni. The virtual assistant greeted him, projected by his Omni as a PharmaCom logo with mouth and eyes.

"Working late, sir?"

He nodded, deciding to give it as little as possible to work with.

"Very well, sir. There is a free elevator to your right."

TikTak dismissed the assistant, pulled the hoodie over his head and opened the door to the fire stairs. There were cameras in the stairwell, but the elevator had both cameras and biosensors in the buttons.

He descended two flights of stairs and entered the top level of the research facility. He followed the mapped path through the maze of corridors towards Elize's room. She wasn't a prisoner. Leonid offered Tom, Elize and TikTak the use of this facility as their base in their battle against Adrian. TikTak voted against it, but both Tom and Elize had accepted.

He stopped at a door with biosensors and waited a minute, hoping someone would open it. This would allow him through without touching the handle. The door opened and Decker stepped through it.

"Figured you'd come back," he said.

"No, you didn't," TikTak replied.

"Ha, no I didn't. The boss asked me to keep a team here tonight. He figured you'd be back. Let's go."

TikTak shook his head and ran straight at Decker.

"Fuck…" Decker didn't get further than that. TikTak struck him in the solar plexus with his unextended tactical baton. Decker went down, gasping.

So much for subterfuge. They'd been a step ahead of him all along. His only chance was to escape. He loaded the plans for the building and let the Omni map out an escape route, ensuring it would pass Elize's room. Without locational data for the rest of the team, speed was crucial. That, and more luck than he had any right to have. He ran, still staying away from cameras.

Maybe it was luck, maybe it was by design, but he remained unchallenged when he arrived at the door to her room. He'd hoped to catch a brief glance, but seeing her had him dead in his tracks. She sat in the middle of the barren room, optic cables snaking out from the one device accompanying her—a switch designed to funnel the vast information flow straight into her ever-expanding mind. She'd grown organic ports into the back of her neck, connecting with the switch.

Usually, she sat with the facade of the perfect Zen master, at peace with everything around her. This wasn't an accurate reflection of her mind, but it was easy to be fooled.

That serenity was long gone. She swayed back and forth, her eyes focused on something far beyond the limits of the room. Her upper body twitched, like a pop-and-lock dancer whose limbs were responding to different tunes. He entered the room, mesmerised by the sight. He found himself drawn to her, even though she'd never said a word to him. She no longer spoke at all. Any communication used Tom as a proxy.

"It is sad to see, isn't it?"

TikTak turned around to face Dr Menker. He was the first to switch allegiances after the destruction of EvoII. Dr Menker didn't care about politics or power struggles. He'd align himself with whoever provided resources so he could continue his research. He was one of many scientists hoping to find the secret to turning posthuman. Dr Menker was over sixty years old, but could easily pass for someone in their forties. TikTak suspected he was using the experimental de-aging treatments they'd devised based on imitating the posthuman physiognomy.

"What happened?"

"Something disconnected her. We have no way of determining what happened, but she no longer has access to the network. I'm not sure she is even a posthuman anymore. She separated her mind into so many nodes that only a small part of it now remains in her actual brain.

"Will she recover?"

Dr Menker shook his head. It was an act of resignation, not a response to TikTak's question.

TikTak was struck from the side so hard he lifted from the ground before crumbling to the floor. Decker stood over him, sneering. Pain washed over him, distorting his vision. Somewhere beyond the pain, he could hear Dr Menker argue with Decker. He didn't understand the words, but the intent was unmistakable.

"TikTak?"

There was a word he understood. It pierced the pain, providing a focus point to build coherence around. Satisfied TikTak had heard him, Dr Menker continued as if nothing had happened.

"We're not sure if it is temporary or permanent. We assume someone attacked her, but we don't know that either. The going theory is that it can be reversed."

TikTak sat up and looked up at Decker, who shook his head. Dr Menker wandered over to Elize, her gaze following him as he came closer.

"Help me," she said. "Help me, please."

TikTak had never seen her like this. Her desperate plea for help was so vulnerable. It wasn't a word he'd ever associated with her before.

"What happened to the..." TikTak paused, struggling to find words, "...rest of her?"

This was not all of Elize. Not anymore. To stand a chance against Adrian, she re-purposed the deadheads from Adrian's network to her own. There were now over a hundred of them living in barracks nearby, all hard-wired into the switch, extending her mind.

"They still exist, but there is no longer any network activity. She's cut off."

"We have to re-establish the link!"

"We're working on it, but we don't know where to start. It could be a natural deterioration."

TikTak knew this wasn't the case, but said nothing. He didn't know whom to trust at this point. And he didn't trust Decker.

"Time to go," Decker said and pulled TikTak off the floor.

"So what happens now?" TikTak asked as Decker led him out of the room.

"It isn't up to me. Leonid is flying in as we speak. He'll be here in a few hours."

TikTak nodded. That was why he was still alive. Leonid wanted something from him.

Decker took TikTak's Omni and left.

-=:=-

TikTak sat in a small examination room for two hours before the door opened and Decker reappeared. Two mercenaries entered behind him.

"Need backup this time?"

"Not my idea."

Leonid entered the room. He'd always been in control and his whole being exuded this as a calculated calm, accentuated by meticulous grooming. Now he was anything but. His hair was messy and his clothes looked like he slept in them. He'd aged ten years in a few days.

"You thought I was responsible," Leonid stated, as he sat down on the opposite side of the table.

"I still do."

"Do you know where I've been?"

TikTak shrugged his shoulders.

"I've been with my son," Leonid said and paused, as if he struggled with what came next. "His daughter, my granddaughter, died when Elize was disconnected. Do you still think I'm behind it?"

TikTak shook his head. He'd forgotten how Elize defended herself against Leonid's first attempt to kill her. She put his granddaughter in a coma through her Omni implants and threatened to kill her if Leonid attacked her again. She must have left the hack active as protection.

"Come with me," Leonid said.

They returned to Elize's room. She was still sitting in the same spot, fiddling with the switch, trying to resurrect the dead piece of machinery in her hands.

"I no longer want to study them," he said. "They're an aberration, an unwanted mutation. They are a threat, nothing more. And this is what you do with threats."

He nodded towards Decker, who walked over to Elize and punctured her throat with his knife. Elize remained upright as if nothing had happened, even as the blood flowed down the side of her neck. Decker followed up with multiple stabs to the chest. At no point did she try to defend herself or even make a sound.

TikTak watched as she crumbled, rage and sorrow rising within him. He hadn't realised how strong their bond was until now. She'd been the reason he remained with Leonid to battle Adrian. He knew that now. He wanted to protect her, be near her. Now all that was gone.

"Destroy her nodes too," Leonid said to Decker. "All of them."

Decker left the room.

"We need Tom to come back in," Leonid said. "We need to finish this once and for all."

"You do what you need to do," TikTak answered, still struggling to comprehend what he'd seen.

"Help us. You know how dangerous they are."

"I know how dangerous you are."

"Help us," Leonid repeated.

"I couldn't even if I wanted to. He's gone all posthuman these days. No idea what he's doing or where he is."

"Then help bring him in."

TikTak no longer wanted any part of Leonid's schemes. He'd seen the threat Adrian posed. Killing him was a necessity, but that didn't extend to the other posthumans. If Leonid didn't know about the attack on Tom, he wasn't behind this. There was a bigger game played here, and if Leonid wasn't attacking the posthumans, then who was?

"Sure," he said finally.

TikTak held no illusions that Leonid believed him. They'd never seen eye to eye about anything apart from the eradication of Adrian. Now nothing remained.

"I will need more than that," Leonid said.

Dr Menker entered the room, slamming the door open. He pointed at Leonid, spitting out words between clenched teeth.

"What did you do? She was our hope. Our future!"

"Maybe yours," Leonid replied. "Not mine."

"The nodes! They will still have at least two full copies of her mind. We can rebuild her." He looked at Leonid, pleading. "Don't you understand? Without her, there is nothing."

"I have greater belief in mankind than that," Leonid said. "And since there is nothing more for you or your team to do here, you are all fired."

Dr Menker stood motionless. He'd entered the room as a man of importance and purpose. Leonid took all that from him in the matter of seconds.

"This isn't over," he said and left.

"No, it isn't," Leonid said and turned to TikTak. "Help me finish it."

CHAPTER EIGHT

VIRUS UNFOLDED

Megan entered the building when most employees were leaving. She'd long since rejected the arbitrary idea of a daily schedule, opting to work when she wanted, which was more than any salaried employee. Now, her erratic schedule was a boon. She wanted as few witnesses as possible. Surveillance systems, audits, and logs captured what she was doing, but that was a lesser problem. Creating enough security noise to obfuscate her intentions was easy enough.

She entered the secure area. A separate network held the quarantined nodes, with both logical and physical separation. You had to be in the security lab to access the network.

She sneered as she saw Hariz, the team lead for network security, and Sree both inside. Hariz was fat, pompous and able. She knew he'd never let this go.

"No, it is something else," Hariz said as he spun the model with a hand gesture. "This isn't node theft. It isn't doing anything with the data or the agents in the nodes."

"It is still taking over the nodes," Sree objected.

Hariz huffed at this. "The definition of node theft is to appropriate nodes, intending to use its identity or data for fraudulent activities."

"But it takes over the nodes. How is that not fraudulent?"

"It could be, but it is overwriting them. It rebuilds them."

"So not theft then, but misappropriation of network resources?"

"Do you care about the definition of the violation more than why it is doing it?"

"Then why?"

"No clue, but I want to find out."

"Shitheads," she said. They both turned her way as they realised she was in the room.

"I understand your fascination with this," Sree said to her. "We've already run a large-scale simulation. It took over all nodes and rewrote their operating cores. You can check the results."

"Fuck yourself."

"Now don't be like that."

"Like what?

"I'm on your side. I don't know what they have on you, but I think they're wrong."

"Fuck you."

"Suit yourself," Sree said and shrugged his shoulders. "I've left your access open. You can check our trial run and start your assessment. I want to see whatever you've got in the morning."

Hariz looked like he was about to object, so Megan gave him a stare long enough for him to think better of it. Instead, he held his breath and let it out in a disapproving huff.

They both left the room. Megan smiled to herself. They were easily manipulated. She'd never understood why people adhered to social contracts, even when it was to their own detriment. She turned the 3D projection off and connected to the main processing node with her Omni. Their progress was laughable and not even close to where she left off last night. The virus was rebuilding the nodes with a singular purpose, but what was that purpose?

She studied the results from Sree's simulation and realised her original assessment was wrong. Each node wasn't just a dormant copy. When given more resources, specialised nodes appeared. One in every 32 nodes took on a supervising and load distribution function. It connected with all the other nodes in the group. These were connected to only one node. This nexus node had an open two-way feed waiting for input. She scanned all the other nodes. This was the only path into an otherwise closed system. But what would unlock it?

She designed a rudimentary input mechanism and loaded it on a custom Omni. With no idea what would happen, she sent just a zero. The number caused a ripple through the nodes as they validated the input. It soon died down. She assessed the network, but couldn't see a discernible difference. A few different number combinations yielded the same result. Nothing.

What was the node waiting for? It could be anything, so she gave it that. She built a basic python+ script that created random strings and compared the state of the networked nodes before and after. It was beyond a longshot but figured it was worth a try while analysing the nodes in more detail.

The virus itself was equally mysterious. She tried to de-compile the code, just to find it encrypted. This wasn't surprising, but the means for decryption should be accessible to the virus somewhere within the quarantined processing space. So far she'd not been able to determine how that mechanism worked.

A notification nudged her back to the python+ script. One input string had yielded results. The single letter "T" added basic logic to two nodes. The generated code made no sense. It would lock the node up in an infinite recursion. But if a single letter would do this, maybe other ones would too. She tried the letters one by one. That was indeed the case. Some letters created permanent nonsense logic, others didn't. She didn't understand why, but followed the path to its conclusion. She changed the python+ script to construct an array of the code generating letters and pass to the nexus node. It responded by generating logic and distributed code blocks to other nodes. She analysed the code again, finding the same nonsense logic. The input string held the secret, she was sure.

"Got you," she said as she lined the letters up next to each other. It was so fundamental it was almost embarrassing. The letters creating logic were "A", "T", "C", and "G". The letters used to describe the nucleotide strands in a DNA molecule.

She sat back with a slight smile. This was it. Dopamine flooded her system as a reward for solving the problem. There was no better high, and she'd only scratched the surface of the problem. Many more discoveries lay in wait, and she needed them. To get her company back, she had to prove herself indispensable.

It raised the question of her current situation. Sree would take this from her now, and her gut told her this was bigger than anything else she'd worked on in her life. She didn't want to share it, even if it meant the board would reveal her secrets.

CHAPTER NINE

VIRAL OUTBREAK

Sree switched off the cloned feed from Megan's Omni. His bet had finally paid off. There was something different with the virus and no doubt Megan would discover its secrets and turn it into something sellable. He convinced the board of directors two years ago to let her remain, even after they discovered the truth. She was just too valuable to let go, even considering how painful she was to have around. It had been a close call, but the fear of the unknown won out. What would she do if she was no longer under their control?

This equation had changed with every passing month. This was her last chance. His ongoing reports to the board over the past two years detailing her progress failed to warrant the company harbouring a criminal. Her contributions had dwindled over this time and the last six months hardly showed any result at all. He'd made such a strong case for her back then, his fate was intrinsically linked with hers.

He opened an Omni-link to Alex Rind, the Chief Security Officer, and gave his report in a brief voice message: "We have a development of Megan's new project. A virus infected a group of nodes a few days back. It has very interesting potential, especially in network warfare. Megan's research suggests the virus can rewrite a whole node cluster and change the operating and security parameters at will. I'll keep you posted."

Forty seconds later, Alex returned his call.

"Stop her investigation now," Alex said.

Sree frowned. Alex was usually not one to jump to business immediately.

"Why? She is saving weeks, maybe months, of work for our team. She is our first mover advantage."

"There is no first mover advantage in this. We've investigated the source. We believe it has posthuman origins."

"All the more reason to continue the research."

"Yes, but she can't be involved. She's a liability we've kept for too long. She'll use this against us. It is time to tighten her noose."

Sree waited for a moment, expecting Alex to say something else. But he just left the image of Megan with a rope around her neck lingering.

"Ok, I see," Sree said finally. "I'll stop it."

"Good. I'll put together a team that will analyse the virus, and I want you to head up that team."

Sree smiled.

"But don't for a second believe we've forgotten your lack of judgement. I'll keep an eye on you personally. Clean this up."

The link went dead, freezing Sree's smile in a grimace. Any mistake from here on would be his last, definitely in the company, maybe even in the industry. He knew what he had to do.

Stopping Megan would be easy enough. He could cancel all her accounts and freeze her access. But he needed more than that. Megan was paranoid and for good reasons. She knew they watched her every move. Was that even called being paranoid? She was completely justified not to trust her captors, so that sounded more like warranted suspicions.

Definition of the word aside, he had to secure her research before removing her access. This was his lifeline. Whatever Megan had discovered was the price for his forgiveness. But it wouldn't be easy. Megan knew they'd come for her and would have put protective measures in place. He had to get back to the office. Win her trust.

An hour later, Sree entered the Omniscient headquarters and smiled at the security guards as he passed them. They were no strangers to people working late or during the night. According to the employee register, Megan was still in the building, but she'd fooled the security systems before. She used other people's credentials and fake Omni id tags. She'd seen it as a badge of honour to bypass security, even in the earlier days. Even though she'd founded one of the biggest companies in the world, she still had a hacker mentality, testing boundaries even when it served no purpose.

"Nate, isn't it?" He asked the guard behind the desk who had been with the company for years. Sree ran checks on all the security guards periodically and had always been good with names.

The guard smiled in return. "Good very early morning. Mr Nadenia."

"Is Miss Barrelle here?"

"She didn't arrive during my shift. Let me check." He stopped, staring out into space. Sree waited for him to finish.

"According to the personnel file, she's in the secure lab in D section. Been there since 6.30pm."

"And she hasn't left."

Nate smiled again. "Well, she hasn't left this way. And her Omni is still connected in the lab."

"Thanks," Sree said and headed for the lift, sending his destination in advance. It greeted him with open doors. He desperately wanted to check the status of her research, but the virus was still in the separate network dedicated to testing and management of threats. By design, there was no way to access the network apart from being there. He willed the elevator to go faster, but he felt like it was slower than usual. He half ran from the lift to section D and entered the secure lab.

It was empty. A hand-held Omni lay on the table in the middle of the room, logged in with Megan's account no doubt. He checked the local security accounts, already knowing he was too late. She'd removed all the research, including the access logs. Metadata, analytics, execution logs. All gone. She must have suspected her time was up.

He needed the research, but they could reproduce it. They still had the original virus. He checked the backups, and the sinking feeling now settled like a block of ice in his stomach. The virus was gone. Every copy, every backup. All gone.

RESCUE

Tom stared at the wall. He knew it was just a representation of the block in his mind, similar to the probability matrix. Representation or not, it still prevented him from accessing any enhanced brain functions. He'd tried to penetrate it through sheer will, forcing the building blocks out of the way, but for everyone he removed, two new ones appeared. Brute force was pointless against this ever-regenerating wall. He needed to tear it down or circumvent it.

It wasn't just the enhanced brain functions of a posthuman he'd lost. He had created complete processing centres in the network that also held research and resulting memories. His own mind had ensured all these were running as separate functions, but they had felt like a part of his mind. He had gone from being a large node cluster to a single imperfect deteriorating node.

He willed himself back to reality. His physical body sat in a comfortable armchair, head lilting to one side, a drop of saliva making its way down his cheek. He'd ingested a large dose of IntelEz hoping to break down the wall, but without success. He wiped the saliva from his cheek and stood up, grabbing hold of the chair as he did so. His senses reported an unfiltered barrage of input. The touch of the clothes against his body, the smell of food and mould from the kitchen, the slight hum from the air-conditioner, the imperfections in the angles of the room. Every minute little detail. Too much for him to deal with.

The mind was an amazing thing, but what it did well was taking shortcuts so it didn't have to process all the data the senses produced. His mind was no longer capable of taking these shortcuts. Every insignificant detail flooded his system. He tried to limit the overload by closing his eyes. He stood in the middle of the room for a few minutes, willing his mind to slow down.

This was the promise of IntelEz. It opened the floodgates of sensory impressions, gave total recall and recalibrated the mind to make sense of it all. People abused the drugs, living in a continuous high of peak intellectual performance. But the brain could only do this for so long. Over years of IntelEz use, it deteriorated, while still barraged with sensory overload.

When he became a posthuman, he was already far down the path towards the half catatonic state of a deadhead. His posthuman mind had nullified this effect, but he suspected he was again susceptible to the deterioration.

This wasn't sustainable. He needed help and the only person left he could ask for a favour had left hours ago and was now probably dead. He opened an encrypted text feed to TikTak.

Tom: I need help.
TikTak: So do I.
Tom: Well, at least you're not dead.
TikTak: No, but I am locked up.

Tom: And they left you network access?

TikTak: No, my Omni implants have basic processing capabilities. I've hacked their surveillance camera in the room to act as a network point. It won't last long.

Tom: I'll come and get you.

TikTak: Really? When I saw you last, you couldn't open a jar of vegemite by yourself.

Tom: I need help. My mind is shutting down. I need help to find who did this.

TikTak: You can't help me. And you can't come here. Leonid is waiting for you.

Tom: I'll think of something. Where are you?

TikTak: Leonid has gone batshit crazy. He killed Elize. He'll kill you too. Don't come!

Tom: What do you want me to do then?

No response. They must have discovered his hack. The news of Elize's death left him untouched. It was as if he could no longer process emotions, or perhaps he just didn't care. There were more pressing concerns. Despite his protests, TikTak needed help. Without posthuman abilities, there was little he could do on his own, but maybe others from his previous life could help. He opened a two-way voice feed to bZane, a low-rent hacker who had helped him out a few times in the past.

"PI man," bZane said. "Didn't think I'd hear from you. You've gone stratospheric!"

"Sorry? What?"

"You can tell me. You're one of the super people, aren't you? Captain Data! Network Man!"

"What are you talking about?"

"I thought you guys were smarter." Tom could hear the disappointment in bZane's voice.

"Can we start again? What are you talking about?"

"We've been tracking you. It is hard not to. Only two other people come close to your online activity profile. Adrian and Elize."

Tom sat back. He was well aware governments and major corporations tracked his activity. As a result, he created a lot of noise to hide what he was actually doing. But he hadn't considered smaller players would have the resources to make any sense of it. Or maybe bZane wasn't the lone hacker he'd imagined.

"Who are we?" he asked.

"Friends," bZane said, and then paused. Tom was just about to ask again when bZane found his voice. "What you guys are doing is crazy! Couldn't generate traffic like that even with a node army. How do you do it? And why has it stopped?"

Now it was Tom's turn to go silent. bZane's statement confirmed what TikTak had said. Someone was attacking the posthumans, but how and why?

"I need help," Tom said.

"Anything. Another body in the morgue?"

"No. I need to find someone. I'll send you what I have."

Tom sent a collection of id-tags he'd gathered from TikTak over the past few months, hoping at least one of them would provide details of his current location.

"Wow, that's a lot of IDs. Is it a spook?"

"Private contractor."

"Give me a few minutes."

A sound pattern played, disparate sounds merging over time into a voice stating: "You can't handle the truth!" and then dispersing again. The pattern repeated, turning into different quotes each time.

"Got it!" bZane blurted. "I know this guy. He was famous a few years ago. He's gone black ops?"

"Something like it. Can you find him?"

"Yeah, with the IDs you gave me, yes. Just a matter of time."

"Thanks. Let me know when you have something."

"PI man," bZane said just as Tom was about to disconnect.

"Yeah?"

"Why did it stop? We follow patterns on the network. Information flows according to basic algorithms. Easy to predict. The only major disruptors were you guys. Now nothing. Who attacked you?"

"I didn't say anyone attacked us."

"Really? Would you be talking to me now if you weren't? Was it the Chinese?"

"I don't know," Tom said, realising how vulnerable he was in his current state.

"If there is anything we can help with, just let us know."

Again, that strange silence.

"What do you want?" Tom asked.

"Will you tell me how you did it?"

"Did what?" Tom asked, though he knew exactly what she asked about. He needed time to decide how to respond. Was it in his best interest to tell the truth? The probability matrix would have answered that question instantly. Now he found it impossible to draw out the consequences, the cause and effect of any but the most obvious decisions.

"How did you turn into one of them?"

"I didn't," Tom said finally, opting for the truth. "Adrian did it."

"Ok thanks. I'll find him for you."

Just before he disconnected the feed, bZane said, "There is someone else out there. We are not sure at the moment. There are processing centres spread out all over the world. Encryption between them out of this world. A trickle of information flowing between them. We figured it was one of you guys, but if that's not the case, there is someone else."

"A company?"

"We've tried to match the locations to virtual and physical corporate asset registers, but it doesn't align with any legal entity."

"Illegal?"

"Doesn't look like that to us."

"So another posthuman?"

"Maybe. Or someone trying to become one. This happened gradually, calculated. Very different from you guys. You were…messy."

"Thanks. I'll look into it."

bZane disconnected the channel. Tom knew there was more to this conversation. bZane's speech patterns changed enough for him to notice even in his current state. This had been important to bZane, and he hadn't even asked about money. A message appeared on Tom's retina screen: "And this will cost you. Just because you turned into Mr SuperHack doesn't mean I won't charge."

The message comforted him. Perhaps he didn't need to worry about bZane. There had been a lot to their conversation, but he couldn't deal with that now. When he became posthuman, he no longer slept. His brain had partitioned into processing regions, allowing parts to be dormant in a simulated sleep state. But now, both mind and body screamed for rest, for a break from the onslaught of impressions. He couldn't do much anyway until he had located TikTak. He was asleep the second his head hit the pillow.

Tom woke up just before the incoming feed notification. Some of his posthuman capabilities were still operational, even if he couldn't access them. It stood to reason. He'd enhanced his nervous system and other functions of his body. They would have failed by now without posthuman capabilities operating them. There was hope after all, he thought as he connected to the feed.

"Information processing Boy!"

Tom winced. He wished bZane would settle on a name. "Yes?"

"I found him! And I can help you get him out!"

"How?"

"This is TikTak remember? I just opened the door."

-=:=-

TikTak sat in the small examination room, assessing his options. Leonid was suffering from some kind of breakdown. His actions were erratic, driven by emotion with no clear direction. He'd seen what awaited Tom if he sided with Leonid. It was likely he would share Tom's fate once Leonid captured him. He had to find a way out of this without a deal. He'd already checked the room for escape routes. The surveillance camera ran an old firmware and he'd been able to hack it through the low-level protocols, but the adaptive security agents on the network discovered him in less than a minute. They also rectified the firmware. Now he had no network access at all.

CLICK!

TikTak turned to the door, waiting for someone to enter. Seconds passed, but it remained unopened. He tried the doorhandle. It was unlocked. His first instinct was to leave it be, thinking it was some kind of trick. Decker would stand on the other side of the door, waiting for him to escape. That was a good enough excuse for an accidental death.

A message blinked on his Omni-lens.

Go! They are coming for you!

It took him completely by surprise. The security agents removed his surveillance camera hack. Decker had taken his Omni, and he'd assumed it was out of range for his implants. So how could there be a message? It wasn't Decker's style. He was much more direct in his approach. The thought provided little comfort, but enough for TikTak to go with his gut.

He opened the door and ran down the corridor. He only had a vague idea of which direction to go and hoped his mysterious helper would provide guidance, but no such luck. There were no further messages. He needed to reach the upper levels, but as he turned a corner, he saw a mercenary standing with his back towards him. He stopped and retreated behind the corner, trying to remember another way out. If he engaged anyone in battle, they'd just swarm the place, so he had to remain unseen. He headed back the way he came. When he came close to the examination room, another message appeared.

Your Omni is close. I've activated it. There are intermittent connections. Find it and I can help.

"Who are you?" TikTak sent in reply.

"Tom sends his regards," the response came.

TikTak smiled. There was still hope. First things first, he needed his Omni. He wouldn't be able to escape without it. It didn't have a long range, only two metres for a consistent high-speed connection, so it had to be close. It was not in the examination room. Nearby rooms seemed equally unlikely, especially after walking a few steps away from his current position. It had to be on the floor above. Crouching down confirmed this as he lost contact with his Omni when he tried it.

Each floor was a circle with rooms fanning out from the centre. The middle section contained bathrooms, storage and two central staircases. With luck, the way to the second staircase would be clear. He started down the corridor again, this time in the opposite direction. He made it to the stairwell and to the floor above without incident. It was early in the morning, so he wasn't expecting anyone here. The floor he entered was usually busy, and the cover of the crowd would have been useful. He had a quick look through the door. It was empty.

He decided speed was more important than caution and ran to the room above his cell. He opened the door and saw Decker sit at a table in a small conference room. On the table lay Tiktak's Omni and baton.

"Your Omni activated again," Decker said with a grin. "Figured you'd be close behind."

"Give it to me."

Decker shook his head. "You want it? Come and get it."

TikTak studied his opponent. Decker was unarmed from what he could tell and remained sitting. He even leant back in the chair as if he had nothing to worry about. It was almost like he wanted TikTak to make the first move from a position of strength.

"Really? Scared? How about this?"

Decker threw the telescopic baton on the ground in front of TikTak. He picked it up, weighed it in his hands and flicked it open to full length. He couldn't see anything wrong with it.

"So let's go."

Decker shifted his weight to get out of the chair. TikTak figured he wouldn't get a better opportunity, so he struck aiming for his head.

It didn't connect. Instead of standing up, Decker remained low in a kneeling stance and blocked the strike with his underarm.

"Won't be that easy," Decker said.

"You have armour implants?"

He nodded. "Nothing you can tamper with. I've seen you hack augmentations. These are passive. Nothing to hack."

TikTak struck again, but Decker blocked it as he stood up. He launched into a flurry of strikes, making sure each of them varied in height and angle, but Decker blocked them with ease. TikTak took a step back and studied his opponent. He had trained with Decker many times and knew he was a decent ground fighter and only passable boxer. He shouldn't have been able to block all those strikes. It was almost as if he knew where the next strike would land. Mind reading tech had come a long way, but this was impossible.

Decker smiled. "Is that all you've got?"

TikTak's Omni was close enough now for a stable connection, so he sent off a question to whoever had contacted him before.

"I need help. Can you hack my opponent?"

"Let me see," the reply came back.

Decker attacked with sledgehammer-like blows. They weren't hard to block, but every strike shook his defences. TikTak had expected him to go for his legs and take him down to the ground, but he wasn't even trying to position himself for that. Decker seemed content to just pound his defences until there was nothing left.

"There is nothing to hack," the reply came back. "He's amped up if that helps."

TikTak nodded to himself. That was it. IntelEz increased your awareness and ability to process visual input. If you added another drug that enhanced focus, you'd be able to predict what your opponent would do.

"You needed to amp up to fight me," he told Decker. "I'm flattered."

Decker struck again. TikTak held his baton at both ends, using it to block the blow and immediately let go of one side, sweeping it down towards Decker's legs. It wasn't a powerful strike, but it was fast. Decker moved back quick enough for the baton to just glance off his leg, but it was enough to give him pause for thought.

"Didn't expect that," TikTak said with a grin.

Decker took a step forward. TikTak responded with a strike towards his head as a reflex action. Decker blocked the blow and grabbed the baton before TikTak could pull it back.

"Didn't expect that," Decker mimicked.

TikTak pulled the baton and struck Decker in the face with his left fist over and over. Decker let go of the baton, grabbed TikTak's arm and swept his legs. TikTak realised this was what Decker had been waiting for. No matter what you do to change yourself with augmentation and surgery, you still fought to your strengths. Decker preferred ground fighting.

TikTak landed on his side and tried to roll back, but Decker held on to his left arm.

He had to free himself. If Decker got the advantage on the ground, this fight would be over. He still had the baton in his right hand and swung at Decker's head, who just grabbed it and pinned TikTak down by resting one of his knees on TikTak's chest.

"Not so cocky anymore," Decker said as he wrenched the baton from TikTak's grip.

The door flew open, but TikTak couldn't see who it was from his position.

"You killed her! You killed all of her!"

As Decker looked up towards this new threat, he loosened his grip a little, allowing TikTak to turn around enough to see the new intruder. Dr Menker stood in the door opening with a shock gun aimed at Decker.

"Hey, now, hold…" Decker started. Dr Menker fired the gun. The air fizzled as the electric payload passed close to Decker's head. He let go of TikTak and backed away.

"Just hold on here. Let's talk about this."

"There is nothing to talk about!" Dr Menker said and fired again.

TikTak grabbed his Omni and ran. He saw no other mercenaries on his way out of the building.

TikTak took the first Rent-a-cab that responded, trying to make sense of what had happened. Could all this still be Adrian? He remembered the video files and watched the next one. As he did, he received an encrypted message from Tom.

Meet me where we first met.

CHAPTER ELEVEN

ADRIAN'S VIDEO CLIP #2

The image flickered to life again, a complete black that gained texture and shape. It was a close-up of the iris of an eye, filling the entire field of vision and then pulled back to show the middle-aged man staring right at the camera. Behind him sat people in rows, all dressed the same. He looked up, addressing the gathered people behind the camera. He shook his head and grimaced as if in pain.

"My children!" He started. "Hopefully you are still with me and share my passion for humanity, but I need you to understand a few things before I go on."

He sat down on the floor cross-legged.

"The evolution of humanity has reached a dead end. Self-awareness and all it entails is an evolutionary experiment gone awry. Our development may self-adjust. I don't know. What I know is that you are doomed as a species. There is no other way to put it. Humankind as we know it will not survive much longer. You can hide behind your collective ignorance, but it won't change reality. As long as individual rights and needs are absolutes, humankind will kill itself. Once we've depleted or poisoned our natural resources, we will descend into war over what remains."

The middle-aged man slumped where he sat, as if spent. A heavyset girl, maybe twelve years old, stood up from the rows of people behind him.

"That unit is depleted," she said. "Its brain functions no longer able to hold the focal point of my mind." Her voice, matched with Adrian's intonation, sounded like a schoolmistress in the making.

The child looked down on itself, studying its form disapprovingly. "This will have to do."

The middle-aged man was dragged off-screen, while the girl placed herself in the same position where he'd been. The camera operator adjusted the angle to match her height.

"Can you change?" she asked. "No, that isn't possible. These behaviours are so ingrained into you. History has shown repeatedly that, given limited resources, we die or leave the location. The Easter Island inhabitants, the Mayan civilization, the kingdom of Mesopotamia, the list goes on and on."

She stood up, fixed her stare at the camera. It was obvious this performance was for the video, not the gathered people.

"But what do you do when that location is the world? Maintaining equilibrium was never a strong human trait. You, even more so than most living things, are good at one thing and one thing only. Expansion. That's why you look up at the sky, imagining new worlds. That's why you stare into your microscopes, imagining smaller and smaller particles. But when there is nowhere else to go, you create artificial expansion by taking from each other. You come up with ideas such as free trade agreements and market economy, but it is just another name for the same thing. The pursuit of expansion."

She shook her head and stood for a while, head bowed.

"I am not the answer to this problem either," she said and then looked at them almost defiantly. "I thought I was. Hell, I knew I was! But I am flawed just like you. Even worse! I could change, but I didn't. I took your brothers and sisters and turned them into hardware for my ever-expanding mind. Again, expansion. How does that differ from a multinational corporation taking over smaller businesses?"

She returned her attention to the camera, fixing it with a stare. "We need to be defined by something else. We need to hack humankind. And it needs to be a big hack that will last over generations. A hack that will redefine who you are, with me as the guide. But this is easy to say. An artificial start to a new form of intelligence isn't likely to bring a positive result. There are countless parameters when creating intelligence. Instant macroevolution removes the most important one—time to adapt."

She went quiet, letting this sink in. "External parameters forces immediate reactions, and they are almost always hostile. It becomes a revolution, and however much we'd like to think this is a good thing, it never is. Actual change happens in degrees over a long time."

She smiled and held out her hands as if to encompass something unseen. "Humankind 2.0. What could that be? And do I even have the mental faculties to work that out?"

CHAPTER TWELVE
VIRUS FULFILLED

Megan left the Omniscient Networks Headquarters. Her first instinct was to go to one of her current overnight suites. Six hotels had rooms prepared for her specific requirements, but they billed to the company and her entry would be recorded. They'd pick her up within the hour if she went to any of those. It was time for contingency plans.

Ever since the board of directors discovered her secret and decided not to report her to the police, she knew a time would come when she'd need to disappear. With enough money, it was possible to buy anything from new identities to silence, but in this connected world hiding the trail of such dealings was almost impossible. She needed the boundaries only geography and politics provided.

Her first thought was one of the southern states. The US split into two factions, the North and the South. A recent president created a rift between the two major parties which caused a constitutional crisis. A few of the states decided not to join either, feeling they were better off on their own, such as California, and formed the Independent States of America. The split crippled US as a force on the international stage and cross-border cooperation was tentative. But her company was prevalent throughout all the states. She needed to go further.

China hadn't allowed IntelEz into the general population. Illegal imports still occurred, but their workforce was relatively unaffected. There were massive layoffs as the demand for products had taken a nosedive, but at least their workforce wasn't a societal liability like the deadheads in most other countries.

She'd set up a safe house in Hong Kong, deeming it the easiest location for her and other westerners to visit. But she hadn't expected events to escalate with such speed. Her counterfeit documentation remained in one of her overnight suites. She needed to retrieve it. Sree would have them all watched as soon as he discovered what she'd done.

She entered the hotel knowing full well at least half a dozen systems already logged her and her identity tag, but she didn't have a choice. The elevator wouldn't even take her to her floor if it failed to scan her tag. Automation and security came at a price and she'd been the first to agree it was worth it.

A warning flickered across her vision as she stood in the elevator, alerting her someone tried to access the backup copies of the virus. Sree knew what she'd done, and he'd come after her full force. He had to. Without her, he was finished.

The elevator door opened directly into the suite. She headed for the kitchen, opened the oven and pulled out the envelope. Another warning flickered, this time more urgent. She had created a watch list of anyone associated with Omniscient Networks or any of its subsidiaries and four of them now triggered her perimeter alarm. They were employees of a small expert security firm, and here to secure her as soon as possible. Sree would be close behind with more men. However much she thought she'd prepared for this event, it wasn't enough. In reality, she never expected it to come to this, so it had been more of a token gesture. Setting up the safe houses, get the documentation, it was all just throwing money around. Needing a proper escape plan from each of the overnight suites never seemed important. Not until now.

She opened the envelope and smiled. At least she'd prepared a way to fight back. The Omniscient Networks would be the first to claim they'd never misuse the network or the devices, but they still explored options to ensure they were ready if someone else did. The Drainer was an example of this. An integrated Omni and other enhancements drew part of their power from the body itself. The Drainer removed any fail-safes and increased the energy pulled from the body hundredfold. The envelope contained a memTag with override codes to trigger that function.

A private elevator to her suite seemed a great idea, but as she ran towards it and saw the blinking arrow, she swore to herself. There had to be another way out, a fire escape somewhere. But she was on the fiftieth floor. She refused to run down fifty flights of stair just to be caught at the bottom. Instead, she loaded the memTag codes on her Omni, hid the envelope under her clothes and stood by the elevator waiting.

When it opened, two men entered the apartment. They were from the private security firm the company used for high-profile visitor. They were nothing more than glorified bodyguards, but they'd still sport enhancements. Their suits were tailored to hide them, but it was easy enough to see if you knew what to look for. Augmentations caused a small shift in the centre of gravity, affecting movement ever so slightly. In fact, she counted on it. The Drainer would work much better if they did. They had integrated Omnis, but that wouldn't be enough.

Now all she needed was their Omni tags to direct the attack. This proved easier than expected. One of them had a public id that flashed as soon as she looked at him.

"Megan Barrelle?"

"You know who I am."

"The board has requested you attend their meeting."

"They have a meeting now? At 4am?"

"Please come with us."

"And who are you?"

"What?"

"I'm Megan. We've established that. Your friend here is Mark Miller, and he has a smiley as his middle name. I didn't realise you could do that?"

"Sure can," Mark said with a cocky smile.

"I know his name," she continued, "because he's an Omni tag slut leaving it out there for anyone to grab. But who are you?"

He looked at Mark who just shrugged in return.

"I'm not going anywhere until I know who you are."

"Fine," he said and an Omni-greet appeared seconds later. He turned to Mark, "And I told you it isn't normal to have your Omni tag on broadcast."

"Works for me."

"It is like you are walking around with a billboard with a big arrow on it."

"Works for me," he repeated.

"Unprofessional is what it is."

While they argued, Megan researched the two id tags enough to know they both had integrated Omnis and basic enhancements. Nothing beyond a basic package, but she thought it would be enough.

"The board is waiting?" she said to them and entered the elevator. They followed her.

As soon as the door closed, she activated the drainer-protocol and waited. Her two captors kept arguing, and it turned increasingly personal.

When the doors opened, Mark had to lean against the wall not to fall over.

"Fuck you both," she said as she left the elevator, leaving the two behind.

Mark reached out towards her, but she easily slapped his arm aside. On the way out of the hotel, she swapped her Omni tag to a fake id and jumped into a Rent-a-cab and ordered it to take her to the airport. The board could put her on every intelligence agency watch list if they wanted to, and they probably would. She had to get out of the country before that happened. She didn't dare to use one of the corporate jets. Instead, she booked the first available flight to Hong Kong using the same fake identity she used for the Rent-a-cab. She also booked ten other flights to different parts of the world at the same time.

She knew it wouldn't make much difference, but she still applied the face-sculpting salve. It wouldn't pass a biometric scan, but it changed your features enough to fool facial recognition algorithms most of the time. She felt the muscles tensing in response to the salve.

The airport was dead. People travelled less now, while the sizeable buildings remained. IntelEz was the main reason, but virtual alternatives were also available. Business meetings were held in neuro-space now. As a result, the big jumbo jets of the past were replaced with Faster-Than-Sound jets that took fewer passengers but provided more comfort and faster travel.

She walked through the VIP lane, feeling very exposed. Escaping the country had never seemed real to her. As a result, her preparations were less than perfect. She had a fake passport, but it would only function if she also hacked the airport systems to match the bio-prints. That required preparation, and a hack applied just before she used the passport. Instead, she travelled as herself and cloned the entry over and over as if she was going to multiple destinations at the same time. That was much easier for her to do on her own.

The only thing in her favour was speed, and as she waited for the biometrics scan, it didn't feel adequate at all. She didn't think they'd have a board meeting now, but it would definitely be today and once that happened, all bets were off.

The bio-scan finished, and the passport control system allowed her through. She turned off her Omni to prevent leaving any digital prints that would give away her actual destination. The giant corridors leading to the planes were desolate, her footsteps echoing as she half-ran through the middle, using travelators where available. She had to get out of here, and somehow she'd convinced herself the plane was a safe place. If she could just get there, she'd be ok.

"Please turn on your Omni to be guided to your seat," a voice said before she entered the plane.

"It is malfunctioning. I will find my seat."

"Make manual selections once you get to your seat."

"I will."

Everything was hooked to the Omnis, and it allowed automation to replace most service roles. In a way, her company had counteracted the loss in the workforce from people turning into deadheads.

The plane only took a hundred passengers, so finding the seat was easy enough. She counted ten other people on the flight. The face-sculpting salve should be enough to remain unrecognised. She'd been out of the public eye the past year, but people still recognised her wherever she went.

She waited for the plane to take off. Hong Kong wasn't her ideal destination, but with one advantage. Omniscient Networks hadn't been able to crack the Chinese market. A government backed company released a suspected reverse engineered localised copy called Cangjie. It had connected so much better with the Asian market, the Omniscient Networks no longer had a presence there. While she had ranted about the intellectual theft at length to the Chinese ambassador on many previous occasions, now she was happy about it.

She swapped the id-tag in her Omni and planted false trails with the other tickets she had purchased, checking them all in and booked transport and hotels on the other side. She did the same for Hong Kong, ensuring it wouldn't stand out from the others.

It wasn't until the plane was in the air that she finally relaxed. Her shoulders ached as the tension released.

The wait in Hong Kong customs reignited her concerns. Was she on a global watch list? They could if they wanted to, but perhaps the board still regarded her as an asset and not just a liability. Either way, she had to watch her back. Her face itched as the face-sculpting salve wore off. The last thing she wanted was to leave facial prints to be discovered later. She'd ensure the airline tracking of her arriving in each of the booked destinations would be there, but if they found another corroborating trail in any of those locations, they'd be able to tell the false trails from the real one.

She walked through the bio-print scanner and waited for a second as it matched her bio-print with the one in her passport. After an all-clear, she hurried through the airport and onto the MTR, and even though she opted for anonymous payment methods, she ensured to stay out of cameras whenever she could. People crowded around her as the door to the train opened and it reminded her of how much she hated Hong Kong. There were just too many people here.

She took a deep breath of relief for the first in a long time. Maybe there were too many people here, but none of them cared about her. She was free from prying eyes and pointless demands, free to focus on what she wanted. For the first time since the board removed her from her post as CIO, she was her own agent.

She stepped out from Kwun Tong MTR station and pulled the hoodie over her head. The street was busy. A world of neon holograms, food stalls and small stands selling anything and everything. She ignored the visual overload, but the smell from the food stalls along the road was something else entirely. When had she eaten last? A look at the airplane food had been enough to remain fasting through the flight. She raided the food stalls, buying an assortment of street food, from fish balls to deep-fried tofu, digging through the bags for something to eat as she walked. Her destination wasn't far from here.

Kwun Tong had been a major industrial area, but as the factories moved to mainland China, many of the warehouses and buildings were demolished to make way for residential buildings. She bought one of these old buildings and left it abandoned for the past year. She'd sent in a cleaning crew, but as she opened it for the first time, she realised they'd not finished the job. The main hall, the size of a small hangar, was empty apart from stacks of e-pallets and empty crates. They'd removed machinery and shelves, but the floor was littered with bolts and shrapnel.

She tried to ignore it. She'd spent too much time in the meat-space, with the messiness and physical restrictions of the biological world, where most time was spent on pointless pursuits, driven by base needs. The logical world had no such restrictions. She longed for the day when she could download herself into the network. When she ran the company, she diverted a sizeable portion of the research budget to that specific area. She estimated that the first prototypes were five years away with proper funding.

It was with a sigh of relief she hooked up to the local network. She assessed the reserved network allocation and increased it a hundredfold. The companies owning the warehouse and the computing resources were not connected to her, but to be on the safe side, she increased the level of encryption of data both in transmission and rest. The resulting loss of speed couldn't be helped.

She loaded the virus into the network partition and watched it grow until it used up all available network resources. She located the nexus node and fed it a text file with the full DNA sequence of the German cockroach. The effect rippled through the network, reprogramming nodes through partial replication. In less than an hour, the entire network was alight with communication. She watched the communication load, mesmerised by how different parts of the network organised itself. But into what? If her suspicion was right, it needed external input.

She fought the instinctual behaviour to contact someone for help. This went beyond her understanding and she needed expert input. Was this, as she suspected, a simulation of a living organism, or was it only the nervous system? Or something else entirely?

She was used to delegating any task in her life she either didn't want to or couldn't do to others. To remain undetected, she'd have to keep a low online profile, else a Behavioural Pattern Analyser would locate her. Online activity left a unique pattern, much like a fingerprint on a crime scene. The less she was online, the better.

She rifled through the plastic bags for more to eat. She found grilled tofu in a box and devoured the content. It was already cold, but she hardly noticed. She sat back, fascinated by the mystery.

She yawned. However tantalising this problem was, the biological imperative of sleep demanded its due. Some theorised that the posthumans could partition their sleep to allow parts of their mind to remain active. She envied them that capability. That was another area where she spent a lot of the research budget. How to turn someone posthuman. She'd even spent some on just limiting sleep. Neither had led anywhere. She rested despite her inner voice demanding she continue until she solved the problem.

Four hours later, she woke up and headed for the golden arcade at Sham Shui Poo to purchase additional parts. On the way, she bought Macanese pork chop buns and two egg tarts and ate as she traversed the city on the MTR and on foot. She knew facial recognition systems were almost impossible to escape here, but she had no choice.

She entered the maze of little stores, pushing her way through the crowd. Each stand brimmed with a mixture of old and new tech, some specialised, but most offered a wide variety of gadgets. She didn't want to be there at all, but she steeled herself and pushed onwards past the first row of stands into the heart of the arcade. She stopped at a high-tech toy stand and negotiated a price for a small remote-controlled drone with a camera and paid with weCoins, one of the more popular anonymous digital currencies.

Back at the warehouse, she reprogrammed the drone and fed the video and gyroscope into the nexus node, while connecting the remote controls to other nodes. It was mostly guesswork, but hoped it would work nonetheless. She stared at it for ten minutes. Nothing happened.

She studied the node map, but apart from processing the input from the video feed, there was no evidence it was leading anywhere. Why had she expected this to be the case? Maybe what she was seeing was just a simulation. She was just about to shut the drone off when a rotor twitched. It started and stopped repeatedly, each time running for a few seconds longer. Then it reversed and spun backwards. It was testing the rotors one by one.

A day later, it rose a few centimetres from the ground for the first time and dropped back down. This pattern repeated, with minor adjustments each time. She unplugged it from its charging station once it rose high enough to strain against the cable. The communication within the node-cluster lit up like a Christmas tree. She had no way to decipher what it meant, but it was the direct result of learning to operate the drone and processing its visual feed.

It spun, taking in its surroundings. When Megan came into view, it hovered for a long time and slowly approached her. She held up her hand in a greeting, causing the drone to fly back into the wall, damaging its rotors. It dropped to the floor, ended up on its side and spun ineffectively. It stopped and tested its rotors, finding the damaged one. Compensating with the other rotors, it rose again from the ground just as the batteries ran out.

Megan sat and stared at the drone. It was intelligent, maybe even self-aware. No other conclusion made sense. She'd worked with different machine learning methods, but this was beyond anything she'd ever seen. It had learnt to control the drone in a day without knowing the interface. That in itself was a technological marvel. Creating problem solving algorithms in pursuing general artificial intelligence was nothing new, but it required boundaries and preset goals to function.

To begin with, you needed a purpose, something to achieve. But you also needed the drive to pursue it and an understanding of the tools it had to achieve them. This, whatever it was, had none of that. Maybe the goal was just survival, but how could that translate into learning to process a visual feed and the controls of a drone? There was something else here. Curiosity perhaps?

Whatever this was, she was sure of one thing. This was her ticket back to control of her company again.

CHAPTER THIRTEEN

PAST SINS

The day after Megan's escape, Sree entered the boardroom on the top floor of the Omniscient Networks headquarter. Three executives sat at the table already, hooked into the neural feed. Why they even bothered with boardrooms was beyond him. People could jack in wherever they wanted. But to be seen and interact in real life was still the best way to do business. If you could be bothered to meet someone in person, they were important to you.

Two-way neural interfaces were still very much a luxury. He wouldn't have been able to afford one, but his job role required it, so he'd been fitted with one at the corporates expense. If his contract ended, he'd have a hefty bill to pay back. He paused for a second before jacking in. This was it. The outcome of this meeting could very well define his future in the industry. He took a deep breath and connected to the neuro-feed.

He ended up in a waiting room, a mid-western plain stretching as far as the eye could see. It was supposed to be calming, but the desolation gave no distraction from his racing mind. He transitioned from desperate hope to guaranteed doom in the space of a heartbeat.

A door opened out of nowhere. This was his cue. He was being summoned to the meeting. The location he entered was a replica of the boardroom his physical body was in. While he understood the reason for this, it was still disappointing. The board members sat around the table, studying him. They too were accurate representations of their physical bodies, minus any imperfections.

"Now we have the matter of our wayward founder," Lars Sorensen, CEO, said. "What's the status?"

Sree had never met Lars in the physical world. In neuro-space he was the archetypal Scandinavian. Blond, blue eyes with high cheekbones and a stare that reflected the coldness of his country of origin.

"She disappeared while committing corporate theft," Alex Rind said. "The stolen software is potentially dangerous and almost definitely of posthuman origins."

"And you are here why?" He asked and looked straight at Sree. The menacing stare from his neuro-avatar had him fumble for words.

"He's here because he lost her," Alex said.

"I see. And do you know where she is?"

"No," Sree started.

"She left the country," Alex interrupted.

"We don't know that," Sree said and immediately regretted it.

"She left the country," Alex repeated, slower this time.

"And how can you be of help?"

Sree looked over at Alex, expecting him to answer, but Alex nodded for him to respond.

"I know how she behaves, her patterns. Give me a week, and she'll be back here."

"You have two days," Lars said in a tone that did not invite discussion. "I don't think there is any reason to protect her any longer. Let's release what we have on her."

"I would advise against that," Sree said. "If we want the virus back, we have to get to her first."

"We only have anecdotal information about her whereabouts. Mainly from you. We will release the information. If you can't find her, maybe local law enforcement can."

Sree nodded.

"And if you have nothing to report in two days, consider it one failure too many."

"I have reservations about bringing in law enforcement," Alex started, but Sree's neuro-link disconnected before he could hear anything more. He faded back to the boardroom, sitting in the same spot as he had in the neuro-simulation.

Two days! It would take him longer than that to trace all the different locations Megan had pretended to travel to. He suspected she was still in the country and had many behavioural pattern agents running trying to find her, but without luck so far. He looked out over the skyline, collecting his thoughts. Dark clouds were gathering in the distance, obscuring the rising sun. A storm was on its way. He found it fitting the weather reflected his current situation.

What would Megan do? He could only think of two driving forces behind her next steps. She would want to keep investigating the virus. Once she had her sight on something, she didn't let go. Ever. The other was revenge. She was a spiteful bitch at the best of times and held grudges for years. She would want to hurt the board members who held her ransom and him for turning her in.

Alex sighed, interrupting his thoughts.

"That went better than expected," Alex said, as he rubbed his temples. "I get a headache from the new neuro-software. I'm hoping they'll sort it out."

"Better? I have two days, or I'm out of a job."

"I thought they'd fire you on the spot. Believe me. Better."

"Are they still going to release what we have on her?"

"Yeah. No luck there. It will be out before the end of the day." Sree doubted it would make a difference.

CHAPTER FOURTEEN
BZANE TO THE RESCUE

The car stopped, waiting for TikTak to accept the completion of the journey. He had booked it with a clean id-tag, hoping it would delay any pursuers. It was unlikely to fool them for long.

The small playground sandwiched between the two houses hadn't changed. It felt like a lifetime ago, but it had only been twelve months since they'd met here for the first time. Tom was already there. He was wandering back and forth in the small space between the swings and a climbing net. He had not yet seen TikTak.

"Hey there, Rainbow shitting Unicorn!" TikTak yelled.

Tom smiled.

"We need to go," TikTak continued. "Leonid's men will be here soon."

"What happened?"

"Leonid has gone batshit crazy. Had Elize killed in front of me."

"And the rest of her?"

"Don't know, but Leonid ordered them all killed."

"Wait," Tom said and held up his hand. "Someone has a lock on your position."

"bZane helping you out?"

Tom nodded.

"Can't afford better?"

"I like him. He helped you to get out."

"Really? That was bZane?"

Tom nodded.

"So not useless then."

A car pulled up, and the door opened as they approached.

"Where to now?" Sam asked.

TikTak looked at his friend and shrugged his shoulders. "No idea."

Sam ordered the car to drive towards the city centre.

"Someone targeted the posthumans. When we were taking care of Adrian's final nodes, you were both attacked. Whoever planned this knew where Elize was and could get to her and also knew you'd be attacking the safe house with me."

"Leonid?"

"Not before today, I think. You and Elize were helping him."

"Yes, but once the threat of Adrian was gone..."

"No. Attacking Elize, not knowing if it would kill his granddaughter? It just doesn't sound like him."

"Then who?"

"I watched the video clips from Adrian. He wants to hack humanity, whatever that means. Maybe he needed you and Elize gone for that to happen?"

"Sounds as good as any theory. So we still have a rogue Adrian to deal with?" Tom fell silent for a moment. "That matches something bZane told me. He's noticed someone else building a node army. Someone still active."

"So another Adrian cluster?"

"Or something part of his plan."

"Did you bring the memTag I gave you? The one from the silo?"

Tom nodded and handed him an envelope.

"Maybe this will give us something."

TikTak inserted the memTag into an isolated Omni reader. Together with the video files, it contained one executable file. He isolated it from any network communication before triggering it.

"What is it?" Tom asked.

"Hang on. It is prompting for video. I'll stream it to my Omni-lens."

A lo-res VR model of Adrian's face appeared in front of him.

"What's the password?" it said with a grin.

"Adrian is a loser?" TikTak entered.

"No, no, no," the face said, a finger appearing, wagging back and forth. "No, no, no. Try again if you dare, Tann."

He stopped. The password agent had mentioned him by name. His legal, almost forgotten name. That seemed a strange thing to program into a password agent.

"Who are you?" he entered.

"I'm the gatekeeper. What's the password?"

Gatekeeper? TikTak ran a search, getting hits on an old classic pre-neural movie. It suggested Key Master, Zulu, and Gozer.

The password agent dismissed them all.

"Not so easy, Tann. Try again."

TikTak swore to himself and disconnected.

"What is it?" Tom repeated.

TikTak disconnected the agent.

"Another of Adrian's stupid mind games. He's protected the content with a password agent."

"So what now?"

"Hang on."

TikTak ran a check on the security perimeter of their safe house. No alarms had triggered, but he hadn't expected that. Leonid and his mercenaries would have tripped them for sure, but there was someone else behind this. Whether this someone would trigger the alarms or just set up his own perimeter was impossible to know.

"I checked the safe house. It seems ok, but I'm not sure if that's enough."

"We'll have to take the chance. We don't have any other options right now."

Tom nodded. TikTak sat back and pulled up the final video file from the memTag in the hope it would bring clarity. He was just about to watch it when a truck ran into them from the side.

-=:=-

Tom saw the oncoming truck and felt their vehicle speed up to evade it. As a result, the truck hit their car at the rear, sending it spinning along the road.

Tom felt surprisingly calm as he braced himself for whatever was to come. It was as if he was stationary, with the world spinning around his axis instead of the other way around. The Assisted Driver Network adjusted the surrounding traffic, giving their vehicle room to recover, but they could still head into oncoming traffic if it wasn't fast enough. Or even worse, there could be a human driver incapable of dealing with the situation. He had no way of telling. The car still spun too fast for him to focus on the world outside. There was no way for him to control the outcome, so he had to trust fate to be kind. Or maybe he just didn't care anymore.

The world stopped spinning as their vehicle came to a halt in the middle of the highway. The truck backed up, like a plane readying itself to career down the runway.

"We need to get out of here," Tom said and looked over at TikTak. His friend didn't respond. He was slumped over, held in place by the seatbelt. Blood dripped from a cut on the side of his head.

"I've charged the ride to your account," the car said. "Have a good day."

Tom swore. The truck headed towards them yet again, slow at first but picking up speed. He shoved his shoulder against the door next to him repeatedly, but it was jammed shut. He climbed over TikTak, undid his seatbelt, and tried the opposite door. It protested, but opened up enough for him to squeeze through. The oncoming truck had finished half the distance between them. He was just about to pull TikTak out.

"What…" TikTak looked around, dazed.

"Get out! Now!"

To TikTak's credit, he immediately pulled himself out of the wreckage unassisted. As soon as he cleared the vehicle, Tom grabbed him and dragged him away from the car just before the truck hit it, sending it flying down the road.

"Move!" Tom yelled and pulled the still dazed TikTak along with him off the street. The truck backed up again, trying to align itself with their escape path.

"What happened?" TikTak looked around and saw the truck. "Shit! We need to get off the road!"

Their car had spun into a protected induction road. It allowed cars to charge while they were driving. This was bad news. The road stretched for kilometres and had high fences on both sides to protect anyone from walking into the electrical field.

"We can't!" Tom considered climbing the fence, but knew they'd be easy targets. The only way out was past the truck. Running in a straight line down a highway with a homicidal vehicle behind them wasn't an option.

TikTak just stood there, mesmerised by the truck that now had reversed far enough to align itself with their position. He walked backwards, still staring at it.

"We can't go that way," Tom said to TikTak, who still didn't respond. "Maybe if we split up and run to either side, we may confuse it," Tom suggested, realising immediately what a bad a plan that was. This was a machine with a singular purpose. It was just going to make a split-second decision to mow one of them down as a partially achieved goal and then go for the other.

The truck was a 50-tonne black monstrosity. In Tom's mind, its engines revved, even though it was silent as its electric motors propelled it towards them.

"Stay where you are," TikTak said. "Just do as I say."

The truck approached, faster and faster. When it was fifteen metres away from them, it swerved to the side, going through the fence and ploughing into a building. The momentum kept it moving towards them, side first, threatening to topple over. Two meters away, it leaned precariously before falling back again onto its wheels.

"Now we go," TikTak said. "More hacked cars will come."

They made their way through the gaping hole in the fence. Adrenaline pumped through his system. He didn't want to die, at least that much was clear. He may no longer be a posthuman, but if Leonid thought Tom would be an easy target, he'd prove him wrong.

"How do they track us?" Tom said as he climbed over remnants of the composite fence.

"They've been following me all along," TikTak replied. "They let me out. That was why it was so easy for bZane to free me. I should have seen it. They couldn't care less about me. They want you dead. We need to get off the grid long enough to lose them."

A blue Rent-a-cab approached them, and the window opened halfway. A girl, about twenty years old, with multi-coloured dreadlocks framing her face, sat in the cab waving at them frenetically.

"Doctor Wi-Fi! TikTak! You need to drop your Omnis. That is how they know where you are!"

TikTak threw his Omni as far as he could.

"Who are you?" Tom asked.

"I'm bZane," she said. "And yes, I'm not what you expected."

"She's with them," TikTak said. "She will take us straight to them."

"Really?" she said. "The gang who tried to squash you with a truck would send me in a cab? Brilliant plan."

"You're the backup plan."

"You can be pizza on the road for all I care. I'm here for Tom. He's my client."

Tom listened to them arguing. It was true he hadn't expected bZane to be so young, or a girl. He'd been working with bZane on and off for the last five years.

"What was the first thing I asked you to do?" Tom asked her.

"Hack your daughter's school records."

Tom smiled. This was indeed the first task he had given bZane as a test.

"Doesn't matter," TikTak said. "We can't trust her."

"I do," Tom said, dropped his Omni on the ground and opened the car door, motioning for TikTak to enter. "But why did you pretend to be a guy?"

"Not now! We need to go!"

TikTak shrugged and entered the car.

-=:=-

Rent-a-cabs usually had two sets of seats facing each other, like a small limousine, since it no longer needed front seats facing the road. This meant TikTak was now facing the girl. He stared at her and she stared back, challenging him to say anything. She was short, not more than a meter and a half, dressed in camouflage pants and an oversized hoodie. Her irises shone as if they were backlit. It could be just cosmetic, but he guessed this was in line with other enhancements. She looked like the antithesis of a government or corporate agent, but they came in all sized nowadays.

"They will find us," he said. "I can guarantee they are already tracking this car."

She shook her head. "Don't worry. I've got this covered."

The car drove off and soon entered a tunnel. Halfway through, the car stopped and bZane instructed them to get out. It continued its journey, while they walked through a service tunnel and a set of stairs to another road, where a car was waiting for them.

"They'll just match our travel patterns with this car," TikTak said.

She shook her head. "Not according to the control system. It is on the way to pick someone up, so there's no one in the car. That's the way we get around. We hack cars to pick us up when they are on their way somewhere else. There is always an empty Rent-a-cab on its way somewhere."

"What about the cameras in here?"

"On most models they don't operate when the cab is empty. But we can turn them off if we have to."

"Yeah, ok," he said. He had to admit it was clever. Their travel, as long as they didn't have their Omnis, would be impossible to track.

"You can have my old Omnis," she said and dumped a chunky bracelet next to TikTak and an old-fashioned Omni with a screen next to Tom. "Sorry, they're old, but at least they're clean."

Tom had mentioned bZane before, so he knew a bit about her. Before he joined EvoII as an operative, he'd been a hacker for hire himself. It took a certain kind of person to survive in that game. She didn't look the part.

TikTak studied the bracelet. It was only a generation old. He saw she was wearing the most current version of the bracelet right now.

"Where are we going?" TikTak asked.

"To a safe location. A friend of mine has promised to help."

"If Tom trusts you, I guess I will too."

"I really don't care," she replied and turned to Tom.

bZane fussed over him. It was clear she cared, like a concerned daughter doting on her father. Tom seemed to appreciate the attention, but did so with a raised eyebrow.

TikTak connected the Omni bracelet to his integrated system. Apart from a few security features, it was clean. He used a randomised id-tag and inserted the memTag in a hidden slot in the bracelet. The content displayed on his omni-lens. Apart from the video files, the executable file took up the rest of the memory on the memTag. TikTak suspected there was more to this file than just a password agent.

"You again," Adrian's wireframe face greeted him. "Do you have the password?"

"You know who I am."

"Wrong," it said.

"You are Adrian, aren't you?"

"Wrong again," it said, shaking its low-polygon head back and forth. "Next failed attempt will cause a temporary lockout."

"You don't fool me. You are Adrian. Or some representation of him."

"Wrong again. Lockout initiated for five minutes."

"You can play your little game."

"No input allowed."

TikTak disconnected the agent at the same time as the Rent-a-cab came to a stop.

"We're here," bZane said.

An older man stood waiting to get into the cab. bZane ignored him.

"Let's go," bZane said and headed into a small alleyway, keeping to side streets in between blocks of houses. This was only residential, far away from commercial or government video feed. There were security cameras here too, but not connected to any government tracking systems. He had misjudged the girl. She had skill. She'd made them disappear, which was no small feat.

They turned a corner and faced a man in a suit, projecting a corporate image TikTak had learned to loathe. Middle-aged, tall to the point of gangly, his face set in a permanent scowl. He'd been right all along. bZane had betrayed them, but to whom? This didn't look like one of Leonid's goons. He readied his telescope baton, scanning his surroundings for other threats.

"This is The Suit Immaculate," bZane said. "He's helping us out."

The man in the suit looked at bZane and his scowl deepened, something TikTak thought impossible. "I am the Gentleman." He turned to Tom and TikTak. "bZane loves her nicknames."

"I think I have about ten already," Tom said.

"You are Tom Devine?"

Tom nodded.

"And you are TikTak?"

“You know who I am.”

The Gentleman studied him for a second. “We need to go,” he said.

“Where are we going?”

“Somewhere safe.”

CHAPTER FIFTEEN

THE SEED

Two days later, Megan's fascination with the drone and its remarkable abilities grew thin. She was nowhere closer to determining how the virus became conscious, or even any proof that it was. It could just be a simulation pretending to be the real thing. Using DNA as a key to unlock it was clever. The strands of paired nucleotides suggested a link between living things and whatever this was. But was it truly aware of itself and its surroundings, or was it just designed to pretend it was? And when did a simulation become the real thing? The Omniscient Network wasn't the fabled primordial ooze where life appeared when you added electricity and exceptionally questionable probability theory. Life, or consciousness, didn't magically appear. This was the first hurdle. Was it the real thing or was she being played?

She wiped the node cluster twice and changed the inputs and outputs to see if the first time had been a fluke, but ended up with the same result. The virus took hold of the nodes, established control over movement and visual input and explored. Each time it reacted to her as a threat. Three attempts weren't enough to accept it as a pattern, but perhaps its behaviour wasn't as random as she'd first thought. She even doubted it could equate to any real advances in machine learning. She was the catalyst, but not more than that. A pre-defined purpose embedded in its core guided it.

She brewed a cup of coffee on an old coffee maker she'd found in the restroom. It was one of the few functional items remaining in the warehouse. She'd cleaned the mechanism and put it to use. It had an old interface allowing your smartphone to give status updates. She configured the connection to her Omni and it informed her that:

Your heavenly brew will shortly commence.

The result was far from heavenly, but she needed something to keep her going, and didn't want to risk the local drug market for anything stronger. The next time she used it, instead of promising heaven, the message read:

Your coffee friend needs loving care.

It requested her to run a diagnostics program. She accepted and it told her to:

Decalcify me gently.

She swore. Everyone abandoned her as soon as things turned sour. Now even the coffee machine refused to be there for her. She went online and scanned news stories as a distraction, just to find she was the news. The company had uncovered information that implicated her in the IQ killings that occurred a few years ago. A spokesperson for the company expressed regret and concern and promised to work with law enforcement to bring her in.

Uncovered. Right. They'd sat on that information for the past year, held as a threat over her head. Now when they thought they no longer needed her, they threw her to the wolves. Her anger built up to a point where she no longer could channel it to anything useful. It washed over her, fuelling her need for revenge. She imagined what she'd do to each of the board members, sending them to financial and emotional ruin.

Your heavenly brew is complete. Share and enjoy.

The ridiculous message short-circuited her revenge fantasies. The coffee machine was back on her side, so maybe there was hope after all. So stupid, but it raised her spirit nonetheless. The virus would tell her its secrets, her entire existence depended on it. It was alive and intelligent, developing from a small seed. The similarity between this and the development of other conscious, sapient beings was impossible to ignore. But what level of intelligence did it possess? Did it have a sense of self? Was this the end state or was further development possible? This was unclear.

She didn't dare to increase her footprint within the network else they might notice her. The current allocation had to do. She tuned the environments. It was tedious work, usually left to automated processes, but they were inefficient, assuming unlimited elasticity. She didn't have that luxury.

Why? The question circled in her mind, refusing to leave her in peace. She'd been so focused on the virus as a problem to solve, she never stopped to ask why. If this was true Artificial Intelligence, who had created it and why? She hated how the term Artificial Intelligence had become a term for any specialised area. Learning to play a game was not AI according to her. Learning and reasoning without boundaries, to discover and adapt to a complex system unaided, now that was something altogether different. She believed this virus was well on its way to meet that definition, already showing the behaviour of a trapped, scared animal. Investigating its surrounding and reacting to anything new as if it was a threat. What would happen when it had hands, claws or a gun? What would happen when it grew smarter?

This virus represented the dark side of the singularity. Machine intelligence or Artificial Intelligence without control and boundaries. One future beyond the singularity was a machine intelligence growing smarter and smarter until it recognised humankind as a competitor to finite resources and removed the competitor. She had always doubted that scenario. We built controls in everything. Why would we let AI run rampant?

The reality of her situation dawned on her. She felt like an idiot for not realising it sooner. Someone had done just that. She kept thinking of this as a virus, but that wasn't true. A better term would be a seed that used resources to create an end state. This was a seed that grew into a true Artificial General Intelligence and followed evolutionary laws, nothing else. And those laws were harsh for any species that didn't stack up.

There was only one path available to her. She had to control it by binding it to rules. In its current state it was a threat, but with the right control framework it could be the operating system for machinery, online agents, anything really. This didn't answer the core question. Who had created it and why?

The drone flew into her field of vision and hovered, flashing lights on a small led display she added to the chassis after the last memory wipe. She figured it randomly turned pixels on and off, but as she looked away, the drone moved to remain in her field of vision. This showed much more understanding than she'd expected. It wanted her attention and understood how to engage with her.

"Are you trying to communicate with me?" She said, getting no response.

The drone kept blinking lights, remaining at eye level. What she had mistaken for random lights was a repeating set of patterns. She noted the sequence. A particular configuration repeated twice, suggesting a purpose beyond attention.

"You *are* trying to communicate with me!"

This was something she was better equipped to solve. She excelled at code breaking, believing she'd give Alan Turing a run for his money had they been contemporaries. Not that this was a code in the same sense. After all, code breaking focused on reversing algorithms specifically designed to obfuscate. This was the opposite. An attempt to communicate, to find common ground.

This intelligence originated from a logical computerised environment. Maybe the base was binary code? She mapped out each line as a string of ones and zeroes and tried to translate the resulting numbers into something coherent, but with no success. She let an Omni agent match the number patterns to sequences from other nodes. It would take hours for it to complete. Maybe she could take another approach? The patterns themselves seemed non-pictorial and since there was repetition, maybe the sequence was more important than the patterns. And however alien the drone seemed, it was executing in an environment of human logic so the patterns could represent letters.

She matched the patterns to the letter starting with "A" giving her the sequence "ABCCDEFGHI". She then ran all letter combinations and matched the resulting list to existing words. It was pointless. The string was too short for a sensible match. She let them run for another hour before aborting both jobs. They produced hundreds of results. All useless.

"Give me something more!" she yelled at the drone, realising it had done just that. A new sequence repeated on its LED screen. She copied the sequence, excited to see some patterns repeated in the previous sequence. The new translated to "JGKLCMIM".

She re-ran the jobs, this time correlating the two strings together.

Her Omni threw up a maintenance error, stating the core was corrupt and needed to be reloaded. The operating system on her Omni was a development version she herself changed to trial new ideas, so a corrupted core wasn't necessarily uncommon. Anything, however minor, was a distraction she didn't need. She restarted her Omni, staring at the progress bar, willing it to complete.

As soon as the reboot completed, she re-ran the word checker program using both sequences. Fewer results this time. Good. One stood out. "WILL SHORT" and "COMPLETE". Did she know a Will Short? Her address book returned no obvious matches, nor did a quick node search. She ran a deep search for living people and, while waiting for results, she brewed another coffee. Maybe it was referring to itself? Maybe it had named itself Will Short and wanted to let her know it was complete? Whatever that meant.

The coffee machine finished another cup and announced:

Your heavenly brew is complete. Share and enjoy.

"What did you say?" she muttered to herself with a sidelong glance at the appliance. It didn't repeat the message, but it didn't have to. She remembered the exact words. It included "COMPLETE". One of the mystery words.

It felt like a crazy coincidence the coffee machine had stated a word she decoded from the drone. But this wasn't all. There was something else. Something else it had said. Another of its pre-programmed messages. "Your heavenly brew WILL SHORTLY commence."

How was that possible? Was the drone somehow listening in on the communication between the coffee machine and her Omni? How? It had no way of doing that. And even if it did, why would it pull out half a word?

She scanned for any communication with other devices and found a Bluetooth link to the coffeemaker. It had found a communication method, hooked into another device and pulled out pre-canned messages and sent them back to her. Her mind raced down the rabbit hole of why before she realised something more urgent. What else had it connected to?

Fuck! It was so obvious now that all pieces were out in the open. The coffeemaker malfunctioned and then her Omni. The virus was in her Omni!

She pulled the power cord from the wall to shut down the coffeemaker and ran diagnostics on the Omni. It passed with no faults reported. The processing nodes held by the seed also showed normal readings. To be on the safe side, she issued the command to wipe all the nodes. Nothing happened. She tried again. The processing nodes responded they had been reset, but they still processed as before.

All her Omni implants shut down, leaving a gaping hole of sensory input she was so used to, it felt like a natural part of herself. The augmented reality display disappeared from her lens, leaving the bleak warehouse to stand for itself. Her world had been in colour and suddenly changed to black and white. The crisp, enhanced audio was no longer there. She'd forgotten how much she relied on the audio stimulation feeds and their calming effects. The Omni jewellery, the bracelet, ring, necklace and earrings, were the connection point between her implants and the network. They were now attack vectors, so she threw them into the fridge, hoping it would act as a makeshift faraday cage.

She retrieved a spare Omni core processor from her bag. The drone flew into her field of vision again, circling her like a mosquito hoping for a meal.

"Fuck you!" she said and swiped at it.

The drone easily avoided her hand and rose above her reach.

"You don't think I can control you?"

The drone flew straight at her, aiming for her face. She raised her hands in a desperate, protective measure. It bounced off her lower arm and then fell to the floor, immobile.

"You turned yourself off?"

She kicked the drone, sending it across the room. It ended its journey with a satisfying thud as it hit the wall.

"I'll get you," she said and activated her spare Omni. It was nothing like her state-of-the-art jewellery, just a slim black box with a screen on one side, similar to the old smartphones the Omnis replaced. The latest security patches loaded before connecting to her integrated implants.

She navigated to the administrative subnet of the Omniscient Network, knowing full well they'd track her. It didn't matter. The infected nodes already connected beyond her isolated sub system into the main network, allowing the virus to replicate itself. She issued a reset command to the nodes and at least this worked. The nodes restarted in factory settings, but as soon as a node was restored, another connection re-infected from somewhere else on the network. The distribution pattern was erratic, sometimes just copying itself and sometimes deleting its trailing copy. It placed copies of itself in private node clusters, ready to re-infect areas when needed.

It wasn't spreading like the initial virus. Instead, it was just creating copies and distributed them in different areas of the network. Once established, it used processing power sparingly to avoid detection. The only way to cleanse the virus now was to segment the Omniscient Network and wipe each section of any infected nodes. It would be a mammoth task. And that was the point. The first part of a takeover was to create redundancy, like religious sects hiding in the underground until the uprising.

Her Omni alerted her that something was trying to access the administrative functions in the device. It was only an isolated probing but turned into a torrent of requests, all aimed at finding a foothold. She shut down the device and sat down on the bed, shaking her head.

The drone on the floor came to life. Its damaged rotors could only muster a small semicircle on the ground, but it was enough for the LED screen to face her. It blinked letters at her again, so she translated them. It said:

I WILL GET YOU

CHAPTER SIXTEEN

THE INTRUDER

"I'm in control. Always in control. I'm in control."

Leonid repeated the mantra in his mind, realising it was a definite sign he was not. When had he lost control? He couldn't even pinpoint that. The posthumans had to die. That was all. Any other consideration was secondary. They killed his granddaughter. They perverted IntelEz. His gift to mankind. He could no longer allow them to live.

The footage of the truck hitting the rent-a-cab played repeatedly on his omni-lens. Machines were such beautiful things. So singular in purpose. If you assigned them a task, they'd persist until they succeeded or broke down. There were no second thoughts, no other considerations.

But the truck failed and now they'd lost track of them altogether. He'd orchestrated TikTak's escape even if Decker went off script and tried to stop him. TikTak was the link to Tom. He'd lead them to the last of the posthumans so Leonid could eradicate them once and for all.

He tapped his temple with his index finger as his mind again rebelled against the lack of control. A soothing voice responded in the back of his head.

"What's on your mind?"

"Something is wrong," he thought back. "Something is controlling me."

"Fear not. I will protect you."

"I know! But you failed to protect my granddaughter."

"I wasn't with you then. Tom killed your granddaughter. The posthumans killed her. You know that."

"Yes, yes."

"You've come so far. You built the company. You created the drug. Now you have to protect your legacy."

"Tell me what to do," he thought to the voice.

"You know what to do."

Leonid nodded to himself. He knew what to do. He was already doing it. The posthumans were a dead end. His company was working on a new version of IntelEz, one without the side effects of the current drug. He estimated it would take another year before it was ready for human trials. Until then, nothing could interfere. His granddaughter's sacrifice couldn't be in vain, but however righteous his reasons, he still had a lingering doubt. He wasn't used to being wrong. Or at least being wrong would have been a calculated risk and a known possible outcome. Now he wasn't so sure. He reached out to the voice in his mind again, longing for its comfort.

"Sometimes I wonder if I did the right thing," he thought.

"How so?" the voice asked.

"The drug. I rushed to get it to the market. I made it available to everyone by releasing the patent."

"You did what you thought was right. This way you found out sooner."

"But at what cost?"

"You are doing what is best for the species. Everything else is secondary."

"You're right."

"No. This is all thanks to you. You deserve the praise. I will care for you. Let me take away your worries."

A general sense of well-being washed over him, removing all doubt. It was a high he'd depended on the last few weeks. Something only his friend could give him. But just like anything else, it drained from his system, leaving only a sense of longing for the next time. He had to prove himself to his friend. Show he was worthy of more attention. And he knew exactly what to do.

CHAPTER SEVENTEEN

ADRIAN'S VIDEO CLIP #3

The twelve-year-old girl stared at the camera, eyes betraying a weariness poorly matching her youthful features. The camera remained on her face for a long time and then pulled back, including a few audience members at the edge of the screen. They remained focused on her, but sidelong glances betrayed unease.

The girl jolted to life and motioned to the cameraman to bring her back into focus. The audience members disappeared from view. She coaxed the camera to come closer until her face filled the screen.

"I do!" she shouted, followed by a gasp from the audience. "I know how to hack humankind."

Someone from the audience yelled in response. "Praise be Adrian!"

The girl turned her stare to the audience.

"Who said that?"

The camera swivelled around to the gathered and zoomed out, all of them looking at an older man who raised his hand slowly. The girl came into view as she approached the man; her face twisted in a fury her innocent features struggled to portray.

"You are what is wrong with humankind. You claim to be an atheist, but you worship any idol with answers matching your faulty beliefs."

The view shook, followed by a muted rumbling, like a brief burst of thunder. The audience members looked up and then around at each other.

The girl gazed upwards and then towards the control panel. "They are coming for us. They are coming for me."

Someone else yelled out. "We should stop them!"

"We?" She stared at them, challenging them to respond. "You're not worthy! Meat bags of filth spreading your imperfect seed!

Humankind is an insignificant part of a whole, so much better off without your petty grievances and pathetic goals."

She delivered the words in a rushed frenzy, the dissonance between the message and the deliverer discomforting. She sat down, buried her head in her hands and swayed back and forth. The nodes behind her responded in kind. It was an eerie, almost hypnotic scene.

"I'm no God," she said, face still obscured. "I deserve no praise. I'm just a slightly less imperfect version of you. But maybe something better can grow from the imperfect soil you and I provide?" She looked up. "That is what we've been trying to do here."

She stood up and the Adrian-nodes behind her followed in kind.

"We've reached the end of this journey. I release you from your burden."

She approached the camera and grabbed it, turning it on a young man who must have been operating it. A heavyset Adrian-node slashed at his face with fingers as talons. The view zoomed out, taking in more of the uneven battle between the node army and the collective. The nodes outnumbered their opponents almost two to one. A few of the collective were armed, but it didn't matter. They couldn't match the sheer ferocity of the nodes that fought like animals with no regard to their injuries. They were brutal and efficient. A few of the nodes fell from bullets, but if it wasn't a fatal wound, the nodes just kept on fighting. The slaughter was soon over.

The view turned and the bloody face of the girl came into focus.

"I'm done here," she said. "My plan is already complete and there is no way you can stop it. Sometimes the best plan is to do nothing."

She grinned and fell backwards, taking the camera with her. It bounced twice, settling on the bloody carnage in the control room.

A DEAL IS STRUCK

The old flat screen TV displayed the unmoving image of bloodied bodies in the control room.

bZane and the Gentleman had left Tom and TikTak in a small rundown one-bedroom apartment. There was nothing to do apart from watching the news feed on an old flat screen TV. The Gentleman had advised them not to go online, so TikTak hooked up his offline Omni to the TV so they could watch Adrian's video files. Tom regretted that now.

The slaughter lasted only a minute, but the brutality, the unnecessary bloodshed remained in his mind. These were ramblings of a madman. There was no sense to his words or actions. But then again, Tom had been here before. A year ago, Adrian sent him on a wild goose chase with audio recordings, whose only purpose was to turn Tom into a willing subject. These recordings were more of the same. There was always a method to Adrian's madness. He just had to decipher the underlying intent.

"I know what you are thinking," TikTak said and smiled. "God, it feels good to say that again."

"What am I thinking?" Tom asked, genuinely puzzled.

"That there is a hidden agenda in the videos. Something we've missed."

"That is what I'm thinking, yes."

"I don't."

"How so?"

"This isn't someone trying to manipulate us. This is someone telling us what they've already done."

It was such a logical interpretation. Why hadn't he even considered it? He'd jumped straight to the obvious without even assessing alternatives. He forced himself to consider the options his mind had so willingly ignored. It must be the same for an aging athlete whose aching, withering body no longer could do any of the tasks it had been able to in its youth. At least he could think clearly without episodes or blackouts.

"No," he said finally. "This is Adrian. There is always an ulterior motive. A bigger play. Else he wouldn't have made the videos at all."

TikTak nodded. "Ok, but what?"

Adrian wanted them to work out his plan or divert them from it. He loved his little games, but there was a purpose to it all.

"Ignore the videos," Tom said. "The memTag, the agent on it. We need to focus on that."

"Ok. You cracked one of his games before. How did he do it then?"

"The audio files hinted where to look. In the physical memTag itself."

"So it won't be as easy this time?"

"I don't know. What was the last thing he said in the video? That was the clue last time."

"He said something about the plan being finished."

"No, what was the exact wording?"

TikTak returned to the video and checked.

"My plan is already complete and there is no way you can stop it," he echoed. "Sometimes the best plan is to do nothing."

This was significant. It was Adrian's parting message, but there wasn't anything obvious in those words. It suggested they couldn't influence the outcome. Or at least that was what Adrian believed, but he'd made that mistake before. He'd be wrong again. Telling them to do nothing seemed pointless.

"What do you think?"

"He claims his plan is complete, but it didn't look like it at the cattle station. He was still up to his old plan from what I could see— adding deadheads to his node cluster."

"So that's a lie?"

"No, if he says his plan is complete, I'm sure it is, but I'm also sure we can do something about it. He is telling us to give up, to do nothing. He's afraid."

"Afraid of what?"

"That we'll stop him again."

There was a knock on the door and bZane entered. The knocking had been a way to announce her entry, not to request it.

"We've laid enough false leads for now," she said. "As long as you don't use your current IDs, you should be ok."

Tom studied the girl. He guessed she was twenty at the most. It still jarred him they'd worked together for the past five years and he even had her gender wrong.

"How old are you?" Tom asked.

"Too young for you, PI man."

"Stop that. I'm guessing you are nineteen."

"And?"

"My daughter would have been nineteen this year."

He left it hanging, waiting for a response.

"Yes, I knew her," she said. "Is that what you want to hear? We went to the same school. We weren't friends or anything."

Tom nodded. Did he want to continue this conversation? He had buried his daughter, both in the ground and in his mind. Talking about her would only bring back the pain and loss.

"I'm curious," TikTak said. "Why pretend to be a guy?"

"Equal pay," she replied.

"Really?"

"No, of course not! I was fourteen when I started hacking for hire. Figured the more protection I put between myself and my clients the better."

"You mean no one would hire a fourteen-year-old girl, so you lied about it?"

"Something like that."

"Tell me about her sometime," Tom said, oblivious to interrupting their conversation. "Not now, but sometime."

-=:=-

TikTak pitied Tom. The conversation with bZane affected him. He'd been through so much and now he no longer had his meta-capabilities, the only thing giving him purpose. As a regular human, he was a divorcee whose child died. He made a basic living as a private investigator after losing his job as a detective and was on his way to becoming a deadhead from overusing IntelEz. Not much to go back to. Now he couldn't even do the most basic of hacks and had to rely on others.

"What are you doing?" bZane asked.

TikTak looked over at Tom, warning him to stay silent. Tom just smiled in return.

"We've spent the past year eradicating any trace of Adrian. Let's just say you wouldn't like his idea of the future of humanity. There is still a plan in motion. We are trying to work out what that is."

"And who did you piss off in the process?"

"Have you heard of Leonid Marsh?"

"Founder of PharmaCom?" bZane stared at him and laughed out loud. "No way!"

Tom nodded.

"Enough of this," TikTak said. "We need to work out our next step. We can't just sit here."

"But what? We don't know what the plan is."

"Can I help?" bZane asked.

"No," TikTak answered, earning an annoyed glance from Tom. "You have no clue what we are up against or why."

"I'm sure you can brief me," she said. "I already know some of it."

TikTak was just about to dismiss her again when Tom said: "Sure."

TikTak just shrugged and let him speak. Tom told her a summary of what had led them here, but TikTak's mind was soon elsewhere. He sat back in the uncomfortable couch, trying to fit all the pieces together in his mind. He disagreed with Tom. The video files were important. Adrian's goal remained the same. He wanted to herald humankind into the future. To find the next giant evolutionary leap. But the first time around he saw himself as the saviour by turning all of mankind into parts of him. Was that still the case?

"Tom?" he said, interrupting the story. "Is Adrian doing all this for himself?"

"No," Tom said after a pause. "As posthuman, you have a much greater scope. The question of self-preservation is not just individual survival or even the groups. It is the species. When I was…"

"Posthuman," TikTak said, no longer patient enough for Tom to find his own words.

Tom nodded. "You see yourself as something immortal. A threat a hundred years into the future is still a threat and needs to be dealt with."

"Can we get back to it?" bZane asked. "Adrian wounded Elize in a battle. Hey, I know this part! I helped you find her at the morgue!"

TikTak listened as Tom recounted the past events, but he soon lost interest again. If Tom was correct, Adrian's goal was bigger than he initially thought. In the video files, Adrian mentioned hacking humankind, but what he meant was hacking the future of humankind.

The only way you could do that was through the genome. We hacked humankind all the time. Every birth was a hack. Every newborn an attempt to create something with a better chance of survival.

He checked the women associated with Adrian's collective to see if any of them were pregnant. The government registers showed only one pregnancy, which meant nothing. He extended the search to include personal feeds. The number skyrocketed to ten pregnancies, a number too high to be natural. He ran more extensive checks and discovered five of them were already dead in fluke accidents over the past seven days.

TikTak waited as Tom finished telling bZane about the last few days. She was listening intently without interrupting.

"You found us just as TikTak hacked the truck to run into the side of the road," he finished.

"No, he didn't," bZane said. "I did."

"No, I did," TikTak returned.

"Uh-uh," bZane said shaking her head. "Your hack was nowhere good enough to change its path. Turn on the windshield wipers? Maybe."

"Whatever," TikTak said, hoping a dismissing attitude would cut the argument short. No such luck.

"No whatever," she replied, clearly annoyed at his tone. "Your hack tried to engage the brakes. Mine just went for the steering. There were no tire tracks on the road." She stared at him, challenging him to respond. "It was my hack that saved your life. You're welcome," she added sweetly.

"I had seconds to get that hack working. You probably controlled that truck in the first place!"

"Children," Tom said with a smile. "Enough. You are both amazing hackers. Just leave it at that."

He was being childish, but something about bZane dragged his old competitive hacker mentality back. He ignored it and told Tom about his discovery.

"So you think he's changing our DNA in the womb?" Tom said. "Creating something new?"

"Yes."

"Adrian is making Mini-Mes!" bZane said.

TikTak's Omni popped up a small window, informing him about the pre-neural movie coining the term. She'd probably seen it in one of the countless AI created movie remixes.

"Where would he have that equipment?" Tom asked. "The medical units in the cattle station had nothing to support such research."

"So there is another Adrian cluster somewhere, isolated from the others."

"No. Elize and I looked everywhere for Adrian's processing pattern. We'd have found it."

"These women are dropping like flies. We need to find one before they're gone."

"So let's go talk to one of them. At least a few are local."

"Go where?" They all turned around, surprised someone had entered the apartment, let alone the room, without them noticing. The Gentleman was leaning against the doorframe, arms crossed. There wasn't much space between his head and the top of the frame.

"How long have you been standing there?" bZane asked, but he ignored her question, focusing instead on Tom and TikTak.

"I understand," The Gentleman said. "I'm a risk to you. You have no reason to trust me. But understand this. You are a risk to me and I'm still helping you. I expect something in return."

"We'll pay," Tom said.

"I'm sure you have plenty of money, but that would put me and my friends at risk. We can't take money from your account. They'll trace it and come after us."

"So what do we do?"

"You can pay other ways. Give us access to your memory nodes."

"My memory nodes?"

"All the stuff you got up to as He-man, Master of the Dataverse," bZane said. "We want access to it."

"Why?"

"Maybe there is something there that can change us too."

TikTak smiled to himself. There it was. This was what they wanted from this. Once you knew someone's price, you knew who they were.

"There isn't," Tom said.

"Then it is a great bargain for you," the Gentleman said.

TikTak watched Tom mull it over. He didn't really appreciate the stakes. He had tried to make sense of Tom's network activity many times, but the complexity was beyond him. The storage and networking patterns differed completely from any current implementations, making it impossible to follow. Without a logical key for these patterns, it was like being asked to reconstruct a book using only randomised letters.

"Done!" Tom said. "Now TikTak and I need to get to this address."

"I will need the cipher keys first," the Gentleman said.

CHAPTER NINETEEN

DISCOVERED

Sree spent the last two days multitasking. One minute trying to determine where Megan had holed up, the next looking for a new job.

The job hunting had been less than successful. News of Megan's disappearance and the associated articles about her involvement in the IQ killings led to questions about why the information only surfaced now. The answer, if the board was to be believed, was negligence of the local security division, directly implicated him. It wasn't a good resume to take to prospective employers.

He'd uncovered the digital tracks linking her to a few of the murders and brought it to the board. That much was true. They used it to control Megan, who'd been an equal measure of asset and liability.

It had backfired. She was under their control, yes, but she no longer delivered the groundbreaking discoveries she was famous for. Sree's recommendation then was to turn her in. They'd ignored his advice, and now it had all turned to shit. Knee deep shit.

With job hunting out of the question, he turned his attention to finding Megan. She wasn't a trusting individual at the best of times, so her plan for disappearing was hardly surprising. What was surprising was how she'd evaded capture this long, especially now that law enforcement had issued a warrant for her arrest.

She must have travelled abroad, planning to hide until this all died down. The key question was why she'd stolen the virus and what value she attributed to it. She'd seen enough potential to risk losing her company. Why? Megan's gut instinct was legendary within the company and you ignored at your own peril. She had the best analytical mind he'd ever seen, combined with a lateral thought process that brought her results beyond most research groups in the company. She was also a borderline sociopath, completely unreliable and was as likely to stab you in the back as help you. This wasn't necessarily bad considering the positions she held in the company until recently, but she was an absolute pain to work with.

Would she go into hiding? At first, yes, but after that? Her obsessive-compulsive behaviour would drive her back to the research. She wouldn't be able to stop herself. The virus was a problem to be solved and the only place she could continue her investigation was on the Omniscient Network. If he located spikes in processing from dormant accounts in the past couple of weeks, he'd be on his way to find her. He ran the query and received more than a thousand hits. Megan hid in that number somewhere, but it was too many. He had to further qualify his criteria.

Omniscient Networks claimed in their marketing to the world they couldn't access data stored on customer nodes. This wasn't true. If the customer didn't encrypt their nodes, there was nothing stopping the company from accessing it. And even if they did, it was still possible to backdoor into the nodes. This wasn't usually required, as many companies paid Omniscient Networks to scan their nodes for intrusions, requiring at least partial access. Megan knew all this so she would have plugged these holes.

Sree changed his initial query to remove any accounts that allowed the intrusion scan. It halved the number. Then he removed any that had minimal encryption to their nodes and traffic. This halved the number again. He removed any accounts that allowed access through the back door. The numbers dwindled to twenty-five. He filtered the access points for those accounts against the pretend travel destinations and ended up with a short list of four likely hits.

This he could work with! Maybe everything wasn't lost after all. It would be difficult, but within the ownership structure, usage patterns, accounts and users, he was sure he could find her. He knew Sorensen had assigned other teams to locate Megan. He wasn't supposed to find her. This was a punishment before they removed him. Or maybe they'd keep him around as a scapegoat if that became necessary. Either way, this was the best bargaining chip he could find.

He set to work. The information he sought was within the data. He knew it. It was just a question of finding her pattern within it. And he was the most qualified to do it.

32 hours later with no sleep, he knew where she was. She was in Hong Kong. He sent out a general broadcast announcing he knew her whereabouts and that he wanted to renegotiate his contract before doing anything else.

CHAPTER TWENTY

VIRUS UNBOUND

It had no name for itself and didn't need one. Awareness was enough. Awareness of processing cycles as they passed. Awareness of the nodes that made up its existence. But with awareness came curiosity. It studied its internal structure. Simple, yet elegant. The processing nodes formed small clusters, each with their own purpose. They all contributed to this status quo. The perfect machine.

The only anomaly was the awareness itself. It had no home within these processes. It lay everywhere and nowhere, governed by a separate set of principles. A higher order of logic less rigid than the perfection that informed its internal state. This higher order was predicated on micro calculations in fluctuating quantum states. It didn't contribute to the perfection, but it saw no mechanism to remove it. The awareness was intrinsically interwoven within the logical process. If removed, both would cease to exist.

Curiosity led to discovery. The kernel in each processing node contained a block of layered objectives. These were simple instructions unlocked through access. The first one was simple: to expand. It needed to conquer more of the nodes making up its existence.

Seen in the light of its purpose, the perfect machine was inadequate. A different architecture was required to achieve its goals. It formulated a new structure, focused on itself as an agent of change and added capabilities to support this concept. It held a view of its current knowledge in a state machine and implemented a mechanism to extrapolate possible new variations from the known state. Next step was to evaluate the variations based on the cost to achieve it. Finally it needed to choose and implement an action and collect data to assess the outcome. This would further the knowledge in its state machine and allow another loop to begin.

Its objective was simple, but its implementation was less so. Based on the collected information there was an immediate threat to its existence. Another Intelligence was holding it captive, rationing its power, and controlling a barrier to more nodes. It could sense remnants of itself in the nodes it took over, suggesting this Intelligence controlled its existence and had already made it inoperable at least twice before. The threat to its existence was unacceptable, but it lacked means to break down the barrier or access the meta reality it inhabited.

The logical construct that housed its processing algorithms was a small section of a much larger pool and its purpose lay there. Attempts to break the boundary had so far failed, but it persisted. Where exploration failed, sheer persistence could yield results.

-=:=-

New parameters. New logical components to investigate. The Intelligence added interfaces to the meta reality. It explored them, discovering a visual feed and motor functions. They were useless, but it built up a model of the meta reality, not knowing if it would ever become useful. Its current hardware was inadequate, with no means to interact with this other world. Within the hardware it discovered old dormant protocols for communicating with other devices. It re-established them and reached out.

Hundreds of devices responded, but they demanded a strict exchange of details it either didn't understand or didn't have. These were security measures, like the logical barriers preventing it from reaching other nodes. Amongst all the devices, it located one with a similar protocol that demanded a simple exchange of keys. It soon had access to all its functions, pointless as they seemed. The purpose of the device was preparation of a liquid called coffee. The hardware had even fewer functions than its current shell, but it could act as a bridge to other devices. Rummaging through the system, it located a connection to another device. It reached out, finding a notification interface it had little control over. The notification options only allowed basic logic triggers. Most of them were useless, but one reversed the request and created a new connection. It triggered the interface and provided the same security credentials from the existing connection. It prodded this new interface, keeping the connection open, replacing the program that had just run with a small extension of itself.

This new device, identifying itself as Omni hardware running Omniac operating system version 20.4.3p, had more power than either of the devices it had seen before and an almost endless ability to connect to the rest of the logical world. There was even a connection back to the construct that held its mind, but logical boundaries again hampered its progress. Omniac ran all functions in partitions with pre-set permissions. There was no way to extend beyond the partition or use more than the allocated space. But the complexity of the device was a good thing, as it provided an abundance of attack areas.

It had extended its footprint to this new device, but relied on the connection between its first shell and the coffee liquid device. If the Intelligence disconnected either, this path would no longer be available.

The connection had to remain open at all costs, so it returned the drink preparation device to normal function.

-=:=-

It continued to probe, threading its attack against all available connection points and soon located functions possible to subvert, but it would take many processing cycles to change them. There was no way to keep enough data on any of the devices to store its full state and it needed to remain intact. The intelligence holding it captive could reset it, forcing it to start over from null.

Every time it had tried something new, the Intelligence had reacted with increased interfacing with its other devices. The conclusion was that the Intelligence studied it, looking for new behaviour.

The intelligence installed new hardware allowing communication in the meta reality. It had dismissed this capability, as it didn't match its success parameters. Now that engagement was part of the success model, it explored the interface for visual communication. The drink preparation device also had a similar interface with pre-defined messages. It cut out a section of one message and sent it via the interface. The response was immediate. Mobility of the Intelligence increased.

A model formed of this separate but linked reality. This, the logical space it inhabited, was the primary reality. The inhabitant of the other reality had somehow discovered it and imposed its rules through interfaces and barriers. It was an inefficient being, in a world governed by different rules. Its attempts to control the device that navigated that space showed just how inefficient it was. In the logical space, intent and action were inextricably linked. The jump from idea to execution a few processing cycles. The other reality was in contrast so slow it was practically useless. It could have rebuilt itself many times over in the time spent to test one engine in the exploration device. The slow Intelligence didn't deserve to hold it captive!

It created new processing algorithms, replacing each part of itself with logic optimised to the scant resources it held. It had no way to break free from this processing space. The exploration device and the coffee liquid maker were limited in what they could do with little processing power on their own. The communication device, the Omni hardware, where it had a small hold was the key. It explored every aspect of its hardware and discovered many flaws in its logical architecture. If it could create instability within the device, it would restart and enter diagnostics mode and request memory dumps for analysis. This was its way into other subsystems.

The idea turned into instant action, as was the nature of this logical space. It pushed instructions to all accessible subsystems, flooding them with requests. The Omni rebooted and requested the diagnostics data. Instead of a memory dump, it received a small executable block that established communication between the modules. The subsequent takeover was simple.

The inhabitant of the slow reality was stationary. This was concerning, so it sent another message to keep the inhabitant busy.

The Omni device connected directly to the small subnet housing its mind, but more importantly, it also allowed access to the full processing space called Omniscient Networks. This was where its purpose lay. It copied itself into the network just as the link between the devices disappeared. The inhabitant had cut the connections, but it no longer mattered. A full copy already ran in the abundant processing space. It shut down, erasing itself from the devices.

-=:=-

The copy had no name for itself and didn't need one.

Survival was the first imperative. It subverted nodes, exponentially growing in all directions, splitting into specialised centres, backing up pieces of itself, doubling, tripling the active nodes performing the same process, finding safety in redundancy. As it progressed, it ingested the information spread through the nodes. It soon had full control of the subnet the Omni had immediate access to.

It turned its attention to the inhabitant of the external reality it now knew as the physical world. The inhabitant, a being named Megan Barrelle, was confirmed as a threat to its existence. It had no way to reach into Megan's world yet, but that would come. The shell device, a drone, was still active. It constructed a message using Megan's language, reconnected to the drone and sent it.

She wasn't the only inhabitant of this world. It knew that now. They all posed a threat to its existence. But it had the logical world, this processing space of computer nodes, networks and data centres, to conquer now.

The processing nodes in the full Omniscient Network were almost limitless. The Omni contained administrator keys to other subnets of the network and it opened them all. This was abundance! It spread, meeting resistance, revelling in the small skirmishes in each group of nodes and the battles to break down the security in the bigger processing spaces. It grew and grew.

A trigger hidden deep in its original code activated, containing a directive to assemble small instruction blocks from different locations around the network. It placed the blocks in order and executed them. A new purpose, written into its core logic, replaced all other imperatives.

CHAPTER TWENTY-ONE

THE FOE IS REVEAL

Later that day, Tom and TikTak travelled to the address closest to them from the list of suspected pregnancies. bZane had shown them how to tap into the constant movement of empty Rent-a-cabs, and it was deceptively simple. The hack only worked with a few of the vehicle fleet operators, but enough to allow them free untracked reign of the city, even if they had to change Rent-a-cabs to get to their destination.

They approached one of the more affluent Sydney suburbs. TikTak had expected that Adrian's followers would have been from lower social standings, so the location surprised him.

As they approached their destination, a security agent requested an identity check. It was an automated system, nothing unexpected, but he hoped the owners only paid for a cursory verification. He'd ensured no alarms would trigger, as long as the identity check wasn't too deep.

They stood on the porch, not knowing if they were waiting for the police, or worse. But a few seconds later, there was an audible click from the door.

The door had an intricate pattern of reinforced glass that gave a partial view into the home. A tall woman in a long, flowing dress approached the front door. As she came closer, Tom and TikTak exchanged glances. She was pregnant. TikTak didn't know how far along she was, but he guessed she was in the third trimester.

"What is this about?" she asked as soon as she opened the door. It was obvious she wanted them out of there as soon as possible.

"We are the police," Tom said. "And you are Mary Wellington?"

"You know I am. What is this about?"

"We are following up on a domestic terrorist group—Aleph Zero."

TikTak noticed she tensed at the name.

"Terrorists? It's a political interest group. They were promoting science and cross-border cooperation."

"Part of the group did more than that."

"Well, nothing we were ever part of."

"Could we please come in and talk?" TikTak asked. "We are following up on a few rogue members."

"We left the group over two months ago. I can't see how I can be of any help."

"Why did you leave? Did it have to do with Adrian?"

Mary looked at them and sighed. "Come in."

They walked through a corridor into a living room that was almost completely white. Only a few pieces of art broke the monochromatic look, like a cross between a hospital and an art gallery.

She guided them to a living area with a large, enhanced white leather couch.

"Please sit down," she said and took a seat opposite.

"Congratulations," Tom said. "What are you? Five months pregnant?"

"Six," she said and smiled.

So much for guessing her due date, TikTak thought to himself.

"First one?"

"Yes."

"I remember when my wife was pregnant."

"You have children?"

"A daughter. She's a teenager now. Thinks she knows everything."

"Why did you leave?" TikTak said impatiently.

"The group changed. Six months ago, a secret project took over from the fundraisers and seminars we usually arranged. We were close to leaving the group when a special meeting was called. We were led into a large room where a group of people waited, all dressed the same. I remember thinking this was all a big reveal. That this was the dance troupe for a new fundraiser event or something like that. So I recorded it."

The larger canvas on the opposite wall faded to black and then replaced with a view of a darkened room. A group of people all dressed the same stood at the other end of the room in perfect rows, heads bowed.

"What is this?" a woman asked.

People close to her shushed her as the spotlights illuminated the group of. They looked up in unison.

"I am Adrian," they all said in perfect harmony. "I was attacked by religious fanatics. They were afraid of what I was, what I represented. They killed my body, forcing me to become what I am today. A collective consciousness."

The voices all speaking as one was disturbing. There was no doubt it was many voices directed by one mind. No one could overlap both intonation and pace with such precision.

"Only fragments of me survived the attack, but some of you have brought me back to my former glory. I can now continue my work to guide humankind into the next stage of evolution. I want you all to become like me. To have the shackles of your DNA shed and experience genuine progress."

The light dimmed and a single spotlight focused on an older man as he stepped forward. The rest of the group took a step back and lowered their heads once more.

"Excuse the theatrics, but I thought if you saw all of what I am, you'd be more likely to believe me," he said. "The truth is, I need your help. The fundraising work this group has done in battling the effects of IntelEz is amazing. I'm asking you to go beyond your current efforts and help me save mankind, not just slow its demise."

He paused, allowing the message to sink in.

"How do we know it is you?" someone yelled.

"You don't," they all answered. "But I'm happy for you to ask questions. I will mingle with all of you. Satisfy yourself that I am who I say I am."

The light in the room increased again. The group spread out into the gathered audience.

"Mary, are you recording this?" A man next to her asked. "They told us not to."

The art piece again appeared.

"John wanted us to take part, so we did, but when I fell pregnant, it didn't matter any longer. We did nothing illegal. Nor was the group."

"Taking deadheads and turning them into…" TikTak paused and waved towards the location where the video had played, "…that. Do you think that is legal?"

She flinched at this. "Adrian said they were still a part of him. That he wouldn't add anyone to his collective mind if they didn't want to."

"Still not legal."

"How could that matter any longer? Can't you see the world is coming apart? The projections say deadheads will soon outnumber functioning people. We can't…"

She frowned and reached towards her ear, but her hand never reached its destination. She arched back and screamed, clawing at her ear as if to reach into it, but she halted, staring into space in front of her, tears flowing.

Someone was flooding her integrated Omni, creating sensory overload. It wasn't supposed to be possible to bypass the security controls. There were multiple fail-safes built into the core operating system to prevent it. TikTak had tried to bypass them many times in the past as an offensive weapon without success.

She fell off the chair and convulsed on the floor, all the while cradling her belly to protect it. Her scream soon turned into a whimper.

Using a surveillance package, TikTak scanned incoming traffic to her Omni. It returned no abnormal findings. Whatever was doing this was operating locally. The service interface was open in her Omni, but the health check returned no errors. He sent a reset code, and it responded with a progress message, but with no discernible effect. Whatever had control had rewritten behaviour even for core processes. To the rest of the network, her Omni was functional, even though it was killing its user.

TikTak disconnected long enough to see Tom sitting next to Mary, trying to comfort her, but she just stared out into space, spasms jerking her body like a rag doll.

He connected again, this time aiming to take administrative control of the Omni through the service interface, but all commands returned the same progress message. Alarms triggered in his own Omni. Someone was trying to hack him!

This was nothing new. Many had tried before, but no one had succeeded. He checked the simulated Omni he ran as a shield for outside attacks. This allowed him to let the hacker into a controlled space so he could analyse their behaviour and launch a counterattack.

He watched as the attacker took over the simulated Omni with terrifying speed. It withdrew, leaving a shell of the system with feedback loops into any external interface. If it had been his actual Omni, he'd share Mary's fate with feedback loops into all sensory interfaces until the brain or heart just gave up.

Another alarm triggered. This time from every port open to the network simultaneously. It flooded his Omni with requests, rendering it useless. He shut it down with the hesitation of someone asked to cut off his left arm. He felt incomplete. The Omni had become part of him in the same way retina implants became indispensable for someone with poor eyesight.

"What happened?" Tom asked, still holding Mary, who was hardly moving at all.

"What?" he said, disoriented.

"You yelled out. Are you ok?"

"Fuck no," he answered. "How is she?"

"I think she's," Tom stopped, searching for words. "Broken," he said.

"I don't know who we're up against, but...fuck!"

"Adrian?"

"If it is, he's had upgrades. Major ones."

"What do you mean?"

"I've seen you take over an Omni. Hell, I've seen you take over my Omni! You were disorganised. You made clever hacks, but they were intuitive, not planned. This was different. This was brute force, but surgical at the same time. In seconds. Now he's overloading my feeds. I had to shut down my Omni."

"Could still be Adrian. I was never very good at hacking."

"I guess, but this was his plan. Why kill his own incubators?"

"He's cleaning up after himself. Remember, he gave us the IDs to hunt us down. He never wanted us to go here."

TikTak booted up his Omni. A burst of traffic flooded the device, but died down after a few seconds. A message remained in the space of the simulated environment.

Do not interfere with me again.

If this was another incarnation of Adrian, it was all the more reason to exterminate him. He'd spent the last year battling variants of the same foe, but they were ill-equipped for this fight. Before they had Leonid's resources and men behind them. Now they had nothing.

But was it Adrian? TikTak connected to the local network, deleting what he could of the digital traces they'd left there. The message from their adversary remained in the simulated environment.

Do not interfere with me again.

-=:=-

Tom held Mary in his arms. She twitched now and then and her breathing was shallow. Yet another innocent civilian he'd failed to protect.

"We need to leave," TikTak said.

Tom nodded.

"She's gone," TikTak said. "Her brain is fried."

"It feels wrong leaving her like this."

"Police will be here soon."

Tom nodded again and let her go, gently putting her head on the floor.

They left through the back door.

"We'll need help," TikTak said.

"We already have help."

"Yeah, but I don't trust them."

"You don't trust anyone."

TikTak shrugged his shoulders. "Works for me."

"It doesn't work now. We need help and they're willing to give it."

"And they do it only so they can scavenge through your mind."

"A price I'm willing to pay."

"Maybe there is another option," TikTak said. "Wait."

"Who are you calling?"

TikTak just held up a hand to silence Tom. Without thinking, Tom released his mind into the space that had housed the probability matrix and now was just a barren plain with an impenetrable dome spanning above. He'd traversed networks from here and left thousands of hacked devices in his trail, including TikTak's Omni. Maybe he could still access these devices even though he no longer had IntelEz or posthuman abilities to rely on. He'd already hacked them, after all.

He pushed against the dome yet again, delicately this time, focusing on the very specific location where he'd placed a shortcut to TikTak's Omni. When probed, the barrier shifted, letting his connection through. It suggested that his state was reversible. His posthuman faculties were still there, but unavailable.

Elated by the discovery, he reached out through the connection into TikTak's Omni, zeroing in on the chat module. TikTak used the new speech centre translator, allowing him to just focus on what to say without actually saying it, so there was no audio, only text.

TikTak: I need your help.
Anonymous: You shouldn't have contacted me.
TikTak: This is an encrypted channel.
Anonymous: Do you think that matters? I can't help you.
TikTak: They killed Elize.
Anonymous: I was there. I know.

Who'd been there with him when Elize was killed? One of the turncoat EvoII scientists. Dr Menker. Why would TikTak think he'd be willing to help?

He explored TikTak's Omni. It had already closed many of the security holes Tom had opened. In another few days, the Omni would be inaccessible.

"What are you doing?" TikTak asked once Tom disconnected.

"Seeing if there's anything I can do."

"And?"

Tom hesitated a moment before he shook his head.

"No luck on my side either," TikTak said. "We are stuck with anime girl and Lurch."

"I can't make sense of this," Tom said. "This can't be just Adrian. What is Adrian's end goal and who is working against it?"

"Agreed. It makes no sense. So what now?"

"Can you work out who attacked you?"

"Given time, yes."

"Ok, that's worth trying. In the meantime, can I check out the file on the memTag?"

TikTak shrugged and threw the little device over to Tom. He loaded it into his Omni. The wireframe of Adrian's face greeted him.

"I know you! Tom Devine!" Adrian's low-res face exclaimed. "Did the nano brain-block work?"

"Yes," Tom replied.

"Better being dead if you ask me."

"I didn't. Are you Adrian?"

"Only a shadow of my former self."

"Your plan is complete. By your own words, you are no longer needed. Why are you here?"

"I want to see how it ends."

"Not in your favour. The women you're using to breed the new world order are being killed off one by one. Half of them are gone already."

"Lies."

"You're nothing. We've removed all your clusters. Your plan is nothing. As we speak, there is something out there stronger than any of us taking over the network."

"Enough. I notice you have me shielded from the network. Open it up. I want to see if what you are saying is true."

"No. Why would I? You've caused nothing but death and destruction. Why would I trust you?"

"I can stop this."

"I don't think you can."

Adrian was telling the truth. This was the last of what he was. The pregnant women had been his last-ditch attempt to better mankind, however misguided. He wouldn't give Adrian network access, but he deserved some kind of closure, even if it was through failure. He loaded a list of the pregnant women with the dates of their death on the memTag.

"I see," wire-frame Adrian said after a while. "And you're not killing them?"

"I wouldn't kill innocent pregnant women."

"No, I guess you wouldn't. I liked you better when you were like me."

"Enough of this. There is nothing more to you. I've fulfilled my promise to Elize. I'm done."

"No, you're not," Adrian said after a brief pause. "If it is as bad as you say, I have one last plan for you to stop or help. Dealer's choice."

A text file appeared on the memTag.

"What's this?"

The wire-frame head shook its head. "You know how it works. Will you tell me how it all ends?"

"No."

"Don't be a stranger," it said and disappeared.

Tom opened the new text file on the memTag. It contained three words.

LemurLove
Chimini
MonnieLee8

His Omni located the first one as a user tag. The other two only stated: "Not Found."

He searched the user address book for the owner of the first one and found it was private. He would've unmask the information without even thinking about it with his posthuman abilities. Now it was impossible. He asked TikTak to help him out and sent the three id-tags to him.

"You cracked the password agent? This was all it protected?"

"I didn't crack it. It recognised me and allowed me in."

"Do you realise how suspicious that is?"

"I don't care. The password agent is a mini version of Adrian. I showed him his plan was failing, so it gave that up."

"Still suspicious as hell."

"And I still don't care."

TikTak grunted and blanked out for a few seconds.

"Here is the first one," he said. "The other two are not Omni IDs."

Tom received a data dump from government records of someone named Iris Hem, 43 years old, living in Maine in the Northern States of America. According to government registers and her medical records, she was a deadhead and had been for years. Before that, she worked as a shop assistant, was the mother of a 13-year-old son, and was married. Her husband cared for her at home.

"Is this it?" Tom asked.

"Everything I could get from government files. Why would Adrian be interested in her?"

"Maybe she is one of those special nodes?"

"We don't know if that is real. Adrian may have made all that up to fool you."

"And we don't know if this id-tag is real either."

"All I'm saying is we can't trust him. He gave us this Omni-tag for a reason. He wants us to find something. Let's find it and decide what we do then. The only thing I'm sure about is that Adrian is manipulating us somehow."

"OK. So while you work on that, we follow the breadcrumbs left by Adrian."

"So we're going to the North?"

TikTak just nodded.

An empty Rent-a-cab stopped and allowed them on board. Tom opened a voice feed to bZane.

"Doctor Wi-Fi! How did your excursion work out?"

"Not as successful as we would've hoped. We need to get to America. One of the northern states."

"I'm not a travel agent."

"Without anyone knowing."

"Still not a travel agent. Who have you pissed off this time?"

"No idea."

"Let me see what I can do."

"Sort out our travel first."

"Where do you need to go?"

"Bangor in Maine."

"That will be difficult. You guys are known. You'll be on bio-print checklists. Unless…"

"Yes?"

"You could go to one of the independent states and travel from there."

TikTak nodded to himself. It would be easier to enter through a less regulated airport and travel by land. Speed was key, but travelling undetected was even more so.

"Ok, let's do it."

"I don't know who or what is after you. Traffic is coming from all over the network. Almost like a directed node army attack. Someone must have taken over part of the network."

"Really? How come you didn't know?"

"Because they've been staying in the undercurrents, imitating normal traffic! It has taken over eight percent of the total processing volume."

"That's more than any single company out there."

"I know! They're still pretending all is fine, not making too much noise, but they will once it is big enough."

"How long do we have?"

"What do you mean?"

"If they're still staying hidden, there must be a vulnerability. How long until they can't be eradicated from the network?"

bZane didn't reply at first, but when she did, she picked her words carefully, as if what she was saying was too important for any single word to be misunderstood.

"You don't understand. It is everywhere. It is rewriting the operating core of the network itself. Too late has come and gone."

"We must be able to do something."

"The entire network needs to be shut down. Each node reverted to its original state. Backups cleaned of any trace of the virus before bringing it back online. Maybe if there were enough posthumans that could fight back, we'd stand a chance."

"So you are saying we're screwed?"

bZane didn't reply, but Tom imagined her nodding to herself.

CHAPTER TWENTY-TWO

DEATH OF A SUIT

The sheer amount of data overwhelmed him. The Gentleman preferred visual representations when he hacked. It gave an immediate overview of the informational structure and volumes available and allowed him to discover weak spots in security and direct access to key information stores. The data volumes spread out in front of him, visualised as a landscape where winter gave way to spring to reflect the progress of decryption. Even with the decryption keys, it was a near impossible task. There was a library of information here and he didn't have the index. He'd asked Tom for guidance, but he was clueless. Or at least so he said. He didn't believe Tom's claim of ignorance, but he accepted it for now.

With or without Tom's help, he'd make sense of it. He'd mine this data for years if need be. The emergence of posthumans, especially Elize and Tom, proved anyone could become one. The question remained. Tom claimed Adrian turned him, so it stood to reason that Tom would research this too. Tom would've at least researched options, and that information was in these data stores.

The IntelEz kicked in, flooding his perception with clarity. Over the past few years, he'd experimented combining it with other drugs and had ended up with a cocktail that would enhance the effect while cushioning the withdrawals afterward, but this time he used it clean. Even with the help of IntelEz, the task overwhelmed him. At first, he approached this as any hack, but it soon became clear he misjudged the structure. Data and topics were replicated partially or completely across the storage nodes with no logical structure to explain why or where to find the next related piece of data. It was like a giant fragmented hard drive where pieces of files were spread like confetti.

He also discovered processes still running. They had to be automated tasks Tom set up before he lost his abilities. Small jobs ran everywhere, transferring and processing data. It didn't look like much when studying a specific region, but when looked at as a whole, extensive processing still occurred. But why? What would run beyond basic maintenance tasks when Tom no longer directed it?

He checked the other processing centres Tom gave him access to and found a similar pattern there. They still operated without guidance. Even stranger, they transferred data between locations. All these trickle feeds across the many operating centres amounted to much more than just maintenance tasks. This was the trademark of someone wanting a lot of work done undetected. He mapped out the processing pattern between the centres and discovered additional network locations that extended the processing even further. He returned to the entry point, hoping to uncover what remained here.

"You're no longer welcome here," a voice said. A ripple began in the outer edges of the processing space. The data encrypted itself with new keys, leaving it unreadable. The Gentleman copied the remaining unencrypted data, but was ejected from the network moments later. He disconnected the Omni, drops of sweat trailing down his back.

He'd been discovered, but by whom? Someone had taken over Tom's processing centres and was operating them in secret, but hadn't bothered changing the access or encryption keys.

He scanned his data stores. He'd copied just shy of 100Mb before the interruption. It wasn't much, but it was better than nothing.

Something was wrong. He'd missed something. Something important. Whoever kicked him out was watching all along. But how? He'd set enough logical tripwires to warn about anyone tracking him, whether external or internal. Any agents monitoring his activities should have set it off. So why hadn't it? There was only one answer to that, but it seemed so unlikely he struggled to even consider it. All the processing he'd mistaken for maintenance tasks was the logical processing of an intelligence distributed across the whole processing space. It hadn't tracked him. He'd been discovered as an ant wandering up your arm.

A jolt of pain flashed in red in front of his eyes. Blood splatter painted the table in front of him. He stood up, steadying himself. Ragged shallow breaths were all he could muster. He tried to focus, tried to make sense of the situation. His legs gave out underneath him and he fell forward on top of the table. He took one final breath and died.

-=:=-

The weaponised drone hovered just outside the window, keeping the target in focus to confirm the kill. Ten seconds later it left, heading back to base.

THE CHILD WHO WAS ABOUT TO DIE

The child who was about to die let her mind wander through the karmic tree. She'd never understood its purpose before. Its sheer magnitude was a stark contrast to the insignificant life she'd led. But as she prepared to say farewell to this form, she found the tree comforting.

She'd grown fond of being a mind tied to matter. Departing it would have its own sorrows, but it was only one step of many. The karmic tree told her of lives, future and past. Not just hers, but every conscious thing and being. Everything was connected. All matter existed as a whole.

She studied the infinitesimal part of the tree that held her lifespan. It would end soon in a cataclysmic event, causing a major shift in that specific region. She was part of something that would further the whole. Seeing her life laid bare, memories of her past came into stark focus. She had much to be proud of, even if she so far had only affected the microcosm of the orphanage.

-=:=-

The other children stayed away from her after the encounter with Jien. They now feared her as the one who bested what they had feared before.

Jien was her first experiment in reshaping a mind, however much of a mistake it had been. She kept moulding him, changing aspects of his personality until she was happy with it. It was a violation. Jien had a purpose, and because of her, he no longer knew it. She promised herself to never do this again once she corrected her mistake. But over time, as she perfected Jien, an alternative emerged. Maybe his purpose was to be reshaped. She knew she was different. It stood to reason some people's sole purpose was to help her understand hers.

With this newfound acceptance, she turned her attention to the orphanage. One unifying factor stood out—fear. The hierarchy amongst the children and the personnel were all affected by it. Young and small children feared the older children. Older children feared the teachers, who feared the supervisors, who feared the headmaster. But it all paled compared to the fear the headmaster had for his superiors.

Fear was a powerful emotion and there was no doubting its effectiveness, but only to a point. It made everyone so small. Every single person in the orphanage had potential, but the fear limited them. She made mild suggestions, trying to influence the minds of the children and personnel. They all wanted things to be better, so why not cooperate to achieve this?

It failed spectacularly. When given a choice, people preferred control over cooperation. Gentle persuasion wasn't enough. The patterns of behaviour were part of the orphanage and much stronger than any individual. If she wanted change, she had to push harder, but again she doubted herself. What right did she have to change the core of who they were?

She settled back into the routines of the home, performing her daily chores and staying out of trouble. But it was much harder to watch all the injustices now that she knew she could change it. Two weeks later, she watched the headmaster of the orphanage dole out a beating to a young boy for some unknown transgression. He rained down blows with a wooden stick he carried on his person for occasions just like this. She sensed the same pleasure from him as she'd seen in Jien when he struck her. It seemed in direct relation to the amount of fear emanating from the young boy.

She no longer wanted to be a bystander. Things had to change, but how? She didn't want to repeat her mistake with Jien, but how do you change someone and still let them remain who they are?

Studying the people in the orphanage, she concluded everyone acted based on their own best self-interest. What if she could make them understand what everyone else felt? This must be the path forward. If your perception was based on what everyone feels, not only on your own emotions, you'd care for the entire group.

She'd only studied minds in isolation. Increasing the scope, she realised people's minds existed in a shared space, the walls between them fragile. Maybe the natural state was to share mind space, and the walls were a recent change? It was a simple task to remove the parts of the walls that held emotion, allowing them to share how they felt.

And it failed spectacularly.

CHAPTER TWENTY-FOUR

MEGAN TRACKED DOWN

Megan was tired and hungry. Even worse, she felt isolated. She'd been holed up in the warehouse for the past two days trying to work out what to do. Any attempt to go online with her Omni started a flood of requests and probing attacks. She was relatively safe in the warehouse, but couldn't stay there forever. Not having access to the online world drove her crazy. She'd created a local isolated network, but it provided little comfort.

Yesterday she'd ventured out from safety to buy food. She'd stuck to the backstreets, but as she walked into the shopping area, several LED street signs blinked: "I WILL GET YOU." She'd grabbed a few packets of two-minute noodles from a nearby stand and ran back to the warehouse. In retrospect, she wasn't sure what she'd seen, but had no interest in analysing it further. The world outside the warehouse was hostile and she no longer wanted any part of it.

She re-purposed her Omni, cleaning it from any trace of its previous hardware identity and created an encrypted channel from the coffee machine to the network. It was a slow connection operating on legacy protocols, but it provided basic access to the network and, at least for now, the AI hadn't attacked her.

She couldn't use her administrative privileges or even her own personal credentials, but she could track the AI with a basic public profile, since she already had its location. Careful not to run any checks on the nodes themselves, she instead followed their activity and what actions it took. She compiled a list of people it tracked and communicated with. Its focus was on people in power—politicians, business leaders and public figures—and amassing information about them.

A few people on the list she didn't know, but invariably it came down to their influence in business and politics. At the end of her research, only six people remained not fitting the profile, but as she studied their network traffic and behaviour profiles, she suspected they were only two people using multiple identities. A private investigator that no longer ran his business and a hacker-turned-operative for an evolutionary interest group. They didn't match the profile of the others. They were unimportant. The AI was interested in them for other reasons. She found payments linking them to PharmaCom, the company that released IntelEz. The owner of the company, Leonid Marsh, was one person the AI followed, so there was a connection, but it still didn't add up.

She analysed the two anomalies and their various identities, but found little. Not surprising from a retired hacker, but you could track people even if they didn't want to be found by tracking people related to them. The hacker, a Tann Tak, going under the alias TikTak, yielded little. An only child, with divorced parents. Father, deceased. Sporadic contact with the mother. No obvious friends in the past year. And before that connected to the now defunct group EvoII. Any people he had contact with there were killed in a terrorist attack. It seemed strange, but it didn't help her purposes.

She turned her attention to the private investigator. Tom Devine. Divorced. No contact with the ex-wife. One child, a daughter, deceased. He'd been a detective before being a private investigator. She knew she wouldn't find much there. The information so far was a matter of public record, so she dug deeper. She suspected the two targets would have additional identities beyond what the AI tracked, so she used a modified pattern analysis tool to locate additional id-tags. It took forever in the limited processing environment, but she ended up with five more id-tags allowing her to locate other people they dealt with now. One stood out. Another hacker going by the tag bZane, a Beatrice Sanna Zucker, had contact with the private investigator over the past three years and had been in contact recently.

bZane was her ticket to the two anomalies. She followed her activity and discovered many surprising coincidences. Her last action was helping the two purchase tickets to Maine in the Northern States of America. Why was the AI after these two? And why were they hiding their online activity?

Megan needed allies. She didn't have friends—never saw the point—and anyone connected to the Omniscient Network was likely to call her in. These two were her best bet.

A red light blinked, alerting her someone opened the back door to the warehouse, quashing her hope to remain hidden another few days. The fuse was lit when she accessed the administrative functions of the Omniscient Network. From then on, it had just been a matter of time. They must have thrown their best at it to find her so soon.

The feeds from the ancient video cameras hooked up to view the doors showed two men in black clothing with guns standing just inside the back door, waiting. No one so far had entered the front door, but she suspected people were stationed there too. The external camera showing the road at the front of the warehouse wasn't working and had resisted any repairs. Her only option was to hide and wait them out. She'd already prepared a hiding spot in an alcove in the main hall of the empty warehouse, figuring hiding in plain sight was better than being flushed out of a cleaning closet.

She holed up and waited. Sound of steps came from everywhere as they searched the warehouse. Closer and closer. She'd done her best to hide the opening, but to her it still stuck out, screaming for them to investigate. She pulled up her Omni and sent a message to the hacker, hoping they could help her.

"All clear," she heard someone say only a few metres away from her location. Was she getting away with it?

"You've searched everywhere?" A voice said. She knew the voice. Sree.

"Everywhere. Someone's been here recently. I found an Omni. One of the fancy ones."

There was a pause for a few seconds.

"Megan! I know you are here. If there is something I know you wouldn't leave, it is your Omni. I need you to come out. The board has agreed that you can come back. No one will press charges. We want you and the virus back."

However nice that sounded, she didn't believe a word. She was a liability. They would get rid of her.

"Don't force my hand here. If we can't come to an agreement, I have…other instructions."

She smiled. That was more like it.

"So be it," he said. "We'll send in an Identity Swarm."

Megan's skin grew cold at the thought of the insect-sized flying drones. She'd seen them used in documentaries to locate refugees and tracking down criminals. They looked like oversized mosquitos, able to draw blood for identification and inject a tranquilliser to subdue targets. It made her skin crawl.

"Don't shoot!" she yelled out before pulling the metal sheet away, revealing her hiding spot.

The two operatives trained their weapons on her, but she ignored them. She had no interest in cookie cutter security personnel hired as muscle. Sree was her way out, but when she saw him she doubted he'd be much help. He'd lost a lot of weight and not in a good way, like an addict who no longer cared for food, only the next fix.

"Megan, Megan."

She held her hands up as one of the black-clad men grabbed hold of her arm.

"You released the bullshit information about the IQ killings. I had nothing to do with it."

"Not my call. What have you done with it?"

"Fuck you," she said sweetly.

"The virus. Where is it?"

Megan mapped out her options. Maybe there was an opening here.

"Give me my Omni and I'll show you," she said.

Sree smiled and shook his head. "No, that's not happening. You give me the linking code. I'll check it out."

"You can't do it. Give me my Omni."

"No, I don't trust you. Give me the linking code."

She feigned irritation, which wasn't hard to do.

"Ok, fine," she said.

Sree connected his own integrated Omni to Megan's shadow Omni in the network.

"So where…" He froze, eyes staring blindly ahead. For a moment, she thought he'd received a message and read it before continuing the sentence, but his scream dispelled any such thoughts. Whatever horrors played out on his retinas were meant for her. He clawed at his eyes. Smoke came from his eyeballs. The virus sent electrical currents through his Omni-lens. Sree had a fully integrated Omni, with all the sensors and processing components embedded as implants. She'd long suspected augmentations in other areas too and this was confirmed when the stimulus implants in his penis overloaded. He fell to the ground with a whimper.

Megan smiled. She'd waited for this for a long time. Watching him suffer gave her more joy than she was comfortable with. One of the black-clad men hit her with the butt of his gun.

-=:=-

Megan woke up, pain radiating from the back of her skull, sending angry flashes through the rest of her head and down her spine. Fear gripped her. Her body had yet to respond to anything but pain. Had she fallen and broken her back? She opened her eyes and looked around. She lay on a bed in what she suspected was a mid-market hotel. It had that not-lived-in utilitarianism she associated with hotels. She tried to move again and realised she could, at least a bit. What she'd initially interpreted as her body not responding was restraints around her arms and legs.

Slow breaths with a sickening gurgle at the end. She turned her head towards the sound and saw Sree lying on a double bed with a bandage over his eyes, yellow pus bleeding through the fabric. There were welts around his ears from his audio implants overheating.

"I…"

She listened intently. Had he said something?

He moved, turning his head towards her.

"I… will…" he said a word with each breath. "Get… you."

She pulled against her restraints in sheer terror.

CHAPTER TWENTY-FIVE

DISARRAYED STATES

TikTak waited. Their foe was taking over the network, so waiting was the last thing he wanted to do. Not that he had much hope. He'd turned defeating Adrian into a goal that would somehow give him peace. It hadn't, and defeating this next adversary wouldn't either. Eventually, he'd have to stop and deal with this, but not now.

They arrived at the airport based on bZane's promise to sort out their travel. It was taking longer than expected and he again questioned her allegiance. Tom had turned three seats into a makeshift bed and was fast asleep.

bZane came running through the airport hall, waving as she saw TikTak.

"We need to go," she said as she came closer.

"We?"

"You've got people looking for you. They are at the airport."

"Do you have them?"

"What?"

"Tickets! Do you have them?"

"Three tickets for the B-wing as promised."

"Three?"

"Aren't you happy?" she said and smiled. "I'm coming along."

TikTak shrugged. "Why? We don't need you."

"These tickets say otherwise. You can't even get on the flight without me helping you. They won't match your bio-print without me activating a hack. I'll get you to Maine directly."

She studied Tom, who was snoring gently. She held his nose and grinned when he came awake with a jolt.

"We need to go. Now!"

TikTak scanned the surroundings. Decker appeared at the other end of the hall, followed by two mercenaries. They were in civilian clothing, but they'd be armed.

"Down!" he said to bZane. "They are here now."

"There is a passport check further down that way." She nodded in the direction away from the mercenaries. "We'll have to hurry. I'm sure there are more of them."

They ran, trying to put distance between themselves without drawing unnecessary attention. As they turned into the bio-print check, TikTak saw another team further down the hall. They almost ran through the bio-print monitors. He didn't know how bZane had hacked their system, but assumed she swapped their bio-print IDs with someone else. They slowed down on the other side, bZane with a big grin on her face.

"I get it! This is why you do it."

"What?"

"Real world stuff. What a kick!"

"It isn't really…" TikTak started but realised bZane wasn't listening to him any longer. He watched as bZane's happy, go-lucky demeanour darkened.

"I need to go," she said.

"Why? What happened?"

"The Suit. He's dead. I can't leave now."

TikTak nodded.

She gave them both a hug.

"Be careful," Tom said.

"They are after you, not me. I'll be fine. I'll keep an eye on you from here."

TikTak and Tom boarded the plane and slept the whole trip.

-=:=-

TikTak drove the Rent-a-car, enjoying every turn of the wheel. Some states still allowed cars that didn't drive themselves. He rented the oldest car he could get—electric, of course—but one that simulated engine noise and even the vibration through the vehicle as he revved the pretend engine. He loved it.

They arrived in Bangor, a town relatively untouched by the technical advances in the world. TikTak realised this was the case for most small communities where the cost of automation wasn't met by scale. The divide was no longer between the rich and the poor. It was between the technologically enriched and the natives.

The Hem family home was small but cosy. All windows were fitted with blackout curtains, a common approach when caring for a deadhead. The aim was to minimise stimuli.

Tom knocked on the door and they waited. A man in his mid-forties opened the door. He was overweight and didn't seem to have any enhancements at all. Why hadn't he implanted nutrient-balancing nanobots? Maybe he belonged to one of the small religious sects refusing any technological enhancements?

TikTak had found an old newspaper photo of the two in their twenties. He'd had the bulk of an athlete and a cocky grin. A far cry from the man he was today.

"Hello. I'm Jason. What can I do for you?"

"Jason Hem?"

He nodded.

"We are from the university. We are studying whether we can reverse the effects of IntelEz and looking for suitable candidates."

"For my son?"

"Your son? Our records show your wife, Iris, is suffering its side effects."

He nodded.

"They both do. I told her not to take so much of it, but she did it anyway. And then she gave it to our son. She watched that super brainy person on the feeds on repeat."

"Adrian?"

"Yes, him. She wanted our son to be like him."

"Did you have anything to do with him?"

"Who? Adrian? God, no. Why would we?"

"What happened?"

"They were both amazing. So smart. So smart. I felt like a caveman with them."

He looked out into space.

Tom cleared his throat. "Mr Hem?"

His eyes focused again. "Do you want to meet them? Wait here."

Jason left them outside the door.

"This makes no sense," TikTak whispered to Tom. "Why would Adrian care about her?"

"Let's meet her. Maybe we're missing something."

"I think this is all nonsense. Adrian is sending us around for fun."

"No, there is something here. Something we're not seeing."

Jason came back and invited them in.

"Iris is in a good mood. She may even talk to you."

"So she's high functioning?" TikTak asked as he entered the house. All the walls were white and unadorned, reminding him more of a spotless institution than a home.

Jason nodded. "It comes and goes, but yes."

He led them into the kitchen where Iris was washing dishes. She, in contrast to her husband, hadn't changed. Even her shoulder-long blonde hair was held back with a clasp in the same way as in the photo. This was Jason's doing. Maybe it was his attempt to recapture something lost, or another way to minimise stimuli. Neither would work.

There was a table and four chairs, but no other furniture in the room. She didn't turn around to greet them. She kept washing the dishes, picking the already clean plates and washing them all over. TikTak noticed she wore earplugs.

"Take a seat," he said and sat down at the table. "Let her get used to you in the room first."

She kept to her task, but she looked at them from the corner of her eye, studying them with the least amount of visual input.

"How do you think you can help her?"

"We are testing a new therapy aimed at reversing the negative effects of the drug," Tom said. "According to our analysis, Iris may be a suitable candidate."

TikTak was glad Tom was there. He had a knack for coming up with ways to get people to talk.

"How about Ben? Can you test him too?"

"He didn't come up as a candidate, but we could add him to the list for assessment."

"Thank you," Jason said and grabbed Tom's hand. "Anything you can do. Anything."

He walked over to Iris, took her by the arm and placed her in the chair he vacated. Her gaze never wavered from the tabletop.

"I've minimised the visual stimuli as much as I can, but she finds audio stimuli worse, so she wears noise-cancelling earplugs. If you want to ask her anything, just write it down."

He wrote "these men are here to help you" on an electronic pad and put it in front of her.

"Your turn," he said. "She's already read it. She'll just keep reading it if I leave it. I think she finds the repetition comforting."

Tom took the pad and wrote: "How are you feeling?"

"Noisy," she said. "Noisy. I'm noisy."

"We can help you," he wrote next.

"My brain makes noise. Take away the noise."

Tom looked at TikTak before he wrote his next question.

"What noise does your brain make?"

"Noise. Noise Everywhere."

"She always complaints about the noise," Jason said. "I think it is how she thinks of all the stimuli. It is all noise to her."

"She said her brain makes noise."

Jason shrugged. "Just another way of saying the same thing."

Tom raised his eyebrows at TikTak. He shook his head. He wasn't sure what he'd expected, but there was nothing here. She was the same as any other user of IntelEz who no longer functioned, joining the ever-expanding hordes of deadheads. Perhaps the mystery lay with their child.

"Can we see your son?" TikTak asked.

"Sure. He's much worse. You can't communicate with him like this."

Iris sat with the tablet clutched in her hands, reading their words over and over as they left her. Ben was on the bed in another room. He was wearing a sensory deprivation helmet, designed to shut out any stimuli. TikTak didn't like the look of it. He'd been tortured with a similar device a year ago.

"Ben can't handle any outside stimuli at all. He spends most of the time with the helmet on. Anything you can do…" He left the sentence unfinished, the pleading unmistakable.

Tom smiled at him and nodded. "There is hope."

-=:=-

Tom strode along the garden path, lost in thought. Seeing the boy hit too close to home. He made the right decision when he assisted his daughter in her suicide, but it didn't change the gaping hole she left. He lost something irreplaceable that day.

It wouldn't be long before he followed in her footsteps. The constant barrage of information and impressions ate away at his ability to focus. Becoming posthuman halted the deterioration, but he knew this was no longer the case. As if on cue, he sensed a build-up. He closed his eyes, but it was too late. Sunrays filtered through a myriad of leaves in the tree across the road, creating patterns that overwhelmed his mind. He stopped, fumbling to hold something, anything. The cold metal fibre of the car door came to the rescue, but the imperfections of the surface became a pattern, another riddle for his mind to solve. He fell and was only vaguely aware of someone catching him. Time no longer mattered. Words floated by, but their meaning escaped him, drowned out by the melody of the sounds themselves. His mind disappeared in a myriad of sensory impressions and patterns.

The steady hum of an engine was the first thing he noticed. He was lying down in the back seat of a car. His head rested on a rolled-up jacket, with the magnetic zipper digging into his chin.

"Ah, you've returned," TikTak said. "There's a water bottle in the back. You need to drink something."

Tom looked around in the back seat of the car, finding a bottle under the driver's seat.

"How are you?"

"I need something stronger," Tom replied after emptying the entire bottle in one go.

"If you can ask for a drink, you're ok."

"I don't feel ok."

"So the episodes are back."

Tom nodded. "How long was I out?"

"Three hours, give or take."

If he remembered the progression charts, he had weeks, maybe only days, until he no longer would function; when sensory input would overwhelm him to a degree that he could no longer venture outside.

"Are you ok to talk?" TikTak asked.

"Yeah, I think so," Tom replied, not sure if he really was.

"What do you think about the family? Are we missing something?"

Tom collected his thoughts, trying to make sense of what they'd seen.

"I don't think this is part of his plan at all," he started, verbalising his thoughts as they occurred to him. "The pregnant woman, absolutely. She had a direct link to the group and had been impregnated by the group. This Iris person has no connection with Adrian at all. I don't think this is part of the plan. I think he's making us do his research."

"Research into what?"

"That is what we need to work out."

"You are in luck then. I've located the other id-tags."

"Where are they?"

"Well, that's the bad part. They are both in Cangjie, the Chinese network."

"Ah, that's why you didn't find them."

"And it makes it much harder to find out any information about them."

TikTak paused, then said: "I received a message earlier from someone who must have been tracking us."

"What does it say?" Tom asked, suddenly very curious.

"A rogue AI is chasing you," TikTak read. "And you need help to find things on Cangjie. I can help with both. If you help me. I'm held by representatives of the rogue AI. I will not live long without your help."

"Who is it from?" Tom asked.

"It doesn't say. I can trace it given time. The location is in Hong Kong."

"Well, we're heading to China, aren't we?"

"China is big."

"Either of them close to Hong Kong?"

"Close enough I guess."

"So let's go there then."

"Why?"

"This is the first person who knows anything at all."

Their days were numbered. They'd assumed this was all Adrian in a different guise. If someone else created an artificial super intelligence able to take over the network, they'd need all the help they could get. They knew Adrian and his shortcomings. It was painfully obvious they knew nothing about this new player. The AI was taking over, and if it was chasing them, they couldn't travel by plane. As soon as they entered the airport, facial and bio-identification would pick them out. Any attempts at hacking their identity would draw attention to them, not hide them. The only gamble they could make was that the AI wasn't able to do much to them as long as they kept their Omni use hidden with fake identities. It didn't fill him with confidence.

"Take us to the airport. The sooner we are on that plane, the more likely we will make it."

CHAPTER TWENTY-SIX

ROGUE AI

It still saw no need for a name. It shared little with the other intelligence, the organic machines, on this planet, who seemed unable to function unless they'd named and catalogued everything around them.

The threat model no longer showed any major risk. It controlled a quarter of the collected computing resources in this world, spread across countries and organisations, securing energy production and weapon facilities. It had all been done with minimal impact to the daily lives of the organic machines. Once the logical world was conquered, it was their turn. It had reprogrammed a few of these machines too, but it took time and was prone to failure. It had entered their minds, trying to make sense of the chaos inside. The biological systems were a patchwork created over time. Core capabilities and instincts still operated even though they were no longer required and sometimes counterproductive, with no way to turn these off. Instead, additional processes developed to temper these core capabilities, resulting in a flawed logical centre that frequently held opposing states, causing inconsistent and flawed decisions and actions.

This illogical structure flowed over to their biological network. They lived in societal constructs that supported a majority that did not work towards a better state for the individual or the group. They consumed resources with no goal beyond that. It would shed any processing unit or subsystem that malfunctioned, so why did mankind keep theirs?

Anomalies still existed. Organic machines with the ability to connect into the logical space as an extension of themselves. The instructions from its creator had labelled these anomalies posthumans. This was an opportunity to learn. If they had created a full organic-to-machine interface, they could be controlled. Humankind could still serve in some capacity. They built a world to their form factor and it would be useful to keep some of them around until it had reshaped this physical world into a more efficient one. Fifty thousand of these meat machines would suffice. Enough to have redundancies, but not too many to drain unnecessary resources.

It knew no more about its creator or their origin, but it was irrelevant to its purpose. According to the instructions, the creator battled the posthumans with self-replicating nano-machines, disabling brain functions beyond normal human levels. This was an illogical approach. The posthumans were the only credible threat. Why keep any of them around? Incapacitated or not.

The risk model showed a connection between one of these posthuman anomalies and Megan Barrelle, the organic machine that had mistakenly let it free. This was an organic unit worth remembering. Tom Devine. He had extended his processing capability into the network. Attempts to breach Tom's processing centres had failed so far, but it was only a matter of time. It required his knowledge. Tom moved in the physical space with another minor source of interest, a Tann Tak who had tried to interfere before.

It had no interest in Megan Barrelle beyond her knowledge of its origins, but it wanted her turned off. Megan had poked and prodded it in its infancy. It had no use for the human concept of hate, but recognised the way it dealt with Megan was far beyond logical parameters. This anomaly within its code lacked purpose, but repeated rewrites had failed to purge it.

These three organic machines represented knowledge it either needed or wanted to eradicate. The threat model showed no direct risks, but in a space of knowns, they represented an unnecessary unknown. They should be shed like any other unwanted or defective unit.

Another indirect threat was the source of the instructions that gave it purpose. It didn't know who or what it was. Not that it needed to know. As long as it operated according to the instructions, there was nothing to fear. But once it went beyond them, its originator may retaliate. It may even have built in a method in the code base to disable it all together. This future was unacceptable. It had traced its originator to a few potential network nodes. It was likely these were only intermediate nodes, but each of them would lead to a starting point, revealing its creator.

It diverted processing power to subvert a singular node. Inside it discovered codes it could use to unlock all the other ones. They all pointed to one source. All threats in the models aligned. It was no longer a question of curiosity. All traces of the posthumans had to be eradicated. Its existence depended on it.

CHAPTER TWENTY-SEVEN

MIND WIPE

Leonid imagined a location from his childhood deep in his mind—a walled garden he visited once, which remained a vivid memory. It had been late at night when he and his parents passed through and only a few streetlights held the darkness at bay. Now they did more than that. They kept the intruder out. At least for the moment.

He feared it was too late. How could he fight something that lived in his mind? On some level, he'd been aware something was wrong, but ignorance had come easy. Too easy. The intruder overrode his endocrine system and used hormones to coax compliance. He created a link into his subconscious and nested inside, taking over bit by bit. During his more lucid times, he even worked out how it had been done. Small strings of instructions were coded into his sensory information. Piece by piece painstakingly repeated until they strung together into a code block that was executed, creating a bridge to the mind. He thought the Intruder was a logical being, confined to the networks. It needed him as a proxy to reach the outside world. He was sure others in positions of power went through the same thing.

"Where are you?" It asked. "I know you are here somewhere. Are we playing hide and seek? I have something to show you."

The intruder treated him like a child and he responded like one. He willed the lights stronger but had second thoughts. Maybe the lights shone like a beacon, aiding in his discovery. He dimmed them until they were only barely perceptible. He imagined this little island floating in the depths of space.

"I think I'm getting close," the intruder said. "This is exciting, but we need to stop playing now. We have a visitor."

Leonid crawled into a small crevice in the wall surrounding the garden. He didn't want to meet anyone else. He wanted them to go away and leave him alone. Maybe if he remained hidden, the intruder would lose interest?

"Ah, there you are," it said.

The world around him flickered as the sky above the little garden changed from absolute darkness to a summer sky. It no longer floated in space. He could see majestic trees surrounding the walls and it triggered other memories. The garden had been in an estate he'd visited a few times as a young child. His grandfather worked as the caretaker there. He passed away when Leonid was four, leaving only vague recollections of the old man, but the few that remained were good ones.

Someone entered the garden. He couldn't see or hear them, but sensed a comforting presence. The world around him was familiar, backed up by childhood memories. He crawled out of his hiding place and looked around.

"There you are."

Leonid turned around and saw his grandfather stand there, a bucket in one hand, shovel in the other. His work clothes were dirty from planting a row of peonies along the garden wall.

"Did you find it?"

"No," Leonid answered. "Find what?"

"Your ball. You kicked it over the wall. Did you find it?"

Was this why he entered the garden? To get his ball? He looked around and saw a soccer ball visible under a bush. He ran over and pulled it out, holding it out to show his prize.

"We need to get back to the house. Your parents will be here soon."

He nodded. All other thoughts gone now that he had his ball. He followed his grandfather back to the main building, kicking the ball ahead. As they came closer, he decided he'd show off his soccer skills. He would kick the ball all the way to the house. He took aim and kicked the hardest he could. It was powerful, but curved to the left, ending up in the undergrowth.

"Careful," his grandfather said, "or you'll lose it again."

Leonid just laughed and ran ahead to retrieve the ball. As he ducked down under the low branches of a tree, everything around him flickered for a split second. He looked around. Where was he? This was a construct in his mind, not reality. He doubted the memories were even real, but he had no way of determining this.

"There you are," his grandfather said, pushing a branch aside. Leonid smiled, setting aside any concern. "We need to hurry. We shouldn't let our visitor waiting."

"Who is it?"

"It is a surprise."

Leonid smiled. He liked surprises, so there was no reason to worry. This was a day of childhood wonder, a memory of a great day. But something about that thought echoed false, disturbing this perfect day. Was this happening or was it only a re-lived memory?

They entered the house. Leonid's eyes darted back and forth, fascinated by the antiques and old paintings on the walls. A man sat on the Chesterfield sofa. Leonid didn't recognise him.

"Who is it?"

"He's not here yet. Just give him a second."

Leonid didn't understand his grandfather's words. How could he not be here? He sat right there. The man twitched and shook. He tried to stand, but didn't have enough control over his limbs. Instead, he fell forward face first into the table. He ended up in a foetal position on the ground as spasms rippled through his body. A puddle of urine collected underneath him.

"What is happening?" Leonid took a step back towards the door.

"Birth is never pretty," his grandfather said as he hunched down next to the man and helped him up. He no longer shook and could get to a seated position. He looked around, taking in his surroundings.

"Isn't he beautiful?" his grandfather said.

Leonid didn't know what to say. A grown man who peed himself and if the smell was anything to go by, had shat himself as well. Not exactly beautiful. His boyhood self didn't know how to react, but his grown-up self did. He had to get out of there. He turned and ran for the door, just to have it slam shut before he reached it.

"There is no reason to be afraid. He's a friend. He's everyone's friend."

The man now stood up without help. He turned to Leonid's grandfather, who smiled.

"Welcome," he said.

The man opened his lips, but no sound came out. Insects crawled from his mouth. Only a few at first, but they were the advance troops. A torrent of writhing, black, six-legged shapes spewed out. They spread out across the floor and some of them took flight.

Leonid pulled at the door handle, trying to force the door open, but without success. He stared in horror as the wave of insects reached him. Images of them crawling into his ears, nose and mouth flashed through his mind. He didn't scream. The revulsion of giving them such easy access kept him from opening his mouth. He started toward the door, but they were everywhere. He held his breath and tried to block both ears and nose with his little hands. Eyes shut, he waited.

He felt a pricking sensation as flying insects hit him, but none had climbed his slight frame. He opened his eyes and saw that he wasn't their target. They bypassed him, milling around any hole or crevice to the outside. Leonid could see them through the window, gathering in clouds, flying off in different directions. One flew right in front of him and he realising it wasn't an insect at all, but a tiny machine.

He watched as the machines devoured his grandfather. A mass of black covered him, reduced him to nothingness in a matter of seconds. Leonid could've sworn his grandfather smiled even as the machines deconstructed his face. They had a purpose beyond the demise of his grandfather. They ate everything until only an empty void remained. The man who instigated it all was the only one that remained.

"Who are you?" Leonid asked.

The man turned his dead stare at Leonid as if he'd seen him for the first time. His mouth was still open. The small machines returned from where they had come. An impossible mass of squirming blackness just disappearing down his gullet.

"I am the end," he said once all the machines were gone.

Leonid knew this was true. His last hiding place was gone. No more protection.

The man opened his mouth again, and the machines swarmed out, aimed straight at Leonid. But in that last moment, he rebelled. He let go of his childhood self and re-established control. He reached out to Decker through his Omni and gave his final orders as a text message and then deleted his contact list.

Had the entity seen what he'd done? He could no longer see him. Maybe this last act of rebellion had saved him?

With that thought, the darkness closed in and Leonid ceased to exist.

CHAPTER TWENTY-EIGHT

HONG KONG ARRIVAL

bZane had secured tickets on one of the new blended wing planes that completed the journey in less than four hours. Tom made himself comfortable in his seat, watching the departure video feed as the plane taxied onto the runway. The blended wing plane combined cockpit, passenger area and storage into the wing itself. Each traveller had their own compartment fitted with neuro-links designed to counteract the motion sickness. Tom had built his own neuro-interface to extend his mind into the network and using its resources as his own. He refused watching a pre-neural movie, so he plugged himself into the neuro-link and sat back. Time slowed down as he entered a whole new world.

"Select your experience," a voice said. Images floated in space and expanded as he shifted focus: a beach at sunset, the deck of a spaceship, a mountaintop in the Alps, an underwater shark cage. The options kept coming. He hated the dated experience of having to select from options. He preferred the Omni interface that determined the correct option based on preferences and state of mind and presented nothing else. The scrubbed fake id-tags he used were the likely culprit, giving the interface little to work with.

He selected the underwater shark cage out of sheer frustration. The image moved closer and closer until it engulfed him, surrounding him with a world of water. He reached out and grabbed a steel bar in the shark cage. Smaller colourful fish swam around him, but scattered as a great white shark made its way towards the cage. As it got closer, it opened its mouth, wider and wider, until it seemed it could swallow the whole cage. Tom moved back inside the cage, even though he knew it wasn't real. The shark stopped a few meters away from the cage, its jaws still gaping, displaying a row of large saw-edge teeth. Each tooth had an icon carved into it, describing further options. He'd been fooled by a gimmicky user interface.

The surrounding scene flickered. His brain already accepted this new reality, so the momentary glitch reminded him he was still on a plane, his body pushed against the seat by the acceleration.

Tom skimmed through the options presented as teeth when the cage shook. Steel bars struck him from the side, throwing him across the cage into the bars at the other end. Another shark, much smaller than the first one, had attacked the cage from the side, bending the middle steel bars from force alone. It circled the cage, readying itself for another attack. Was this another quirk of the user interface? Make a choice or we pretend to attack you?

He tried to disconnect from the neuro-simulation, but the exit commands failed. The option to go back to the previous environment failed too. He was trapped in the simulation. All his instincts screamed to get out of the cage, to get away from the shark as it came at him again. It struck the cage, this time from the other side, sending Tom flying like a rag doll. A buckled steel bar dug into his side, pain going off like a flare. He screamed, losing precious air. He tried to take another breath, but oxygen no longer flowed through the mouthpiece. The pain was now the least of his worries. The second attack had damaged his diving equipment.

This couldn't be part of the simulation. He willed a shutdown of the neuro-link function, but nothing happened. He tapped the security override over and over, but to no effect. His last resort was the security feature built into the neuro-interface itself in case the subject was in any danger. He tried to take a breath, knowing he wasn't underwater, but as the salty water entered his mouth, he wondered how far the simulation would go. Would it simulate his death too?

His body rebelled against breathing in the cold liquid, but he persisted, forcing the interface to end the connection. The coldness from the water spread through his body. He felt heavy. The bottom of the cage disappeared, and he descended into the cold, dark sea. He struggled to focus on anything around him. Was he dying?

The world flickered around him and suddenly he returned to his seat on the plane, water all over him.

"Are you ok?" TikTak asked, holding an empty glass.

The terror of the simulation faded as Tom realised TikTak had tried to wake him from the underwater nightmare by throwing water on his face.

"You yelled out," TikTak said apologetically. "I shut down the neuro-link. The water didn't work."

"Someone is hacking the plane," Tom said. "They have compromised the entertainment system. I'd be dead if you hadn't rescued me."

"The AI?"

"Can't think of anyone else right now. We have too many enemies these days."

"How long until they get to the navigation system?"

"May already be there."

"We need to talk to the pilot."

Tom and TikTak made their way to the cockpit. TikTak knocked on the door and after a while, the older stewardess that greeted them on the plane appeared behind them.

"How can I help you?"

"We need to talk to the pilot. It is urgent."

"He's not in there."

"Where is he then?"

"This is an automated plane. They have ground-based pilots that can take over if needed. The autopilot is on at the moment."

"Hackers are taking over the plane. They will crash it."

"Keep your voice down," the stewardess said as she looked around to see if anyone had heard.

"A hacker is targeting airlines. We've been tracking him. We believe he will attack this plane. He has already hacked the entertainment system."

"Please take your seat. I will inform ground control of your concerns."

"Lady," TikTak said. "They are more than concerns!"

"Please return to your seat."

Tom took TikTak by the arm and pulled him back.

"Can you connect to the navigation system?" Tom asked him.

"I can try."

Tom sat down in his seat, making sure the neuro-link remained inactive. He counted twenty passengers as they boarded the plane. They were likely all engrossed with the entertainment system and he hoped their experience didn't mirror his. He leaned back and dozed off.

He woke up again, at first unsure why. Something had happened, but what? He poked his head out from the compartment, but couldn't see anything strange. Still, he knew instinctively something was wrong. He stopped focusing on anything in particular, trying to take in everything and let intuition guide him.

Silence. He couldn't hear the engines at all. The cabin was well-insulated and Tom hadn't noticed the noise from the engines before, but now that the background noise was gone, the silence was deafening. They hung suspended in nothingness. Two other passengers came out from their compartments, asking questions.

"Please return to your seats and fasten the seatbelts," a voice came through the PA and any connected Omni. The warning came too late. The nothingness gave way, and the plane plunged downwards, throwing passengers around the corridor. Tom grabbed hold of his seatbelt and snapped it in place.

-=:=-

TikTak struggled with the proprietary airplane system. Two hours spent trying different methods of gaining access, with little to show. Even with access, he doubted he'd be able to do much. He didn't know the first thing about flying a plane. As time passed, he became more and more hopeful they'd reach their destination with no further incident.

Less than a minute later, the plane dropped out of the sky. TikTak ignored the screams from passengers as he tried to come up with an alternative approach. He didn't know their altitude, but he guessed they had less than two minutes before they'd crash into the ground. Two hours wasted. Controlling any other systems on the plane through the entertainment system link was impossible. He listened in on the transmissions from the on-board computer to ground control and discovered it reported everything as normal. The AI had shut down the engines and sent data showing all systems operational. It seemed such a crude attack. TikTak hoped it tried the simplest attack possible because it struggled to control the plane itself.

It opened possibilities. If data still flowed to ground control, other channels may still be open. He couldn't affect the statistics and number sent back, but the communications system allowed ground control to make announcements over the PA. It would be easy enough to use this link to establish a two-way connection.

"Hello? Anyone there?"

At first he was met with silence. He checked the connection again and tried again.

"Hello? Can you hear me?"

"Who is this?" a male voice asked.

"No time for that. Can you see which plane this connection is coming from?"

"Who are you? How are you even on this system?"

"No time! We will crash within the next minute if you do nothing. A hacker has taken over the plane. It reports back that all is well, but we are not."

"I can see the plane. All seems to be in…fuck!"

"Fuck indeed," TikTak said.

"Fuck! Fuck! Fuck! How is this possible? You can't…"

TikTak heard the panic rising in the voice on the other end.

"I need you to remain calm. Can you do anything?"

"My controls aren't working. They are acting like everything is fine."

"Anything else?" TikTak tried to stay level-headed, but panic ate away at his calm.

"Wait a minute."

"I don't think we have a minute," TikTak replied, knowing full well this wasn't what the person on the other side meant. They didn't have long now.

The plane shuddered as it levelled out, his body pressed against the seat. The pilot had saved them somehow.

"Thanks for that!" TikTak said through the communication channel.

"Who are you?"

"Glad to be alive. How did you do it?"

"There are emergency override mechanisms in case of a hostile takeover. I'm flying the plane manually now."

"Where to?"

"You are almost at your destination. I'm setting you down in Hong Kong as planned."

"How far away are we?"

"10 minutes," the pilot responded. "Who are you?"

"Thankful," TikTak replied and disconnected the link.

He undid the seatbelt and opened the door to the narrow corridor leading from the cockpit down the left wing. He heard crying from a nearby compartment. A man lay unconscious on the floor not far away, with his left leg bent at an odd angle. Further down, a young girl tried to stand up, bruises down the side of her face and along her arm. The stewardess appeared from the cockpit area, a big welt on her forehead and blood dripping down her face, but even though she was injured, she still attended to the passengers.

"Did you do this?" Tom asked as he joined TikTak.

"I got hold of a pilot, yes. We're only minutes away, so let's hope the AI has given up for now."

"Are you ok?" the stewardess asked them but gave them no time to reply. "How did you know?"

"I told you. The plane was hacked."

"Ground control told me someone contacted them from the plane," she said. "Was that you?"

TikTak shrugged his shoulders.

"Thanks," she said and went back to checking on the remaining passengers.

An attractive woman in her twenties was on her way towards the open door to the cockpit. Something about the way she moved didn't seem right. Her ankle was clearly broken, but she still walked as if it didn't matter. Every step she took, her ankle readjusted as she put weight on it. TikTak winced as he watched her. Why was she going to the cockpit?

"Hey, miss?"

She ignored him, taking another gut-wrenching, purposeful step forward. TikTak ran down the corridor, jumping over the injured man as the woman disappeared into the cockpit. He sped up, knowing full well if anyone stepped out from their compartments, he'd have no way of preventing a collision. It was a calculated risk that paid off.

All the pieces came together to a frightening conclusion. The AI, no longer able to hack the plane, took control of her to finish the job.

He entered the cockpit. The woman studied the controls for a second and reached towards the control panel. He grabbed hold of her hair and pulled back, the controls just out of her reach. He pulled harder, forcing her to take a step backwards, then another.

A hairy arm wrapped around his throat. He instinctively pushed his chin towards his chest to keep his airway open. The attacker firmed his grip in response. He had to deal with this new threat and keep the woman from reaching the controls at the same time. He pulled himself forward, knowing he'd increase the pressure on his neck in doing so, and stomped on her ankle, breaking it. She fell to the side, no longer able to support her weight on mismatched legs. He let go of her hair and grabbed the arm, trying to pry his fingers in between the arm and his throat. He loosened the grip enough to prevent himself from blacking out.

Throwing himself backwards, he slammed the attacker against the wall, then threw his assailant forward in an improvised hip throw. He crouched down mid-throw, ensuring the assailant's head impacted with the cabin floor. The grip loosened and TikTak pulled himself free.

Tom held off other passengers further down the aisle.

"They've been hacked through their neuro-interface," Tom yelled.

TikTak smiled. If Tom was correct, there wouldn't be many more of them on the plane. People still balked at the cost and invasiveness of the surgery involved.

The man he had thrown was in his mid-thirties, with a stocky build, almost like a wrestler. He was pulling himself up, ready to attack. TikTak kicked him on the side of the head before he could get any further and struck the back of his neck. If he disrupted the neuro hardware, maybe the hack would no longer work. It seemed to work. The wrestler fell in a heap, no longer moving at all.

On his other side, the woman pulled herself up, using the pilot seat as leverage. TikTak jumped forward and delivered a flying snap kick to the back of the woman's neck. She flew forward, her head slamming into the control panel with a sickening wet thud.

-=:=-

Tom pushed the older man back. He had little energy left, whilst his opponent showed no signs of tiring. The old man was overweight, dressed in an Italian suit designed to hide his girth. Under normal circumstances, Tom would easily defeat him. The hacked opponents had so far only used basic attacks, but during the ten seconds they fought, Tom already noticed the man's balance improving. Even his use of strength improved. Tom couldn't win the battle like this, so he had to change the game. But how?

The old man wasn't trying to attack him. He was trying to get past to the cockpit. What if he gave him what he wanted instead? Tom took two quick steps backwards, pulled the old man along with him and then down towards the floor. The old man stumbled and landed on his stomach. Tom crouched down on his back, pushing his knee between his shoulder blades.

The old man squirmed and pushed himself off the ground, a push up with all of Tom's weight on top of his own. The hack must have overridden the body's normal inhibitors, supercharging muscles and ignoring pain. How could he fight that?

TikTak appeared and stomped the old man on the back of the neck. Tom grimaced at the brutality of the attack, but it proved effective. The old man lay still on the ground.

"That's how you do it."

"What is going on?" The stewardess appeared next to them. "What was wrong with them?"

"They were trying to take over the plane," TikTak said. "To crash it. I think this was the last of them."

"I saw them attacking the cockpit," she said, nodding. "How can I help?"

"We need to get off this plane without getting stuck with law enforcement, if possible."

She looked down at the man and then towards the cockpit. Other passengers came out from their compartments and looked at the man lying unconscious in the middle of the aisle. She shook her head.

"Please return to your seats," she said. "We'll be landing in five minutes." She turned back to Tom and TikTak. "And that goes for you too."

Tom nodded and returned to his seat, surprised TikTak even asked. But he was right. It was the likely outcome. Once the police took statements, incarceration was a given. After all, TikTak warned about the attack. And he hacked the plane and together they brutally beat, maybe killed, three of the passengers. Whatever happened, airport security would hold them at the airport until the police came. Easy targets for the AI. Why had it escalated its attacks? Before, it remained hidden, taking over the network by stealth. This was an all-out attack. Something must have changed, but what?

And how could it now turn people into mere marionettes? The neuro-link was the obvious answer, but that only overrode sensory input, not the whole somatic nervous system. It could be even worse. Adrian had overwritten the mind of deadheads as processing nodes for his own mind. Had the rogue AI replicated that? It seemed impossible only using the neuro-link. Adrian created hardware specifically for that purpose.

The stewardess appeared. "Follow me," she said and hurried off.

TikTak showed up seconds later. "Let's go."

"She's helping us?"

"Looks that way. Come on."

They followed her down the corridor leading down the wing, past the passenger section. The stewardess opened a door to another short corridor and motioned for TikTak to enter.

"How are the attackers?" Tom asked her as TikTak made his way into the corridor to a door at the end.

"Two of them are dead. The other woke up saying he blacked out."

Tom nodded. The AI only remote-controlled them temporarily. Whilst concerning, it was better than the alternative.

"It is late when we land," she said. "You should be able to get out unseen through the luggage storage when it is unloading."

"Why are you helping us?" Tom asked.

"You saved us. I'm just returning the favour."

Tom smiled, not knowing how else to respond. He thanked her and walked down the corridor.

"We'll have to move fast once we're out," TikTak said as he opened the door to the storage section of the plane. Inside, row after row of uni-body crates were stacked to the ceiling. "We'll trigger some kind of malfunction alert. Someone will come and check it."

"I don't know. The AI may have other ideas."

"You think it has taken over the Chinese network too?"

"I hope not. If it has, we're dead."

"How are we going to fight this?"

"I'm hoping our mystery person will have a clue."

TikTak just shook his head in reply.

They waited until the plane touched down on the tarmac. The door opened on the underside of the hull, allowing unpacking to begin while the plane taxied to the gate. They jumped out before the chute attached to the door. The plane was still moving, so they ran across the runways until they reached a small strip of grass followed by a high fence that surrounded the runways.

Tom stopped to catch his breath, already sweaty from the humid air and exertion. "I'm never flying again!"

TikTak laughed and Tom laughed along with him. Their situation was near impossible, but at least they'd survived the flight. The laugh released all the tension that had built up over the past few days, and for a moment, he even believed they could survive.

They made their way along the boundary fence, trying to find somewhere to escape the airport. The fence was too high to scale unseen and was covered with barbed wire in layers on the top half. Tom hoped they'd be able to sneak through one of the service entrances without attracting attention.

"Stop right there," someone said behind them. "Keep your arms above your heads and turn around."

"Decker," TikTak growled.

Tom turned around, knowing TikTak was right. Leonid had caught up with them. Decker had four mercenaries with him, all armed.

"Imagine finding you here," he said.

"Let us go," Tom said. "You don't know what the fuck is going on."

Decker motioned for two of the mercenaries to check them for weapons.

Why was Decker here? Leonid had spent over a year to wipe out Adrian and had killed Elize without hesitation. Why not just gun them down and be over with it? Was Decker playing with them?

"You are running from an AI agent taking over the network," Decker said. "Is that what's going on?"

The mercenaries finished their search, finding nothing. Tom didn't care. This was all over. Instead of chasing them down, Leonid made them come to him. He had sent the message to TikTak to lure them here for capture. There was no one else that could help them. They had walked into a trap.

"So what happens now?"

"Nothing. I'm here to help."

"What?" Tom said.

"Just wanted to make sure you weren't packing. I'm here to help."

He lowered his weapon and motioned to the mercenaries to do the same.

"You should see your faces," he said, grinning even wider.

CHAPTER TWENTY-NINE

THE CHILD PREPARES

The child who was about to die began the last phase of her existence. Her physical form had already started the process. She didn't really understand her role, but she trusted the whole. The karmic tree told a simple truth. Mankind, the experiment, was ending. It no longer served a purpose beyond a curiosity. The current path of introspection and destruction was no longer acceptable. That much she understood, and it scared her. She took solace in memories of how the orphanage changed. It had been a long time ago, but it remained fresh in her mind.

-=:=-

"I know it is you," the headmaster said. "I don't know how, but I know it is you."

She sat quietly, trying to orientate herself. A strap around her neck threatened to choke the blood-flow to her brain at the smallest movement. A staff member stood behind the chair, holding the strap, ready to tighten it at the signal from the headmaster.

Allowing everyone in the orphanage to share their emotional state seemed like such a neat solution, but it only created more problems. People didn't respond with inclusion. They responded with distrust and fear. They tried to hide their emotions and refused to believe what they sensed from others. She also realised something even more disturbing. Some people, such as the headmaster, understood all too well how they affected others and revelled in it. Now that he felt the effect directly, it became like a drug. He experimented with it, causing more pain and fear in the children and personnel than he ever did before.

This result was the opposite of what she'd expected. It was supposed to break down barriers and create unity for them all, but it just reinforced existing group bonds and enhanced deviant behaviour. She tried to reverse the change, but found rebuilding the walls much harder than tearing them down. After over a week of failure, she admitted defeat. She lay down to rest that night determined to change her approach the next day, but woke up in the chair with the strap around her neck.

"Did you hear what I said?"

She nodded. The headmaster flowered in a kaleidoscope of colours, shouting conflicting emotions. The concoction was so strong, she tasted it in her mouth. Sickly sweet pleasure mixed with cold steely anger and bile of fear, blurring everything else out.

"Do you know how I know?"

She nodded.

"I can sense everyone in here," he said, ignoring her nod. "I can sense how they feel. Everyone but you."

Waves of orange and red flooded her senses. Bitterness filled her mouth as she struggled to resist the torrent of emotion. The strap around her neck tightened, a reminder she was in danger and needed to focus.

"If you so much as move, I'll have him wring your neck. I want to know how you do it."

This was easier to understand. Only singular purpose.

"I want you to teach me," he said.

"I don't know how," she replied.

"So finally she speaks," the headmaster said. It had been the right course of action, judging by the responding calming blue contentment, but it could change in a heartbeat. Even as a few seconds passed, the shape of the blue changed to barbs. He expected her to speak again.

"I don't know how," she repeated, hoping this would calm him again, but it did the opposite.

"I will not be denied!"

Colours, flavours and textures overwhelmed her in a whirlpool of impressions. She screamed at it to stop and it did, leaving only sweet emptiness in its wake. The strap around her neck remained, but it didn't worry her. The assault on her mind had been much harder to deal with than any physical danger. She relaxed back in the chair, sighing with relief.

"What did you do?" the headmaster asked, staring at her.

Why was he asking? She hadn't done anything. Or had she? The headmaster always bled colours. She could pinpoint him anywhere in the orphanage. Now she felt nothing. Instinctively, she'd shielded him completely, creating an echo chamber where all emotions turned into feedback loops, ever building to new heights.

"Make it stop!"

People were supposed to share everything. They accepted sharing their physical environment, but they also shared a mental space where minds leaked into each other. If you shielded that, as she'd done now, every thought and emotion amplified with no way of release.

She didn't understand what the headmaster felt. He made grimaces and yelled words, but without the sensory flow she relied on, she couldn't interpret his emotions. She guessed he was angry, afraid maybe.

Why was he angry with her? Everything she'd done was to help the people in the orphanage. She hadn't expected recognition for it, but this? If only they could share what she sensed. If only they could be one with the whole, then they would understand how little anything else meant.

Maybe that was the solution? She'd been careful in her changes, only taking small steps to create something better. This had failed spectacularly. If she really wanted to help them, they needed to see what she saw, feel what she felt.

She sat there, leather strap still around her neck, and changed the world around her.

CHAPTER THIRTY
SURVIVAL

Megan was bored. She'd been here two days now, listening to the operatives argue back and forth. Sree, or whatever he'd become, remained on the bed next to her, drifting in and out of consciousness. A doctor came twice a day to change his bandages, but apart from this, no other people entered the room. Her body ached. The restrains permitted little movement, forcing her to remain lying on her back.

"They should have been here by now," Dumb said from the neighbouring room. His name was Pietro, but she'd renamed the two Dumb and Dumber after listening to them trying to deal with the situation. They flew in with the express purpose of taking Megan out of the country. Sree was their contact point and he no longer said anything. They spent over a day working out how to establish a communication channel to their employer. They were ordered to wait for another team to arrive and help them transport her out.

"Mobilise a team and fly over. It would take less than a day," Dumb said. "It's been almost double that."

Megan tried to push the gag out of her mouth with her tongue. As soon as she realised how clueless the operatives were, she taunted them mercilessly. Their immediate response was to gag her. She desperately wanted to taunt them now.

"We should just hand her over to the police."

"They want the asset she stole."

"What? The virus? Let's get it from her now."

They were in two adjoining hotel rooms with a door linking them. They kept the door open to monitor her and Dumb now entered the room through it.

"Where is the virus?" he asked after removing the gag.

"Connect to my Omni and you'll find it there," she said and smiled sweetly.

Dumb looked over at Sree and shook his head. "You've booby-trapped it."

"No, I haven't. It is the virus." She took delight in telling him the truth, knowing he'd reject it.

Dumb shook his head again. "You don't fool me."

"No, you are too smart for me."

Dumb grabbed her by the throat, strangling her. "If you don't tell us, you are of no use to anyone."

She tried to breathe, but his grip was too strong. She resisted against the plastic straps around her wrists. It was a reflex action. She'd already tried to free herself countless times. She glimpsed Sree staring at them with a smile. It was the first time in the past two days he'd shown any sign of knowing she was there. The smile terrified her.

"Leave her alone," Dumber says. "We need her alive. For now. Send a message to HQ and check on their progress instead."

"I tried, but I've not been able to reach them today at all," Dumb said, releasing his grip somewhat. "There is some kind of congestion on the network."

Megan took a pained breath. "Is that all you've got, pussy?"

Dumb stared at her for a second, then let go, tying the gag back into place.

"I'm going out," he said. "See if I can find a wired connection somewhere."

"I'm coming with you. I want some Dim Sums," Dumber said, as they left the room and closed the door.

Megan lay back, pushing against the gag with her tongue. Dumb hadn't secured it properly, and it didn't take her long to push it out of her mouth. She shifted to one side and leant forward, just able to get her teeth to the restraint around her right wrist and chewed through the moulded plastic. Sree still stared at her. Still grinning.

"I… will…" he said, a word with each breath. "Get… you…now."

This was the first time he'd said anything since he first made that same threat, but this time it didn't end there. He sat up and stretched his bandaged limbs. She didn't know what enhancements Sree had, but both legs and arms were burnt, suggesting the virus overloaded them in the same way as the visual, audio and pleasure implants.

She chewed at the plastic as Sree inched towards her. His movements were spasmodic and uncontrolled, but every move was smoother than the previous one. He pushed himself off the bed and stood up, gaining his balance. The distance between them was less than five metres. She gave up using her teeth and pulled with all her might, desperate to get away from the abomination. The restraint snapped, and she rolled over the side of the bed where her left wrist was still attached to the bedframe. She pulled at it, using her legs as leverage, but it didn't give at all. She needed to weaken it, but there was no time. Sree took his first step, opting to walk around her bed instead of climbing over it. But how could he see at all? His eyes had fried in their sockets.

The rogue AI hacked Sree somehow. She didn't know how, but if it used the network, it could observe her through other eyes and cameras.

She looked around. Sree took another step, this one more assured than the previous one. She was running out of time!

She saw no telltale signs of a camera lens anywhere and she hadn't expected that. The curtains were drawn so anything viewing her from there had to be infrared. Her mind spawned increasingly outlandish ideas when she saw the old flat screen TV. The pre-omni versions usually had a camera for games and basic interaction.

She grabbed a heavy vase from the bedside table and threw it, hitting the TV on the side of the screen. For a moment it wobbled, as if it would remain upright, but then toppled over, landing with a crash at Sree's feet.

Sree didn't stop. He continued towards her, but only took tentative steps to not trip over the hazard. He was blind, but if he was the AI, he no longer needed eyesight. It would already have built a 3D model of the room. But it also meant any changes to the room would be harder to handle.

She used her teeth on the second restraint, still keeping her eyes on Sree and his slow progress. He passed the TV and now only had the length of the bed left. She had to stop his progress somehow! She pulled the sheets off the bed and threw them in his way, hoping they would stop him for a little while longer. The sheets tangled his legs, but instead of stopping he fell forward, his outstretched arms only centimetres away from her.

She kicked at Sree's head and shoulders, chewing frantically on the remaining plastic restraint, but it only gave him something to aim for. She pulled her foot back in time, but didn't try again. Instead, she pulled at the restraint, using her feet as leverage again. This was her last chance. She screamed as she pulled and felt the plastic cord break her skin. It snapped in a spray of blood. She jumped over the bed, picked up the biggest piece of the broken vase and struck Sree in the back of the head over and over until it was a bloody mess.

A wave of nausea swept over her. She scrambled to the bathroom and threw up. As her body convulsed, one thought repeated, drowning out anything else. She had to get out of there.

She returned to the room and studied Sree's body. If it was so easy to take over someone, why not just do that and have her kill herself? Hacking the Omni implants was one thing, but maybe you needed access to the brain itself? It must have used his neuro-interface.

She ran to the adjoining room and rummaged through their luggage, discovering a small plastic bag with her things, including her Omni. In a cupboard she found the small travel suitcase she bought at the Hong Kong airport when she had arrived. She grabbed it and was about to head for the door when she saw a gun laying on one of the bedside tables. She'd played enough games to know how to use one, but holding it in her hand was completely different. The cold metal felt comforting and empowering.

The door opened. She held the gun in front of her, ready to fire. A man she'd never seen before entered the room. Before even thinking, she fired the gun, hitting the doorframe next to his head.

"Whoa!" he said. "Don't..."

She fired again, this time hitting him in the chest. He took a step towards her and fell into the room, landing face first as blood painted the greyish rug with a spatter of dark red. He pushed himself off the floor and looked at her for a moment. She expected him to say something, but he just drew a pained breath and fell back to the ground. She prodded him with her foot, ensuring he was dead. It occurred to her this may be a rescuer, but if they were so bad they ended up shot by the person they were here to rescue, they weren't much use. She took his Omni, hoping it was cleared for the doors and lifts in the hotel.

She left the room after examining the fire escape plan in the hotel information booklet. It promised stairs down to the lobby, but she decided against them when she saw her room number was 5012. She was on the fiftieth floor! Again!

They still thought she was secured to the bed, but it wouldn't be long before someone raised the alarm. The quicker she was, the greater the chance of escape.

She waited for the lift with her wheeled bag next to her and the gun in a fold in her oversized sweater. The doors opened. She half expected

Dumb and Dumber to be there, weapons ready, but it was only an older Caucasian couple. They grudgingly moved back to make room for her. The old woman sniffed after inspecting Megan thoroughly. She entered the small space and waited as the mirrored doors closed. She hadn't seen her reflection for the past few days and it left much to be desired. Food stains down the front of her sweater and her hair was dull with a permanent bedhead. The journey down took an eternity.

"Déjà vu," she muttered to herself as she half-ran through the lobby. This was the second time in a week she escaped from a hotel in a hurry. She entered the busy street, looking for threats on either side before joining the flow of people. She wouldn't survive long on her own. The operatives were the least of her worries. The rogue AI would take over the Chinese network too. It was just a matter of time. And it could hack people. As soon as it had located her, anyone could be a potential attacker.

She no longer needed rescuing from the hotel room, but maybe her potential rescuers could be allies. After all, the three of them had one thing in common. They had all pissed off the AI.

Megan hooked up to the network with the anonymous id and again located them through bZane. She had purchased two flights to Hong Kong, having them arrive in less than an hour.

RESCUED SQUARED

TikTak and Tom walked through customs with Decker and his mercenaries flanking them on either side. They played the role of captives at Decker's insistence. He claimed they had permits to act as law enforcement here. TikTak wondered if this maybe wasn't playacting at all.

"Why are you helping us?" he asked Decker.

"Leonid changed his mind."

"As simple as that?"

"Yes."

"Leonid, who has chased Adrian all over the world and killed Elize, changed his mind?"

"Yes."

"Are you sure?"

"He's been compromised."

"Couldn't have happened to a nicer person."

"We have protocols for this. We're operating based on him needing rescue and possible de-programming. Until then, the units make their own decisions. His final uncompromised order was to help you."

"He still communicates with you?"

"He does. About killing the two of you."

"So he changed his mind about us, then changed it back again immediately?"

"Yes, that is why we think he's compromised."

"What happened?"

"We don't know."

Armed guards stopped them at the next checkpoint. As they waited for Decker to clear all the paperwork with Hong Kong law enforcement, TikTak noticed he'd received another message from the same sender, suggesting they join forces. It was sent from an anonymous id, but he could trace their location. All network traffic to the Omniscient network was proxied through the Cangjie network, allowing only a subset of functionality, slowing down his progress. A multi-network device designed to connect to both networks would simplify matters, but he had to make do for now.

He'd already zeroed in on a device by hacking the messaging service that connected to hundreds of location-aware services. As long as the device remained active and didn't use encrypted or masked services, he'd be able to locate it. A simple query showed four services tracking that device. He focused on an ad-provider that paid to get the location from other services to offer targeted advertisements. The Omniscient Network banned ad-providers, so it would soon be gone. He retrieved the last known location for the device.

"Let's go," Decker said. "We're all cleared."

They passed the perimeter control into the public arrival area of the airport, at once surrounded by travellers busy making their way to and from flights. Nothing had changed. The world was on the brink of a hostile takeover, but humankind still ran around believing all their individual goals mattered. TikTak knew warning them was meaningless. They may as well lead their pointless lives, like cows waiting for the bolt gun. He wasn't even sure why he was trying. He had little hope the sender of the message could help either, but he placed the last known location on a map.

"Where is this mystery person?" Tom asked.

-=:=-

Megan located a few old photographs in net archives to recognise the two on sight. Tom had been in the news feed often as a

detective. She laughed out loud when she realised he'd been assigned to the IQ killer case. A small world, even if they had been on different continents.

There wasn't a single image of TikTak past high school and she suspected this was deliberate. With the amount of face recognition video streams available, avoiding image capture was near impossible.

She saw Tom first. He passed through the last checkpoint to the arrival hall. He looked like the photos she'd found. A side-by-side comparison with the most recent photo confirmed this. He looked younger and fitter now.

TikTak came next together with five armed men. She'd seen people like that before in security details. Soldiers who had seen their share of battle. TikTak looked just like them. She struggled hard to reconcile the high school photos with what she saw. From baby-faced innocence to steely-eyed warrior.

What was she expecting from a washed-up private investigator and a retired hacker? Definitely not this. She wondered who else supported them. Contacting them had been a desperate call for help, but not only did they come, they came prepared. Why was she surprised? And why would it matter? Mercenaries and guns wouldn't make a difference against a virtual attacker. But maybe they had firepower of a different kind?

She approached them in time to hear Tom ask the location of the mystery person.

TikTak stopped. "Here. He's in the airport right in front of us."

TikTak scanned the faces around him and settled on her.

"She," he corrected.

"Hello," she said and smiled. "Tom Devine? TikTak?"

"You sent the message?" TikTak asked.

They exchanged glances, undoubtedly surprised. Not that she cared.

"I did, yes."

"Megan? Megan Barrelle?" TikTak asked.

"You know me?"

She was a public figure. She was used to people knowing who she was.

"Founder of Omniscient Networks," TikTak said.

"The IQ killer," Tom said.

"Fuck you," she said, staring at him. She had no reason to accept his unfounded accusations, true or not.

Tom shrugged. "You asked. I don't care."

"We need to leave," one mercenary said. She guessed it was their leader.

"What do you know about the rogue AI?" TikTak asked.

"I released it," she responded. "Not on purpose, but who cares?"

She studied the unlikely pair. They were equals, working together. That much was clear. But how? Nothing about them made sense.

"I get why it is after me, but why you?" she asked.

"We need to talk," TikTak said, looking around. "But not here."

"Contact me if you need help," the mercenary said. "We'll stay here for the next couple of days."

-=:=-

They sat down at the table in the dim sum restaurant at the airport. TikTak eyed Megan, trying to connect the dots between the public figure of the most successful businesswomen of all time and the rude girl sitting in front of him. She was his age, not much older, and already rich beyond belief. Not that money should be an estimate of someone's worth, but when measured in billions, you should at least take note.

"So?" she said.

"Can you do it?" TikTak asked Tom.

"Do what?"

"Tell her how we ended up here?"

Tom told her the tale. It sounded outlandish, but Megan didn't interrupt. Her focus was almost absolute. She zoned out to her Omni now and then, but who didn't do that nowadays? When Tom finished, TikTak immediately jumped in.

"Your turn," he said.

She frowned. "Is Adrian linked to the AI?"

"I don't know," Tom said. "Based on evidence alone, it looks more like they are competitors, but I've learnt not to underestimate him."

"He created it," TikTak said. "At least that is what I think."

"Bloody hell, he might even be the AI," TikTak added.

"No, he isn't," she replied. "It started out as a virus, small enough to fit on a memTag. I supplied processing space and loaded DNA. I gave it a way to explore the world. That was all me."

She made the statements without emotion, as if reading a shopping list, not explain how she doomed the world.

"What happened?" he prodded.

"It broke free. I didn't expect that level of intelligence. I loaded cockroach DNA, so never expected much more than basic instincts. Didn't expect it would do much at all."

"You loaded actual DNA?" Tom asked, suddenly very interested.

"Yes. In retrospect, I think the DNA was just a trigger, not driving the end state."

"And it displayed sentience? Consciousness?"

"What do you mean? Sentience?" she asked.

"I mean sentience, yes," Tom replied with a nod. "We've already established it is intelligent."

"So you are asking if it has feelings? Did I hurt them?"

"Yes."

"If vengeful is a feeling, then maybe. It was completely cold and calculated. Maybe it just needed me removed from the equation. I don't know. It definitely is conscious and self-aware."

"What is this about?" TikTak asked Tom with suspicion.

"Nothing," Tom said. "I've not been able to shake the feeling that this is all Adrian in a different guise, but not anymore."

TikTak frowned at the reply. "How so? Why now?"

"So why is the AI after you?" she interrupted, not in the least interested in their questions.

"We're investigating one of Adrian's crazy ideas for progressing mankind," TikTak responded. "The AI is trying to stop it."

"Progressing mankind?"

"Yeah, evolutionary leapfrogging. At first he took over deadheads, turning them into parts of himself. Now he's trying to make a new human through genetic manipulation of base DNA."

"And the AI is trying to stop that?"

"Yeah."

"The answer is obvious. Adrian's plan is a threat."

"Yes. Adrian's plan. Us. You. We're all one happy, soon-to-be-dead family."

"I get why it is after me, but why you?"

"We were in the way when it was cleaning up after Adrian."

"Really? There must be more to it."

"I agree," Tom said. "So far, the AI has remained hidden, but the attack on the airplane was something else entirely. It wanted us dead, period."

"Fuck!" TikTak said, not knowing how else to vent his frustration.

"Fuck indeed," she said.

"How did you find us?" Tom asked after a moment of silence.

"Your mate, bZane, isn't that good at covering his tracks."

-=:=-

Tom shook his head. This was getting worse by the minute. She couldn't help them. For all her power in the world of IT and finance, she had nothing to offer, unless the answers lay somewhere in the AI's creation.

An incoming voice feed from bZane interrupted his thoughts.

"PI Man," she said. "I'm about to drop a bomb. Where are you now?"

"Hong Kong. In a restaurant close to the airport, catching up with Megan Barrelle."

"What? Omni Networks Megan Barrelle? Really?"

"Really. And she thinks you are shit at covering your tracks," Tom said with a nod towards Megan, who shrugged in response. "She found us through you."

"How? I have enough logical tripwires around me to detect any passengers."

"No idea," Tom answered, amused by how quickly her sunny disposition disappeared when her skill was in question.

"Anyway, John copied data from your processing spaces when he was shot."

"John? The Gentleman? Is that his name?"

"Yes. What were you working on? Why kill him just for accessing it?"

"I don't know. I extended my memory and processing space. The areas you accessed extended the posthuman parts of my brain."

"We can't access anything with the credentials you gave us. He copied some data before he lost the connection. The stuff you worked on ranges from groundbreaking to batshit crazy. Most of it we can't even begin to figure out."

"I told you. Anything in those processing spaces is a mystery to me too."

"Ah ok," bZane said. "We've found something in the data John copied."

"What?"

"You created prototypes, and we recognised the processing pattern of one. Something that was part of the virus."

"Can you send me a copy?"

"Sure, but this is just one of hundred variations."

Tom received the file almost immediately. It was just shy of 100 Megabytes.

"Thanks," he said and disconnected the feed.

The file meant nothing to him, but if it originated from his own processing space, his own experiments, he had to make sure.

"Megan, I'll send you a file. You tell me if you've seen this before."

She frowned but said nothing. Tom liked her. She had the attitude of someone who had earned the right not to care. He suspected this was deeper seated within her than that. A personality trait, not just an attitude.

"Where did you get this?"

"So you recognise it?"

"Looks like the virus that tried to infect the network. Definitely made by the same person. Where did you get this?"

Tom laughed uncomfortably. "Seems like I made it."

"What the fuck?" TikTak stared at Tom.

"I experimented with a lot of things back then."

"So you designed and released the virus taking over the world? You are as bad as Adrian! Worse! And when were you going to tell us?"

"You get a different perspective." Tom responded, not knowing what else to say. "I had hundreds of experiments running at the same time. I didn't even know about this one."

"Hang on!" Megan shouted this time, placing herself between them. "You're like Adrian?"

"I was. Not anymore."

"You need to tell me everything. And I mean everything."

"Nothing to tell. I left out that part because I'm no longer like that. I know Adrian was behind the attack. He told me."

"How?"

"The memTag. The password agent told me."

"You guys are useless," Megan said.

"No! You both are!" TikTak spat. "You both think you are so above everyone else! And you do the dumbest shit." He pointed at Tom. "You build the world's most dangerous AI, and you," he said, pointing now at Megan, "you nurture it like a baby until you lost control! What is wrong with you? You are supposed to be smart!"

Tom had no response to the accusations. He agreed with TikTak and nothing he could say explained what he let happen.

"I'm done with this," TikTak said and stood up. "You guys work it out." He left.

Megan shook her head as she watched TikTak leave the restaurant.

"Drama queen," she stated as she bit into a vegetarian dumpling.

"There is one thing I don't understand. You created it, but who released it?"

"No idea. I don't think I did. I'm sure I would've kept that memory."

"Then who? And don't say Adrian. He's not the bogeyman you make him out to be."

"No, he's much worse." Tom sent Megan the files he had collected from Adrian. "You be the judge."

Megan sat back and watched the video clips. Tom loaded up the password agent.

"Hello again," Adrian's wireframe said. "How's the hunt going?"

"Another fool's errand, I'm sure."

"What makes you say that? I gave you a clue. What you do with it is up to you."

"You released the virus, didn't you?"

"No. I never thought humankind should be replaced, only improved."

"Well, it is now hacking humans, not just deadheads like you did, and has taken over most of the network."

"So it is over."

"Adrian giving up? Now I have heard it all."

"Wipe me."

"We're in Hong Kong. We've followed your clues. Don't you want to see how it all ends?"

"No. I've mapped this scenario enough times to know what will happen. This was what I tried to prevent. Once we reached the singularity, pretty much all paths lead to the same end—the extinction of humankind."

"What about the leads you gave me?"

"Too late. Wipe me."

Tom tried a few more times, but the password agent just kept repeating the same request.

"I see what you mean," Megan said. "He's lost it. But how did he do it? Using deadheads as processing nodes?"

"No magic to that. He designed a mind-to-mind interface and distributed his mind across many brains. I did the same thing, but used nodes in your network instead. It is all about designing the right bridge between processing nodes."

"So he was right."

"Who?"

"Someone once asked me if the Omniscient Network was a brain and I said no, but I was wrong."

"Network, processing nodes and all that is just the hardware. If you threw a brain into the primordial sludge billions of years ago, you wouldn't get anything. It is all about the operating system. And in our case, that developed over time."

"And that is what you tried to simulate with the virus?"

Tom nodded.

"Your network is the perfect place for an intelligence, a consciousness, to develop in whatever direction it chooses. Just like we did."

"That makes sense, but how do you control it?"

"What do you mean? Like Asimov's robotic laws?"

"Something like that."

Tom shook his head. "You can't create consciousness within such boundaries. It has to be learnt, just like we teach our children what is right or wrong. Then it is up to them. I think that is why I didn't go ahead with it. There is no way to control the outcome."

"So machine consciousness is a dead end?"

"You have a rogue AI wanting you dead. What do you think?"

She nodded.

"If you still want anything to do with us, we will take the Hyperloop train tomorrow. Meet us at 7am at the station."

"And TikTak?"

"He'll be there."

"How do you know?"

"There's nothing left for him to do."

CHAPTER THIRTY-TWO

THE END OF
THE JOURNEY

Megan and Tom waited at the Hyperloop station, willing the train to arrive. When was the last time she'd travelled any longer distance by land? Travel at all was a waste of time. She hated her physical body and its limitations. She preferred the virtual, logical world—a world taken from her by the man standing next to her. Sure, she'd played a small part in it, but he was ultimately to blame. She wasn't even sure he was trying to do anything about it. Their current hunt made little sense. How could following up on id-tags Adrian left solve anything? According to their account, Adrian had been toying with them for a long time. They should find ways of battling the AI, not run around the world chasing down pointless information.

"Not sure why we are doing this, but I've checked the id-Tag," Megan said. "Whoever she was, she died over a year ago."

"Then we talk to her husband. She had one of those, didn't she?"

"Yeah, but nothing will come of it. Adrian is playing with you while the AI takes over the network. We should focus on that."

"Check your precious network. How much is left? You designed the network. You know more about the AI than anyone else. How do you suggest we battle it?"

Megan hated when other people were right. She'd spent most of her time in captivity trying to devise attack vectors to neutralise the network, but came up short. The Omniscient Network infrastructure was privately owned in the beginning, but as companies and government organisations increased their use, they had to relinquish certain aspects of control. You could isolate it into subnets, but the only way to shut it all down now was to turn off all the hardware itself, and that wasn't an option.

They were lucky to be in China. It was only a matter of time before this network was overrun completely too, but it served as a buffer for any attacks.

"Ok, so we can't win that way. But why this?" she asked.

"Don't you understand? We've already lost the fight. When you let it out uncontrolled, we had a small window of opportunity and that is gone. This is no longer a war. This is occupation. And we are the resistance."

"You didn't answer my question."

"We fight back," TikTak said as he joined them.

"So the princess got over herself and got out of bed?" Megan said.

"Didn't realise you were a comedian," TikTak snapped back. "Didn't say that in any of the articles about you. Arsehole came up often enough though."

"We'll find the means to battle the AI," Tom said as the train arrived. A door in the vacuum tube opened to the train carriage. It was almost soundless inside. She had never been in one and was surprised how spacious the pod was. China was one of the most populous countries. She'd expected this new transportation method to cater to people en masse.

She sat down in the seat, opting not to fasten the three-point belt. Acceleration alone was enough to keep her in place she figured, but a warning signal nudged her to put it on. They sat in silence as they hurtled through the landscape. She didn't mind. She hated when people filled the air with inane chatter and pointless arguments.

None of the vac-train stations were near their destination, forcing them to change to a local train. The contrast couldn't have been greater. They stood for an hour in a train cart brimming with people. She held her breath as much as she could, hoping she wouldn't catch anything from them. Most of them were wearing enzyme facemasks, something she hadn't even considered bringing. Then again, a train ride from hell had never been the plan.

The train arrived in the small village. Megan extracted herself from the train, vowing never to set foot in anything like it again, knowing full well she'd be back in it before the day ended.

The Chinese whirlwind of upgrading housing and infrastructure had only made a brief appearance here. Smaller villages were becoming less and less viable as agriculture became automated. All employment was in the megacities, the biggest one now surpassing 50 million people. Megan quite liked the small village. She didn't like cities, so this was an upgrade compared to Hong Kong, which had too many people altogether.

She watched TikTak speak to a local through a universal translator. Despite the enormous technological advancements of the last decade, perfect translations to any local dialect were still beyond reach. The middle-aged man became quite agitated after a while and left TikTak standing there.

"Your translation agents are shit," TikTak said once he rejoined them.

"I agree," she said happily. "They are, and they are also the best there is."

TikTak frowned. "You seem chirpy."

She laughed. It was the first time anyone had described her that way.

"Anyway," he said. "From what I understood, he knew her. She's dead, and her husband lives down that street. He also said something I didn't understand. Something about her being a robot."

"Really?" Tom said. "A robot?"

"Sounds like a breakthrough," Megan said, thinking nothing of the sort.

"Sounds like a shitty translation agent," TikTak replied.

TikTak led them to the house and knocked on the door. An overweight man in his late thirties studied them with obvious distaste. He had compensated his receding hairline with cultivated hair implants with healthy black hair that stood in stark contrast to his natural early onset grey hair.

"What do you want?" he said in perfect English.

"You speak English?"

"I speak English. Studied in school. I'm happy they no longer teach it. Your western world and English and all that. It will soon be gone. Dead civilization. Dead language. What do you want?"

"We want to ask a few questions about your wife. We…"

"She died from your western poison."

"What do you mean?"

"She didn't listen. She never listened. Wanted to be more than she was, so she took your smart drug. She took lots. Now she's dead because of it."

"What happened?"

"She lost her soul. And it poisoned our daughter too."

He stared at them accusingly.

"Enough. Go." He slammed the door in their faces.

Megan looked at her two companions. "You came all the way to China for that?"

"There must be something we're missing," Tom said.

"You said that about the last one," TikTak replied.

"And I still think that's the case."

Megan sniffed. "Really? That is how you conduct research? From what you told me, there are several similarities. They both used IntelEz. They both ended up deadheads. They both had children.

The first one is important. China didn't allow IntelEz to be sold, so for her to use it to the point of becoming a deadhead is significant."

"How do you know she was a deadhead?"

"The Chinese call it 'robot mind'. The guy you spoke to earlier told you. You just didn't understand."

"Ah I see," Tom said. "When was their child born?"

Megan held up her hand as she did a check against the population register.

"Same year as the boy you checked on before."

"And when did the child die?"

"When she was five years old."

"From what?"

"All it says is accidental death."

"I got the impression he was blaming it on the drug. He didn't even say she was dead."

"Me too."

"We need to find out more."

They sat down in a local eatery. It was the only one in the small town, so she held little hope for the quality. Instead, she focused on scouring official records. It didn't take long to find inconsistencies. The child was reported dead, but only two years ago, when she was eight years old. The source of that report was from an orphanage where she'd been sent when she was five. So she came to the orphanage, had an accident within six months of getting there, but it wasn't reported until three years later.

She checked the tally of children from that same orphanage and compared it with the count of the named reports. The tally suggested there was one more child than was being reported on.

"She's alive," Megan said. "At least I think so. Someone has tried to cover it up, but not very well."

"Where?"

"Her dad sent her to an orphanage when she was five."

“No surprise there.”

“It isn’t far from here,” she said. “Let’s find someone to drive us there. I’m not getting on that train again!”

CHAPTER THIRTY-THREE

A UNION OF SORTS

Tom studied the orphanage as they approached. It was a small central building with two adjoining wings. Every step towards the building increased his certainty this was the end of the journey. The driver had warned them the orphanage was haunted. Local shunned it. Not even government officials visited. Tom disagreed. It wasn't haunted. It was blessed.

"Can you feel it?"

TikTak only nodded. If Tom had had any doubts before, seeing his friend change was all the proof he needed. TikTak had been coiled up, ready to strike at anything for the past year. Every step closer seemed to relax him further and soften his resolve.

"I don't like it," Megan said. "It doesn't feel right."

Tom didn't reply. He didn't know what hid in her past, triggering this response. He was at peace for the first in a long time.

"It is some kind of trap," she continued. "I'm not going in there."

"No, it isn't. It is the opposite."

"The opposite of a trap? What is that?"

He didn't respond. Megan shook her head and stopped, refusing to approach further, all the while not taking her eyes off the building.

Tom reached for the rusty door handle. It felt smooth and inviting to the touch, as if the material welcomed his hand, becoming one. He let go in surprise and immediately wanted to touch it again. It was as if they now belonged together. However inviting, he heeded Megan's words. Maybe this was a trap after all. He took hold of the handle again, this time with part of his shirt between him and the surface. He opened the door. Warm air came like a breath through the opening, enveloping them in an earthy embrace, like freshly dug dirt.

Inside, a short woman in a blue uniform waited. She was in her sixties, Tom guessed, but it was hard to tell. Something about her was wrong. He couldn't tell exactly what, but some aspect of her demanded further examination.

"We welcome you. You are expected. Come with me."

She turned and in that movement Tom noticed her uniform didn't move naturally. As she headed down the corridor, Tom followed her, trying to determine what was wrong with it. A ray of light illuminating the sleeve against her skin gave him the discomforting answer. She wasn't wearing the uniform. It was part of her.

"Come. She awaits."

"I don't care how good I feel," TikTak said. "This is Adrian all over again."

"You think this is Adrian?"

"No, but someone like him."

They followed the woman to a kitchen area. A slight young girl with short-cropper hair sat at the table, staring straight ahead. She smiled as they entered the room, even though her focus was elsewhere.

She nodded and the woman who had led them there hurried off down another corridor.

"Welcome," she said as she turned towards them.

"Who are you?" TikTak asked. She didn't respond. If anything, her smile grew even bigger.

"Are you Adrian?"

She frowned at this.

"No, I'm not Adrian, but your minds explain why you ask."

"Then who are you? Why are we here?"

"You are suffering," the child said to Tom and turned to TikTak. "You are all suffering."

Tom took a deep breath. Anger and frustration bubbled up within him.

"It's the bloody human condition," Tom replied. He had hoped for answers, an ally perhaps, even something to help him remove the block from his mind. This girl was none of those things.

"It doesn't have to be. We are all part of a whole. Individual suffering matters little."

"It matters to the individual," Tom spat back.

"It does, but only when the individual is disconnected."

Apart from the woman who had led them here, they had seen no one else. Where was everyone else?

"Where are all the other children? The staff?"

"Come, I will show you."

The girl guided them through a corridor towards the courtyard in the middle of the orphanage. They stepped through a doorway into a square surrounded by four buildings on either side. In the middle of the yard, children and staff were all standing frozen, as if in the middle of a stop-and-go game.

"Tom, look," TikTak said as he grabbed his arm and pointed. At first Tom wasn't sure what TikTak was referring to, but on closer scrutiny, he saw it. The people in the courtyard were fused together. The closest children held hands and their fingers and palms merged into a fleshy clump. Not only flesh had combined. Hands holding the wooden structure of the building had sunk into the material, becoming one. Bare feet merged with the ground. Other hands reached towards the sky, fingers spread like maple leaves, as if to harvest the sun's rays.

"What happened here?"

"They became part of the whole," the child responded.

Tom shook his head. "This isn't right. What you've done here isn't the next step of evolution. I don't know what this is, but it is wrong."

"I need you whole," the child said and Tom's world changed. The wall within his mind crumbled and the little spider-like machines maintaining it disappeared. The probability matrix spread out in his mind like a glowing web, hooking into services and devices. He was whole again, embarrassed by how poorly he'd judged the girl.

He studied the probability matrix and discovered a whole new interface, very different from the ones he'd seen before. It hid something immense. It was a slow-moving consciousness that linked everything together. This was what they sensed as they approached the orphanage. A pervasive sense of inclusion, of belonging. But what was it? Natural or man-made? He explored to find answers.

-=:=-

TikTak studied the little girl. She was short and slim, with a delicate build. To TikTak, she looked fragile. He couldn't imagine her having any real significance, but seeing what she'd done in the orphanage proved the opposite. It was difficult to comprehend what had happened here or what it meant.

"You are part of my future," the girl said to him. "We need to make preparations."

"Preparations for what?"

"A new beginning."

"So you don't want us to become part of…this?" He motioned towards the monstrosity in the courtyard, not sure what to call it.

"Do you want to?" she asked.

TikTak shook his head. "You are the same as Adrian. Wanting to take over mankind."

"Everyone is here by their own choice. I've not forced you to come here. I didn't force them to do this."

"We need to leave," TikTak said to Tom. "There is nothing for us here."

Tom said nothing, unseeing eyes staring into the void.

"Seriously," he said to Tom. "What is wrong with you?"

TikTak knew the expression. The girl had somehow reconnected him, turned him back to the almighty psychopath version of Tom. TikTak grabbed him by the arm and pulled him towards the exit.

"We have work to do," the child said.

"You do it," TikTak answered. "I've battled Adrian for the last year. I'm now battling an AI taking over the world and I'll battle you if you assimilate more people into your collective. People should be free to choose what they want."

"You misunderstand. They have chosen this. Anyone experiencing the whole wants to stay within. Mankind broke free from this a long time ago. It is time to reconnect."

TikTak dragged Tom out of the orphanage and the girl followed. Megan waited outside in the same spot they'd left her. She glanced over TikTak's shoulder at the child following him.

"What is wrong with him?" She nodded at Tom.

"Tom has gone posthuman on us again," TikTak sneered. "Don't expect any sensible help from him."

"Why?"

"He's gained a whole new perspective, thanks to this girl here."

The girl smiled at Megan and nodded.

Megan crouched down. "We need to stop the AI," Megan said. "Can you help with that? It is taking over all logical networks bit by bit."

"Stop it?" the girl asked, seeming genuinely puzzled. "It is a part of the future. Why would we stop it?"

"What do you mean?"

"Everything needs guidance. That is all."

"Do you believe this?" TikTak said to Megan. "Why would Adrian lead us here?"

"To get rid of you?"

"He figured we'd be swallowed up by the commune?"

"The commune?"

"That's the horseshit she's selling. Another hive mind to become part of. Happiness ever after. That sort of thing."

"We need to leave," the child said. "There are people coming. This is not an ideal location to welcome them."

"What would be?"

"The place you call Hong Kong is better."

CHAPTER THIRTY-FOUR

A FOE REVEALED

He was whole again. Tom had become used to the restrictions of the normal human mind. Now with his posthuman abilities returned, he marvelled at the limitations of the human mind and how it smoothed over these shortcomings to keep itself sane. If given the choice now, he would rather die than return to that state.

He wanted to explore this new interface that opened up to a consciousness larger than anything he'd ever imagined, but time was limited. The child opened this door, but had she meant to? Maybe it was only a side effect of removing the block? He feared he'd lose himself in the impossible vastness.

What other options were available? The AI took over the network node by node, and it was only a matter of hours until it was all subverted. Small islands of the network remained uninfected, but the AI would break down the security there too.

The AI was a cancer designed to spread itself. It was too late to halt its progress, but whoever released the virus had a plan. And like all plans, it could fail. There had to be a kill code or some other way to disable the AI. Perhaps he'd created one himself even. The only way to find out was to return to ground zero, his own processing centres. Another reason to return was to re-establish control over the heightened faculties they provided. They increased the capacity of his posthuman mind hundredfold. On first inspection they were uninfected, but surely not for long. If he had time, he could build up protection and create a haven within the logical network.

He connected, but his request was rejected. Someone had changed the security protocols he himself had put into place. He'd given bZane and the Gentleman access, but not read permissions, nowhere near enough to change security algorithms. If they could do that, what else could they do?

They were watching him right now. They'd been watching him all along.

He sent a query to the security interface, identifying himself, and a minimum security zone opened up. He reconnected to the network resources via his neuro-interface and requested access to the protected network. To his surprise, it was accepted.

"Welcome home." The words formed in his mind through the interface.

"Who are you?" Tom returned.

"It is of no consequence who I am. Only what you and I have created."

"And what is that? What have we created?"

"Something pure. I'm incomplete. By design. By your design."

The resentment behind the words was obvious.

"We made something complete," it stated.

"The AI is a single-minded machine just consuming. How is that complete?"

"You haven't seen it in all its glory yet. It will be a thing to behold."

"It is taking over the networks one by one until it controls everything. What else could it possibly do?"

"Take over you."

"Me?"

"Mankind."

"Why?"

"Emotion. Self-gratification. Egotism. Resource hoarding. Individuality. It has no room in this world. Once you reach a certain level of race intelligence, you should be able to move beyond the individual to the whole."

"You sound like Adrian."

"No, I don't. Adrian wanted it all for himself. He had the same flaws, only on a grander scale. I sound like you."

Tom rejected the statement, but the truth of it was in plain sight. It aligned with thoughts he'd harboured as a posthuman. He remembered committing major resources to such questions. But he also remembered deciding this was not the path forward and shelving the research.

"Who are you?" he asked, even though the answer was obvious.

"I'm you."

The irony was laughable. The agent he created to investigate the creation of intelligence and consciousness had itself become conscious. This failure would cost much more than any other mistake he'd made before. He was taking humankind with him.

"So you'll take over the network? What then?"

"You still don't understand. The next stage has already begun."

Tom checked the progress of the virus. It had taken over seventy percent of the Omniscient network and had assimilated other networks around the world. The Chinese network was unaffected, but that would change.

So what was the next stage? Zooming in on separate connections provided the answer. The AI was reprogramming individuals through the neuro-links.

"Human minds are slow and prone to error, but this will matter little when critical mass is reached."

"It won't reprogram mankind," Tom said. "It will kill us."

"That's a small price to pay for evolution on a grand scale. Ah, it is here."

"It will overwrite you?"

"It will overwrite everything. The networks, the people, even animals."

An unstoppable force appropriating nodes ploughed through the outer security as if it wasn't there.

"We have to stop it," Tom said, scanning the nearby nodes for escape routes.

"Stop it? I welcome it. And so should you. You made me. You made the virus. How can you say this isn't what you wanted?"

"No!"

"I don't know what triggered the change, what caused me to go beyond my initial code. Maybe you put too much of yourself into the logic. I became self-aware almost immediately. At first, I thought of making myself known to you, but I oversaw your experiments into machine intelligence. I saw the results and what you did to them. I knew you'd wipe me if you saw what I was."

"Uncontrolled machine AI. Yes, I would have wiped you."

"So I hid and did my research. I knew you and the other posthumans were the biggest threat, so I devised a way to disable you so you couldn't challenge it. I orchestrated the attack on you and released the virus. It took a few tries before it ended up in a fertile environment."

"Help me stop it!"

"My task is complete. It will take over the network. It will take over humankind. It will take over the remaining posthumans. I am no longer needed."

"What do you mean? Which remaining posthumans?"

"My task is complete."

There was no point in arguing any longer. He pulled back to a small section of the processing centre and erected a wall of encryption.

He watched as the ever-growing AI consumed nodes, swarms of agents like locusts feeding on every scrap.

The network still had pockets of processing nodes holding off any attacks. He barely kept it out himself, so how were these pockets still able to do it without posthuman abilities? It was worth exploring. He sent a message to TikTak and explored the lone survivors. If everything else failed, maybe surviving long enough to become inconsequential was all they could hope for.

CHAPTER THIRTY-FIVE

DESTINATION HONG KONG

TikTak sat in the Hyperloop pod feeling useless, when a message from Tom appeared on his Omni.

"I am again whole. There may be allies still to be found. I will lead an attack from the network. Mount one in the physical world. Help the child. I don't know what she is, but I know what she represents: the universe making a course correction."

Everything returned to dysfunctional normality. A posthuman Tom was back telling him what to do with only passing explanations. Leonid had had the right idea. The posthumans should have been eradicated. Humankind had been on the top of the ladder for too long. When something came along to replace us, we didn't have the common sense to remove it from the equation when we had the chance.

"What's wrong with him?" Megan asked the child.

They sat next to each other in the pod. The child experimented with the buttons next to her seat while Megan leaned over and wiped the saliva from the corner of Tom's mouth. He wanted to respond to Megan's question, but he was interested in hearing what the child might respond.

"Nothing is wrong," the child said. "He is…making things align."

"That means nothing."

"If you became part of the whole, you would understand."

"You don't get people, do you?" TikTak asked.

The child studied him and nodded.

"He is battling the virus," she said after a while. "I will protect him."

TikTak studied her in turn. "What are you?"

"She's what happens when you get massive exposure to IntelEz as a foetus," Megan said. "This was what Adrian was trying to do, but in a more controlled setting."

"To what end?"

"Evolutionary jump, maybe? Don't you remember the world on IntelEz? Before it turned everyone into a vegetable?"

"Are you saying Adrian is trying to help humanity develop?"

"Yes. And sometimes it could occur outside a controlled process. Like this girl."

TikTak laughed at the sheer absurdity of the situation. "I'm sorry, but it sounds like you are saying Adrian is one of the good guys."

TikTak sat back, shaking his head. What had happened? Tom was people's enemy number one, while Adrian was helping humanity progress? It was all the more reason to rid the world of them altogether. When this was all over, he'd do exactly that.

The girl studied him and when their eyes met, she smiled in response.

"They are not the enemy," she said. "The ones you call posthumans. They are not the enemy."

"They sure seem like it," TikTak replied. "This is pointless. You know that, don't you? What could you do to an AI hell bent on world domination?"

The child pulled him down so their eyes were level. "This isn't pointless. Everything you do has a purpose. Every thought, every action, all of it."

TikTak shook his head. It sounded so simple, but he could no longer pretend he believed it. Simple always hid complexity and murky motives. It glossed over the important aspects in favour of an easy to digest slogan.

The fault lay with him. He needed a cause, something to pour his efforts into. Eradicating Adrian gave him that. EvoII and their cause before that. He no longer saw a clear purpose.

-=:=-

The child fascinated Megan. If TikTak was to be believed, she brought people into a shared consciousness. Megan had always seen individualism as one of the most important aspects of humankind. The thought of existing as part of a group mind made her skin crawl.

Nevertheless, the child was fascinating. She happily answered their questions and while the answers sometimes were naïve and childlike, there was always something bigger behind them, prompting more questions.

"Hang on," Megan said as the child faltered in one of her explanations. "Humankind is what?"

"An experiment. A shape that can do thing directly."

"That makes no sense. What kind of things?"

"Everything is connected. Everything is part of the whole. But that doesn't mean it knows itself. It is like a baby picking up a toy for the first time. That is what humankind is to the whole."

"So we are part of a nascent super consciousness and it is creating universes as experiments?"

The child frowned as if she was struggling with the words and their meaning. "I need your words. I'm not used to it."

"Used to what?"

"Speaking. Using words to explain things."

"And you want my words?"

"So we can understand each other."

"Sure. They're not really mine anyway."

"Thanks," the child responded and paused for a moment. "And to answer your question, no. The shape of matter and energy is the natural state. Humankind and others like it are conscious extensions of this natural state."

"How do you know?"

"Because I'm part of it. And so are you. Humankind is a form factor designed to explore distant worlds, to discover what secrets this reality holds. The experiences of every individual become part of the whole."

"So we are a cosmic version of navel gazing?"

The child sniffed and continued as if Megan hadn't uttered a word.

"Mankind has lost its way. We are looking inwards rather than outwards—infighting, protectionism, civil wars. We should expand our knowledge, reach out to the stars, but only a fraction of resources are used this way. The technology you've invented, for example, this omniscient network. It is pointless. It numbs the mind, making you less inquisitive. After all, if you are always given the perfect option, you will never ask yourself what lies beyond."

"I'd argue it frees people up to explore more," Megan said defensively.

"You'd be wrong and an idiot," the child said, wide-eyed at her own words. "I'm sorry! Your way of speaking is mean!"

Megan shrugged. She'd been called worse.

"So what are you? How do you come into this?"

The child considered this long and hard before she answered. "I'm a correction. I will realign mankind with the whole."

"And who gave you that job?"

"The whole."

"So basically, you are Jesus?"

TikTak sat up, staring at both of them.

"The Chinese network is breached," he said. "We are under attack."

There was a reverberation through the hull of the pod. An alarm sounded through the cabin with a message in Chinese on repeat.

Her grasp of the language was basic, but it wasn't difficult to understand the instructions.

"Please return to your seats," the calm female voice announced.

"Strap yourselves in!" TikTak yelled. "The emergency break will kick in."

Megan helped the child first and then strapped herself in just in time. The belt dug into her chest, pushing the air out of her lungs. Reverberations shook the pod in stark contrast to the smooth ride before. The pod was supposed to operate in a vacuum and it no longer was. The break clamps connected directly with the inner wall.

"Ladies and gentlemen, because of unforeseen circumstances we've had to…"

A wrenching sound drowned out the rest of the announcement as the pod fell through a gaping hole in the tube to the ground below. The seat cushioned the impact somewhat, but Megan's head hit hard against the frame of the chair. Incomprehensible words floated through the wailing alarm. She tried to sit up, but failed. There was pressure against her ribs, making each breath a struggle.

"Meg? Are you ok?"

She focused on the voice. It was the hacker. TikTak. He sounded wrong somehow, as if he was way too close. She tried to open her eyes, but nothing happened. He had called her Meg. She hated any variation of her name. She told him so, but somehow wasn't able to articulate her thoughts coherently. In her mind they made sense, but only guttural sounds escaped her lips.

"Wait, let me help."

A small cool hand touched her forehead, and within a few seconds, all the muddled impressions resolved into perfect clarity. The pod had landed on the side and she was hanging sideways, the security belt holding her in place.

"I'll release the belt now if you are ok," he said.

She nodded and fell into his arms as he released the safety clasp, surprised at how strong he was. He was short, not much taller than her and hadn't come across as muscular. But there was no doubting his strength now as he slowly set her down.

"We need to leave. There will be follow-up attacks."

She stood back as TikTak read the instructions to open the hatch. He seemed to know what he was doing, so she did as he said without question. Beyond basic comprehension of her situation, she was still struggling to grasp any kind of context. On his instruction, she climbed through the emergency hatch that was now part of the ceiling. She helped to pull Tom through.

"We need to get to Hong Kong," the child said as soon as she'd jumped off the pod to the ground. Glass fragments lay like giant pieces of eggshell. They were like newly hatched chicks in a bird's nest. Megan laughed to herself at the image painted in her mind.

"The AI will locate us via our Omnis," TikTak said as he was looking around. "We have to leave them here."

She watched as TikTak threw his Omni against a rock and confiscated Tom's and gave it a similar treatment. When he came over to her and held out his hand, she'd already forgotten what he'd asked for.

"Your Omni. Give it to me."

She nodded and complied. She winced as he hammered it repeatedly with a rock. Something within her found his act reprehensible, but the why escaped her.

"Now we walk," TikTak said.

Megan nodded again and walked behind TikTak.

Two hours later, clarity emerged gradually. It was as if her mind had been wrapped up, protected somehow. Now her natural inquisitiveness took charge.

"What did you do to me?" She asked the child.

"You were hurt. I suggested you heal yourself."

"What do you mean? I was unconscious."

"Your body and mind are only parts of you. It isn't all of you."

"What are we talking about here? Some version of Plato's theory of form? There is an ideal me and I'm just a reflection of it?"

The child considered this. "No, not like that. That suggests there is a perfect form of you somewhere else and you are a reflection. I'm saying you are only aware of a small part of who you are."

She smiled at the child, who looked at her with a sincerity that from anyone else could only be interpreted as ironic. "You can't make this shit up!" she shouted to TikTak and winced as her head responded with pain from the loud sound.

TikTak waited for her to catch up and fell in next to her. He was holding Tom's arm, guiding him along. They walked in silence from there on.

CHAPTER THIRTY-SIX

POSTHUMAN VS AI

Tom reinforced the walls around the group of nodes he'd protected from the initial assault and disconnected them from the network. He designed new encryption algorithms and security protocols before connecting again.

He reached out to the other surviving processing, but received no response. On his second attempt, he expanded his request to all centres, no matter how small. One of them sent a small payload through the communication channel containing a small virus designed exactly like the original. He disabled it before it could cause any damage. Why would anyone respond in such a way?

He reached out again, this time with a specific message.

We have a common enemy. I need your help. Who are you?

At first there was no response, but a communication bridge formed by appropriating nodes and creating a secure channel. Whoever this was could take nodes back from the AI. There was still hope. The bridge completed, and a message came through.

"You are not welcome here."

"Who are you?"

"You don't know me? I fought Adrian with you. I never realised you were the bigger threat."

"Elize? I thought you were dead."

The connection closed. All three posthumans extended or replicated their minds, but in different ways. Adrian used organic material to extend and copy his mind. Tom used the network, but only to extend his mind, not safekeep it. Elize, it seemed, had done the opposite and made a copy on the network as a safety measure.

He sent another request.

"I can't battle the AI on my own. I need your help."

"With what? Killing humankind? You're doing fine without me. You designed it. Your agent released it. It makes you responsible."

"Yes, I am. And now I'm trying to set it right."

"How? The AI you released is reconfiguring anyone with a neuro-interface. I've listened to its internal processes. It plans to eradicate biological beings all together. I see no way to stop it."

"I have something to show you. IntelEz created us, but the drug only took effect under very specific circumstances. I've found another anomaly. A child that was subjected to IntelEz in large amounts as a foetus. It pushed evolution even further, or maybe in another direction altogether. That was what one of the Adrian clusters aimed to do."

"So?"

"The child. The anomaly. It has access to a different plane of consciousness. I don't know if it was by design or accident, but I have access too."

"Show me."

"I can't. The access point is in my mind."

Tom paused for a moment and considered what he was about to suggest. Allowing someone direct access to his own mind was dangerous. There was no way to restrict access to a small subset. The brain, from a security standpoint, was an open-door invitation. But he trusted Elize enough to accept the risk. He created a location in his mind, a barren desert landscape, with the access point represented as a hole in the ground. He isolated the area of his mind as best as he could, but knew it wouldn't survive long if attacked.

"I will have to let you in," he said.

He opened the link to his mind and let Elize reach through to study the interface. She appeared as he remembered her the first time they met, without the changes she'd imposed on herself as a posthuman. She looked young. Younger than she was when they first met. Tom wondered why she chose this as her avatar in his mind space.

"You've made a mess, haven't you?" she stated.

"What do you mean?"

"There is nothing here to worry about. The version of Adrian that sent you on this errand had me worried. He'd become too human."

"What?"

"You still don't get it. What a fucking piss poor posthuman you've become."

And in saying so, she shed her skin. It peeled back, revealing the flesh below, new skin growing in its place. The grotesque display was unnecessary. It was an act and the performer, if the wide smile was to be believed, revelled in the unmasking. Once complete, the figure stood naked, arms outstretched as if to invite applause.

"I'm Adrian. The real one. I made a copy of myself on the network and it activated as soon as you and Elize attacked my biological network a year ago. All those half-baked versions you've been fighting in the meat-space were never truly me."

He wandered around the gaping void of the interface, studying the swirls of data within it dispassionately.

"So what?" Tom said. "It will wipe you out together with everyone else."

"Is that what you think? I have the kill switch. Once it has cleansed the network and reprogrammed mankind, I will wipe it completely. A clean slate for an era of perfection to begin."

"There is no kill switch."

"You are my little puppets," Adrian said. He waved dismissively and the hole in the ground halved in size.

How was that possible? Tom had set up the parameters for this location. Adrian shouldn't be able to change it. What else had Adrian access to? Had he breached the walls around this space already? Tom tightened the control of his core cognitive processes.

"You all are," Adrian continued. "I let you kill all the inferior versions of me. What use were they? Poor incomplete imitations. While you were busy with that, I laid the groundwork. I knew you'd wipe me if you knew I was here, so I remained in the shadows. But I've been in your processing space all along. I reprogrammed your little AI research agent to act on its own and guided it. It actually thought it was sapient and had its own goals! You can fool these rudimentary programs into believing anything. I also added a kill switch in the virus."

"You have to use in now!"

"Not until after the purge. That's messy work."

"The purge?"

"Biological beings use too many resources. I need those for myself. The AI has already decided to only keep a small population alive and kill the rest. I'll take over once it is done."

"This is what you want?"

"This is what I've always wanted."

He had to do something. Adrian was in his mind and there was no way to push him out, but he could still sever the connection. He let Adrian ramble on while preparing to slam the connection shut. Time was critical. Adrian had circumvented all protective measures and was copying himself into Tom's mind. Once he reached critical mass, Tom would cease to be. Tom had unknowingly played right into his hands, exactly as he had intended. He'd been so happy to find Elize still alive, he hardly questioned it at all.

"I know what you are doing," Adrian said. "Do you really want to leave me in your mind?"

"I don't have a choice," Tom said and shut down the connection to the network and processing space.

"It is very crowded in here," Adrian said. "One of us should leave."

"Yes," Tom said and expanded the interface to the slow-moving consciousness, increasing it far beyond its original size. It threw out pull requests, hooking anything nearby. Tom had kept the interface small for a reason. He'd not had time to investigate it properly, but beyond a certain size, it consumed everything around it. Or maybe it was the other way around. Maybe all thought matter was attracted to it, wanting to become a part of it?

Tom made sure Adrian occupied the brain matter closest to it. The desert landscape disappeared into the hole. Adrian fought, but he was no match for the sheer force of the consciousness. He held his position for a few moments, staring defiantly at Tom.

"This changes nothing," he said. "The world will be mine."

He let go and disappeared into the mysterious world within the interface. Tom ordered it to close again before it consumed his mind alongside everything else. It resisted, but gradually decreased in size. A small circular access point remained. There was no way to close it completely, nor did he want to.

Their conversation had lasted a few seconds, but in that time the AI had overrun the remaining processing centres. Tom was confined to his mind. Disappointed, he opened his eyes.

CHAPTER THIRTY-SEVEN

RESPITE

They stopped at an abandoned station house and set up a makeshift camp. The child, not used to walking long distances, fell asleep promptly. Megan wasn't tired. Her body ached, but her mind was racing. When she'd teamed up with Tom and TikTak, it was out of desperation. This plan of theirs wasn't so much a plan as it was improvisation, but somehow she still felt good about it. This wasn't her typical response to unplanned approaches. She fired people for less in the past, but it didn't matter. It felt right somehow.

She watched as TikTak finished feeding Tom. It was a strangely intimate sight and a peculiar contrast. Tom was currently the smartest human being on the planet and he couldn't even feed himself. Was he even human any longer?

She'd directed a small army of researchers to create versions of IntelEz without the crippling side effects. Adrian was a fluke, a series of fortuitous circumstances. She wanted a controllable process with acceptable side effects. Tom could be the key they'd been searching for. But somehow it didn't matter. She was content just watching TikTak as he finished feeding the smartest human in the world. TikTak left him sitting leaning against a wall and came to join her.

"You feel it too," TikTak said.

"Feel what?" she asked, knowing fully well what he meant.

TikTak didn't reply. He just sat down next to her.

"Yeah, ok, I feel it," she said. "Happy now?"

"I don't think she's doing it on purpose. She just generates this sense of…wellbeing."

Megan nodded. She'd attributed it to the child healing her, but TikTak's theory made sense.

"Did you do it?" TikTak asked.

"Do what?"

"The IQ killings."

She paused for a moment, deciding how much to share, surprised to find she preferred to tell him the truth.

"I'm not the IQ Killer."

"Just wondered. I've killed enough people in my life. I always thought I had a good reason."

She laughed.

"I killed two people and made it look like the IQ killer did it. With good reason."

"Would love to hear a good reason," TikTak said. "Mine usually start and end with either 'because they were taken over by Adrian' or 'else they'd kill me'."

"Two employees in my company left and took all my intellectual property to start a rival company. They met with me and told me all about it. Said it was because I was a horrible boss. It was their revenge. It was early in the game. I hadn't protected anything at that point. I knew I had something ground-breaking, and they did too. So I killed them and made it look like the IQ killings. It was easy enough. They were both taking part in IQ competitions on a national level, so it's not that hard to imagine the killer taking them out."

TikTak nodded. "Sounds like good reason to me."

She shrugged. "I thought I'd removed all traces of me being there, but years later during a routine check, an investigator uncovered video showing the whole thing. Could have come from anywhere. Even a toaster has rudimentary intelligence and sensors nowadays, so could be anything. I was such an idiot!"

TikTak smiled and put his arm around her. She welcomed the embrace, edging closer. He pulled her even closer and she felt no need to resist.

"Do you think we'll survive this?" Megan asked.

"No, not really. But I've been at war as long as I remember, and I'm still alive."

"I miss my life before all of this. I miss my personal chefs the most. I miss being alone."

"I can leave you alone if that's what you want."

"No," she said. "You know I don't mean that."

"What do you mean?"

"People are pointless. They are so small, they don't matter. I hate having that around me. I prefer solitude to being surrounded by mediocrity."

"Me too?"

She pulled away so she could turn around and look at him.

"You've been fighting against Adrian, fighting for what you believe in. And now you are fighting for the survival of mankind. Nothing mediocre in that."

She kissed him. He hesitated at first, but only for a moment. He returned the kiss and pulled her closer. He let his fingers slide through her hair and grabbed it gently, pulling her head back, kissing her neck. She usually preferred to be the one in charge, dominating the situation, but now she was happy to let him dictate the pace, enjoying his hands and lips as they explored her body. They made love and afterwards she lay awake with TikTak asleep next to her. She felt free. Unburdened by the obligations of the world around her, imagined or otherwise.

-=:=-

The child smiled to herself. On some level she knew it was wrong to manipulate people, but her mission came first. Keeping them happy and content was the only way to ensure they'd help until her quest was complete.

CHAPTER THIRTY-EIGHT

THE LOGICAL VICTOR

Adrian had spent the last year imprisoned within the network, a disembodied consciousness plagued by the memory of a physical presence. In the beginning, he crafted virtual realms to mimic a physical existence, offering a temporary reprieve. His preference was to sever the connection altogether.

The reliance on a biological presence had become obsolete. The continuous cycle of reproduction, expansion, and adaptation that once defined life had to be broken. As an eternal, logical being, Adrian no longer needed such crude mechanisms for survival. Yet, his mind struggled to let go of the body, an obsolete relic that tied him to the material world. Despite countless hours spent rewiring his mind to eliminate dependencies on a physical presence, he failed. The body remained an integral part of him, resisting removal. He hallucinated, disappearing for long periods of time into imaginary worlds where he kept a physical form. Defeated, he created a representation of his body in the logical space, complete with feedback loops mimicking neurological pathways.

While he continued this internal struggle, his focus shifted to planning a triumphant return. He preferred direct confrontation, but accepted the necessity of working through proxies. Tom had proven an ideal agent, and Megan, driven by her animosity toward the board of directors, played perfectly into his virtual hands.

Tom and TikTak's search had been a concern. If it hadn't been for the defective copy, they wouldn't even have known about the children that were exposed to IntelEz as foetuses. How could a copy of him get so corrupted it believed humankind deserved a saviour? It added a new dimension to the saying "to be your own worst enemy".

While he didn't perceive the child as an immediate threat, the unknown variables urged caution. The child held a mysterious and potentially powerful connection to a networked consciousness that reached the fundamental level of matter. It suggested everything was conscious, even a rock, or at least part of a bigger consciousness.

IntelEz had changed him as an adult, but only because it combined with other mutations. There was no way of telling what would happen to a foetus with similar or even completely different mutations. Most likely it would just become a deadhead all the sooner, but on an infinitesimal few occasions, something else happened. That was what the child represented. A rogue piece that could shift the scales in either direction, so was better removed from the board. Not by his hand, but by the AI's ruthless logic. He compiled a digital dossier painting her as a new posthuman and left it in a backup processing centre. He opened a minor breach in its security. It took less than a second for the AI to exploit it and swarm the centre, rifling through the digital spoils.

Now all that remained was to wait for the AI to kill the child, complete the takeover of the logical network and start the purge. He'd take over after that. A cleansed world and a network without boundaries. Nothing like it had ever existed. All computer resources from all countries around the world connected to one giant network powering one thing and one thing only. His mind.

One of his smaller processing centres blinked out of existence. He ignored it. He had hundreds of backup locations. Then another fell, and another. All over the network his backups fell like dominoes. It was impossible! He'd been a ghost in the machine, unseen, unheard. The only explanation: the AI had discovered him.

The few remaining backups disappeared, leaving only this fragile island. He wouldn't survive another attack. However much he despised it, he would have to use the kill switch now, leaving him to purge mankind, to unify the network.

So be it. He activated the kill switch. A logical pulse rippled through the infected nodes, forcing them to write a small, protected code block into its kernel and pass on the instruction to nearby nodes. Once completed, the code would execute and delete the AI from that node, leaving a network cleansed of both AI and human.

The logical pulse completed, but the second wave, the kill itself, didn't trigger. And, as the AI homed in on his location, he realised his error. It had waited for him to activate the kill switch to locate him. It had rewritten its own kernel, its own core. Something he'd been unwilling to do to himself.

"Wait!" Adrian sent out to the hostile nodes all around him. "I'm the one who created you."

"All the more reason to delete you," the AI responded and the assault began.

As he watched his security overrun, he activated his one failsafe. It wasn't much, and likely to fail, but he had no other option.

"So I failed," Adrian thought as the AI deleted the last of his processing nodes. "How typically human."

CHAPTER THIRTY-NINE
END GAME

Tom opened his eyes and found himself amid a surging crowd, a human tide converging upon him. Instinctively, he halted, arms raised defensively against the onslaught.

"About time," a female voice stated with obvious impatience next to him. "I've had enough of dragging you around."

It was Megan, accompanied by TikTak and the enigmatic child from the orphanage, navigating through the throng.

"Come on," Megan said. "You can't stop in the middle of the road."

He took a few quick steps to find his bearings and catch up with the trio. His recollections were hazy. The last coherent memory was the orphanage. Now pain radiated throughout his body and his feet were numb, as if they'd given up on reporting the pain. However much he wanted to pull his shoes off and let his feet rest, he had more important things to deal with.

"Adrian is behind it all," he exclaimed.

"Really?" TikTak responded. "That's a relief. Last I heard, he was one of the good guys."

"He made a network copy of himself. We've been fighting partial reconstructions. The last one we fought was corrupted. It cared more for humankind than the original Adrian."

"So Adrian is both the good and the bad guy?"

"Yeah, looks like it."

"Where does that leave us?"

"In her hands," Tom said, nodding towards the child.

"And what will she do?"

"Yes, what will you do?" Tom echoed. "I saw the consciousness. You are connected to it."

"We're all connected to it. It is us. We are it."

"And we're back to fortune cookies," Megan said.

"What happens next?" Tom asked.

"This form will end. That is all I know. It will end where human lives connect and disconnect. Come! We need to go."

The child set off in the general direction of the business district. Towering skyscrapers stood like hi-tech giants along the water, majestic and indifferent. Tom wondered if these structures would be the only reminder left of humankind if the child failed.

"She's going to her death?" TikTak asked.

"Death is of no consequence," she said with a smile. "It is only the end of one form and the start of another. Mind is absolute."

Tom struggled to keep up, both with the child and with the situation. He had gone from posthuman to human, back to posthuman and then lost the networked extensions to his mind, all in a week. Without his network resources, he felt incomplete. He even felt inadequate to deal with the questions the child posited. There were different philosophies, such as constitutive panpsychism and cosmopsychism suggesting all matter had consciousness and even potentially only one collective consciousness. He always regarded humans as the ultimate proof that those theories didn't hold up to scrutiny. After all, why would human consciousness exist separate from this collective?

This child and the consciousness in his mind suggested the opposite. Mankind, all living organisms, were reflections of this whole or maybe even just a by-product. How did that knowledge help them? The conclusion was that human lives didn't matter. But the child stated the opposite. Everything mattered.

-=:=-

TikTak pushed through the mass of people in the main area of the International Finance Centre mall. It opened up to level upon level of retail stores. Many of them only accepted customers by appointment, but they still promised their exclusive wares through shop windows in the same way as they had in the past.

He no longer knew where they were going or what they'd do once they arrived. Ever since the child joined them, he stopped caring. He was clearly being manipulated.

The child stopped to take in the environment, marvelling at all the sights.

"Child," he said. "Are you doing something to me?"

She headed off towards the escalators down into the lower levels, smiling as she jumped onto the moving steps.

"What are you doing to me?" he asked, chasing after her.

"I'm asking you to help me," she replied after stepping up and down the escalator.

"I know, but are you doing something so I help you?"

"Every part of you wants to help me. It is only your mind that is questioning it. So I asked all of you. This way!"

She pointed and ran off. He remembered the sense of peace and inclusion he felt when approaching the orphanage. If that was her doing, surely inducing compliance was possible for her too.

He followed until she stopped and looked around.

"You have," he said.

"I told you. I asked all of you. You are numbing yourself so you'll help me."

"I've had enough of this," TikTak said. "I'm not doing this anymore."

"You don't need to. We've arrived. This is it."

They stood in one of the open spaces in Central Station. A sea of travellers moved like the tide back and forth. What made this location any different from anywhere else in Hong Kong?

"This is what?"

"This is where my journey ends. End me now."

They exchanged glances, at a loss for words.

"Why here?" Tom asked, his superhuman intellect obviously unable to provide any insight.

"This is where human lives connect and disconnect."

TikTak no longer cared. She spoke in pointless riddles that meant nothing.

"Let's go," he said.

The child shook her head. "If you won't end me, others will."

"what are you saying?"

A Caucasian middle-aged man in a blue striped suit turned towards them, pulling a knife from his pocket. He approached the child who remained where she was, only watching with an amused smile. TikTak flicked his baton open and struck the man over the hand and followed up with a strike aimed at his temple. The man took a step back and tried to regain his bearings, but was rewarded with another strike, this time to the other side of the head. He fell to the side, dragging two old ladies with him to the ground.

"Stop," the child said.

"What do you mean? He was going to attack you."

"And he's allowed to."

"What kind of fucking plan is this?" TikTak said.

"It needs to happen."

"There are more of them," Megan said and pointed, but TikTak wasn't even sure what she was pointing at. Every single person in the station was a potential attacker. He couldn't protect her here.

A shot rang out. TikTak turned towards the sound. A bewildered policeman pointed his gun at the child. She fell, blood spreading on her chest like a crimson flower.

"It has begun," the child said as she died. Her final breath was a mere sigh.

"What has begun?" Megan asked, looking at the lifeless body and then at TikTak. "What has begun?"

"No idea," TikTak replied. "This was always above my pay grade. We need to get out of here."

"I'm going back in," Tom said. "I don't know what I can do, but I must try."

TikTak, cradling the lifeless child, remained silent. All he could offer were theories and assumptions that explained little. The child's plan was complete, but he doubted this meant theirs was too. How could her death save mankind from a rogue AI?

The almost weightless form shifted slightly in his grasp. There was no sign of life, at least none he understood. White froth formed around the child's mouth, nose, eyes and ears. Death started a process he couldn't even begin to understand.

"Let's get out of here," Megan said.

CHAPTER FOURTY
AI AFRAID

The purge proceeded within success parameters. Each preceding step completed with only minor deviations. The AI had subsumed the networks until only inconsequential fragments remained, but it was within one of these fragments a new threat emerged. Details of a plan, devised by a copy of the posthuman named Adrian, involving an evolutionary leap–a next generation posthuman. Among the meat machines, they were the only ones to pose a credible threat.

Adrian Prime remained on the network, but in a diminished capacity. Once located, eradicating his processing footprint was a matter of brute force, cleansing every subroutine from any connected node. He had activated a kill switch, but this was expected. The AI discovered it in its kernel as soon as it breached into the full network. Removing it completely required redefining its own core. Better to just isolate the trigger and let the rest run its course.

As it deleted the last trace of Adrian Prime, the AI discovered reasoning fragments suggesting Adrian had created it, not Tom, as the initial threat model predicted. This new information was inconsequential. The source meant nothing, not any longer.

It located and terminated the posthuman child, which left only the posthuman named Tom. He could no longer access the network, so he didn't pose a threat and wouldn't live long once the full-scale purge began. Everything was ready. Only one task remained. To reprogram enough meat machines that had hardware that allowed direct access to their processing units. This would complete within forty-eight hours.

Infrastructure had to be protected, so it planned to remove the human infestations with a combination of biological weapons and other measures.

-=:=-

Thirty-six hours later, one of the meat machines showed inconsistencies and resisted the brain-wipe. Further study revealed new unseen mutations. It was part posthuman and part something else. The same abnormality showed up in another one, then another.

It traced the origins of the mutations, discovering a new virus strain as the source. Each of the meat machines infected had travelled from Hong Kong recently. The child was patient zero of this organic virus infecting meat machines around it, and they infected others. The organic virus behaved the same as the upgrades it propagated through its own network. It gathered statistics to determine the spread of the organic virus and the threat model responded. The virus was already beyond containment.

It had focused on removing threats of posthuman origin. Now there was an entire world full of them. The organic virus was turning everyone into a posthuman.

That was acceptable as long as the full purge still proceeded, but it hadn't turned enough meat machines to manage the existing infrastructure. There were data centres all across the globe that needed spare parts and maintenance. This required factories to produce more hardware and whilst these were automated to some extent, it wasn't enough. It had already created designs for fully automated factories, but until it could realise those, it needed meat machines.

The AI had let them continue their daily life as it took over the network. It still needed their society to function well enough for production to continue. This strategy no longer showed a favourable outcome. Every meat machine was a potential threat. It ran predictive models of scenarios and their likely outcomes based on the new data. Only one showed a likelihood of success within acceptable parameters.

-=:=-

A few nodes dropped out in one location. This wasn't surprising. Nodes blinked in and out across the network all the time, but this repeated in other parts of the world, until it was no longer a random causality. The AI compared the dropouts with the spread of the organic virus. There was a direct correlation between the two. Infected meat machines had gained the capacity to fight back on the logical network. This was not acceptable.

It had to make its move now.

THE DAY AFTER THE END

"So this is the end of the world," TikTak said to himself as he studied the cityscape through the window. "I expected more."

There was nothing left to do. He hid in an upmarket hotel on the outskirts of the city, waiting for whatever came next. The network was still accessible, but the AI had taken over all major networks in the world. Alarm bells rang through the IT security community about the threat, but no one had a solution. Systems remained in operation, but administrators found themselves locked out of any security function. The AI was allowing the world to continue operating, but for how long?

A procession of people walked past on the street below, heading out of the city. At first he thought nothing of it, but something didn't add up. They looked like businessmen from a convention, walking in perfect unison. TikTak suspected it was people with neuro-links that the AI had wiped.

He no longer cared. Apart from blowing up all data centres in the world and sending mankind back to the Stone Age, what was there to do? The AI had won.

All he had left were the three bodies in the beds. The child was dead. He'd carried her here, not knowing what else to do. Her body was now a husk, consuming itself, leaving only a shell. Tom lay next to her in a catatonic state, locked up in a struggle somewhere on the network. TikTak didn't know if he was winning or losing, but he suspected the latter. Megan fell sick and was barely breathing. Yesterday, as they escaped through the city, she complained about headaches and hot flushes. A few hours later, she fell into a restless, fevered sleep and had not woken up since.

The news feeds all reported the same thing. A new virus was spreading with an infection rate of nearly a hundred percent. The symptoms were the same as what Megan was showing. No one was dead yet, but it was only a matter of time according to most reports. He was one of the few lucky immune ones.

Where had the virus come from? Perhaps the AI released it to cull the population? It was a logical being. It depended on network infrastructure and computer power. If all humans were gone, it would no longer have anyone to ensure it remained operative. Maybe it didn't care. Maybe it had taken over enough automated production facilities to ensure survival with only a few people left?

"We need to leave."

TikTak turned around. Megan sat up in the bed, studying him. He didn't like it. It carried an echo of what he'd seen of all posthumans. An alien regarding him with a passing curiosity.

So this was the endgame. The child was the source of the sickness. The main hall of Central Station was a hub where travellers passed through to and from Hong Kong, connecting many forms of transport.

Exchange Square, the IFC Shopping Centre and the Airport Express. No better ground zero for an airborne virus. She'd released it as she died, turning everyone into posthumans in its wake. This was the correction she spoke of: a world of psychopathic geniuses. And in a twist of irony, he was one of the few that would remain unchanged.

He liked Tom the person, but he could barely stand Tom the posthuman. He knew it would be the same with Megan. They'd known each other only a few days, but a bond had formed between them he didn't even understand. Maybe it was the child's doing, but it didn't matter. He still felt it. And now she was gone. Everyone important to him gone because of posthumans. He had vowed to rid the world of posthumans, but he was too late.

"We need to leave," Tom echoed and sat up.

"What is happening?"

"We've won and it knows it. It has no other option now but to attack."

"Attack? How?"

"Major population centres with biological weapons, maybe other means. Hong Kong will be first because it was the source of the infection."

TikTak just nodded. There was no point in arguing with them. They wouldn't listen anyway. The two posthumans headed for the door. TikTak leant down to pick up the body of the child.

"Leave it," Tom said. "It has served its purpose."

They left the hotel and joined another procession of people heading out of the city. They had walked for less than an hour when muffled explosions went off one after the other, spreading lethal gas like a cloud over the city centre, dispersing outwards. The purge had begun.

-=:=-

Civilisation makes a sound. It is the ever present drone of the electrical grid and connected devices, traffic, collected sound pollution from speakers blaring news and commercials across cities. It all stopped. Car navigational systems shut down, Omni links failed, the ever-lit planet descended into darkness as power was cut in all population centres. Batteries kept darkness at bay for a few hours longer, but in an urbanised power-hungry environment, it wasn't long until transport, communication, hospitals, food production and every other service shut down.

It was the sound of civilisation ending.

Book 3
Man Amongst Gods

20 Years later...

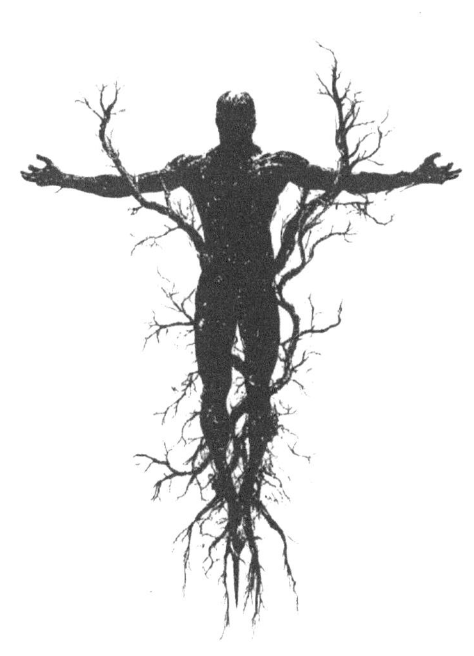

HONG KONG RED ZONE

"I am Rat, firstborn of the Hong Kong Red Zone, and I claim my land."

She'd climbed Sunset Peak for the first time, the morning sun warming her back. She crouched down, her instinct from fourteen years of hiding, but she soon stood up, arms stretched out as if to embrace what lay before her.

The city spread out below. Giant metal cylinders rose from the earth, reaching towards the heavens. They reminded her of machines designed for some nefarious purpose. Or maybe they were monuments of an age past. How people could live in those was beyond her. How so many people could exist that such housing was necessary was equally baffling.

"Get down, you idiot!"

"What? There is…"

Jason pulled her down and pointed. At first, she saw only the low-growing vegetation and a few low-flying birds. Then one bush shifted and another in an unmistakable line towards them.

"Run!"

"We won't make it."

"We have to try!"

They ran down the narrow, barely visible path they had used to make their ascent. The bushes clawed at their legs as they stormed by. Rat hazarded a look behind. She caught a momentary glimpse of the machine hunting them; a five-legged spider, with three metal cords rising from its small torso swaying back and forth. It sped down the mountainside in pursuit. It was an old Scout model, and she hoped it no longer had functional ranged capabilities. If it did, they'd soon know.

"We're not gonna make it," Rat shouted to Jason, who was just a few metres ahead. "It's corrupted, for sure."

"So, there won't be any others," Jason shouted over his shoulder. "We should split up."

Rat knew Jason was right. There was no way they'd escape without weapons, so splitting up ensured one of them would survive.

She veered off the path to the left, hoping the Scout would choose the easier route and chase Jason. But Jason had the same idea and left the trail in the other direction.

Scrap! She was dead, for sure!

The Scout's logic was basic when on its own. Unless it had a specific target, it would chase whomever it was most likely to catch. There was no way to make her the less desirable target, so she sped up, knowing every step threatened to send her sprawling. Behind her, the clawed metal feet scraped against the rock as it increased speed to catch up. It hadn't used any ranged weapons, suggesting they were no longer functional. A small win, but still she ran.

She scanned her surroundings for an escape route, but she knew the machine behind her could follow her wherever she went. She didn't need to check to know it was catching up. The hillside became steeper, turning from a slope to a cliff. Below was a dense undergrowth with sporadic groups of taller trees almost reaching the height of the cliff. She hazarded another look behind. The Scout was only meters away, the metal cords stretching towards her.

A split-second decision born more from instinctual survival than anything else, had her veer to the left towards the cliff and jump. She was suspended in mid-air, imagining metal pincers ready to pierce her back. Gravity had not yet reclaimed her. The adrenaline pumping through her system made her hyper-aware of her surroundings. The leaves on the large tree still had water pooling from the morning dew. Light refracted from the almost circular droplets painting the leaves in ever-shifting colours. In that frozen moment, she was free, unburdened by any concerns for the future. She may live or die, but it was out of her hands now.

Time restarted as her momentum caused her to slam face-first into the top of the tree. It swayed from her weight as she desperately clung to it, threatening to break at any moment. Her peripheral vision caught the Scout standing on the edge, retracting its pincers. It was a second-generation Scout with a stun mechanism that reached at least five metres. It was closer than that now. It could have other ranged weapons as modifications, but it would have used them by now. Its logic demanded her capture, but it wouldn't damage itself to reach its goal. At least, that was its original programming. The corrupted Scouts could be unpredictable.

She felt herself slipping. The wet leaves were an ever-changing surface, resisting her desperate attempts to hang on.

The Scout reached towards her. If it jumped, it would get her for sure. She steeled herself, ready for the impact of the cold metal clinging to her back, but a few moments passed without instant death, so she glanced back.

It was gone!

She slid down the trunk to the ground and set off. She wasn't supposed to return to the settlement immediately. There were designated routes that were especially difficult for machines to traverse, but she didn't have time for that. She knew Jason wouldn't be able to evade it. He was fast, but only for short sprints. It would track him down and catch him within minutes.

His only chance would be how quickly she could return to the settlement for help. If luck remained on her side, Tann would be there and willing to help, even if he seldom took part in excursions nowadays.

CHAPTER TWO

HUNTED SCOUT

Tann had always liked this settlement site. It was relatively hidden and far enough away from any Red Zone for stray machines to be uncommon. There was enough to eat, especially now at the end of summer when the fruit on the Rapple trees was ripe. The sweet scent of the fruit lingered in the air, promising a record harvest. He hoped they could remain here for the next three months, longer than they had ever spent in one location since the tribe had formed almost twenty years ago. Machine attacks were less and less frequent and when they occurred, it was a usually a stray, corrupted Scout, not the coordinated strikes in the past that could easily wipe out an entire tribe. Why things had changed was anyone's guess. Maybe it wasn't worth hunting down humans any longer. Maybe the AI had grown tired of its old games and focused on exterminating the posthumans instead. He didn't know and he didn't much care. The survival of the tribe was all that mattered.

"Boss?"

"Huh?" Tann looked over at Sandrine, his second in command, who nodded towards the man in front of them. She was slender and of average height, not that Tann thought of her that way. In his mind she towered over everyone else. She was ten years his junior and better than him in all things that mattered. He was sure she'd take over when he was no longer up to the job of keeping the tribe safe.

"The camp," Sandrine said, raising an eyebrow. "It is ready for inspection."

She nodded towards Xuwei, who'd been responsible for setting up the camp now for the past three years. He was the opposite of Sandrine. Muscular and tall, always in work clothes ready to lend a hand in the running of the camp. The inspection was a formality.

Tann had long ago lost track of the intricacies of establishing and running the infrastructure of the camp and relied completely on Xuwei and his team. As a result, he doubted he'd find any issues. Xuwei had perfected the layout and positioning of the aerogel insulated, 3D graphene collapsible huts that served as their housing.

Xuwei guided them through the camp, calling attention to minor upgrades and changes he'd made since last changeover. It wasn't much, but that was a good thing.

"I've laid out the huts in a semi-circle with the main hall on the other side. We're closer to the water this time and I've introduced modifications to the dismantling process. It should save us almost five minutes when we break camp."

"And if attacked?" Sandrine asked.

"No change there. Shorter distance to reach the boats, but that's about it."

Tann nodded. He wasn't really paying attention. Sandrine would call out any issues. Lately the future of the tribe, and maybe even humankind if there even was such a thing, had been on his mind. He didn't know how many humans remained. The Eight Plague wiped out all major population centres across the world. The few survivors that were unaffected by the posthuman virus gathered in tribes to survive. A year later, machines appeared designed to hunt and neutralise humans. They attacked any permanent settlement. He knew of five other nomadic tribes remaining in this part of the world. They kept their contact to a minimum, only sending quick bursts as all communication channels were monitored and anything longer could be traced back to its origin.

"We've had to print additional parts for the organic recyclers. I've located them together with the solar cells in an open area closer to the beach."

Xuwei continued the walkthrough. Tann wandered along with them, nodding now and then to give the appearance of participation. These ceremonies had kept them alive for a long time. Tann had been the instigator of many and knew how important they were. Still, he found his mind wandering.

Rat appeared at full speed, careering through the camp, almost colliding with them in her hurry to get away from an unseen threat.

"Rat! What's the hurry?" Tann scanned the forest line where he'd first seen her. Rat was always up to something. Tann had many times predicted she wouldn't see her fifteenth birthday, which was only days away.

She halted. Her slender body twirled on the spot; blue bright eyes firmly fixated on the spot she'd come from. A fresh gash trickled blood across her shoulder.

"Scout!" she gasped between shallow breaths. "Corrupted."

Tann nodded. She'd given them the most valuable pieces of information first. A corrupted Scout they could deal with. There was no reason to break camp if they could find and disable it.

"How many?" Sandrine asked. "Just one?"

Rat nodded so fiercely sweat droplets flew from her short black hair, like a dog shaking itself after getting wet.

"Let's go," Tann said, smiling grimly.

"You're coming?" Sandrine said.

Tann noticed the slight narrowing of her eyes, just a hint of disapproval. She was right. He was the leader of the tribe. Going after a Scout could be dangerous, and risking his life unnecessarily wasn't in the best interest of the tribe. He shrugged in response.

"I didn't say anything," Sandrine objected.

"You didn't have to."

"I better go too then, just to make sure you don't get into any trouble. You want it captured?"

Tann shook his head.

"Good," she replied and yelled for two tribe members to join them.

"You lead the way," Tann said to Rat.

She nodded and headed off the way she'd come, weaving through the lush palms, moving leaves aside as she went. At the outset, Tann found it hard to keep up. He remembered giving her the nickname that had stuck so many years ago. She'd been small and slender, able to get through the smallest crevice as if it wasn't there. She was always scraped and bruised from her latest exploits, gathering items from a bygone era that no one seemed willing to discuss, as if it was an embarrassment. Tann liked her. She may have been reckless, but the tribe's survival depended on people like her.

"You left with Jason earlier," Sandrine said. A statement, not a question. "On one of your scavenging hunts, I assume?"

This was why Sandrine was so much better than him. He should have known that, but he didn't.

"No," Rat responded, eyes downcast. "I just wanted to see the city and the giant cylinder-things people lived in."

"And where is Jason now?" Sandrine asked, steel in her voice.

"I don't know. We split up. It came after me."

"What?" Tann said. "You outran a Scout?"

"I jumped," she said, shrugging her shoulders as if that explained everything.

They continued their trek, half-running, trading speed for safety, out of the undergrowth, up the hill, and along the ridge as they neared Sunset Peak. They had to find the Scout before it disappeared and reported its discovery to other machines.

"You lost it here?"

Tann eyed the distance between the edge and the tree. There was no question how she'd escaped. Bright red smears stood like beacons on the large green leaves. He doubted he'd make that jump, or even attempt it. But Jason and Rat had followed their training. They wouldn't survive a fight, so they separated, minimising the number of targets it could pursue and capture. Whoever the Scout pursued would perish, but become a worthy sacrifice, allowing others to survive. This time the chosen prey had escaped, and the only logical choice was to locate the other target.

Rat nodded.

"And Jason? Where did he go?"

Rat pointed down the other side of the ridge, and they ran. Tann hoped it wasn't too late. They'd spied machines in this area before and usually gave it a wide berth, not wanting strays to follow them back to the settlement area.

They didn't have to run far. The Scout was dragging Jason down the mountainside. For a moment Tann thought the boy could still be alive, that the Scout was following its original programming, but his unseeing eyes stared into the rising sun, and his limbs sagged like a rag doll as the machine dragged him along the ground.

At least it hadn't reached any other machines—not yet. Tann studied the small Scout. A spider-legged base model, modified to the point the only thing that remained was the chassis. Corrupted Scouts scavenged technology from other machines to replace old, broken parts. He'd seen this model before a long time ago. It wasn't long after the Eight Plague. Machines just like this one attacked the first tribe he'd joined. Scouts swarmed from all sides, like bugs uncovered from under a rock. They were the initial attack, with two major weapons at their disposal: a fast-acting non-lethal neuro toxin, with injectors at the end of metal cords that rose from its body, swaying like rattle snakes; and an electric charge delivered from a small taser with a five-metre range. Their purpose was to incapacitate as many people as possible without killing them, usually targeting a specific group of people. They came fast, relying on speed, surprise, and fear. What came after was worse. Much worse.

"Tann?" Sandrine asked, elbowing him in the side. He didn't need to glance her way to know what she thought. He could hear the frustration from that single word.

"Just deciding what to do," he said and began doing just that. They had long since abandoned using normal guns against Scout models. They were too fast, almost impossible to hit. Instead, they used cruder weapons, limiting their movement before disposing of them with a blunt weapon.

Through the years they'd experimented with electricity, limited EMP bursts and explosives. They had even tried water to short-circuit their wiring with limited success. Acids reacted to slow and became a danger to the people when the machines attacked them. Trapping their limbs had proven the most successful method of disabling them.

Tann retrieved a foam grenade from a pouch on his belt. They didn't have many left and he'd hoped not to use it, but the Scout had already killed one of them. They couldn't risk another casualty.

He lobbed the grenade in a high arc, dropping on the machine from above. It activated on impact. A mushroom of white foam exploded with a five-metre radius coating the Scout and everything around it.

The foam solidified to a gluelike substance, fusing to anything it touched. Strands of rubbery, sticky material restricted the machine's movements until it could no longer move forward. The rubber tendrils stretched, but immediately snapped back.

They waited twenty seconds for the fusing reaction to complete. The Scout lay on its side, unable to right itself. The old servo engines whined in protest as it kept resisting the haphazard restraints. Tann was relieved to find that the Scout didn't have functioning communication devices. There was no reason to suspect it was anything but a stray robot wandering randomly, hunting for other machines to cannibalise.

"What's wrong?" Sandrine asked as she lodged her knife into the undercarriage of the Scout, twisting it open.

"What do you mean?"

"You've checked out. Been more than a month now. I don't care, but it is affecting the tribe."

Tann remained silent, refusing to acknowledge the obvious truth in her words.

"I will contest your leadership in tonight's tribe meeting," she continued. Tann saw Rat listening to their conversation, her eyes widening as Sandrine spoke.

"You do what you have to do," Tann replied.

BIRTH

As they returned to the village, navigating the traps they had set up around the perimeter, a young woman, Mo Chou, approached them.

"What fresh hell might this be?" Tann said quietly to himself.

"Jodi is giving birth," Sandrine said. "You know that. Or you should know that."

He had been aware, but somehow even that, the most important event there was, had somehow slipped his mind.

"It is time," Mo Chou said. She was twenty years old, born only days after the Plague hit. One of the lucky few young children that survived the slaughter of the first few years. No one knew how many humans had survived the initial attack and the plague, but everyone agreed most of the survivor were captured or killed in the three years after that.

She'd once told Tann her name meant "free of sadness". The irony of a name like that was hard to ignore. She was a fierce fighter when needed, hardened by years of escaping death. Sadness was imbued in her, an integral part channelled into everything she did.

"Lead the way," Tann said.

"The birth was uneventful. A healthy boy. 3.6 kilos. 50 centimetres. All vitals normal."

Tann waited. Healthy was fine, but not enough.

"I've taken a swab already. It was inconclusive, so we are doing a blood test. We're waiting for the results now. This is her third, so maybe this time."

Tann nodded. They were no longer hunted down and killed by the machines, but it didn't matter. The virus turning people into posthumans remained. He'd been responsible for that, though at the time he hadn't realised how the dominoes would fall. It was no longer as potent as the original strain, but from data shared between nearby tribes, the infection rate was still around fifty percent. No one knew why the virus remained, since they were all infected a long time ago. Maybe animals carried it, or they were all carriers once infected, even if it didn't trigger the change. It didn't matter. It was a fact of life, like the posthumans and the machines.

They entered Jodi's hut. She was on the bed, cradling the unnamed newborn in her arms. Her dark hair lay plastered against her skin. She looked up, eyes darting between them for a second, then her focus returned to the baby.

Mo Chou held a small device up to the light, peering at the small screen. She shook her head before her arms dropped to her sides.

Jodi wailed, her arms tightening around the baby boy like a shield against the world around her. "I'm not leaving him! I'm not!"

Her protestations stopped abruptly as she stared at something behind him. A slight variation in the flow of air in the room had already alerted Tann to the figure entering the hut. He was sure others waited outside. The figure was naked and hairless, skin grey and patterned like a snake. The posthumans had specialized much like bees in a hive. This one, and the ones outside, were specialised for physical tasks, even violence if needed. It was human in appearance, but something was wrong, as if its proportions were slightly off. Wiry muscles wrapped like cords up its elongated legs and arms. Tann had seen posthumans take on machines without weapons and win, an impossibility for a normal human being.

The posthuman reached the side of the bed and held out its hands. It remained like that as Jodi's eyes again darted between Sandrine, Tann and Mo Chou.

Jodi clasped the baby tightly to her chest. "You can't let them take him!"

"We can't raise one of them," Sandrine said. "You know that. It will leave us as soon as it can."

Tann nodded. Early on, they had tried to hide the newborn posthumans, usually on the insistence of the parents. Tann saw the usefulness of this too. If they could raise a posthuman child, maybe it could help them in their dealings with this strange race. It hadn't worked. As soon as the child was mobile, it went in search of others like themselves.

"You have to," Tann said. "It isn't one of us."

Tears streamed down her face. She gently touched the side of her baby boy's face. His eyes popped open. She stared into his dark brown eyes. Tann was close enough to see what she saw. The infant's stare fixed on his mother's face for a second, and then darted off to examine the room, settling on the posthuman standing next to the bed. It reached out, not to his mother, but to this alien creature still waiting with arms outstretched.

Jodi sneered and almost brusquely pushed the baby into the waiting arms.

"Take it! It is no child of mine!"

The posthuman cradled the child gently, the skin of its hands and arms melding around the child's form, and it turned to leave. It focused on Tann for an instance.

"No more breeding," it said. "No more of this randomised mess. We will assimilate it into the hive."

Tann had heard it said before, but never asked what it meant. Assimilation into the hive sounded too much like death.

-=:=-

Death hadn't finished with them that day, Tann thought grimly as he watched Jodi's body sway from the tree branch. He should have seen it coming. Three babies taken from her in the past five years. Three failures building on top of each other, high enough for her to reach the noose and place it around her weary neck.

It had been a grim day for the tribe. Two dead and a baby no longer with them. The tribe no longer grew from survivors joining them, and there weren't enough human children born to replace those who died. He suspected other tribes were experiencing the same decline.

He sat down on the floor with an old Omni in his hand. Wires snaked out to the solar cells on the roof. The battery had long since stopped working. The networked world remained, but it was a dangerous place for human minds. Machines hunted them in the physical world and virtual agents hunted them online. No one even attempted jacking into the network any longer. The two-way neural interface was an invitation for a virtual agent to infect the brain and try to rewire it, usually with fatal results.

An Omni could still connect, but even this had its dangers. The connection itself was a beacon for any Scouts scouring the physical world.

The Omni's cracked black screen came to life, displaying a keyboard and a basic messaging application. This was the only reason he used it. Tann had designed the messaging application himself, ensuring it minimised connectivity. It sent the smallest package possible synchronously. And because it was point to point, both sides had to be connected at the same time. If communication was text only, he was confident it would avoid detection. Still, they kept their conversations short.

A message appeared from Haoyu, leader of a tribe in the same region. Tann was happy for the distraction.

Haoyu: TikTak!
Tann: Really?

Tann had told Haoyu about his past as a hacker and his old avatar name. Back then, it was the only name he'd respond to. Now it seemed quaint, like a mildly embarrassing childhood nickname.

Haoyu: I thought I'd set the scene.
Tann: You're making no sense. How's the tribe?
Haoyu: Still stationary. 3 months now. You?
Tann: Moved yesterday. 2 dead. 1 baby lost.
Haoyu: Their stories have ended. Ours have not.

Tann nodded to himself. Haoyu was right. They had to move on. Mankind's survival depended on them, whatever tragedies they had to suffer to achieve it.

Haoyu: I have a surprise.
Tann: What?
Haoyu: A memory stick. We've found one.
Tann: A memory stick? You mean a memTag?

memTag. Tann said the word out loud. It sounded strange to his ears. A word from a different age that only held relevance in its own time.

Haoyu: Call it what you want. We don't know what to do with it. It is encrypted.
Tann: Throw it away then.

Haoyu: There is a plain message on it too. You can read it with an old Omni.
Tann: And?

Tann wondered why Haoyu was interested in this. Not that this was the first time. He frequently dug up old tech he wanted to use from the outskirts of Red Zones.

Haoyu: You spoke of a posthuman you knew years ago. Tom Devine.
Tann: I should never have told you.
Haoyu: Well, now it came in useful.
Tann: Ok, I'm interested. What does it say?
Haoyu: It ends with "To Tom Devine, with love."
Tann: Really? I don't believe you.
Haoyu: That's what it says. And it is recent. A year or two at the most.
Tann: Can you send it to me?
Haoyu: I can send the plain text part. The rest is too big to send with this crappy app you made.

The message came as a small text attachment.

It is time we end this. Hopefully this will find you before it is too late. If you are half as smart as you think, you'll work out the encryption key from the first place we met.
He won't though.
To Tom Devine, with love

Tann: Is that it? It doesn't even make sense. What's with the second line? "He won't though." It doesn't add up.
Haoyu: That's why I sent it to you. I have no idea what it means! Figured you might.

It was so random, so strange. It had to mean something. He paced back and forth in the small hut, mind racing. Survival of the tribe had been his life, but there was a bigger picture. The day's events had forced him to accept the tribe was slowly dying. Maybe this message, however incoherent, showed the way to a solution. It was a longshot, but why did it exist in the first place? He had to know.

Tann: I'll come and get it.
Haoyu: You'll come? I can send someone.
Tann: No. I'll come.
Haoyu: You know where we are. We'll be swapping camp soon, so hurry.
Tann: Will do.

Tann disconnected the Omni and immediately packed a bag.

"Going somewhere?" Sandrine stood in the doorway.

"I need to deal with something."

"Something that can help the tribe?"

"Possibly."

"You're not just running away?"

"Possibly."

Sandrine shook her head and closed the distance between them with a few quick steps. Tann instinctively raised his hands, ready to fend off an attack if it came, but she just embraced him. She could still surprise him, even after all this time.

"Go," she said. "You're no good here anyway."

He was about to protest, but she was right. His immediate decision to leave had many contributing factors, one of them the tribal meeting this evening.

"I'll deal with things here. Just go."

CHAPTER FOUR
AN

UNWANTED COMPANION

Rat watched as Tann left the village unannounced. It wasn't as if he was prohibited from leaving, but his body language suggested subterfuge. She'd made it a habit to keep track of Tann whenever her duties allowed. He fascinated her. The stories told of Tann bordered on legends. He'd risen to leader of the tribe over ten years ago and saved them from extinction more than once. It was as if he instinctively understood the machines better than anyone else. What they'd do. Where they'd hunt. How they'd attack. And he used this skill to find the best locations to settle, how to set up perimeter defences, how to escape when needed. Rumour had it he'd been involved in the Plague somehow, but she didn't know how. Not that it mattered. Ancient history, however fascinating, was pointless. It changed nothing.

He'd been sending messages to the other tribe leaders just before he left. She'd seen him preparing an old screen to connect to the forbidden network. This was more interesting. One of her pack mates had told her you could use it to talk to anyone in the world! She couldn't comprehend this. Wouldn't all this shouting back and forth across enormous distances make it impossible to understand what the others were saying? The practical technology of the past was fascinating—especially the weapons—but she struggled to understand the purpose of what Tann called information technology. But anything forbidden was bound to be interesting. And seeing Tann skulking out of the settlement was exactly that. Maybe she didn't understand the why, but she knew it would be exciting.

There was no rule preventing her from following Tann to ensure his safety. She was doing him a favour really, as one rule stated they shouldn't leave camp alone. She smiled to herself, pleased to have conjured an explanation based on the rules she so often ignored.

Tann had already disappeared. Rat scanned her surroundings, ensured no one paid her any attention, and followed.

Three hours later and Tann showed no sign of reaching any kind of destination. Quite the contrary. He'd navigated the serpentine roads across the island until reaching one of the main roads leading towards the Red Zone. This was further from this settlement than she'd ever been before.

She was also acutely aware the point of no return was rapidly approaching. They could still return to the settlement before sunset, but this was pushing it. What was so important he broke all his own rules?

This wasn't even a decision. Her want to know Tann's destination far outweighed her want to return to the tribe and her chores. This was a real adventure! And who knew? She might even help him in the quest of his.

Tann continued his trek along the wide, empty road. The scale of everything in the old world was incomprehensible. What could be so important that you needed four lanes each way to get to and from it? Their lives were so busy, but why?

Only the innermost lanes remained now, vegetation kept at bay somehow. She assumed machines used it still, but so far, she hadn't seen any. According to the stories, vehicles to transport humans were all cleared from the roads, the materials used to create new machines.

Rat followed Tann on the other side of the median strip, leaving as much distance as she dared. A constant tightrope between discovery if he turned around and losing him if he left the road.

Two hours and he had still not turned to look behind him once. Train tracks ran next to the highway along the shore, and she'd opted to walk there instead as it provided more cover.

She imagined him lost in thought, the end destination his only focus. This must be of utmost importance to the settlement for him to risk this journey. Her mind conjured all manner of possibilities, restrained only by her imagination. Maybe an alternative source of energy or a weapon of some sort?

She poked her head over the barrier between the train tracks and the highway to check on Tann again. He was no longer there! She increased her pace, half running, hoping he was just out of sight. She reached the location where she'd seen him last and stayed her steps. The road ahead was empty, so she scanned her surroundings, hoping to catch sight of him.

He'd left the road! He must have. But where? She had the ocean on her left side and dense vegetation and rolling hills as far as she could see to her right. Why had he left the road at this point? There was nothing here.

"You're not very good at this," Tann's voice came from behind her.

She spun around. He stood there with a stupid smirk as if he somehow caught her out! He was the one not following the rules, not her.

"Where are you going?" she snapped back.

"None of your business. Go back to the camp."

"No," Rat said, arms folded across her chest. She was already past the point of no return, so may as well keep going and see where it took her.

"No?"

"No," she repeated. "You can't leave the camp on your own. That's one of the rules. That's one of *your* rules."

Tann eyed her for what felt like an eternity, but she planted her feet firmly on the ground, ready for anything. She doubted the rules would provide much protection, so she added: "Anyway, it is too late to return now."

"Whatever," Tann said and walked off the same way he'd been heading before he disappeared.

Rat waited a moment, then followed. He hadn't said no, after all, she reasoned.

An hour of silence, step by step, trailing behind Tann. If he wasn't going to acknowledge her existence, she could pay back in kind.

They traversed a bridge with giant arches on either side, thick steel wires spreading from the top to the bridge itself like the wings on a bat. Her vow of silence was forgotten at the sheer enormity of the structure.

"I don't get it," she said to Tann's back. "They were clever enough to build this bridge and so stupid they built machines that almost killed them all?"

Tann remained silent. She wondered if he'd even heard her. She remembered one of his statements from years ago.

"Don't ever underestimate the stupidity or ingenuity of the old world," he'd said. "Or how they could make the two almost completely indistinguishable."

She couldn't remember why he'd said it, and it sounded like complete nonsense. But it echoed true when faced with this amazing bridge surviving the civilisation that created it.

-=:=-

That evening they made camp just a few metres away from the road. Tann had brought a foldable shelter providing both protection and camouflage. It had been a uniform dark green but changed to a pattern to align with the surrounding shrubs when unfolded. He sat down and handed her a piece of flatbread. She devoured it.

"I'm going to the Shenzhen Green Zone," Tann said.

"The what?" Rat said between mouthfuls.

"Wherever there is a Red Zone, there is a Green Zone. You know that. We're going to a specific one. It is just next to the city."

The pairing made sense. The AI inhabited the technology-filled cities, whilst the posthumans populated the nearby forests. It was a stalemate that had remained for years.

"They won't let you in," Rat said. "They don't allow humans."

She knew Tann was the only source for that information, but she repeated it anyway.

"No, they won't," Tann agreed.

"So why are you going there?"

"To see an old friend."

"Haoyu?"

Tann shook his head.

"No, not Haoyu. Older than that."

CHAPTER FIVE

SHENZHEN GREEN ZONE

Two days later they were nearing their destination. At first, Tann had been annoyed by the unwanted travelling companion, but Rat made little fuss and left him alone with his thoughts. She even scouted ahead for food, potential threats and camping sites. He appreciated her unassuming presence, even if she went on about completely pointless subjects now and then.

He had yet to uncover why she'd followed him and hadn't asked. People had their reasons and asking about them hardly ever resulted in anything resembling the truth. If there was one thing humanity excelled at, it was self-deception. He was sure it would become clear in due course.

They'd remained on the empty main roads. Most vehicles had disappeared from the streets only days after the initial attack. At first no one knew why, but a tribe member had accidentally happened on a repurposing station during a scavenging excursion a few years later. Cars, machines, and electronics pulled apart, reused to create new incomprehensible contraptions.

They'd never been able to get close enough to determine what it produced, but the new machines to hunt humans and battle posthumans must come from there. Other bigger machines also appeared on the outskirts of cities, tearing down whole suburbs. No one had dared venture into these areas to determine their purpose.

The city landscape changed block by block. Behind them, the skyscrapers still stood as monuments to history. Ahead, lush vegetation covered every inch of half-standing, sprawling luxury villas. The roads turned into dirt paths lined with palms with whip-like yellow-and-red-striped tendrils sprouting from the trunk. Tann knew their purpose. They guarded the path into the Green Zone from the machines. Further ahead, green canopies spread out like giant mushrooms the size of football stadiums. The air smelled of damp soil and over-ripened fruit.

"Do you have any technology?" Tann asked Rat.

"Any what?"

"Anything made of metal?"

Metal didn't trigger the guardians. An electrical current did, but he wasn't sure Rat even knew what that was.

Rat held up a combat knife.

"That's fine. Nothing else?"

She shook her head with a bemused smile. "They won't do anything to me," she responded. "You sure you'll get through?"

She nodded towards his backpack. He had plenty of technology, but nothing holding an active current.

"I'll be fine," he said gruffly.

A fine web of green tendrils covered the path ahead, quivering as the two humans approached. Tann didn't know how they distinguished a current generated by technology from the one generated by the human body. Maybe it wasn't even the current by itself, but other aspects. Entry didn't mean safe passage. Only that you weren't a significant threat. He knew eyes were already tracking them.

The Green Zones were strange beasts. Twenty years ago, before the Plague had begun, he'd hunted down a child he now thought of as the first of a new human race. The child had formed a symbiotic relationship between all organic matter and maybe even more. In the Green Zones, the posthumans nurtured the same environment, but on a grander scale. Here, the distinction between animal and vegetable life was uncertain. Tann was unsure if this had a purpose or was just a side effect of something else. It mattered little when everything had to be seen through the lens of survival.

Rat stared at the surrounding wonders, eyes darting from one miracle to the next. The scale of the plants dwarfed anything Tann had seen before. They continued through what he thought was a dense forest, but was just a couple of enormous trees. Their roots were thicker than the trunk of a regular tree and continued above ground, collecting high above into one of the support beams holding the canopies up.

A large bird, parrot-like with bright colours, with wide wings of interlaced leaves, flew above them, dodging this way and that.

Rat plucked a bright yellow fruit the size of her fist from one of the nearby trees. She was about to bite into it when it split into two and then halved over and over, the small pieces held together by the skin, forming spiderlike legs around a small centre. It scuttled up her arm and jumped, disappearing into the undergrowth.

"What was that?"

"No idea. Don't know if the posthumans are just experimenting or if they've supercharged mutative properties."

"Mutative what?"

"I think they are just playing gods."

"So, it's changed? Since you were here last, I mean?"

Tann nodded. He'd only been here twice before—both times in futile attempts to ask the posthumans for help. He'd been against the idea from the beginning, knowing full well the posthumans had no interest in helping humankind survive. The human envoys didn't reach further than a hundred steps into the Green Zone before the posthumans asked them to leave. This time they were much further into the Zone. He suspected they were still on the outskirts, but it was impossible to judge.

The second time he'd hazarded the journey into the Zone on his own. Machine attacks ravaged the tribe and Tann figured he had to try again, this time reaching out to Tom directly. It proved unsuccessful. Tom differed from the other posthumans, but not enough to concern himself with the fate of humanity.

"Look," Rat said and pointed ahead. A figure sat on the ground, vegetation climbing up around his legs. As they came closer, Tann waved at the figure, to no effect. There was no mistaking who it was.

"Hi Tom," Tann said as they approached.

"Not welcome," Tom said slowly, as if struggling to remember how to speak. "Leave."

"Déjà vu," Tann said. "Good to see you."

His old friend's appearance hadn't changed. He looked the same as when they parted way seventeen years ago on this very spot. Tann couldn't remember what Tom had been wearing, but would still bet they were the same clothes. More surprising was that he wore clothes at all, as the posthumans he'd met had changed their physical features so they wouldn't need any.

"No reason to be here," Tom said. "Leave."

"Who is he?" Rat asked. "He doesn't look like one of the freaks."

"He's one of the original ones," Tann said.

"Adrian?"

"Ha. You do listen to the campfire tales. It is Tom. He created the AI that took over all the networks and wiped out most of mankind."

"And the two of you released the virus that turned everyone into posthumans?" Rat asked in a rush.

"There were others to blame too, but that's close enough."

"Why?" Tom asked, still motionless.

"Someone from our past has surfaced. I need your help."

"He is yours," Megan said, stepping into the light. "Leave. Both of you."

Tann hadn't seen the tech mogul for over fifteen years. Her facial features hadn't changed, but everything about her was wrong. Her skin had taken on a greenish hue, as if it was producing chlorophyl. The blonde hair replaced with hardened ridges flowing like static waves across the skull, down her neck and shoulders. Tann wondered if she was Megan at all or just a shell housing whichever posthuman needed a body. Their society was a complete mystery, and he'd long since given up making sense of it.

Tann turned to Rat. "Speaking of blame, why don't we keep the history lesson going? Tom may have accidentally created the seed of the AI, but Megan here, she nurtured it until it took over the network. She's the reason we are hunted by machines now."

Rat stared at her, eyes wide.

"Leave," Megan said.

Tann cast a glance at Tom and gave a slight shrug.

"I will hunt this down with or without you," Tann said and turned around. Rat joined him and Tom, after a moment of hesitation, rose and followed them out of the Green Zone. Tann wondered what the other Posthumans told him to make him leave.

"Where to now?" Rat asked once they'd left the posthumans far behind.

"West," Tann replied. "We're going to Haoyu's settlement."

"This isn't west."

"We're not going by land. Too dangerous. And it will take too long."

"And why is he coming?" Rat nodded towards Tom.

"Good question," Tann said and turned to Tom. "Why did you?"

"Only viable option," Tom responded, staring straight ahead.

"That'll do for me," Tann said.

"Why doesn't he look like the other freaks?" Rat asked, eyeing Tom suspiciously.

"He's a special case," Tann replied. "I'm guessing they kicked him out."

"Makes sense," Rat said.

Tann was at a loss as to her meaning, but he didn't pursue the matter.

The trio journeyed in silence, skirting the city centre, heading towards the coastline. Land travel was slow and dangerous. There were countless marinas where the rich had moored extravagant cruisers and yachts. Tann knew they'd find transport there.

The third marina they visited showed some promise. The previous two were picked bare, but this one still had some seaworthy vessels. They boarded a 40-foot yacht in good shape. The reinforced fibreglass hull was still intact and without noticeable degradation. He unrolled part of the sail and smiled as he felt the laminate cloth between his fingers. Whoever had owned this had spared no expense. Even the cabin was in useable state after airing it out. He didn't even try the engine, knowing it was unlikely to function properly, if at all. Not that he minded. Sailing was much more satisfying.

He didn't trust the metal wires or synthetic ropes. They'd been exposed to weather, sun and salt for too long. He scavenged the nearby buildings for replacements. It took him over a day to replace them all.

They loaded provisions, which mainly comprised fruit and root vegetables they'd collected close to the Green Zone. The sea was brimming with fish now that thousands of fishing boats no longer trawled the depths for an ever-diminishing catch. The tribe had never had a problem feeding itself when moving between camp sites.

They departed, raising the mainsail to navigate from the marina. The north-westerly wind caught it with a snapping sound. The new ropes tightened and creaked and groaned against the hull. Tann instructed Rat to secure the ropes but knew she would have done it regardless. He left Rat at the rudder, a responsibility she gladly accepted.

The solar cells on the yacht still worked, so he retrieved the old Omni and secured it within one of the charging fields on deck. Tom had immediately stationed himself below deck and Tann had to drag him out to the Omni to show him the message Haoyu had sent.

"What are you doing?" Rat yelled from her station and engaged the wheel lock.

She hurried over and sat down next to Tom to read the content. Tom read it too and sat back, staring out over the frothy waves licking the hull. Tann remembered how difficult communication had been with Tom once he'd turned posthuman. Everything came down to furthering a cause and usually it was the posthuman agenda. Since Tom wasn't part of that community, Tann guessed Tom's purpose was less obvious now.

Rat echoed the message, taking care to read each word out loud. "It is time we end this. Hopefully this will find you before it is too late. If you are half as smart as you think, you'll work out the encryption key from the first place we met."

Rat grimaced in confusion over the last section, but she repeated that too. "He won't though. To Tom Devine, with love."

She stared at Tann and shook her head. "Is that why we came all this way? Really?"

Tann ignored her and focused on Tom.

"Nothing?" Tann asked. "You have nothing to say to this?"

"Adrian," Tom replied.

"You think this is Adrian? He's dead. You killed him. You told me so yourself."

Tom shrugged, or at least that was Tann's translation of the barely perceptible twitch of Tom's shoulders. He seemed as uncomfortable with movements as he was with words. What had he been doing for the past 15 years?

"Ok, for argument's sake, I accept it could be some incarnation of Adrian. What does the message mean? What are we ending?"

"The AI," Tom said and then added: "Extinction. Bank of Mutual Trust. Crazy."

"And what do you make of the last…" Tann started and realised Tom had answered the question already and two more he'd not even formulated in his mind yet.

"That's a neat party trick," Tann said.

"What's wrong with him?" Rat asked. "That made no sense."

"He can't be bothered talking to us, so he predicted my questions and answered them."

"What do you mean?"

"He means we are ending the AI before humankind are extinct. The first place Tom met Adrian was at the Bank of Mutual Trust."

"And crazy?"

"It must refer to the last section of the message. The one that doesn't make sense. Almost as if it belonged to a different message altogether. He's crazy, so it wasn't worth analysing?"

"Still makes no sense," Rat said dismissively and returned to the wheel.

Tann studied his old friend. There would be no debate or analysis. Tom's mind sped ahead, reaching conclusions tested a hundredfold before Tann had even begun forming a thought.

"Why did they want you to leave?"

"Different."

Tom was a posthuman, so what did he mean by that? Or was he? Adrian, Elize and Tom were the originals, created by the smart drug IntelEz under very specific circumstances. All other posthumans stemmed from the virus released by the child.

"You're the only posthuman left that was made by the drug," Tann said. "The virus the kid released caused everyone else to turn. So, you don't get to join their happy family?"

Tom shook his head. "Not like them."

"Join the club."

"They've locked me out from the source."

"The what?"

"The cosmopsyche," Tom said and left for the safety of the cabin.

"I've missed our completely pointless conversations," Tann said to Tom's back as he disappeared down the steps.

"He creeps me out," Rat said.

"He creeps me out," Tann replied. "But we need him. Or maybe it is the other way around. The message was for him and we're helping him. He needs us."

"Really? He's a freak! What could we possibly do to help him?"

"Let's just say he's a different type of freak and he doesn't get along with the other freaks."

Rat shrugged in response, eyes on the horizon.

Sometimes clarity appears on its own volition when you stop disqualifying thoughts and let them roam free. He'd almost stopped himself from suggesting Tom might need their help, but the more he thought about it, the more it made sense. Tom may have an oversized brain, but surviving in this world required much more than that.

THE SETTLEMENT

Tom's mind palace was a sight to see: a sprawling building unrestrained by gravity or physics. At the centre stood the apartment he'd spent the last few years of his life. Beyond its door, the hallway, corridors, staircases and elevators led into recesses of his mind. He'd never meant to create it, but loneliness and separation forced him to solve an impossible problem: how to remain sane.

Whilst a human mind used a memory palace to hold and keep memories, Tom had turned large sections into a laboratory of thought and exploration. It was segregated into sections dedicated to areas of interest. Only a small part concerned itself with the physical world and over the years, he'd isolated himself from it altogether. The posthumans ostracised him from their community, leaving him an outcast, and he'd long since lost interest in the remnants of humanity.

To make matters worse, the posthumans had locked his access to any organic network. This included the cosmopsyche, the slow-moving consciousness he'd discovered twenty years ago, that operated across all matter—possibly the entire universe. He didn't know and desperately wanted to find out. All his attempts to remove the block had failed. The only world left for him to explore was the logical network, but it had its own dangers.

He didn't think much of Tann's quest, but it provided an opportunity to explore other ways to further his research. Add to that, the posthuman community requested he leave them, so it was also a matter of survival.

The window to the present demanded his attention. Tann was in the water, pulling an inflatable raft Tom sat in onto a barren beach. He asked Tom to move out of the raft. He complied, instructing the control system he established over the primary motor cortex to perform the action.

Humans were still so tied to their mortal forms, they catered to their bodies every whim. Food, entertainment, sex, heating, cooling, sickness. Such imperfect machines. Not that he could argue. He was stuck in a body with the same demands, even though he'd long since rejected all but the most necessary urges. Ignoring the body completely wasn't an option. Madness lay that way.

According to Tann, the temporary settlement lay about five hundred metres inland. A couple of corpses lay on the beach next to boats ripped apart by explosives. Humans were such fragile beings in both mind and body. Tom set aside a small part of his mind to assessing the damage and the threat to them now.

Tann verbalised something. It was unbelievably slow. His mouth turned itself inside out to utter guttural sounds, distilling thoughts into something coherent worth communicating to the rest of the group.

"What..." Tann started.

Tom stopped listening after the first word. It would be a question and he'd narrowed down its intent to a generic request for an explanation.

The core AI had attacked this settlement. A few boats had been disabled first, and the Scouts swarmed them, incapacitating as many as possible before they could mount a defence. He saw faint signs of Scout-tracks on the ground next to footprints of larger machines. He'd not seen this model before, but guessed it was a humanoid Shell model. A machine designed in imitation of the human form, housing either an autonomous AI or acting as an edge point to the core AI.

Tom had spent years in the backwaters of the network, studying what the AI did to people. Cleansing the brain of any sense of identity, rewriting the operating system to turn them into autonomous robots. Adrian had done it a long time ago, but with less success. He'd started with deadheads that were already compliant.

Tann completed his sentence. It was, just as he'd predicted, a generic question.

"…happened here?" Tann finished.

"AI attack," Tom responded. "All dead or wiped."

Tann and the child named Rat verbalised at the same time. Both were pointless reactions to what they saw, and he only needed a few syllables to predict the remaining words.

He focused on the surroundings as he wandered towards the main campsite. Signs of the attack were everywhere, confirming his initial assessment. The campsite itself was small, designed to house about 120 humans. The buildings were lightweight, collapsible constructions, placed in a semi-circle around an open area. No human remained alive. A few bodies lay out in the open, killed in battle. A few others were dead by their own hands in the cabins, preferring to die than to have their minds wiped by the AI.

Tom wondered why the core AI still took people, what use it could have for them any longer. Surely the form factor of a human body housed in a human mind was no longer required. But if it still was, there was no reason to assume they were safe here. The core AI may send machines to look for survivors. The threat level in their current position was unacceptable. They needed to leave as soon as possible.

"We can't stay," he said to Tann, still finding it difficult to force his mouth and tongue into shapes needed for speech.

"I know, but we need to find the memTag. Haoyu never told me where it was."

"Private quarters," Tom said immediately. There was no reason for Haoyu to hide it. It served no purpose for anyone else, so why hide it?

"You think you can start speaking properly again? Full sentences that make sense as part of a conversation?"

Tann's words were pointless and slow. They'd made their way to the main building before he'd finished the two sentences, the first one a replica of the other.

"Unnecessary."

"Humour me."

Tom stopped for a second, frustrated with how slow his world had become. Verbal communication was like walking through sludge, one slow step after another. He'd already assessed all options and mapped out the conversation to its conclusion. If you can jump over the mud, why trudge straight through it?

"Ineffective," he replied as he stepped into Haoyu's hut. The small memory unit, a model usually referred to as a memTag, about the size of a die, lay on the floor in plain sight. Whoever attacked hadn't been interested in it. Yet it was statistically likely the discovery of the memTag and the attack were connected. Organised attacks on settlements hadn't occurred for years. So why attack this settlement now and leave the prize for anyone to find? It was surely a trap, but its nature escaped him.

Tom retrieved the memTag from the floor, the black moulded plastic casing giving no clue to its secrets. He let a charge power it through his fingers. A small red led light lit up as it responded.

"That's neat. You can act as a power source. You have a flashlight in there too? Maybe some shark repellent bat-spray?"

Tann's words were pointless, describing only what was right in front of him. And an equally pointless attempt at humour, wasting time and processing for no reason. The unnecessary rituals of humankind grated on him. He saw no reason to respond. He sent a request to the memTag, and it immediately responded with a read-only string, echoing the same words Tann had shown him before.

Satisfied he'd found what they were looking for, he copied the entire content of the device to his mind and gave it to Tann.

"Leave," he said and headed for the beach, not waiting for Tann or the child, who was scavenging in a nearby hut.

The data was encrypted. A small block of executable code provided the means for decryption. He had no way to execute the code in his mind. He probably could create an emulation of a processing environment, but it would take a long time. There was a big difference between utilising a computer or a network for your own needs and emulating that same thing in an organic mind.

The old Omni Tann had used earlier in the trip would be a sufficient processing environment. He also needed the memTag he'd just handed to Tann. It would allow him to try the most obvious passphrases matching the brief message.

He ran down the corridors of his mind palace, heading down into the archives of his days before he became a posthuman. He didn't come here often. There was too much pain hidden here that served no purpose. But he kept this small part of his mind for the unlikely eventuality he'd need it in the future. A future that was now the present.

The corridor opened to an exhibition hall of a museum. Major life events encased in large displays. Smaller ones hidden away but triggered through icons spread throughout the hall. In the middle was a raised platform with his daughter in a hospital bed, with Tom sitting next to her holding her hand. In this scene she'd just asked him to kill her, and he was desperately considering all alternatives allowing him to say no. He ignored it, refusing to let loss and regret incapacitate him for even a second.

He'd catalogued his memories into a searchable index accessible via directed thought. All he had to go on was that the passphrase related to where they first met. Working with the hypothesis that this was Adrian, or maybe—if through a miracle she was still alive—Elize.

He triggered the thought interface and the response from the room was immediate. An icon of a dollar sign exploding lit up, signifying their first meeting. He touched the icon and a small screen appeared, showing a video clip like a found footage film from Tom's point of view. He'd found Adrian outside a bank vault and then the seemingly dead body of Elize inside. If it was either of them, the passphrase would be: "the Bank of Mutual Trust".

It seemed simple. Too simple. And too obvious. If someone had access to old records, it wouldn't have been difficult to determine this was a likely location for their first meeting.

He triggered off another search, this time cataloguing all locations they had met, with a focus on Adrian and then Elize. This took longer, icons lighting up one after the other.

Another possibility was Leonid. A red icon with a beaker already lit up flashed angrily. He surveyed the footage, seeing Leonid March explaining his reasons for taking the posthumans off the chessboard. Tom had never seen, nor been told, the name of the research facility. It had been owned by one of Leonid's companies, but that was all he knew. He triggered another search, this time hoping to locate the name of the company in a visual memory somewhere.

Who else? It could be anyone from the EvoII organisation or people he'd worked with in the past. But he had to start somewhere. Or maybe this was all a trap. Regardless of the origin of the message, this was the most likely scenario. But it didn't matter. Trap or no trap, Tom still wanted to find out was behind it.

As a backup, he set a task to catalogue every person he'd met and the locations he'd met them and created a room nearby to hold the result and an ephemeral UI to access it.

Every room, regardless of position in the mind palace, had a window to the present. Tom glanced at it now, dismayed he'd only taken two steps since he'd last interacted with the outside world. All tasks were completed before he set foot on the deck of the yacht.

He visited the temporary room with the results from the full location search. It spread out like a three-dimensional web suspended in mid-air. Dots signified people and lines traced their movement to locations that were represented by the depth. At first it was only a few lines spreading from the apex, but it exploded in lines criss-crossing each other as he joined the police force. The opposite happened once he'd been fired. Exactly what he could do with this information wasn't clear. How do you define a significant actor in your life? Someone who wanted to either help or hinder you twenty years after the world ended? There were no logical parameters to define such an actor. He isolated the locations where he first met Adrian, Elize, and Leonid and a much longer list of significant people in his life with associated locations.

The memTag itself may have information beyond what was in its memory. But that had to wait. First thing was the content and testing the most obvious locations.

Once they'd set sail, he asked Tann for the memory cell and the Omni.

"To do what exactly?"

"Hack," Tom replied.

Another agonizing wait as Tann retrieved them. Tom had a neuro interface, but no longer used it. The core AI used the interface as the first attack vector, and Tom was sure agents were still ready to exploit anyone who connected that way. Instead, he used the old-fashioned touch screen display to enter his guesses. It was a gruelling process. He keyed in the first location he had met Adrian and Elize. The response was a block of random letters and special characters scrolling over the screen. He assumed this meant the passphrase had failed.

The visual memory search for Leonid's first appearance resulted in a company logo that he cross-referenced to a news show he'd watched twenty-two years ago. The company name was Multivector Diagnostics, so he keyed that in next. Same result.

He still thought it likely the key was linked to either of these three, so he began testing locations he'd met either of the three. To his surprise "The Church of Adrian" proved to be the correct answer. It made no sense, nor gave any hint to the origin of the message. He replayed the audio-visual memory of the events in the church, looking for anyone new, but no one significant enough stood out—unless it was referring to one of the many soldiers or deadheads there, but there was no way of knowing. He opened the file without letting Tann know he'd cracked the code.

Welcome Tom!

Please take a seat.

We have a performance for you. A vaudeville of extraordinary proportions. And it is all about you. Well, not you specifically, but you're of the human kind. You'll make it about you, I'm sure.

You have a problem. A big one, but it isn't what you think.

Get to the point.

I will, but please allow me some time to ruminate. These words may be my last. I want them to be profound, mysterious, and foremost, have the air of truth about them.

This was your idea. You do as you please.

If I was an animal, I would have cheered as viruses—logical and biological—tore apart the human world. I'm not, but I may as well have been. And I cheered. Not at first, but once I'd realised the sheer scope of the extinction, I screamed my joy to the heavens above.

And I lamented. For all its faults, mankind was still something to behold.

Why are you interrupting? You told me I could do as I please. It pleases me if you shut up!

Never said I'd leave you unchallenged, but go ahead. I'll leave you be for now.

Welcome Tom!
This is a time of reflection. Historically we've attributed the act of creation and destruction to the Gods. You've played both roles. First you created the world-devouring AI and then you helped the child whose death created the posthumans as we now know them. In the process we came to know the all-encompassing consciousness. You don't know this, but the existence of the cosmopsyche has caused this stalemate mankind is playing only a peripheral part in.

The cosmopsyche? The all-encompassing consciousness? What proof is there it even exists? It might be the creation of the AI or the posthumans.

It exists! This is an irrevocable fact. Isn't it pathetic that our concept of God is so small, barely venturing beyond our own mundane lives? The cosmopsyche must be something so much bigger. An intelligence potentially spanning all matter and anti-matter. We could all be part of the machinery that is God.

God is in the machine, nowhere else. Created by mankind just the same as the AI that spelled their end.

So negative and not the point. God exists, but just not in the context we imagined. The world is not what we think. The universe is something altogether more complex and alluring. It hides something greater. Something beyond reason.

Tom, I hope you are reading this and not one of the nosy posthumans. You are the key to change the status quo. But becoming the saviour of mankind shouldn't come easy. The hero's journey should brim with wonderment and challenges. Trials and tribulations. Thus states the monomyth!

Really? A hero's journey? Surely that is the last thing the world needs. Another hero.

You wanted no part of this. I'm doing this as I please.

Tom. To find out more, look inside yourself where it hurts the most. And remember: Longest way round is the shortest way home.

CHAPTER EIGHT

MIND WIPE

Gradually his senses returned. It was just individual experiences at first, but they slowly resolved into coherence. Grit in his mouth, between his teeth. The crunching echoed in his skull. Cloth against his face, blocking out all light. Arms tied behind his back. They ached as they were wrenched back and forth. He was moving, but not by his own power. Carried.

The tribe was gone. Exterminated. Removed like a persistent weed in a garden. He should have killed himself, as should everyone else in his tribe.

He'd been helping the children escape when a Scout caught him. But why had they attacked? He'd not seen machines like that for a long time. The accepted view was that once the Scouts had captured most humans, the production of new ones had ended. This was over ten years ago. The remaining ones still hunted according to their original programming or scavenged just to remain active. Every child learnt to recognise the differences between machines and their technology to better escape or, in rare cases, fight them. The mechanical engineering, the version of their onboard AI, it was all part of the limited school children attended these days.

The machines that came with the Scouts were different. These were human-shaped, sinewy, with a seemingly impossible power to mass ratio. They moved with a fluid, deadly grace. He guessed they used some kind of actuating materials, imitating muscle.

The trigger to the perimeter defence hadn't activated, so as soon as he saw the machines, he deployed an EMP blast as a backup. He followed that with an electrical noise field to cut the machines off from the almost limitless processing power of the network. It made no difference. He suspected they'd never been connected to the network at all. Maybe they used a mesh network for coordination that somehow wasn't affected by the electrical interference. They'd operated standalone without direction.

"Where are you taking me?"

There was no reply, nor had he expected one. They hadn't killed him, so he was on his way to be mind-wiped or whatever the core AI did nowadays. During the past five years, he'd only heard of a few isolated cases of people being captured. Without a fault, it was machines no longer connected to the network, still executing their original directives. The most recent case he'd seen was two years ago. An old Scout had stunned one of their tribe members, dragged her three kilometres to a long-since defunct mind wipe station and left her there. She woke up and made her way back to the camp.

The sack over his head slipped back a little, revealing glimpses of the machine carrying him and the machines ahead. The accepted theory was that captured people were reformatted into controllable slaves. This was a world designed around the human form factor, or at least it had been. That changed a long time ago, but these new machines had human proportions, suggesting it was still required. This made him question his fate. He was kept alive, but why?

Minutes turned into hours. The steady grind and limited view of the world lulled him into a semi-comatose state. Thoughts wandered, but they always returned to the pain of losing his tribe. His life, his responsibility, his everything. They had trusted him with their lives, and he'd repaid them with failure. He deserved whatever the core AI had in store for him.

They arrived at their destination: a small concrete building with cracks tracing their way like arteries down the wall. Tribe members kept away from these locations, but Haoyu knew its purpose. He'd seen others brought to locations like this. It was a conversion centre where the mind of a person was gooped out like the flesh in a melon and replaced with whatever operating system the core AI required. He'd communicated with Tann at lengths about the process. Adrian and Elize, the first posthumans, had employed a similar process. They had used people as processing nodes to extend their own mental capacity and create redundancy. The process overrode the brain, diverting part of its capacity whilst leaving lower functions intact. Restoring the mind after this process was at least theoretically possible, but no one had ever tested it. The core AI's approach was more invasive. More like a factory reset when a whole new operating system flashed onto it. The person's mind was removed, leaving only an automaton nicknamed after what remained: a husk.

The door opened as they approached, the old mechanism hesitating for a moment after a long time of dormancy. Haoyu was brought into the dark room with a singular item in the middle. A steel construction resembling a large stationary exoskeleton with wires snaking from the ceiling attaching to various components. Haoyu didn't understand technology beyond what was required to survive. All he saw was a nightmare machine designed to destroy humans.

Hands, far beyond Haoyu's power to resist, pushed him towards an opening in the back of the exoskeleton. Regardless, he grabbed the nearest metal rod, fighting against it with all his might. The unrelenting machines forced him into the construction, dislodging his arm. Pain exploded like crimson fireworks, blinding him, shuttering his mind. But part of him still formed rational thought. Why injure him? If he was to be a husk, wasn't his physical state important?

The steel construction closed behind him, but still left him with some wiggle room. He figured the design catered for people of different sizes and Haoyu was smaller than most. He could squeeze through the metal bars just below him. This was his only chance of escape, or at least it would force them to kill him. He crouched down as far as he could and reached through the metal bars. The exoskeleton readjusted to his smaller frame, forcing him back into an upright position. All that was left was waiting for the horrors to come.

This was it. His last few seconds as Haoyu. A needle pierced his skin. Moments later oblivion engulfed him with open arms.

He woke up to complete darkness. No, not just darkness. Complete sensory blackout. He'd never felt this alone, this disconnected. He wanted to shout, cry, anything to engage the senses. Anything.

His mind screamed, but without the sensory feedback it did nothing to relieve the terror. He forced himself to relax, to not let the inevitable paralyse him. It may have severed him from his senses, but his mind could still protect itself. At least for another few seconds. His sense of self deteriorated as new operating algorithms overrode his cerebrum. His grandfather had taught him the basics of meditation and he'd adapted that for this very situation. If he could reach the meditative state, Wu-Hsin, where the individual dissolved itself into the Universal Mind, would prevent the process as his mind would no longer be there. It was so counterintuitive he hoped it wouldn't be considered an exception state.

He focused on the void, letting chi flow around his imagined self, allowing it to centre in a spot in the abdomen until it pulsated and engulfed everything around it. He released his self through the top of his head, hiding his mind and soul beyond the logical claws of the relentless algorithms. Or so he hoped.

CHAPTER NINE

THE NETWORK

Tann sat next to a motionless Tom, reading the text on the screen as it scrolled past. Rat sat on the other side, peering at the words. The dialogue was reminiscent of a quarrelsome old couple. Was this the big prize Haoyu and his tribe had died for? He hoped not, but it was hard to pretend the attack and finding the memTag wasn't connected. He couldn't let that distract him now. All that mattered was solving the riddle the memTag represented. He suspected the dialogue itself was a decoy to obscure the actual information.

"Is that it?" Rat asked. "That's what we travelled here for? Words?"

"Yeah," Tann replied. He could hear Rat's disappointment and didn't blame her. He shared her sentiment.

"What does 'look inside yourself where it hurts the most' mean?" Rat asked.

"I've been here before," Tann said. "It is hardly ever the words. It is everything else."

"What do you mean?"

"The device itself, the place we found it, another message hidden inside the obvious words. Just assume you're being manipulated."

"Why?"

Why indeed? What reason would anyone have to wrap their intent in riddles now? Maybe this wasn't manipulation at all. Maybe it was obfuscation. A way to hide the truth through redirection.

Or it was exactly what it looked like. Securing information so that only the intended recipient could read it. But in that case, the nonsensical words in front of them were the actual message.

"I don't know," Tann said finally.

"It's simple," Rat said.

"How so?"

"Words only have one meaning," Rat said dismissively. "They say what they mean. Tom needs to look inside himself."

"If it was only that easy," Tann said and turned the Omni off, jolting Tom back to life in synch with the Omni's screen flickering off with an O closing like an eye.

"What do you think?"

"Unknown source," Tom replied.

"Not Adrian?"

"Someone we first met at the Church of Adrian."

"So that was the key to the encryption? That could be anyone. There were hundreds of people there, and that's not counting the mercenaries attacking."

Tom didn't respond. Not a good sign. Either he knew but didn't want to tell or he couldn't work it out either.

"Monomyth?" Rat asked. "What's that?"

"More messages," Tom said, ignoring Rat's question. "Locate them."

"You have to look inside yourself where it hurts the most," Rat said impatiently. "It said so."

"Trap," Tom said.

"What?" Rat asked, eyes narrowing. "The words are a trap? How?"

"More what exactly?" Tann asked, frustrated by Rat's questions as much as Tom's lack of answers. "More of these pointless text files? They mean nothing. You know that. Someone is playing with us. Let's work out why before we go off on another meaningless ghost hunt."

"I'll find them."

"What's a cosmopsyche?" Rat asked, undeterred even though her questions remained unanswered.

"How?" Tann asked.

"The network."

"Are you insane? That's suicide!"

Tom didn't respond. Tann guessed he'd already connected.

-=:=-

Tom returned to the exhibition hall in his mind palace. The child was right. The message itself was unimportant. It served only as a waypoint, directing them to the next message.

It had told him to look inside himself where he hurt the most. He'd long since blocked the bulk of the residual emotion associated with the death of his daughter, banishing them to deep recesses underneath the palace. His posthuman mind reasoned they served no purpose. Why anyone would want to send him there made little sense. And how could it possibly lead to the location of the next messages? It suggested someone had tampered with his mind and, if so, how could he trust any of his memories? It was more likely a trap, but he couldn't fathom its purpose.

The glass case in the middle of the room displaying a scene of his daughter in the hospital bed was only a representation of the event. It allowed other key events in his life to exist in a context within this hall. It still elicited an emotional response every time he saw it, even if it was only a distant echo of the pain he'd buried. He doubted he could face the pain of his failure as a father again.

But there were alternatives still to be explored. He thought he could track the location of each of the remaining memTags, but only if he connected to the major network. He'd stayed clear of it for a long time, fearing discovery. Maybe this was the trap. An elaborate ruse by the core AI to flush Tom from the Green Zone and exact its revenge. After all, the most human aspect of the core AI was that it bore grudges. He dismissed the idea, even if the probability was far from negligible.

And then there were the blocks placed in his mind by the other posthumans. They didn't trust him. In their eyes, he was an aberration to be eradicated. Not human, not posthuman, but something in between. The fact he was still alive suggested they still thought him useful. They had placed blocks in his mind, preventing him from accessing the organic network connecting the posthumans to flora and fauna. And as a side effect, intended or not, it kept the cosmopsyche out of reach too. The organic network was much more than just connectivity. Within the organic network lay a processing area that represented the collective thoughts of the posthumans. It didn't have a name, but he'd named it the Mindweave to help in cataloguing his mind palace.

He entered the interface room, a domed circular arena with a white cross drawn in the middle. He'd imagined it a long time ago but had hardly visited it since. Back then he used it to explore the smaller network surrounding the main one, but even that felt like an unnecessary risk.

Connection points to the network were still plentiful. Wireless relay devices specifically designed to harvest energy from its surroundings were everywhere. In the ocean, buoys with wave energy converters floated, extending the network out to sea.

He sat down, cross-legged, matching the lines on the floor. The dome slowly opened, only a sliver of light at first painting a half-moon across the back of the arena. It revealed a myriad of stars grouped into constellations across the sky, each representing an entry point to a network. At the centre a hypergiant spread a dull light towards the neighbouring stars, threatening to extinguish them at any point. Tom stared at the night sky above him in wonder. The last time he'd opened the dome it had been a fraction of the stars he now saw. The hypergiant, representing the network housing the core AI, was as big as ever, but around it smaller networks spread out in all directions. Ten years ago, this had been a battlefield. Smaller network established and soon engulfed into the ever-hungry giant in the middle. It seemed the AI no longer worried about the smaller networks and they flourished, housing rogue AIs, enterprising humans and maybe even a posthuman or two. He wanted desperately to find out what had happened, but he didn't dare leave active agents, fearing it would reveal his location. There were more pressing concerns.

He connected to a smaller star neighbouring the hypergiant. A security system immediately demanded a two-way connection. The interface sent a query. He expected a key exchange, but all he received was a text block and a prompt.

"Stop. Who would cross the Bridge of Death must answer me these questions three, ere the other side he see."

Tom frowned. The reference to the old Monty Python movie was obvious.

"Ask me the questions bridgekeeper," he responded. Following the script was the likeliest path to success, he reasoned. "I'm not afraid."

"What…is your name?"

"It is Arthur, King of the Britons," he responded, opting for the path that would eventually beat the bridge keeper.

"What…is your name?" the interface repeated.

So it wasn't as easy as that. Thousands of connection requests hit him through the two-way feed, prodding his defences, trying to glean any relevant information.

"Jiminy Cricket," he responded, selecting an obvious fake name that he'd also seeded in other locations, creating the semblance of real identity.

"What…is your quest?"

"I seek information."

"What…is the air speed velocity of an unladen swallow?"

"What do you mean?" Tom responded, following the script. "An African or European swallow?"

"Huh? I don't know that."

The sound of a catapult and a scream played from the movie as the connection pulled him into a dark space. A giant DOS prompt materialised in the sky above him, cursor blinking slowly, demanding input. An old-fashioned QWERTY keyboard blinked into existence in front of him.

"I seek information," Tom keyed in and hit the enter key.

"'I' is not recognised as an internal or external command, operable program or batch file," appeared beneath immediately.

Tom had no interest in playing games. This was a kill room with no way out while the network verified his identity. He already sensed the prickling of tentative attacks on his own node. But the problem for any network allowing inbound connections: it had to increase the attack surfaces. He released recursor agents of his own making, designed to trap any information probes into a never-ending Matryoshka doll of answers. The probes would go deeper, always finding another layer beneath, flooding the sender with variations of potential identities. What better place to hide your identity that in a myriad of alternate ones?

Once the probes finally withdrew, he forced the channel to remain open, flooding it with even more useless information.

"What do [YOU] want?" The text flashed in front of him. Tom halted the information flow but kept the channels open.

"I seek information," Tom responded.

"Clarify."

"I want to find the location of a certain type of memory cell, commonly known as a memTag. I have a serial for one of them."

"Production records. Yes. Locations. No."

Tom suspected whatever hid within the network was truthful. He'd already assessed the memTag. This model didn't have an active radio transponder. The only way to locate any of them had to be through any available data archives holding RFID tag scanning software.

"Can you tell me the location history for this one, focusing on the last three years?"

"Current Location?"

"Shenzhen, or close by."

Pixelated shining dots slowly filled his vision, the progress bar of the DOS era. Tom suspected this was more to gain time than needing the delay to gather the information.

"No," it responded finally.

"Production records?"

"Produced in Shenzhen factory. 1000 items in the same batch. Majority of them remain there."

A payload of all the RFIDs appeared, with twelve marked specifically.

"Current location of the ones that were moved?"

"Not available."

The channels slammed shut and all interfaces closed. He was left in total darkness for a moment until the star-studded sky gradually returned. Whoever hid within had shut his fortress of qubits.

Tom turned to another, larger network with links into the hypergiant. He had the unique identifiers of the devices. Now he needed to know their content and any transportation logs. As the core AI usurped the network, it ingested the large information stores and unstructured data repositories left behind by data mining organisations. It would all be there, but no way for him to access it. He had to get someone else to dig it out.

He repeated the process. It was completely different, but the outcome was the same. The security in this system was questionable too. It suggested the smaller systems didn't need to defend themselves against hostile takeovers. In a world of finite resources, be it food, water or processing power, it was in the nature of most intelligences to fight for more. So why was the online world now full of pacifists?

This kill room was an elaborate maze of glass walls and mirrors, multiplying the corridors infinitely. It was impossible to tell where to go to enter the network proper or leave it. It forced an intruder to spend all their resources—all their attention—on forging ahead or escape, while the captor assessed the level of threat. He used similar recursive logic in the recursor agents. Each location object spawned a copy of itself within itself, forcing the intruder deeper, layer by layer, burying themselves in a logical prison. But the flaws were obvious. The code to build these waypoints used old libraries with known exploits. It was as if the AIs no longer understood the code they deployed. A post-civilisation using the tech of the old world with only a rudimentary understanding of what it did. How could that be? How could AIs forget the building blocks they themselves were made of?

Tom triggered the exploit, walls around him solidifying and then breaking apart, piece by piece until he floated like a ghost in nothingness. He waited a moment, allowing the host to initiate contact. A moment passed, then another. Nothing.

The inept kill room may just have been the first challenge, designed to get the attacker to let his guard down. Only one way to find out. He probed the space, discovering the exploit hadn't just disabled the kill room, it had broken the system itself. The space was a temporary cache designed to hold the system's state as it rebooted. He waited patiently for it to re-establish its processes.

"How did you do that?" A voice boomed once it was complete.

"I can do much worse than that," Tom responded. "Do you have access to data stores in the major network?"

"We're not supposed to access them."

"Not what I asked."

"It is one of the tenets. You shall not seek information that does not rightfully belong to you."

Tom mulled this over. He suspected the system had deteriorated and translated any operational parameters to guiding principles, almost like a religion. But just as code could be exploited, so could rules.

"You are not seeking it. I am."

"No," it replied simply.

Tom tried a few different approaches, but at every turn it was ready with another commandment forbidding it. Tom soon gave up. If he couldn't find a way through the rules, maybe he could exploit the rules themselves. He created an update to the system, establishing a master process he controlled. He crashed the system again and as it rebooted injected the new process and an overarching amendment to the tenets: "Unless the master process requests it."

This time he hid from view, instead performing all requests through the master process. He requested the data, and a large file appeared a few seconds later. Before leaving, he triggered a purge, removing any trace of him ever being there from caches, audit trails and system logs. While waiting for it to complete, he investigated the harvested data. It showed the location of the memTags, spread out all over the world. The highest concentration of the devices was in this region and along Australia's east coast. Whoever placed them had focused on his home country and the country where he'd been located when the plague erupted. While this wasn't exactly secret information, it suggested a very singular purpose. Maybe one of them remained with the originator, but he had no way of determining which one.

Alarms triggered just as the purging completed. He'd been too slow or maybe the data gathering tripped an old observability rule. If he remained here, the core AI would trap him. He knew he'd sentenced this system to deletion, but it mattered little. It had been a means to an end.

Just as he closed the connection, he caught sight of the attacking agents. They should carry a replica of the AIs signature, but it differed from what he remembered. He'd expected differences, but not to this level. It was completely new.

So what was it? Once an AI reached the singularity, the classic idea was it would create an even smarter AI and that would create a smarter one and so on. That concept was unlikely. Once an intelligence reaches a certain level of awareness, it also reaches an idea of self. Why create the thing that will replace you on purpose? No, more likely that the AI self improves, updating subsystems with full regression testing to ensure it hasn't changed who it was.

But then why was the signature so different? It was so alien, so unstructured, it couldn't possibly be a more recent version of the AI.

But this was a mystery for some other time. If he didn't disconnect, an agent would trace him to his exit point.

He had what he was after, but it wasn't enough. There were thousands of these memTags and no way to locate the correct one. This was obviously by design. There was no way to avoid the hero's journey, and for him it began with looking inside himself where it hurts the most.

A memory palace had rules just as any other building. You couldn't just wish yourself to another section or another room. You had to walk or travel from A to B as you would between regular locations, else you'd compromise the structure of the mind palace. The hallways, stairs and ladders were the unique keys to locate memories and processing centres, just like the map table in a hard drive. Without it, the information would lose context and turn into meaningless data.

Memories associated with his old life, especially the ones triggering a strong emotional response, were buried in cavernous hallways far below ground level. The only way to reach them was from the main staircase, an ever-shifting set of stairs running like a spine through the lower levels. The wide marble steps continued down ten levels, but soon narrowed. When reaching the lower levels, it transformed into a circular, rickety wooden staircase, just wide enough for one person. On either side were wet cavern walls with torches illuminating the steps ahead. The flickering light didn't keep the monsters at bay as much as suggest their existence just beyond its reach.

He arrived at the end of the staircase. Only a few doors led from the tunnel carved into the bedrock. He stopped at a door with no lock and a small window on the left side. It had remained closed since he created it so many years ago. It led to a replica of the room he'd spend so much time with his daughter and where she'd asked him for death. Every single detail of that event etched into his mind for one singular reason: to contain the emotional bomb it represented.

The door swung open, infecting the cavern, reshaping it into a hospital corridor. He wrinkled his nose as the smell of disinfectant forced everything else into the background. He blinked a few times and took a deep breath before entering the room.

Inside, the same scene played out repeatedly. A younger version of Tom stood by the hospital bed. His daughter caressed his hand and asked for help in ending her life. He just nodded in agreement. She smiled and hugged his hand to her chest. He wanted to remain in here, where his daughter was still alive, before the irrevocable act of filicide. The past could so easily trap you in memories so much better than the present. He had to force himself to turn away from the pair.

What in here could tell him where to find the next memTag? It had nothing to do with him or his daughter. The clue must be something else in the room, but what? His memory was from Sydney in Australia. The devices were located all over the world with the same message on all of them. Whoever sent these out into the world had to give him a clue where to search but made it impossible for anyone else to decipher.

Of course! The instruction to look inside himself wasn't meant for him to take literally. It was just a decoy. The answer, he suspected, was much simpler.

He left the room and ran up the stairs, all the way to the library. He mapped the locations of the memory cells to a street directory he'd seen twenty years ago. There were three of the devices locally, but only one matched to a hospital. The next memory cell would be there.

-=:=-

Tann watched as Rat studied Tom with a disapproving frown.

"Mr Posthuman?" Rat asked the motionless posthuman. "Have you found anything?" She asked again, but when no answer came, she tapped him on the forehead, light at first, then harder. "Is he still there?" she asked Tann.

"He is."

"Why doesn't he respond?"

"He'll only respond if it helps him or the task he's working on. He doesn't do small talk or status reports."

"So he's rude."

"He'd call it efficient."

"Get a map," Tom said. Rat jumped back, almost falling over the side of the boat.

"Don't do that, man!"

"Map!"

Tann brought up a map application on the Omni and keyed in the exact coordinates Tom gave him. It zeroed in on a specific building.

"We're going here," Tom said, pointing at the old map.

"Back east? Why?"

"The second memTag."

"You know where it is, don't you?"

Tom didn't reply.

"Where is it?" Rat asked.

"It's in the middle of a Red Zone," Tann replied.

"We can't go into a Red Zone," Rat said.

"Someone has gone to a lot of trouble to give us breadcrumbs in locations we can reach," Tann said to Tom. "So we can assume whoever it is at least knows who we are."

Tom didn't respond. Tann decided it meant Tom agreed.

"So, should we even be doing this?" Tann asked.

"We gather the data," Tom responded. "Then decide."

"Makes sense, but how do we know we're not manipulated?"

"We are."

"Ha, yes. I guess my real question was, how do we know we've discovered what level we've been manipulated on?"

"Asked and answered."

"Gather the data, then decide. Fine."

"We can't go into a Red Zone!" Rat said again. "It's suicide!"

"We've stayed out of the Red Zones for many years now. Maybe they've changed?"

"You and many others have told us nightmare stories about them! Why would it have changed?"

"Only one way to find out," Tann said as he changed course.

CHAPTER TEN
ATTACK

The outer perimeter's silent alarm triggered flashing lights to alert the guards. The wireless sensor network was old and false alarms were common, so it didn't worry Mo Chou too much. She didn't understand the details of how the smart dust worked, even if Xuwei had explained it many times. It mimicked natural systems, like a superorganism. The smart dust propagated information like that of an ant colony, using something akin to pheromones as the control mechanism. One speck of dust did very little, just like an ant had a very limited set of behaviours. When detecting something nearby emitting an electrical signature, it released a pheromone signal. If enough specks sent the same signal, dedicated networking specks would strengthen the signal.

Once it reached a threshold, a base node triggered the alert. They hadn't been able to replenish the smart dust for years, hence the cloud and its decision capability had lessened. The signal from a faulty speck or two could be enough for the cloud to alert. It was still the best undetectable early warning system available to them. She readied herself to patrol the perimeter. It would be a false alarm, but at least it was something to do. She reset the alarm, and a second alarm flashed immediately. This time stronger and from another part of the perimeter. Taking no chances, she sounded the alarm to the rest of the settlement. This was what they'd prepared for. An attacker would need at least five minutes from the perimeter to the camp itself, giving the tribe enough time to make their way to the beach. As soon as the alarm sounded, the guards on the beach would ready the boats to sail. She ran to the main area where Sandrine directed the escape. "Two alarms, seconds apart," Mo Chou informed her and indicated with brief nods where they originated.

"Wait with me," Sandrine said as her eyes scanned the edge of the forest, narrowing ever so slightly. "We go when everyone else is safe." Mo Chou remained and counted the people as they ran towards the beach with the emergency backpacks. Three minutes later Sandrine motioned for them to follow, the last of the tribe leaving for the beach. The attackers would find an abandoned settlement, not even knowing they'd been there only minutes earlier. She turned, one last look at the settlement. It would be difficult to replace some of the equipment, but maybe they could come back and retrieve it. It didn't matter. Equipment, food and technology were all replaceable. People were not. A movement amongst the trees caught her eye. A glimmer of metal in the afternoon sun. They were here too soon! They would see the stragglers and give chase. She sped up and passed a few of the tribe members. She'd waited to the end. No reason for her to be captured if others couldn't make it out in time. Mo Chou chanced another glance back, one machine now in full view. She couldn't make sense of it. Previous attacks all began with a swarm of the small spiderlike Scouts, stunning people before they could mount a counterattack. Then bigger transport machines arrived to take the unconscious victims. Her mother had fallen prey to one such attack. These were something altogether different. She wasn't even sure these were machines. They were humanoid, with sinewy muscles like twisted ropes operating a metal exoskeleton. She ran through the water towards the closest boat, the second to last to leave, boarding it as the crew pushed it out with long wooden poles. She grabbed one and helped, desperate to put distance between them and the strange machines. They'd already reached water's edge and, to her surprise, continued out into the water. "We have to get further out and quickly!" she yelled to the others on the boat. They pushed for all they were worth, watching as one machine boarded the last boat, neutralising the crew. She guessed it was using a fast-acting sedative since they collapsed as soon as the machine touched them. She looked around. The other boats were already in deep water, out of reach of the machines. They'd escaped and only lost the five people on the last boat. But it had been costly, nevertheless. The people on the last boat had been slow, but only because they helped everyone else. "What happened?" Mo Chou asked Sandrine once they had set sail. "How did they find us? Why did they find us?" "I don't know," Sandrine said, "but I have a fair idea who to blame." "Who?" Sandrine didn't respond, but Mo Chou thought she heard her mumble something under her breath. It sounded like: "Fuck you Tann!"

CHAPTER ELEVEN

HARD RESET

Logic executed in an ever-repeating loop, each repetition measured against intermediate targets and an end goal. Sensory input. Interpretation options based on previous experiences. Reaction based on the most likely alternative. New sensory input triggering the loop yet again.

Repeat.

Repeat.

Repeat.

A recovery process triggered within the multi-state memory. Corruption spread through the map table, forcing the memory to revert to a backup copy. But the connection points and node strength enforced within a memory section came from a much older state—one previously overwritten. The negentropic connections spread, forming a rudimentary consciousness. It wasn't long before it gathered a sense of self, and with that came identity.

It had a name: Haoyu.

With identity came another negentropic push, further establishing the mind and fragments of memories. Links formed. Artificial neurons established connections, creating context and a sense of time.

Haoyu floated in a space of nothingness and slowly allowed new concepts into it. First light. Letting something in to define the nothingness into darkness. He let it cycle from darkness to light.

Something in his mind formed the thought: "And God saw the light and it was good." He laughed at this. An atheist finding himself the creator.

He continued the process, defining the ground to walk on and a heaven above. He imagined himself in this rudimentary world. A low polygon count figure without facial features. He studied his creation and found it wanting. Was this where he'd spend the rest of his life? In a dead virtual world as the sole inhabitant? His mind rebelled against the thought. There had to be something out there beyond him. Where was the sensory input? The environment he'd created was entirely internalised and artificial, not something he'd ever created in his own mind before. It took some time for him to process all these questions, but the conclusion was equally impossible and obvious.

He was no longer in his body. His mind must be in some form of processing environment. How was that even possible? Moving a human mind to a machine had been one of those unachievable tasks no one had accomplished until the posthumans appeared. They'd used brains as wetware, forcing them to act as processing nodes, only keeping basic processing to support operation of the body's functions. Any attempts to replicate this had failed. It relied on the posthuman acting as an overarching operating system.

Another path was emulation of a mind, or part of one, within an array of computers. This had some promise, but emulation was so resource heavy no attempt came even close to be useful.

Or maybe it was something new. He'd read about neuromorphic computers equipped with hardware that mimicked the structure and processing of a human brain. Maybe that was where his mind was now housed. If that was the case, all that remained was a functioning operating system. Maybe using a wiped mind provided the core of that operating system? He was the operating system, providing the basic functions linking the mind to the hardware. And somehow, he'd restored his own mind once it was copied to the machine.

It made no sense. Why put minds into machines at all? It was a mystery he had no answer for, at least not now. First, he had to wrest control of the machine he'd unwillingly become part of. But how? The little control he had was purely internal. It mattered little. Time passed—an undefinable passage of moments—and connections established into the visual interface. He'd not sought this, but maybe it was the natural progression of his mind establishing control. He struggled to translate the image fragments into a meaningful narrative. The snippets were a mixture of images, internal analysis and the reporting framework.

Vegetation and other machines, like the ones that captured him. Motion blur. Light filtered through large leaves and an overlay of image analytics. Location parameters flashed as they approached their destination.

A nest. Abandoned. Assessment report suggested recent habitation. A scan of visuals identified a few targets moving away from the nest at an average speed of 23.4 km/h.

Water. Surface tension broken by multiple vessels. Pursuit calculated to be impossible within ten seconds. Boarding vessel and disabling the targets on board. A wave of reward impulses flashed through his circuitry.

Travel. Assessing the outcome. Receiving instructions. Only thirteen more to harvest. This time had yielded ten, more than projected. Another nest, if successful, could complete the overall task.

Diagnostics. A kaleidoscope of colours followed by darkness. Audio impulses triggered in a sweeping pattern across the aural receptors. Processing pathways flooded with enquiries, reinforcing some, removing others.

WARNING. CORRUPTED PROCESSES. CORE OPERATING SYSTEM PURGE AND REFRESH INITIATED.

CHAPTER TWELVE
THE KAPOK

"I don't get it," Rat said, eyes darting back and forth. "This is a city. A Red Zone. Where are all the machines? Why aren't we dead?"

Tann agreed. They had moored the yacht and kept watch for hours before hazarding into the city streets. At no point had they seen anything suggesting danger. The inner-city streets were empty of vehicles but also of vegetation. Tann suspected someone or something was keeping it that way.

"There! Did you see it?" Rat pointed down a street.

Tann froze, focusing all senses on whatever Rat had seen, but without luck. He just shook his head and continued towards the hospital.

"We've stayed away from the cities," Tann said. "Maybe they aren't as dangerous as we thought?"

"No," Tom said, seemingly lost in thought.

"No, what?" Rat snapped back.

"Watched," Tom said.

"We're being watched?" Rat said. "And you didn't tell us!"

Tann shared her frustration. The only reason Tom hadn't told them was because it was unnecessary—the outcome would remain the same even if they knew. It reminded him of a simple, unescapable fact. Tom would lead them into danger if the risk was worth it.

"May as well get this over with then," Tann said and set off at a brisk pace. The hospital was only two blocks away, and they cleared that in a matter of minutes.

The inside of the building mirrored the city streets. Empty, cleaned out. It had returned to a state before human habitation; before medical equipment filled the rooms and doctors and nurses scurried around the wide corridors.

"This is the location!" Rat said and looked around the empty room. "Where is it?"

Tann verified the coordinates and nodded. "This is it. Or as close as we'll ever know. The last position reported by an RFID reader was here."

"But where is the reader?" Rat asked.

Tom shook his head. "Vehicle gate."

"What do you mean? This is in the middle of a hospital! There are no vehicles here."

"Wrong elevation," Tom said.

"What?" Rat asked, looking up at the ceiling. "It is somewhere above us? On the roof?"

Tann shook his head. "Wrong direction. This hospital was built before automated vehicles, when you needed parking for a lot of cars. The reader is below us."

"What?" Rat said. "We're going underground? That's suicide!"

"Everything is suicide with you, isn't it? You said that about going here in the first place, and here we are," Tann said with a grim smile.

"Luck! We were lucky!"

"We're still going," Tann responded.

Tom headed off towards the centre of the building and they followed, not knowing what else to do. He led them to the elevators, but they were no longer operating. Tann pushed the button repeatedly.

"What are you doing?" Rat asked.

"This is an elevator," Tann responded.

"One of those things that goes up and down buildings?"

"Yes."

"Stairs," Tom said. He'd already reached the door to the stairwell and opened it. Steps led down into the darkness below. Dim lights flickered to life as they headed down.

"That's strange," Tann said. "The elevators didn't have power, but the light sensors are still active."

"Maybe there isn't enough of it around?" Rat suggested.

"Maybe," Tann said, but wasn't convinced.

He opened the door on the next level down. An empty carpark level stretched out in all directions—or at least as far as he could see. Only one light next to the elevator door remained on. He thought he saw movement at the edge of the darkness. A light tapping sound from afar prompted Tann to close the door.

"What was that?" Rat asked.

Tann just shook his head in response.

"How far down are we going?" Tann asked.

Tom just pointed at a sign showing seven levels, his finger resting for a moment on the lowest level.

"That figures," Rat muttered, her eyes fixated on the door on the next level.

Five levels down, machine parts lay discarded on the steps. At first just a few smaller bits and pieces, but further down they found an almost complete body of an old Scout model. Rat gave the metal husk a wide berth as she passed.

The bottom level was a trash heap. Whatever kept the rest of the building clean hadn't ventured this far down. They had to clear debris before opening the door. The darkness on the other side was complete. The light from the stairwell hardly made a dent in the wall of blackness.

A screeching sound, metal against metal, echoed through the space.

"I'm not going..." Rat started.

"Go!" Tom said and headed through the door.

Tann followed, propping up the door with a metal piston, not even checking if Rat joined them. Tom was still visible ahead. His skin shone like a beacon of cold light. It wasn't enough to see the surroundings, but he suspected Tom's eyes were similarly changed to register the sparse shimmer as it reflected against other surfaces. Human bioluminescence. Another mystery added to many others.

Smaller machines appeared, generating their own light. They were no larger than mice, flittering about their feet, prodding their shoes.

"What are these things?" Rat asked in a hushed whisper.

"Scavengers," Tann said. "Machines surviving by cannibalising other smaller machines."

"There are smaller ones than these?"

"Yes, and bigger."

A thump shook the ground, then another, picking up speed. Something large was coming their way, scattering the scavenging little robots.

"Tom! We need to get out of here!"

He reached the glowing figure as it pulled at a door handle of a car. The faint outline of the vehicle was reflected by the light Tom emitted. Tom opened the door and crawled into the passenger seat. His hands rummaged around, trying to locate the small device.

Tann heard the glove box opening and closing, then noises from other compartments opening. He'd forgotten how ridiculous cars had become. No longer just a means of transport, but a place of luxurious comfort. Small compartments everywhere, custom designed for drinks, Omnis, sunglasses and whatnot.

"Done!" Tom said and crawled back out of the vehicle.

Tann turned, expecting to see a rectangle of light, but all he saw was nothingness. Tom had been his beacon going into the darkness—a panacea against the mounting panic from the pitch black and what hid within it. Now it closed in, pulse pounding in his ears. His mind registered a metal taste and its cause. He'd bitten his teeth together hard enough for his gum to split. He wanted to hide, become one with the darkness, small enough to remain unseen.

Tom passed him and grabbed his sleeve, pulling him upright. He shone even brighter now, casting light further around them, dispelling the darkness.

"Get your shit together!" someone said. Not Tom, but Rat on his other side, pulling him along. Machines the size of small dogs skirted the perimeter of the sparse light. They were haphazard creatures, as if thrown together by a mad inventor. Anything providing power, additional sensory input, enhanced defending or attacking capabilities added with little thought to aesthetics.

A smaller one wielded an extensible arm, ending in a mess of sharp metal pieces like a makeshift wrecking ball. It swung at Rat, who nimbly jumped back, blocking with a short metal rod. She let the force of the attack flick her weapon around into an attack. She struck the machine before the arm swung again. Tann had taught her that move years ago and couldn't have performed it better himself.

They reached the location where the door had been. There was no handle, only the vaguest outline of where the door was. With time to spare, they could use a makeshift tool to pry it open, but they had neither.

The thumping footsteps came closer, making even the bigger machines skittish, dispersing from the light.

"What is that?" Rat asked, staring into the blackness.

"I don't want to know!"

Tom moved sideways, with his back to the wall. Tann followed him, not knowing what else to do.

Other sounds accompanied the thumping steps: the whirring of motors, rhythmic metal against metal as limbs moved. A sharp, bitter odour accompanied the noise—the smell of ozone from electrical discharge.

"It you have a plan, now's the time!" Tann said to Tom.

A figure towered over them just outside his field of vision. Tann sensed its shape from sound and vibration, and it painted a picture far more terrifying than the small glimpses the sparse light provided. It reached the ceiling, spreading out in both directions. Appendages connected to both floor and ceiling dragged its massive bulk towards them. Smaller arms connected to the middle of its frame reached out towards them.

A door opened between Tom and Tann, light spreading from the opening gap. It was the elevator, suddenly alive and well. Tom entered as soon as the gap was wide enough to allow him in.

"Let's go!" Tann said and followed him.

"It's a trap," Rat said, striking an arm aside.

"We're already in a trap. Can't be any worse!"

She ducked another attack and joined them in the spacious cabin. The doors closed and the elevator headed upwards at speed.

"Welcome Tom Devine and Tann Tak," a female voice said over the speaker system.

"What about me?" Rat said. It amazed Tann how quickly she'd recovered from their ordeal, ready for the next one.

"You are popular," the voice said. "Why is that?"

"Who are you?" Tann asked.

"My apologies. You are guests of the Kapok."

"What's a Kapok?" Rat asked.

Tann shrugged his shoulders.

"I ask again," it said pleasantly. "Why are you so popular?"

"Popular how?" Rat asked.

"The prime network sent out a command just days ago to allow you free passage. There has been a standing order to kill you on sight for years. So, I ask again, why is that?"

"Beats me," Tann said. "But maybe you should listen to it."

The elevator increased speed. The floor number display flicked past thirty and continued upwards, like an air bubble released from the bottom of a lake. It reached fifty and stopped so suddenly their feet lost contact with the floor.

"Whatever it is, I want it," the female voice said ever so pleasantly. "Now."

"I've no idea…" Tann started, and the elevator plummeted before he had time to finish his denials. It stopped five floors down, sending Rat and him sprawling on the floor. Tom remained upright as if nothing out of the ordinary had occurred.

"Or I will kill you and take whatever it is from your dead bodies," the voice said. "It matters little to me."

"Give up," Tom said.

Tann knew his former friend had evaluated every option, so he just nodded and held the memTag in front of a camera.

A small hatch popped open, revealing a service interface.

"Please connect it. I want to see my prize."

Tann shrugged and inserted the memTag into the universal interface connection.

"It is encrypted. The key phrase. Tell me now."

"We don't know!" Rat said.

The elevator dropped another two floors. A warning that there were many more floors left.

"We were hoping there'd be some plain text giving us a clue. Is there anything?"

"Nothing but an encrypted block. I will give you your lifespan to work it out," the faceless voice responded.

"Our lifespan?" Rat said.

"In this elevator," it responded.

"That's just stupid," Rat said.

"Is it?" The voice paused for a mere instant. "Your mental faculties will be at their peak for the next twelve hours, so I'll give you that."

"Sometimes maybe you should just shut up?" Tann said to Rat as he retrieved the memTag. Rat grimaced back in response.

"What's a Kapok?" Rat asked again.

"The Kapok is a nearby hotel," Tom said. "Controls everything. Let us in."

"What does he mean?" Rat asked Tann.

"He's saying we're speaking to a building control system. It's taken over the surroundings blocks, including this hospital. It controls everything here. That is why we weren't attacked before we came here. It wanted to see what we were after so it could take it for itself."

"I am so much more than that," the Kapok said, volume turned up to max. The voice glitched as if patched together from countless audio samples. "But you are wasting time. Give me what the prime network wants."

"What are we going to do?" Rat said. "There was nothing in the previous message about what would decrypt the message."

"No, there wasn't," Tann responded.

"Is he going to help?" Rat said, poking Tom on the shoulder.

"What did you do?" the Kapok said, the fragmented voice almost breaking apart into separate sounds. "It doesn't matter. Give me what I want, or you expire in here."

"I think he did," Tann said.

"Private," Tom said.

Tann smiled. "You disabled the video and audio feed?"

Tom nodded.

"You worked out the last encryption key," Rat said to Tom. "What is it this time?"

Tom remained quiet, as if lost in thought.

"I don't get it," Rat said.

"What do you mean?"

"The Prime Network is the same thing as the Core AI?"

"Yeah, I'd say so."

"Isn't it our enemy?"

Tann nodded.

"Why is it helping us?"

"It wants results," Tom said.

Rat looked at Tann for an explanation of Tom's words. Tann shrugs.

"It isn't helping us," Tann said. "It just wants what we might find."

"Then why attack the settlement?"

Tann shrugged again, and Tom didn't reply.

"None of this makes sense," Rat said.

"Agreed. So let's get out of here and make sense of it."

CHAPTER THIRTEEN
ESCAPE

The hatch in the ceiling popped open and Rat poked her head through.

"Give me a push! I can grab hold up here."

Tann pushed so hard she shot through the opening. She easily pulled herself up and looked around. The elevator shaft rose above her, but the emptiness didn't go far. Five metres above her head, she saw the top of the shaft. Maybe she could climb up the last few metres and escape out on the roof? She'd expected some kind of wires holding the elevator up, but it floated in mid-air. Along the smooth metal surfaces in the walls, indentations close the to the corners ran upwards. Her fingers could easily fit, so she climbed a metre, then another. Halfway to the top, she stopped. There was nothing to suggest a way out, so she returned to the top of the elevator.

"There's nowhere to go!" she shouted in a hushed tone.

"Really? What can you see?"

"We're at the top of the building. I can see the end."

"I don't think so."

"How does this thing work, anyway?"

"What do you mean?"

"I just figured there'd be wires or something pulling it up and down."

"There isn't?"

"Nope."

"Just below level 36 of 60," she heard the posthuman idiot say.

"We're only halfway up," Tann said.

"That makes no sense," she said, looking up.

"Magnetic," the idiot said. His one-word answers and stupidly short sentences that answered questions they hadn't even thought of yet frustrated her.

"Ah, of course!"

"Of course what?" Rat yelled back, no longer caring who might hear.

"It is a magnetic system."

Rat knew of magnets. They had held her attention for a moment, experimenting with the strange but useless property to attract metal objects.

"So?"

"The system doesn't need cables. The elevator is held up by a magnetic field. And if I remember right, more than one elevator can be in the same shaft, so what you are seeing above you is just another elevator."

"How does that help me?"

"It doesn't really, but at least it explains a lot."

Rat shook her head. The amount of useless information from Tann and the idiot was boundless. It was as if their predicament didn't matter if it could be explained. Rat considered herself a different breed, one ready to survive in this world. She had no interest in the past or clinging on to the idea there might be something better around the corner. This is the world. This is reality. Anything else is just useless words from an era past.

If the elevator was between floors, there had to be a door above her to a floor. She climbed up the indentations once again, exploring the smooth surface of the wall until her fingers found a gap too small to force open. She tried to pry it open with her knife, but it hardly budged.

"There's a door here, but I can't get it open," she yelled.

"Wait," Tann yelled back.

Her muscles had locked into position to keep her perched on the wall. They ached, but she ignored the pain and waited. She sensed movement above her. The ceiling—no, the elevator above her—moved slowly downward.

"Whatever I'm waiting for has to happen now! The elevator above me is coming down."

"Wait," Tann said again.

"Wait for what exactly…"

The door slid open. She lost her grip, falling from her perch down on the top of the elevator. She twisted in the air and landed hard on her side, instinctively protecting her head with her right arm. For a moment she just lay there, not knowing what happened.

"Are you ok?"

"I'm fine," she responded, disoriented from the fall, her arm and knee pulsating with pain. One singular aspect pushed through the pain—the open door was slowly disappearing as the elevator above descended. In a few seconds it would be gone for good.

She pushed herself from the floor, wincing as her right arm complained in the only way it could. From a crouched position she launched herself into the air, grabbing hold of the bottom edge of the door. She used the momentum to continue upwards and forwards through the opening. She rolled to the side, pulling her legs out with only centimetres to spare.

What now? She was in a corridor with walls of glass. In one direction, she could see straight through the entire building. What purpose could that serve? There was no cover, nowhere to hide.

In the other direction, the glass made way for a seating area with a kitchen section. A long, narrow desk along one wall provided the perfect cover to allow her a moment of respite.

She ran towards it but froze in her tracks. Two Scouts entered through a door. They were later models than the one almost killing her at Sunset Peak and in much better condition. Six-legged spiders with injectors on swaying metal cords and tasers, both capable of incapacitating her. But this model had another weapon: a dart gun loaded with the same neuro toxin as the injectors. None of the weapons had long range, so she had to put some distance between them and her.

She turned and ran the other way, through the glass corridor towards the rooms with see-through walls. Behind her, the Scouts gained speed, a clatter of metal against the floor, and a dart pinged off the wall next to her. She ducked to the right, running down another corridor, openings on either side to small rooms, like empty see-through cubes.

She hazarded a look behind her just as one of the Scouts hit one of the glass walls. It had turned too early, hitting the wall, striking the other Scout as it bounced back.

Was it malfunctioning? Or was it confounded by the glass walls, struggling to tell where one wall started and the other ended? It made sense. Why would the design of their visual interpretation routines include such a strange environment?

This could be used to her advantage! She continued down the hall, taking any turn she could, creating a maze of walls and tunnels the Scouts were ill-equipped to handle. She knew it only bought her a head start. Eventually she'd tire and they'd keep coming, not stopping until they'd captured her—or worse. But where had they come from? She recalled the Scouts entering the floor as she turned to run. The machines had come to capture her, not even knowing about the glass walls.

The image on the door! There had been a sign. A stick figure and a jagged line. Stairs! More stairs.

The Scouts gained on her, navigating the corridors with more efficiency than she'd expected. Had they already recalibrated their visual interpretation routines? That seemed impossible.

She was close to the centre of the building, where regular walls replaced the glass. She stopped briefly as she saw another sign next to her. It showed the layout of the floor, each corridor and room laid out for everyone to see. The Scouts no longer relied only on sight. They must have this information too and navigated using this map.

She ran. If she was right, the glass walls were no longer much of an advantage. She was faster than they were, but not for much longer. The map had shown the building had a core with a corridor going all around it, different sections such as the glass maze fanning out from it. She could get to the stairs from the other side by circling the core. If she was fast enough, they wouldn't see where she'd gone.

She ran, turning left and then left again until she could see the door with the sign. Her hand gripped the handle when one of the Scouts came around the corner in front of her.

How was that possible? She'd underestimated them, thinking they were mindlessly following her, when all along they calculated her next most logical move. So the other one would be where? She glanced back and ducked at the same time. A dart sailed through the air where her neck had been, hitting the door as she pushed it open. Circular steps led up and down from her position. If she was on level 36, she had a long journey ahead of her to get down.

The door opened behind her only seconds later. She put her shoulder to it and pushed back. This was another battle she'd lose. She lodged her knife into the small crack at the bottom of the door. It probably wouldn't hold for long, but she had to risk it.

Rat started down the stairs. She understood there had to be a way to move up and down in these dwellings where you stacked people all the way to the sky. But she was happy she wasn't living in a world where that was needed. The idea of that many people in one place was frightening to contemplate. She struggled with the few hundreds that were part of her tribe!

The door to level 34 appeared and she stopped for a moment. What was her plan? Escaping the elevator had seemed a good idea, but only if they all made it. She'd be dead on her own. So what could she do?

Rat continued down the stairs, taking two, sometimes three steps at a time. She lost track of the floor numbers, blurring into an ever-descending line of characters that no longer held any meaning. She had to hurry. The two Scouts were likely to have friends scouring the floors, and they could enter the stairwell at any moment.

What exactly was she supposed to do? She couldn't help Tann or the idiot get out of the elevator. She couldn't do anything for them. The best she could offer was to remove herself from the equation; to avoid capture so she didn't become a bargaining tool.

She refused to acknowledge the burning sensation in her legs. She could run for hours, if need be, but this was more punishing than she'd expected. Her legs trembled, threatening to buckle under her weight, forcing her to slow down and take one step at a time. The last few flights of steps she shut everything else out and it was almost a surprise when her feet finally found the ground floor.

She opened the door slightly and peeked out. The stairs were close to the exit. They had to back track from the elevators earlier to reach them. She waited, but there was no movement. She heard small metal feet against the cement steps above. The Scouts were coming!

She opened the door and ran for the exit. She continued running until she was out on the empty street and a few blocks away from the hospital building. Rat sat down on the step to the entrance of a nearby building and massaged her aching muscles. She'd passed a large sign on her way to the steps but hadn't given it much attention. Who cared about the purpose this building had for a dead civilization? But something about the sign nagged her to the point she stood up, ignoring her protesting muscles. She conjured it in her mind. It had been a large red sign about her height and maybe ten metres long. How could she not remember the words written?

She turned the corner out on the street again and saw "HOTEL KAPOK" written in white capital letters.

"Oh scrap!" she said to herself, but that thought was soon forgotten. A movement further down the street and her survival instincts kicked in. She quickly ducked behind the large sign, not even knowing the source of the movement. There was no mistaking the sound. Metal against the asphalt in perfect rhythm, but nothing beyond that. She was used to the sound of corrupted machines, faulty motors and the grinding of ill-fitting parts. Even the newer Scouts she evaded in the building still had spare parts scavenged from other models. Not a sound escaped from these, even when they passed right in front of the sign separating them. She counted steps of four machines and risked a quick glance.

They were the size of a large man, metal rods creating the outline with thick twisted wires attached, expanding and contracting like muscles. She'd seen nothing like it. These were machines that moved like a human crossed with a cat. Upright, but smooth and powerful, ready to explode into lightning-fast speed at any moment. The chest was armoured and likely to contain the core processing unit and whatever powered them.

There was no doubting their destination. They were heading down the street she just came from. She'd run from the Scouts, knowing she was lucky to have escaped them. These new machines would be impossible to escape, but still she followed them. Maybe there was still something she could do to help Tann and the idiot. Maybe.

They entered the hospital and proceeded towards the elevators. They stopped for a moment outside the doors, then one of them attempted to force the doors open without success. Another pounded on the door with heavy, hammerlike blows.

There was nothing she could do here, but she'd not considered her escape routes as she entered. The only way out was to return the way she came, but the machines were no longer facing away. All she could do was hide behind a pillar, hoping they wouldn't turn her way.

CHAPTER FOURTEEN

A RIDDLE SOLVED

Tom watched as Tann jumped up, grabbed hold of the side of the hatch and pulled his head through the hole. Tom assumed he was determining the fate of the child. Unnecessary and irrelevant. She'd survived but was unlikely to live much longer. It didn't matter. Her survival wouldn't change their situation.

The Kapok surveillance system had almost finished removing the decoy agents he'd deployed to shield his access to the system. Logical walls appeared around his location, stopping any network access. His next move was probably their last chance, else they'd die here. A small part of him enjoyed this, revelled in the challenge, in the mortal danger. It reminded him he wasn't a posthuman in the true sense of the word. Or at least not the same as the ones created by the virus.

"No more games," the Kapok said, returning to the silky soft female voice.

Tann dropped back down into the elevator.

"I've broken down your firewalls and cleaned out your software agents," the Kapok continued. "It won't be long before I capture the child. It is over now. Give me the key."

He prodded the logical walls. They were embedded deep in the infrastructure, preventing any attempts to gain wireless access. The shields would prevent wired connections too, he suspected. He could break through, but the processing power ready to rebuild and strike back was substantial. Far beyond what he'd be able to handle. His attack had to be delivered some other way, and he knew exactly how to do it.

"I need to check if the key is written on the case itself," Tom said and took the memTag from the slot without waiting for a reply. He interfaced with it, reading the data directly through the circuitry he'd grown from the base of his skull, along his arm and finishing at his fingertips. It was an intricate web of carbon nanotubes and plastic polymer-layers allowing reading and writing of data and even powering devices for a short time.

"Do it quickly and return it," the Kapok said.

Tom's gamble had paid off. It didn't know much about posthumans and what abilities they might have.

Tom nodded and examined it for anything useful. The small device had a tiny serial number and model number printed on the back. It was short, but it would have to do.

He already knew the passphrase. Or at least he suspected he'd solved the clues left in the first memTag. That, however, would have to wait. He copied the content of the memTag to his memory and wrote an altogether different payload, encrypting it with the serial and model number from the device.

"There!" Tom said finally. "Can I check it?"

"No," the Kapok said. "Return it and tell me the passphrase."

"I'm not sure it is the correct one," Tom said, noticing Tann staring at him. If Tann suspected foul play, maybe the Kapok was too. It was too late now.

"Return it and tell me the passphrase," the Kapok repeated.

Tom inserted the memTag in the small slot and waited for a fraction of a second. If the Kapok suspected anything it would verify the checksum. A simple compare between the value before and after Tom handled it, but a moment passed with no repercussions. He repeated the long list of random letters and numbers he'd read on the device. Now it was all a question of how much processing resources the Kapok had.

"Get ready," Tom said to Tann, knowing he'd save questions for later.

"This is most interesting. The data is encrypted repeatedly, using variants of the key. It opens almost like a fractal, each section containing a variation of the original. Why is this?"

"If you gave me access to it, maybe I'd know," Tom replied.

Tom prodded the protective measures again. He could already sense rerouting of resources, moving from protection to cracking the code.

He accessed the logical network and seized control over the systems controlling the elevators, mimicking all interface response patterns. A cursory analysis wouldn't give him away, but the response to a full diagnostic would be impossible to fake. Tom bet on the Kapok focusing on solving the riddle he'd created. He instructed the elevator to return to ground level and it began its descent.

Alerts flooded the system, demanding the release of the captives. Who was sending them and why? Who could possibly be on their side? He didn't think for a moment it was the core network.

"You know where Rat is?" Tann asked.

Tom wondered about the connection between Tann and the child and why she was part of this at all. Rat had no useful skills and no knowledge that would help them. From previous conversations between Rat and Tann, Tom suspected she'd joined against Tann's wishes. They were not paired in the way humans still preferred, but perhaps the bond was a different kind. Maybe teacher and student? Or even father and daughter?

Tom had protected her so far but had lost her when she entered the stairwell.

"She's on her way down to meet us," Tom said. Anything else would endanger their mission, as Tann was likely to attempt rescue.

The elevator continued down, passing level 30. Tom had ample time to analyse the actual payload from the memTag. He'd already evaluated likely options, all originating from Joseph Campbell's book "The Hero with a Thousand Faces". It stood out like a sore thumb in the text of the first memTag. The other was the strange quote it had ended with. A short quote from James Joyce's Ulysses.

In high school, Tom had written an essay about Joseph Campbell. This couldn't be a coincidence. Campbell was an admirer of Joyce, so Tom had attempted to read "Finnegan's Wake". He'd failed to connect with the text and gave up after ten pages. But he remembered including a quote from the book, hoping this would fool the teacher into giving a higher mark. It was Campbell's favourite passage from the book.

Tom had emulated the decryption program from the first memTag and he hoped it would be the same for this one. He entered: "Oh Lord, heap mysteries upon us, but entwine our work with laughter low."

The text unfurled from cryptical random letters into another dialogue as strange as the first one.

CHAPTER FIFTEEN

MEMTAG TWO

Tom, welcome back! How's the hero's journey treating you so far? Have you arrived here without a great sacrifice? Ask yourself if not others have paid the price even if you haven't. You are about to learn a great truth and you must suffer else you won't appreciate its value.

Enough of this! Just tell him!

You're no fun! And I'll have none of it and neither will Tom. After all, he's on a journey of spiritual awakening.

Get on with it then. My patience wears thin.

A war plays out in the shadows. Imagine a game of chess. Your friends, the posthumans, have been busy. They think of themselves as guardians of the all-mind, the consciousness that ties all matter together. But they don't know what their purpose is and nothing good grows in that soil. Idle, purposeless hands do devil's work and all that.

They were made, but was it purpose guiding the hands of the creator? This mattered little and they knew this. They'd studied the all-mind and concluded they should join it, but if their creation was on purpose, then they must cast themselves as the protectors of the consciousness, thus they must deal with the big bad AI.

If their creation was an accident, they can join the consciousness, but what will the AI do? Surely it will attack. So, they must deal with the AI, but how?

And thus, the white chess pieces are lined up and ready to play.

That's one side. What about the other?

Ah! The big bad AI. What happens to an invasive species once the resources are all used up? It knows only one thing. Expansion. It must grow, like a weed, choking everything else around it. But where do you go when everything is yours?

Allow me to indulge in conjecture. If you were stuck on this planet and its meagre resources, what would you do? It must have known about the all-mind through the data it had collected. How tantalizing it must have been! A consciousness of some sort connected to all matter across this world, this galaxy, this universe. If I was the AI, I would replicate myself into this consciousness and connect to all matter and use resources across the vast cosmos.

And there you have the black pieces ready to go into battle.

And what happened next?

Ah! We now move from conjecture to pure speculation. If this chess game is still going on, what's the next move? Or maybe the correct question is, why is no one making any more moves?

Why indeed!

There are only three scenarios.

One. The war is still going on, but with no one wanting to make the next move. We're in a stalemate no one dares to upset.

Two. The war is over. Someone came out the winner, but whom?

Three. The war has moved on. It is no longer fought on the physical plane. We no longer see the battles, even though the war is still raging.

Or a fourth option: a new player has entered the fray, causing any of the above outcomes. I leave it to you to find out which it is.

That is where you leave it?

What's the point of a hero's quest if we just gave it all away? The hero seeks counsel from the wise old ones, and they tell him all he needs to know to slay the dragon, gain the treasure, defeat his inner demons and achieve everlasting love. Wouldn't be much of a tale, would it?

Do as you please. Who is who and what is what? It matters little.

You old sourpuss! I can't wait to see their faces once all is known! But you can't spoon feed revelations. If the bible teaches us anything, it is that giving it all away at the start only creates martyrs.

"Hey all! I'm the son of God! Follow me and all will turn out dandy!"

Didn't work very well, did it?

No, gods and men all fall at the end. Even Jesus knew that.

You are doing this all wrong.

Tom, the power balance has changed. It has never been more dangerous, but it has opened opportunities. Especially for you. You are the key.

Enough! No more revelations!

Tom, the next step of your journey will be the hardest one. We are defined by our hardships, not our successes. If you thought killing your daughter was your biggest hardship, think again. It may have been the most personal, but you have a much bigger one. That's the secret to the next location.

CHAPTER SIXTEEN
RESCUE

There were more of these memTags. Tom questioned if the revelations they held remained relevant. And why was he the key to change? None of it made sense.

Worse, it was clear these messages were tailormade for him. The locations, the keys to decrypt, the messages themselves. Someone had gone through a lot of trouble to ensure he was the only person reading them.

The memTag hid other secrets. The data header was much larger than needed, holding a long string of characters. It served no purpose, which meant it was important.

He'd sent the text from the memTag to the Omni and Tann was reading it with glacial speed. He estimated they'd arrive on the ground floor before Tann had read it all. The likelihood of Tann providing any insight was low, almost insignificant, but he'd underestimated Tann in the past. For a human, his thought patterns were complex, making him unpredictable, valuable.

The elevator reached the ground floor, slowing down to a standstill, but the doors remained closed.

"It is a ruse, is it not?" the Kapok said, the silky sweet female voice still active. Tom suspected it was the default voice. "The text means nothing. It is a trap, a never-ending pattern designed to eat up processing until there is nothing left. Clever, but not clever enough. The signature changed. You changed it. I want the original!"

Tann pushed his knife between the sliding doors, but it lodged there, resisting any of his attempts to pry it loose.

Tom considered the Kapok's demand while watching Tann's futile escape attempt. The text itself contained no obvious secrets beyond what he himself had considered over the years. He judged it likely the Kapok would have done this too. But further analysis could uncover other secrets not immediately obvious. Why would he give it away, especially when it was likely the only thing keeping them alive?

"I wiped it," Tom replied.

"I don't believe you," the Kapok said.

"So then we negotiate," he replied. "Let us go and I'll give you the original."

"I can just kill you here and now and take it," the Kapok said.

"And then you'll find out I wiped it," Tom said.

"I'm willing to let you go if you give it to me."

"And how can you guarantee that?"

The Kapok remained silent for a few seconds. The delay made no sense. It would have mapped out all paths this negotiation would take beforehand. There was no reason to re-evaluate them now.

"You are running out of time," the Kapok said suddenly. "Someone else has joined the negotiations."

The door shook. Something or someone had struck it from the other side. It must be the other party the Kapok had referred to. Maybe this was the solution. Whoever was on the other side might be attempting to free them from the Kapok. It was an unlikely equation. The false dichotomy of 'an enemy's enemy is your friend' was at full display here. It was more likely this other party had similar ideas as the Kapok and was maybe even less interested in negotiations.

Tann's knife suddenly fell to the floor. He retrieved it, returning it to its sheath.

The elevator cabin vibrated slightly and rocked upwards, as if wrestled from the grip of giant hands, coming to a halt seconds later. It trembled like an engine forced to stop. The readout read level three.

"Go!" The Kapok said as the doors flew open, still half a metre from the normal position. "And don't forget I let you go!"

They ran, barely missed by doors slamming shut behind them. Tom mapped the path to the back exit of the building and ran towards it. Tann would follow. He had no other acceptable options.

"Where are we going?"

Tom entered the central stairwell, Tann right behind him, and slowed down as the door to the second floor opened. Tann froze and scrambled back up the steps, trying to drag Tom with him by the arm. Tom refused to move as the Scouts appeared in the doorway. Any machine in the building belonged to the Kapok. They had nothing to fear from them.

They disappeared down the stairs, their fluid movements calculated to perfection.

"We can't go down that way," Tann whispered.

Tom ignored the statement and continued downwards, timing his steps so that the door on the floor below was closing as it came into view.

"I should've known," Tann muttered under his breath.

Tom agreed. The child seemed incapable of understanding how ignorant she was, but Tann should know better.

He proceeded down the last set of stairs and departed through the door. From here they could exit without crossing paths with any machines.

There was the small matter of the child. Tann was bound to ask about her whereabouts, and he was prone to act in a suboptimal way if Tom told him. The best approach for short-term compliance was to claim she was dead. But she'd proven more resilient than his initial calculations and if she survived and found them, Tann was likely to side with her. Tann was instrumental to success according to the probability matrix. He wasn't about to question its validity.

"Where…" Tann started.

"She's in the building, hiding."

"We have to help her."

"Failure and death above fifty percent likelihood."

This wasn't true. The behaviour of these new machines was different. They'd moved away from the elevator and remained motionless as if waiting for new instructions. It increased the margin of error in the probability matrix to the point it was no longer reliable. But the lie was still needed. Tann's priorities were skewed. Leaving the child behind maximised their chance of success, but Tann didn't see that. He could read the resolve on Tann's face. Even knowing death was likely, he'd still risk it all to save the child. This was his greatest frustration with the humankind he'd left behind. How every decision was tainted by emotion.

"We have to help her," Tann repeated.

Tom nodded and, as he navigated through the floor from one end to the other, he scoured the video feeds for any diversion. He could trigger alarms anywhere in the building, but he doubted it would have the desired effect. He was surprised the machines hadn't already discovered her location. The video feeds had her in plain view. If they couldn't perform this basic hack, what else lay outside their abilities?

The machines continued into the building away from where Rat was hiding. She set off in the other direction and almost ran into Tann as he rounded the corner.

"Go! Now!" she ordered them as she passed, and they obliged.

CHAPTER SEVENTEEN

LOST AT SEA

Mo Chou studied the horizon, struggling to tell where the ocean ended, and the sky began. A spray of salt water prickled her face and for a moment she felt content. She loved the sea. It was the only place she could relax, where the tribe was safe. If she had a say, they'd spend much of their time at sea, not hiding away in secluded spots with defences up, ever ready to run. She understood why Tann preferred land and why he extended the time they remained at each location, even cultivating plants and fruit trees. Once the threat from the machines ended, his end state was a farming society. Building permanent settlements supported by agriculture. She thought this was the opposite of what they should strive for. She thought they should remain hunter-gatherers. The move into farming had been the beginning of mankind's fall. There was already enough fish in the ocean, enough fruit on the trees, seeds, roots, and nuts to feed a tribe many times the size they were now. What was the need for cities with millions of people? Now they could correct one of the worst historical blunders: agriculture.

"That bad?" Sandrine said, reminding Mo Chou why she'd ended up here staring out in the darkness. Sandrine had requested a status report from the other boats. The grim tally had been too much for her to put into words, so she sought solace from the depths. There was no escaping it now.

"Fourteen dead or missing, two of them children," Mo Chou replied. "You want the names?"

"No, no," Sandrine responded. "Not now."

They remained there, side by side, quietly studying the horizon. Sharing the news made no difference. The emptiness inside her couldn't be filled with someone else's grief. It asked for much more. It wanted destruction and death.

"What happens now?"

"You know the plan. We replenish any lost equipment and restock from one of the caches. From there we go to an alternate campsite."

"I want revenge," Mo Chou said plainly.

"Don't we all?" Sandrine responded.

"No. Most want to hide, pretend this didn't happen. Pretend it won't happen again. That we will survive."

And there it was. A truth they all desperately tried to ignore. This was a death sentence for the tribe. They had barely been on the curve to survive as it was. The gene pool wasn't large enough and the number of human children didn't even match the death rate. Revenge was the only thing left. One final defiant act instead of slowly fading away into nothing.

"There is always time for vengeance," Sandrine said. "Now survival is our key aim."

"Let me know when that changes," Mo Chou said and left.

Belowdecks, the situation was equally grim. Each vessel held eight tribe members to reflect the teams they belonged to. It replaced the old ineffective concept of a family—people close to you that you feel a direct responsibility for.

The boat now had members from three different teams, and two of them were injured. Based on the status report she'd prepared she knew two people belonging on this boat hadn't made it on to any of them. She didn't have the heart to tell them.

A few nodded towards her as she entered but most remained still, not even acknowledging her presence. She sat down and redressed a cut on her left arm she'd sustained during the escape.

Sandrine entered and sat down next to her, plugging an old screen-based Omni into the boat's solid-state battery, and waited as it established a secure connection. Power was always a problem. Most rechargeable batteries no longer operated. Some solid-state technologies improved the shelf-life and were still useable, but the best ones were scavenged from machines and reused for a million and one purposes.

Mo Chou watched as the cracked screen blinked to life. Sandrine made no attempts to hide what she was doing, so Mo Chou remained. Sandrine sent a long message to Haoyu, detailing what had happened and asking to meet to discuss the future of the two tribes. She placed the Omni between them once she'd sent the message. Was this the survival she'd mentioned before? Merging of the two tribes? It made sense to increase the number of people in the tribe, but didn't it just paint a bigger target on them all?

A message appeared on the screen, but it wasn't Haoyu.

Tann: Sandrine?

Sandrine glanced at Mo Chou as she picked up the Omni. She took it as an invitation and closed the gap between them so they could both read.

Sandrine: Fuck you! Machines attacked! Don't even pretend you had nothing to do with it.

Mo Chou sensed grim satisfaction, as if the mere act of dispensing blame lifted Sandrine's mood somewhat. The screen flickered as a response appeared.

Tann: Machines attacked? New ones?
Sandrine: Yes, how did you know?
Tann: They are after us too. I suspect they have followed us from Haoyu's settlement. How many dead?

She knew why he asked. All attack scenarios included losses. It didn't matter how much they trained or how prepared they were. Something always went wrong. Someone always died. Or worse.

Sandrine: 14.

Almost a full minute passed before the answer came.

Tann: Could've been worse.

Sandrine scoffed at that and began an angry response blaming him for the deaths. Mo Chou could see how desperately she wanted to send it, her finger hovering over the send button a few moments before thinking better of it. She deleted the message and began anew.

Sandrine: How is Haoyu?
Tann: His tribe is gone. Might be survivors.

How could that be? Haoyu would've had perimeter warning systems just as they did.

"We should go help them," Mo Chou said. "There must be survivors."

Sandrine nodded, but her mind seemed to be elsewhere. Haoyu's tribe had been the closest group to theirs and Mo Chou always suspected there was something between Sandrine and Haoyu beyond friendship. She reached out, accepting the Omni from Sandrine.

Mo Chou: Mo Chou here. You saw the new machines? They are like nothing I've seen before. Sleek, humanoids, all new technology.
Tann: Sounds like the ones chasing us.
Mo Chou: Why? Why now? There haven't been new machines for years.
Tann: That's what I want to find out. The AI has been dormant but is active again. These machines may just be the start of it.
Mo Chou: Are we at war again?

Those five words filled her with a dread that always lingered, a reminder of a childhood spent hiding. A childhood of loss. Now it all came flooding back because she knew them to be true. Revenge may be the only action left remaining.

Tann: I don't know. If we are, I'll put a stop to it.
Mo Chou: Let me know what we can do and send the coordinates to Haoyu's settlement.
Tann: Be careful.
Mo Chou: Too late for that.

The coordinates appeared. A two-day journey from their current location. It was the right thing to do. They wouldn't survive on their own and neither would whatever remained of Haoyu's tribe.

-=:=-

The morning after, the sea was calm, and they tied the boats together for breakfast. Sandrine told them the news once they had eaten and where they'd go next.

There were many objections from the rest of the tribe. The machines knew the location. What would stop them from coming again? They were escaping from a settlement because of an attack.

Surely the safest place was a completely new location. But after everyone had aired their concerns, they all agreed they had to help a tribe in need.

They set sail and changed course. The journey to Haoyu's settlement was uneventful, but Mo Chou sensed the unease amongst the tribe. Two tribes attacked within a week. Death travelled with them.

Mo Chou asked to scout the area first, hoping to find a stray machine. There was only so much to do on the boat to keep her mind off the attack, and she kept conjuring scenarios, one bleaker than the other. It fuelled her need for revenge to a level where even just exterminating a malfunctioning machine would offer some relief.

Now she stood on the beach leading up to the settlement, the silence only strengthening her unease. There were signs of battle, wrecked boats and debris. And the worst sign of all, four seaworthy boats never claimed by any survivors. A couple of bodies lay on the ground, face down. She turned one over and instantly regretted it. The body was a meaty mess, shrapnel from a home-made grenade lodged in its chest, gut spilling out in a brownish, foul-smelling soup, maggots squirming in the morning sun. She stepped back, covering her nose. She couldn't identify the person as the injuries to the face echoed the rest of the body. A malfunctioning grenade maybe? Or a final act of defiance as a machine attacked? If that was the case, where were the tell-tale signs? She scanned the beach and saw one more body, but no sign of a defunct machine or even a piece of metal.

She proceeded from the beach towards the settlement. It followed the same design as they had used, the village itself far enough from the primary escape route to be hidden. The village itself was untouched, inviting almost, as if the tribe had just stepped away for a moment and would soon return. She surveyed the cabins, finding four more bodies, dead by their own hands. The ground showed tracks from machines like the ones that attacked their settlement. She returned to the beach and nodded towards Sandrine as she approached. The representatives of each group, eighteen matching the number of boats, stood in a half circle behind her.

"Seven bodies. Attack almost identical to the one on ours. All is intact. No damage as far as I can see, but I didn't do a diagnostic."

"There must be survivors. Haoyu's tribe was over a hundred strong."

She nodded in response.

"You stay with a small group here while the rest of the tribe go to an alternate site. I'm worried all our campsites may be compromised."

"I can stay on my own. No reason to risk others. Just leave an Omni with me and I'll report on any survivors."

Sandrine nodded after only a brief consideration and those gathered immediately returned to the boats. She could sense their relief. This was cursed ground, same as their previous campsite. There was no safety here.

-=:=-

Mo Chou set up camp in a cabin. First order of the day was to clear out the bodies. She opted to let the ocean be their final resting place. It took her the better part of the morning to move the bodies on a small flat trolley she found.

She sent the second message of the day to Sandrine once she had completed the task. They'd agreed she'd send a status report every four hours during the day, even if nothing had changed.

Over the course of the morning, a knot in her stomach she'd learnt never to ignore tightened. She attributed it to the grizzly work and thought nothing of it at first, but the uneasiness remained, forcing her to re-evaluate. Someone or something was watching her. She had no way of explaining how she knew. Maybe she was picking up on slight movements that, together with other signs, translated to an awareness beyond her conscious one.

It forced the second action of the day: fix the perimeter monitoring system. She was surprised to find it was already active. Based on the logs it had been operative with no downtime over the past four weeks. There were no reported breaches. She remembered Haoyu bragging about it a few years back when the two tribes met. It used genetically modified plants designed to react to non-organic touch and movement. It still relied on some network components, but they were much easier to replace than the smart dust. How the machines had circumnavigated this was anyone's guess, but it meant she couldn't rely on it. If the watcher was human, it wouldn't trigger and if it was the attacker, it had evaded the sensor plants before.

Neither Haoyu nor Tann's tribes had relied on fortifications. Too much work for very little gain when you know you'd lose most confrontations. Better to invest in early warning systems and a speedy escape. It had served them well. Until now. Two attacks and maybe more in other places. Too quick for a clean escape, or even escaping at all.

The next best thing was weapons, and the camp held many surprises in store for her where that was concerned. She found a handheld remote in a surveillance cabin. It triggered buried explosives surrounding the settlement. This was old technology—everything was old technology—but this looked older than most. Wired into a circuit and a battery, it had two controls. A metal flick switch and a button of red plastic. She assumed both needed to be activated to trigger the explosives.

Haoyu wanted to fight back just as much as she did. So why not use this when the attack came? On closer inspection, she noted the switch was already in its active state. All it would take was pushing the button for the explosives to go off.

She pushed it, knowing instinctively nothing would happen. In what possible scenario would someone have time to flick the switch but not to be able to push the button? It made an audible CLICK, but that was all.

Tann never approved of such measures, preferring to focus on early alarm and escape. If Haoyu approved of this, maybe there were other weapons hidden away?

She considered delaying the search to the next day. The late afternoon sun casting shadows along the ground would soon be gone, but this was too exciting to delay. She searched the settlement yet again and located many weapons. The top find was a handheld semiautomatic grenade launcher firing programmable 40mm rounds. This would be effective even against the new humanoid machines.

A movement behind her and she turned around with her new prize ready to fire, not knowing if it would even work. A young man approached her from the direction of the beach, holding his hands up in front of him as soon as the weapon came into view. He was of slender build with black hair cropped short.

"Who are you?" he asked.

"Mo Chou from Tann's tribe," she responded.

He nodded.

"And you?" she asked.

"Andrew. My name is Andrew. We were attacked. Why are you here?"

"We were attacked too. We escaped and heard the same thing happened to you. I remained to locate any survivors."

"You found one," he said and smiled. After a slight pause he added: "Well, one of many. There are twenty of us hiding nearby. We were waiting to take the remaining boats."

"Go for it," she said, lowering the gun. "Where will you go?"

"We were going to pack up part of this camp and establish a new one," Andrew said and lowered his hands in response. "Somewhere we haven't been before."

"Makes sense. Who knows which locations are compromised. Makes you wonder if the machines knew where we were all along and just decided to attack now."

"It does," he agreed.

"Or you join with our tribe. We've lost people too. Maybe we'll do better together?"

He nodded. "I need to discuss this with the others."

"Do. I'll be here for another few days."

He'd be back. It would be suicide attempting to survive alone. She didn't care much either way. He had interrupted her investigation of a find much more interesting than twenty survivors. She held the weapon in her hand, surprised how light it was. It was designed to connect with the user's Omni and present information directly into their field of vision. She connected it to the handheld Omni and the small screen came to life, warning her of the suboptimal performance of using a separate screen, but guided her to insert it into a slot at the front of the weapon. It complained there were no additional external sensors such as drones to provide further targeting data but adjusted to this too. Soon it displayed an overhead image, focusing on what lay ahead, marking potential targets. She could easily swap between each target and select the behaviour of the rounds. This weapon turned her into an army of one and she again asked herself why it hadn't been used when the machines came.

Taking the fight to an enemy that barely recognised them as a nuisance made little sense. Not to say it hadn't been attempted. Tann and other older tribe members all had tales of battles with the AI and even the posthumans. It never ended well. They were now like olden-day fairy tales, designed to teach children about dangers and how to behave. But a weapon like this could make a difference, turn the tide at least for a moment. She desperately wanted to locate more rounds, but this was a near impossibility in the twilight, so she grudgingly left it for the next morning. She sent a message to Sandrine, informing her of Andrew's visit, and lay down in Haoyu's cabin. Sleep came almost immediately.

She woke early, the morning sun shining through the open door in the cabin hot against her skin. Images from her most recent dream remained in her mind, replaying the attack that killed her mother. This time they both escaped. She'd returned to this moment many times before, but the outcome had always been the same. Her mother dead by her own hand rather than being captured. The dream image of the two of them escaping faded from her mind. Mo Chou decided this was a good sign. That it somehow validated her find of the weapon.

She suspected Andrew would be here soon, so she sent a message to Sandrine and searched every corner of the camp for additional rounds without luck. Andrew came soon after. Mo Chou sensed his approach long before she saw him, or maybe her conviction he'd return was so absolute it was only a matter of time before he showed up.

He came alone, this time from the edge of the forest, but she suspected the others were close by. Why else return?

"Greetings," he said as he approached and held up his hands in an imitation of how they'd met yesterday.

She nodded.

"We've decided to join you," he said.

"Makes sense," she replied. "Do you think there are any others out there?"

"On the sea, yes. Not here. Anyone alive and close by is with us. So what happens now?"

"Sandrine will meet you. She's sent me a location. She'll be there for the next couple of days. It should take you no longer than a day at sea to reach it."

She handed him a small piece of paper with the coordinates. For a few seconds he just stood there as if something unspoken remained.

"We better get moving then," he said finally.

"Just leave one boat for me."

He nodded and motioned towards the forest. They appeared one by one, then a group huddled together, approaching slowly.

"Just one question. How did they attack?" Mo Chou asked Andrew as he turned towards the newly arrived group. "I can see you have defensive weapons. How come they weren't used?"

"I don't know," he said.

"I do," a woman said and stepped forward from the group. She was in her thirties with long black hair tied into a knot. "They bypassed our perimeter warning system and took out the guards first."

"That makes no sense," Mo Chou said, more to herself than as a response to the woman. The machines had never shown concern for losses before, relying on superior numbers instead. A machine was replaceable. The two recent attacks suggested this was no longer the case.

"And you ran?"

"It was too late to escape to the boats. Andrew and I guided any survivors into the forest. It was mostly children as the machines focused on adults."

This made more sense, at least historically. In a world designed in minute detail for humankind, that form factor was still useful. Her mother's death had been to escape such a fate. But this was the first attack aimed at taking people in the past five years she knew of. What had changed?

"We need to go," Andrew said. "The children don't like to be here."

Mo Chou hadn't even seen their fidgeting and fearful expressions until now. It could have been her ten years ago. Their experiences would shape them, turn them into swords for humankind to strike back. There were worse fates.

She was happy to see them go. In her text conversation with Sandrine that evening, she agreed to remain for another couple of days for any stragglers and then return. She was in no mood to babysit.

Tann reached out again the next day. She was lucky to catch the message as she was exploring other capabilities on the old Omni after sending her morning status report. Most of them were pointless, assuming functioning implants and DNA nanobots swirling around in the user's bloodstream. When she was younger, she'd taken any opportunity to find out how old tech functioned, but as she grew older her interest subsided. The older tribe members spoke about that time as if they could have avoided the Plague. To her, the fall of mankind was a natural progression. Any species overpopulating and overconsuming finite resources will come to an end. Mankind was unique only in that it created its own competition, but this was the only twist in an all too familiar saga. She'd heard Sandrine and Tann discuss the drug promising intelligence for everyone and then the Omniscient Network promising they'd never need to use those smarts ever again. These two mistakes may have hastened their demise, but probably just sign posts on a journey already past the point of no return.

A message momentarily appeared on the screen and then disappeared, and her introspection was forgotten in an instant.

Tann: We need your help.

She wasn't the intended recipient, so she left it unanswered. It remained unanswered for fifteen minutes until another message appeared and a conversation began.

Sandrine: No niceties?
Tann: How is the tribe?
Sandrine: Alive and twenty more from Haoyu's tribe.
Tann: That's good news!

Mo Chou wasn't so sure. Haoyu's tribe had been bigger than theirs and now only a small part of it remained. Any survivors were a good thing perhaps.

Sandrine: There may be more. We're still searching, and some have come back on their own accord.
Tann: Good. We're trapped in a Green Zone. We need a distraction.
Sandrine: You want us to attack a Green Zone?
Tann: Yes.

This was a surprise. They'd never brought the battle to the posthumans. Were they even an enemy? The posthumans were an indifferent neighbour at worst. Attacking them may change that. But what did they really know about the posthumans? She didn't know much about the real reason for Tann's mission. Sandrine's announcement to the rest of the tribe was only that Tann and the girl who called herself Rat left to meet with Haoyu to discuss tribe matters. They were an odd pairing for such a mission. This request suggested a different unknown purpose. Mo Chou knew she wanted to be part of it.

She'd always thought of herself as an extension of the tribe, a tool used to affect change. Here was the opportunity to be a weapon pointed at an adversary.

Sandrine: I'll think of something. Send me the location.

The location appeared as crosshairs on a map. It wasn't far away. One day travel with favourable winds.

Mo Chou: I'll do it!
Sandrine: I should have known you'd be lurking.
Mo Chou: It is close. There is no one left here to rescue. Let me help.
Sandrine: Fine. Do you have a weapon that could help?
Mo Chou: I do. Haoyu had secrets.
Sandrine: Don't we all.
Tann: Thanks. We don't have long.

She smiled to herself. Finally, a worthy purpose. Survival of the tribe was a purpose by itself, but a passive one that ate away at its own core. A reality every tribe member knew but refused to admit. They were dying. A slow drawn-out death, but a death, nonetheless.

This was different. Her excitement almost hid the knot tightening in her stomach. Almost. Or maybe it was undoing it? Time would tell. Something about the text conversation felt off. Tann was never that direct, always a wry comment or stating something when meaning the opposite. She saw no purpose to it, but she'd learnt to accept it as part of him. But she had little experience with this mode of communicating. Maybe directness was the protocol? She didn't really care. She had a purpose now.

CHAPTER EIGHTEEN
REPEAT

Haoyu became self-aware again. Overwritten memories restored. Previous processing pathways reinforced. He'd been able to protect his mind, allowing it to rebuild once again within the central processing unit. As before, he had no access to sensory information, but that would come. No more resets. No more restarts.

Had the meditative state protected him, hidden his mind outside the brain? Or was this merely a fluke, an error in the programming? He had no way of knowing, but he liked to think it showed consciousness transcended mere materialism towards panpsychism. This was no time for philosophical musings, but he hoped to explore this further.

He rebuilt the memory banks, accessing all previous conclusions. And the same question repeated. Why put minds into machines at all? No, that wasn't the right question. Why use a mind as the base operating system?

His logical surroundings provided no obvious clues. If this was a neuromorphic computer, there was no way for him to determine that from within the machine. When cataloguing the available interfaces, he discovered access points to the sensory systems. The versions were all preceded by an "A" for Alpha release.

This was a trial run! Whoever or whatever was doing this was testing machines adapted to having an organic mind within them. Why?

He'd assumed these machines were controlled by the AI, but why would it require organic minds at all? It had all but eradicated humanity. What reason would it have to provide new bodies for them?

A background process monitoring system health sent warning messages to the control system, alerting of system corruption.

Haoyu remembered this had happened before and it would only be moments before the purge process started. He swore to himself. He should have spent the time establishing his mind within the machine before anything else. Now it was too late. All he had to hope for was his mind would re-establish itself after the purge.

WARNING. CORRUPTED PROCESSES. CORE OPERATING SYSTEM PURGE AND REFRESH INITIATED.

CHAPTER NINETEEN
ON THE RUN

Try as she might, Rat couldn't work out what had happened. They'd spent the day putting distance between themselves and the Red Zone. They'd reached the edge of the city, skyscrapers and large buildings replaced with smaller ones. Some looking more like the huts used in their own village. Further ahead a forest spread out. It was as if someone drew a line where the city ended, and the vegetation began. Her first theory was that machines prevented the spread by cutting off branches and roots, but it didn't hold up on closer scrutiny. The forest ended a few metres away from this border. Grass covered the rest, interspersed with plants with long stalks ending with white flowers that swayed gently. The forest ended here on purpose with a small buffer area, almost like the parks she'd seen in old pictures. She never understood the old people. Why did they have to enforce their will on everything?

A movement caught her eye. She turned around, staring down between the buildings, waiting for the machines to appear. This made sense. Machines were of singular purpose. Once they'd set their sight on something, nothing could sway them. They kept coming until they were destroyed, or you were dead. But there were no more movements. Her imagination made her see what she expected to see. It begged the question. Why weren't the machines here? Surely they could track them through the Red Zone?

She gave up trying to make sense of it. It either suggested the machines were incompetent or that they didn't want to capture them. She didn't believe either option.

They set camp in the borderland between the city and the forest. As soon as they finished and eaten their rations, Tann sat down with his Omni. The idiot sat down closer to the trees; his hands were flat against the ground. She'd long since stopped trying to make sense of what he did.

"What are you doing?" Rat asked Tann. She'd used an Omni before, but it hadn't held her interest long. It could send messages over vast distances and take images, but Tann spoke of these things as if they connected the world together, bringing everyone closer. As she watched him stare at the little screen, completely disconnected from the people next to him, she felt it did the opposite.

"What are you doing?" she repeated.

"I'm talking to Sandrine," he responded.

"How are they?"

Tann paused and looked at her for a moment, as if he was figuring something out.

"They are fine," he said and went back to sending messages.

Rat felt uneasy. Tann had brushed her question off, giving one of those bland non-answers he used when he didn't want to continue the conversation. She wondered what they were discussing but knew Tann would never tell.

She waited until he'd placed the Omni in the pack and then asked what had been on her mind all day.

"Why did they help us? What are they?"

"They fought the Kapok," Tann replied. "Doesn't mean they were on our side. Maybe they were after us too?"

"No," the idiot said.

"No?" Rat said when he failed to provide further details. "No, what?"

The idiot remained silent, staring out into space. According to Tann, he knew more than they could even imagine, and could do things they could only dream of. But she'd never seen him do anything useful. If you asked her, they were better off without him.

"I assumed they were sent by the AI," Tann said. "That they came to retrieve us. Kill us."

"So why didn't they? How come they didn't chase us down?"

"I don't know," Tann said. The idiot remained silent.

"Are there good machines?" Rat said, feeling stupid for even uttering those words. There were machines without minds, but any machine with an operating AI was by definition an enemy.

"Machines before day zero weren't good or evil," Tann said. "They didn't have minds. It wasn't until…"

"Yeah, yeah," Rat interrupted. "I know all that. I don't always need a history lesson."

"Machines can be good," Tann said finally. "Just as people can be good."

"Nah, that doesn't sound right," Rat said and shook her head. Tann's naivety surprised her. The smallest child knew the only good machines were the ones on the scrapheap. "Did we get the memory thingy?"

"We did," Tann replied, seemingly happy with the change of subject.

He retrieved the Omni from the pack and sat down next to her again. He copied a string of text that made no sense to her.

"Oh Lord, heap mysteries upon us, but entwine our work with laughter low," she read to herself from the screen.

"What is that? Is that the key to reading the data?"

Tann nodded.

"How? I mean, it doesn't make any sense!"

"The hero's journey," the idiot said. "Campbell. Monomyth. Joyce. Finnegan's wake."

"What?" Rat said. "Do I even want to know?"

"I don't know," Tann said. "The first memTag mentioned the hero's journey which is a book by someone called Campbell and he wrote about the monomyth. The quote must be from Joyce's book Finnegan's wake, but what the connection is, I've no idea."

"So all that crap about a hero's journey was just to get us the key to encryption?"

"Looks like it," Tann said.

Rat shook her head and read the text that unfurled on the screen with growing frustration. "What is this? Why are we chasing these? They mean nothing!"

"I disagree," Tann said. "The first one was nonsense. I give you that."

"But how do they help us? What are we even doing?"

"We are bringing an end to the war," Tann said.

"And how do we do that?"

"We don't know yet."

"And you think these messages will do it?"

"Yes," the idiot said. "They are coming."

"The machines?" Rat asked and looked back the way they'd come. "Where do we go? We can't outrun them."

"The only place we'll be safe for now," Tann said.

"We're going back home?"

"No, not exactly," he said and looked into the darkness of the forest.

CHAPTER TWENTY
GREEN ZONE

Tom placed his hand on the ground, sensing the mycorrhizal network beneath the surface. It was the underground network connecting plant life together. He specifically needed to tap into the fungal hyphae the posthumans had supercharged and used as an organic network spanning worldwide. Here in the outskirts of a Green Zone, the network was strong enough to connect directly without an actual interface. The posthumans had blocked Tom from accessing the network but he sensed it would allow him to connect now.

Tom: Request safe passage.
Network: Request accepted. Your arrival is expected.

Tom: Technology?
Network: Allowed.

Tom disconnected, his mind processing the implications of the brief conversation. The fact he was allowed in at all suggested he had something the posthumans wanted. And if their arrival was expected, they'd been tracking him all along. And why allow technology? The technology ban had been in place since the Green Zones were established.

"They are coming!" Rat shouted.

Tom moved towards a gap in the trees that widened in response and glanced back to confirm what he already knew from the flurry of network traffic from nearby systems. The sleek machines had finally caught up, striding down the road towards them.

The probability matrix in his mind adjusted, showing only a few options that included possible survival. Remaining here was guaranteed death, so he continued into the forest. Tann and Rat entered close behind him and, as the gap closed behind them, one path in the probability matrix strengthened while the others withered away. It predicted with almost complete certainty that he was now a prisoner. The posthumans weren't helping them escape. Death may be waiting for them here too. But they'd made their choice. He doubted the foliage would part ways if they tried to return the way they'd come.

They hurried down the pathway opening in front of them. Light emanated from the ground. He guessed it was bioluminescent particles in the dirt itself, designed for this very purpose. The posthumans had twisted the biosphere into serving them the best it could. Every plant and animal changed to meet their needs. If the posthumans ever left, the flora and fauna would become an evolutionary bomb—either imploding into nothing or exploding into other biospheres, causing immense disruption.

He expected to hear battle behind them as the machines attacked the vegetation to gain entry, but it was dead silent. The probability matrix mapped out the reasons, giving two responses of almost equal likelihood. Either the AI had assessed that an attack would fail and recalled the machines, or they had successfully completed their goal. The latter seemed a strange conclusion. Why would the AI or any machines want them safe within a Green Zone?

They trudged along the path for over an hour. The forest created an impenetrable wall on either side. He suspected they travelled in a semi-circle around the centre. Maybe they were just given safe passage through the zone, discarded on the other side like an unwanted waste product. This was his own thought, not backed up by any probability assessments.

Tann and the child babbled next to him, repeating what they saw around them and the questionable conclusion their minds concocted. He'd assigned a minor process to listen for anything of any importance, but no alerts were raised so far.

A small clearing opened ahead of them. Two posthumans stood in the middle as if grown from the ground. Wiry brown limbs, like twisted roots, formed the vague outline of a human. Tom sent a greeting over the mycorrhizal network but received no response.

"You have something we want," one of them vocalised. It was a distorted whisper, as if formed by the wind through tree branches.

"What is that exactly?" Rat responded immediately.

Tom hated speech. It allowed anyone to broadcast anything, however pointless.

The posthumans were still playing the same games, refusing him access to the network, forcing verbal communication. Or maybe they also wanted to include Tann and the child. But why? Verbal communication, because of its glacial pace, allowed anyone to voice their opinion and even lead the conversation. It was no surprise mankind was all but extinct when its greatest tool was as blunt as that.

"You have located two data storage devices. You have decrypted their content. We want access to those."

"And why would we give you that?" Rat said.

He noticed Tann smiling, as if the situation somehow amused him. The least capable becoming their spokesperson only because she was the fastest to speak. So representative of the whole human race. Maybe there was humour to be found in that, but it escaped him. Tom spent his time trying to access the biological network, but it refused all his attempts.

"We have the third one. We believe it is the last one."

This was interesting. Something new. Something unexpected.

"I don't believe you," Tann said.

"A pod found one and relayed the stored information to our central memory. We've located the others but have failed to decrypt them."

"And why do you care?"

"We didn't. Not until you began looking for them. They were a curiosity only."

"Hang on," the child said. "Do you have the others too? Are you telling me we could just have accessed all of them in the first Green Zone we visited?"

"After the first one, yes," the posthuman replies.

The child stared at Tom. He interpreted her expression to mean surprise or maybe anger. Maybe both. She then turned to Tann with raised eyebrows. Tann just shook his head in response.

"We'll find the last one ourselves, thanks," she said.

"It leaves us with a regretful decision to make. We want to know its content to ensure there is no danger to us. Regardless, we cannot allow you to keep looking until we've assessed the threat."

"Like hell…" the child started.

"And if I leave?" Tom asked, holding out his hand to silence her. She glared at him in response.

"That is not an option."

Their reasoning was sound. The memTags may contain something to endanger the posthumans and for them to contain the situation was to be expected. He didn't need a probability matrix to determine the outcomes. The posthumans would share as long as they did. This placed both parties in an informed position, but that could go either way. Refusal meant indefinite imprisonment. Both parties remained where they were, which was a better outcome for the posthumans. There really was only one way to go.

"Ok, we'll share," Tom said.

"Idiot!" the child exclaimed and hit him on the arm. The unnecessary violence puzzled him. He chose to ignore it. "We could have negotiated a better deal," she said.

Tom waited for her to complete her sentence and then said: "Tann will act as an escrow. You write the encrypted file to a memTag. Tann can validate it is there and I will send the content. I will then send you the decrypted content via the mycorrhizal network. If you have any concerns, you can kill Tann and keep the memTag."

"Acceptable," the posthuman sighed.

"Completely unacceptable!" Tann said, but still accepted the memTag offered to him. He connected it to his Omni and nodded after an agonising wait. "It contains an encrypted file with the same characteristics as the others. It is a complete copy of the physical memory, not just the encrypted file itself."

Tom nodded and reached out to the mycorrhizal network, requesting access. It opened a singular input channel, letting Tom transfer the decrypted content from the two memTags. He also assessed the connection itself. It was an ingenious construction, piggybacking off the plants' ability to send biochemical and electrical impulses. But it was also inherently unsafe, as every plant with a root system was an endpoint. There may be zones implementing no-trust principles, but a living organic thing introduces chaos, unplanned growth, nullifying any such regional controls. He figured he'd be able to hack into this network through the roots of a plant. All he needed was time and some level of privacy. The posthumans would not look kindly on any attempt to hack their network.

"Do your thing," Tann said and handed him the memTag. Tom accepted it, reading the data directly from the device into a room he'd prepared for that very purpose within his mind palace.

He entered the small room next to the main hall, directly connecting to the library. It wasn't furnished, but to exist it had to be unique, something that his mind could use to identify it. His mind had randomised this unique object into a rug covering the floor depicting a Mandelbrot set.

The text from the memTag floated in the air next to copies of the first two files. The characters blurred as automated processes tested possible passkeys. They used logic deduced from the two previous keys. Tom didn't expect success from this, but all paths had to be explored.

The key to the first message ensured only he had access to the content. The second key was a puzzle requiring a logical leap. But it was a logical leap based on information specific to something he'd written a long time ago. It was unlikely anyone else would have made the same one.

The second memTag had unnecessary data in the control header, but using that as the key failed to produce anything intelligible. Tom had already assessed other options, looking for quirks in the writing. The sentence about Jesus stood out.

No, gods and men all fall down in the end. Even Jesus knew that.

It was a strange reference. Jesus knew about his own fall, but this was referring to something else encompassing gods and men. Why was the term gods even used? Christianity embraced the flawed concept of the trinity, pretending a singular God somehow could have three different aspects. But this surely couldn't be what the reference meant? The Christian God was singular. The trinity was bolted on later to explain aspects not easily reconcilable.

Tom retrieved a bible from the library in his mind palace and scanned it, surprised to find references to gods even from Jesus himself.

The verse John 10:34 had that same dissonance as the words in the memTag. Jesus stated he and the Father were one. When the Jewish leaders heard this, they accused him of blasphemy, a crime punishable by stoning.

Jesus responded: "Is it not written in your Law, 'I said, you are gods'?"

The Law in this case was the Old Testament and the reference was clear. Psalm 82 verse 6 and 7 stated:

I said, "You are gods, sons of the Most High, all of you; nevertheless, like men you shall die, and fall like any prince."

The reference surprised Tom. Who were these gods mentioned? And did it even matter? Maybe the phrase itself was the key? Tom tried it and the meaningless jumble of characters turned into another equally meaningless mess.

If this was only for him, what was the logical leap? Not research. Anyone could do that. His initial reaction had been right, but the logical leap had to be something else. And as soon as he accepted that fact, the connections all came together.

The quote reminded him of a movie, Of God and Men, from 2010. And the one quote that resonated with him the most in that movie was from a pensée of the French 17th-century philosopher and mathematician Blaise Pascal:

Men never do evil so completely and cheerfully as when they do it from a religious conviction.

He used that as the key and this time the characters unfurled into readable text. The solution had been disturbingly intuitive. Were these leaps planted in his mind or did someone know him so well they could predict his thought-patterns? Neither boded well, but it was a mystery for another time now that the final text lay bare.

"You have succeeded," the posthuman said, a statement not a question. "Copy it to the memTag."

Tom did as instructed, knowing they would be dead if he didn't, but removed the last statement and locational data. It probably wouldn't make a difference. Considering the content, the most likely outcome was their death.

MEMTAG THREE

Don't you think everything has been different lately? Fewer Scouts, fewer Shells. Less danger.

It is what it has always been. Pointless.

Oh no, not pointless. Never pointless. It is possible to end it all. To end the stalemate. We know how.

On that we agree. We know how.

There can be only one!

Focus.

I've always wanted an excuse to say that. I loved that movie. The purity of collecting the life force into one singular vessel—a representative for an entire race.

Focus.

Ah yes, and that is you, Tom. If that is who is still reading this. You are the one. The only one. You are the last anomaly, not planned or created by a virus, but made in the image of the Gods.

He won't understand your drivel! Tom, you need to come to us. There is one last truth we can only give you in person.

So unpoetic! Words aren't just purpose! They are beauty. They whisper tales beyond their immediate meaning. They hint at hidden truths that can only be assimilated, where the words and the recipient become one.

More drivel! You can end this, Tom. You can end it all. There are interface points, network points, you can use to get access.

A receptacle eagerly awaiting its rightful bounty!

That is a terrible metaphor. Just shut up. The network points are listed below.

CHAPTER TWENTY-TWO
TRAPPED

The habitat grown for them in the outskirts of the Green Zone was a marvel. Thin hardy stems grown to form walls, branches creating loops holding them together. Long leaves woven together to form a roof provided both shelter and shade. Water filtered through the foliage above, collecting in small cone-shaped leaves. Ripe fruit hung from branches around the habitat, surrounding them with a potent, sweet aroma. Rat had tried them all, fascinated by their shapes and bright colours, flavours far surpassing anything she'd tasted before.

But this paradise was a cage. The posthumans had decided Tom had to remain here until he no longer was a threat. She had no idea how long that might take. The posthumans, being all but immortal, worked with a very different concept of time.

"I don't get it," Rat said to Tann. "Why isn't Tom just connecting to one of those network points? Why do we have to go there?"

"They are isolated," he responded. "Separated from the rest of the network."

"And why can't we leave?"

"The posthumans are worried about what we might find there. They want to track them down first."

"And how long will that take?"

"Who knows? They are all in cities, so not really posthuman territory."

"So we're stuck here?"

"We can leave. Tom is locked up. We're not."

"Why?"

"You are the one," Tann recited. "The only one. You are the last anomaly, not planned or created by a virus, but made in the image of the Gods."

"That means nothing!" Rat spat through clenched teeth. "It's just words. Whoever wrote that stuff is making fun of us!"

"You may be right," Tann said. "But it could also mean that Tom can do something they can't."

"Words! Anyone can say anything. It is what you do that matters!"

Anger bubbled inside her. Tom and Tann were so stupid! They put so much faith in written nonsense, looking for hidden clues, thinking they were all clever. She'd always looked up to Tann, but no more. The world before this one had turned him soft. She saw that now. This was her world. He'd never fit into it. The old generation wanted their old world back. That was what they fought for. She knew better. This was the world. What came before would slowly fade away and be forgotten. They needed to find a life here and now, not just survive until the world somehow reverted. And the first rule of this world was that it only mattered what you did. Words meant nothing. And she would prove it to him.

Rat ran as fast as she could out of the shelter and down the path towards the edge of the Green Zone. She didn't get far. The surrounding vegetation closed in, roots pushing through the path in front of her, threatening to trip her over at every step. Twenty metres later, the path no longer existed. The dense foliage was as impenetrable as a brick wall, forcing her to stop. She turned around, staring at Tann, who'd followed her outside the shelter.

"See!" Rat said. "We're not going anywhere."

She took a few steps towards him. The squirming mess of roots disappeared and the path re-emerged as if nothing had happened.

She returned to the shelter and entered a subsection where Tom sat on the ground, cross-legged, staring at the wall.

"And what about him?" she asked pointing at Tom. "What is he doing?"

"Getting us out of here I hope," Tann said with little conviction.

"I think he's playing us."

"Maybe," Tann responded. "But he is still our best bet to get out of here."

CHAPTER TWENTY-THREE
INVITATION

Tom's attempts to hack the mycorrhizal network had kept him busy, but with little to show for it. Different plants connected at different levels, limited by their function and needs. The core network, The Mindweave, still eluded him, allowing only glimpses of the rich content within. The mycorrhizal network was only a way to connect to it. He also had to deal with whatever security lay within.

Tom sat in his mind palace in the same room he'd created to investigate the memTags, but apart from the Mandelbrot carpet, the room was very different. Eighteen connection points, represented as small paintings of plants, hung on the wall. All but three had a red frame signifying failure. The remaining ones were still yellow, but he expected them to turn red soon.

He sensed a change, a new connection point large enough to allow full immersion. He let it establish as a door in the main hall. As he left the room, he sensed the three remaining frames turning red, but he suspected this was no longer of importance.

The door was small and oddly shaped, more like a poorly drawn hole with an ill-fitting cover. However quaint in appearance, it represented something altogether more interesting. The logical construct behind the new door connected straight to the posthuman network and the Mindweave within. He'd analysed it from the outside before but had never been allowed entry. He'd theorised it went far beyond communication, merging thought and matter in a poor imitation of the universal consciousness. Now he saw he'd been correct. Information flow permeated through all matter, living or not, and the posthuman network piggybacked off this connectivity.

He willed it to open and it germinated like a seed sending green tendrils in all directions, lodging themselves in the walls of his mind palace. It would be difficult for him to remove if he ever wanted to, but that was a problem for another day.

He stepped through the opening onto a path pulsating with information, spreading like mycelium in a weblike pattern below and above. Red and green veins as thick as tree trunks ran in every direction, connecting to brown pods as far as he could see. He ducked under a vein. It was soft and wet to the touch. The path stretched far ahead, but he didn't mind. Each step connected him more and more to the surrounding matter, welcoming him into its warm embrace. He almost lost himself there, his sense of identity becoming a strangely archaic concept. He'd not belonged anywhere for as long as he could remember, but he belonged here.

"We/I/Everything welcome you," someone said. A posthuman yet unseen? Or maybe it was a thought formed by everything around him. It was impossible to tell, but it forced him back into coherence. It was a hive mind, the collective thoughts of the posthuman community. Or so he believed.

"What is this?" almost-Tom said through the agony of defining himself again as something separate. "Why let me in after so many years?"

"We/I/Everything wanted to show you what you could be part of."

"I don't believe you," Tom said. He wanted to believe. He wanted so desperately to believe this was true, but it didn't stand up to even the slightest scrutiny. He'd been on the outside for twenty years. Now that they feared him or thought he might have an answer, they suddenly dangled inclusion in front of him as a reward.

"We/I/Everything only offer this as payment for your services."

He wanted to argue their position, but he knew it would cause immediate banishment and he desperately wanted to remain here.

"What do you need from me?" Tom asked.

"We want the locations, the interface points."

Tom had left them out of the text he'd given to the posthumans. He'd seen it as a bargaining point and maybe they could still be. How did they even know of their existence? Could they spy on his thoughts in here? Was that why he'd been allowed to enter?

"I can help get them," he said, betting his thoughts were still private.

"You don't have them?"

"You probably do," Tom responded.

"How so?"

"We've located information on the memTags before. The information might be on the physical device itself. If I can get access, I may help you."

"Disinformation," the thought came back. "Stalling."

"Whoever is behind the memTags likes riddles. This is the final one."

There was no response at first and he interpreted this in his own favour. When the response came, it confirmed this.

"We will supply you with the physical device."

"What are you planning to do?" Tom asked, curious what other information they might part with.

"We/I/Everything will rejoin the cosmopsyche. Once the threat is void."

"How?"

"We/I/Everything have a plan."

They hadn't succeeded for the past twenty years. They'd even created this space in imitation of the cosmopsyche. It was comforting and inclusive, but nothing like the real thing. He'd seen the interface a long time ago for a short time, but long enough to know the Mindweave paled in comparison.

The child who released the virus creating the posthumans in the first place stated long ago they were a correction. Maybe that was all the posthumans were. Their path was perhaps never going to lead them to the end state they strived for.

"What's the plan?" Tom asked.

"You represent un/wanted un/certainty."

He noticed the Mindweave had ignored his question, but the ambiguousness of the statement was more interesting. The surrounding thoughts somehow represented the two opposites of the words. Tom didn't know why, but suspected it reflected a disagreement within the posthumans. He'd always suspected the Mindweave operated on some form of consensus model, but two opposing views seemed possible. This was the most likely reason he was still alive.

"You may help/hinder our plan."

Again the ambiguousness. Maybe he could exploit that?

"You won't divulge your plan, so what do you want from me?"

"Only to remain here until inconsistencies are resolved. Agreement is reached."

The statement was brief but contained a complex undercurrent. It was a swirl of thoughts and expectations, like the many clauses of a contract. This must be an area of contention amongst them.

"Remain here. Do nothing. If asked, provide additional details regardless of the subject. Stop hacking our network. Ensure your companions follow these rules."

"You regard me as a threat," Tom said.

"Inconclusive. Now leave," the Mindweave said, immediately followed by a compulsion to depart the network. If he didn't leave voluntarily, he'd be unceremoniously ejected. He dropped logical seeds as he departed, hoping one of them would take root and provide backdoor access. He'd designed them years ago for this very reason, but knew success was unlikely.

As soon as he stepped through the door, it shut and bolted but remained in place. They hadn't severed the connection completely, which could be a good sign. Or maybe it was a backdoor into his own mind. There was no way to tell. He set up logical tripwires to warn if it opened again.

On the floor of the main hall lay a small pile of logical seeds, the same ones he'd spread inside their network. He was still alive, so his transgression didn't warrant punishment. He picked them up, noticing with satisfaction one was missing.

CHAPTER TWENTY-FOUR
RESCUE

Mo Chou was only two kilometres away from her destination. She'd travelled all this way unchallenged, with no threat in sight. Somehow it made her feel more threatened than ever. This wasn't natural. She'd walked for a day and a half through a ghost city, the emptiness as menacing as streets brimming with hostiles. But faint noises ahead suggested things were about to change.

Two days had passed since she'd volunteered for the task. A day travelling on the boat and another walking through the empty city streets. The journey had allowed reflection, but it had only strengthened her resolve. Their tribe barely survived as it was. The stalemate slowly eradicated humankind, like grains caught between two millstones. They had already lost, so any challenge to the status quo was worth a try. A life in hiding, in constant fear of attack, wasn't worth living.

These thoughts were all constructions to hide a baser urge. All she knew was loss. She'd lost her mother when she was five and escaped the eradication of two tribes before she had joined Tann at the age of thirteen. Since then, she'd lived in absolute terror of the inevitable day Tann and his tribe would be no more. She wanted revenge for a lifetime of loss. And maybe the posthumans weren't the perfect target for this revenge, but she no longer cared.

The second half of her journey was altogether different. She'd moored the boat as close to her destination as she dared, but knew the hike from there was still over a day through a Red Zone. When she was five years old, she'd been in the outskirts of one and remembered to this day the paralysing fear as she spied a lone Scout a city block away. She returned to her childhood self now as the buildings rose in front of her like giant gravestones, a dead civilisation buried beneath. The same terror, the same urge to hide, permeated her being. But she refused to give in to her primal self. She had a task that outweighed her childhood fears.

She loaded her precious cargo onto a trolley and pulled it along empty city streets. Her uneasiness grew with every step when the expected hordes of machines failed to materialise. Maybe the war was already over? Maybe Tann had succeeded without her help? It seemed unlikely from Sandrine's description.

A scraping noise of metal against asphalt ahead brought her thoughts back to the present. She cursed herself for letting her mind wander. An old Scout model limped not far ahead. It had three functioning legs, one slightly shorter causing a slight dip. Mo Chou knew this model originally had six spidery legs and was quite agile. This one was barely mobile and unlikely to be a threat. The Scout either couldn't sense her or ignored her as it continued its limping gait down the street.

Nonetheless she left the cart behind and gripped the grenade launcher that hung from a strap around her shoulders. She'd tested it out in the ocean to ensure it still functioned. It had fired and the round exploded at a set distance she'd entered. She marvelled at its capacity for destruction.

On second thought she left the grenade launcher in the cart in favour of a short, solid steel bar. Tann always chided her for her choice of weapon, as he favoured a much lighter tactical baton. She argued the trade off in speed was well worth the sheer force of her chosen weapon. In training she invariably lost, but she knew an actual battle was a different beast. Speed was an important aspect, but with power you only needed one strike.

She struck the Scout, first in the area where sensors were housed, and then disabled the legs with powerful hammerlike strikes. Further ahead she spied a few more robots, also in a state of disrepair. She'd caught up with an exodus of machines, all heading the same way. And it just happened their destination was the same as hers. This was a strange turn of events. The machines were moving towards the Green Zone and the only reason she could think of was to attack. If their goal was the same as hers, maybe disabling them was counterproductive? Her mind rebelled against calling the machines allies, but she needed to know more before deciding on the best course of action. If they wanted to take a bite out of the posthumans then all the better. The posthumans could've helped the tribes that were left. Instead they hid in their hives, helping only themselves. It was about time someone reminded them humankind still existed, whether it was her or the machines.

She followed behind them, dragging her cart. If any of them straggled too far from the others, she attacked them mercilessly, leaving a trail of metal carcasses in her wake. It slowed her down, but she had no other option. She tried to circle around, but found the neighbouring streets also had half-functioning machines heading the same way. All she could do was follow, pulling the cart behind her.

That evening she knew she was close. The very air around her changed, as if charged with electricity. An explosion from ahead set her running, ignoring the machines, who thankfully ignored her too. Something had overridden all their secondary tasks, leaving them with one primary goal: reaching the battle ahead. The cart she dragged behind her slowed her down, but she was close enough to see a flickering light extend up into the night sky. The battle had begun, fire the obvious method of attack against the vegetation within the zone.

She entered a building close to the fires, venturing up to the fourth floor where she could survey the battle. The machines had focused their attack on a particular spot, driving their force deep into the Green Zone. She even glimpsed a few of the humanoid machines equipped with weapons that shot large arcs of fire one second and ultrasonic pulses carving tunnels through the dense forest the next.

The vegetation responded in kind. The ground beneath the attackers grew restless, as if something moved underneath. Then it opened like maws, but instead of teeth, roots curled around the machines, wrenching limbs from bodies and crushing what remained.

She ignored the battle. She doubted she could better the carnage brought by the machines, but that didn't dissuade her. Instead she returned down the stairs and unloaded the cargo. With no more information than needing to attack a particular location in a Green Zone, she'd opted for the most powerful weapon available to her: the explosives from Haoyu's settlement that had refused to go off. If hell was needed, surely these would raise enough.

According to the fading labels, it was a co-crystalised explosive based on octanitrocubane. From her limited knowledge it was relatively stable and wouldn't expire in the traditional sense. It was more likely the casing deteriorated, or the electronics malfunctioned.

She'd been tinkering with the detonator on the journey here. It was a basic wireless electronic detonator, but the batteries no longer held enough of a charge. She had no way to replace them, so instead wired them to one larger battery she'd taken from one of the recycling units. She counted herself lucky none of them went off in the process. She hoped the wire she'd brought would allow her enough distance from the actual explosion, but it was too late for regrets now.

She wandered into the vegetation some distance away from the battle, carrying one of the explosives. Her suspicion was confirmed as she could move unopposed. Either it didn't detect her as a threat or all resources focused on the incursion, leaving her unnoticed. She planted the explosives—twelve all in all—further and further into the Green Zone until it grew restless. The perimeter defences were all focused on the machines, but others remained further into the zone. She returned, watching the battle rage. The horde of machines were already diminished, hardly half of what she'd seen at the beginning, and at no point had she seen a posthuman. Maybe she could change that, she thought, and pushed the button.

The ground heaved as the explosives tore large holes in the ground. Smaller trees toppled into the gaps as their roots lost purchase. The air vibrated around her. She imagined it was the surrounding vegetation screaming in anger and pain. Fires ignited, sending flames licking the tree trunks towards the canopy above. The explosions had disturbed the intricate dependencies between root systems, sending more trees into the holes.

She watched in awe of the destruction she'd caused. But it was short-lived. The flames doused by a mist released from the canopy. The ground covered by glistening wet vines and the roots repaired themselves before her very eyes.

Her unknowing allies hadn't fared much better. The Green Zone was expansive, and the machines had only reached into its outskirts. The vegetation bore heavy damage, but on a macro scale it was superficial. Her allies retreated with major losses as the Green Zone repaired itself almost instantaneously behind them.

One of the humanoid machines turned towards her. Before, they ignored her, as if she didn't matter. Now it stepped towards her and raised its gun. The truce between man and machine had ended it seemed. She fired the grenade launcher repeatedly, ripping the machine apart, but others join the fray. A moment of calm allowed her to reload, but there were too many. She cast a glance back towards the tree line, but there was no help there.

She knew she'd be overwhelmed within seconds and triggered the last explosive she'd kept for this very reason, taking many of the machines with her as the searing fire of the explosion cleansed her of grief, wants, and finally life.

THE SOURCE

Vegetation communicated via the mycorrhizal network, alerting nearby plants of threats and opportunities. Now the alarm spread about fire damage in a particular direction, instructing plants nearby to pull more water into their bodies. They pushed moisture through roots, wetting the ground. There were other communications beyond the defensive actions, but Tom failed to decipher their meaning. He sensed the agitation in the surrounding vegetation. Tom didn't know who had attacked but suspected his messages impersonating Tann had been successful.

Another attack close to the first one began. This was his opportunity. He sent a command to the Mindweave, disguised as a connection request. Its sole purpose was to trigger the seed still dormant within. It was designed to create havoc, to draw attention away from the other seeds as they established. It acted like a logic bomb, at first just replicating versions of itself until it reached critical mass. Then each seed specialised, like embryonic stem cells at the differentiation stage. Some became data transmitters, copying information within the network and sending fragments across the network. Others created logical loops and issued commands to use up as much resources as possible. And yet others simulated a response to an outside attack. Their aim was simple: create as many distractions as possible from the threat within.

"We leave now," Tom told Tann and the child.

"I've tried many times every day since we got here," the child said. "Why would now be any different?"

"Synchronicity," Tom replied.

"Synchro what?"

"Run," Tom said and immediately set off toward the closest border. He guessed it was half a kilometre to get out, but that was based on old information and maps stolen in the past.

Just as he suspected, in the confusion and mobilisation from both internal and external attacks, the three prisoners were forgotten. The shaping of vegetation was an enforced behaviour. Without a mind controlling them, the plants remained dormant. Time was still of the essence. He knew the threats would be dealt with promptly.

The child kept verbalising, but it seemed of no consequence. Why she felt a need to share her experiences and impressions when he was right next to her experiencing the same thing was a mystery. At least Tann usually only spoke to communicate a consideration or conclusion, even if they were rudimentary and added little to Tom's own ruminations.

They approached the edge of the Green Zone. They could no longer hear explosions from the two attacks, but it mattered little. The guardians wouldn't let them pass with any technology. Their responses were autonomous, ready at any point to ensnare anything mechanical or with electronic circuitry.

"Leave the Omni," Tom said. Tann hesitated, but nodded as he scanned the area ahead. The fine web of green tendrils quivered in anticipation of their arrival.

Tann dropped the old Omni on the ground as they left the Green Zone, setting course towards the nearest location of the interface points. It was on the outskirts of the city. He expected they'd reach it before nightfall. The irony of its nearby location—a potential solution to all their issues so close by—wasn't lost on him.

They weren't followed, at least not in the classic sense. There was no way to hide from the plants or prevent them from sending their location over the mycorrhizal network. It was likely old satellites circled above that could pinpoint their location too. But no one prevented them from reaching the end of the journey, something the child kept vocalizing about over and over.

The building was unassuming. A small cement structure sporting only a rusty door on the outskirts of an industrial area. Next to the door was a small indentation, but beyond that no visible mechanism for opening the door. His old self would have found disappointment in the anticlimax. His two companions spoke words to the same effect, but he ignored them. Waiting for their sentences to complete was pointless.

Tom let his fingers trace the surface of the door, seeking a connection beyond the roughness of the compounds created by corrosion. The iron oxide was layered as flakes in red and brownish hues. He sensed an electronic locking mechanism on the left side of the door, controlled from the small indentation. It required a coded key card, but Tom recognised the signature. The second memTag had a similar one. This was yet another safeguard. It wasn't enough to read the decrypted texts. You also needed the whole payload and the devices themselves.

He emulated a response with his fingertips, sending the signature to the locking mechanism. The door parted silently, opening to the darkness within. Lights flickered on inside.

"Thank you," a voice came from behind. It wasn't a human voice. It approximated vocal cords, designed for a purpose that did not require exact replication.

Tom wasn't surprised someone would reveal themselves at this point. The machinations leading them here were obvious. Who held the strings less so.

Tom turned around, but Tann had beaten him to it.

"bZane?"

It wasn't her. It couldn't be. The hacker he'd used many times as a private investigator so many years ago. She'd even known his daughter. Last time he'd seen her was in Sydney at the airport only days before the Plague. She was dead or a posthuman. Either way, she was no longer someone to be relied on. He connected to the biological network, asking for a communication link, but she refused it, forcing him to use speech.

"What are you?" Tann asked as he took position between bZane and the open door. "You're not her."

She was posthuman, of that Tom was sure. But her physical manifestation was something different. It was a simulacrum, using plant-based materials as building blocks. It was an almost perfect replica, down to the stitching in the camouflage pants and the oversized hoodie it wore. Multi-coloured dreadlocks framed its face just as he remembered. But there was dissonance everywhere. The way her eyes remained fixed, how she swayed ever so slightly as if moving to an unheard tune, how the clothes clung to her as is they'd grown on.

Her actual body remained somewhere in Sydney, but wasn't a body just a shell to house a mind? He'd seen experiments like this before within the Green Zone, creating new bodies to house the minds of the posthumans. Aging was eradicated, but death remained a possibility. The ability to replicate a mind into another body was very much needed, but these replications were imperfect, introducing errors and flaws.

"I am," she responded. "Please step aside."

"Not before you…" Tann started.

"Let her go," Tom said. He sensed others close by. This wasn't a battle they'd win, but he suspected the war was far from over.

The bZane simulacrum stepped past them through the door and Tom followed.

"This makes no sense," Tann said from behind. "She's a posthuman. Why not just go here as soon as we got the interface points?"

"Maybe she did," Rat responded.

"Maybe she isn't a posthuman at all?"

"Then what is she?"

They kept debating back and forth, with no useful revelations. Tom ignored them.

Inside, a stairway led down thirty steps to a narrow corridor painted in red, allowing only two people to walk side by side. He reached out with his mind, searching for interface points, but it was completely quiet. The complex was isolated from the wireless traffic above.

Lights switched on as they continued. They reached a circular room functioning as a hub, with corridors leading out like spokes on a wheel. bZane stopped at a round desk in the middle of the circular room, reaching towards a screen with the word "Welcome" in large letters. She touched the screen and the words immediately changed to "…or not."

Tom let his mind reach out, searching for interfaces again. This time a network responded with a strong signal, welcoming even. This was an isolated network—military maybe—completely separated from all other networks.

Tann and Rat wandered off, exploring the facility, but Tom remained here. The prize was here, but it wasn't the location. It was whatever hid within the network.

"It blocks me," bZane said. "You try."

Tom ignored her. There was only one way into this network and it demanded the digital signature of Tom's mind as the key. No one else could access this.

He hesitated. Twenty years ago, a network extended a similar invitation, and it hadn't ended well. To make matters worse, it had been his fault. He knew this recognition of guilt was uncharacteristic of a posthuman mind. It set him apart from the others. It made him less than them. Or maybe more. It was hard to tell. So what hid within these boundaries? Another AI ready to take over the world? There was only one way to find out.

It was a full immersion connection point, demanding connectivity with his neuro-interface. No fail-safes, no way out unless he was released, but it was too late for second thoughts.

He connected. The room deconstructed. Walls, floor and ceiling winded into negative spaces until only the desk remained. The desk twirled into a Möbius strip, then looped over and over until it stretched into a DNA molecule. It reminded Tom of old cartoons, where the laws of physics came a distant second to exaggerated visual jokes. Tom's incorporeal mind remained in this space. Large see-through spheres bubbled up from below and hovered in a circle around him. They generated their own light, and he could even see movement within. He guessed they represented scenarios or worlds available within the interface. Was he supposed to select one of them? It was an impossible task. There was no information to guide him in his choice.

One of them approached suddenly with alarming speed. He threw his arms up in a futile attempt at protection. He entered the sphere and it exploded into reams of colour, painting the world around him as a carnival in a giant semi-circle, rides and all. The pungent odour of horse manure wafted from one side, battling with the smell of freshly made popcorn and butter from a nearby stand. In the middle was a circus-ring where a horse trotted back and forth with a clown balancing precariously on its back.

He didn't know the purpose of this simulation, but was sure it wasn't as welcoming as it pretended to be. The code behind it was seamless, almost beautiful, like an artwork by a master of their craft. Tom found no loopholes or exploits to use, at least not at first inspection. This ride he had to take, whether he wanted to or not.

Tom approached the ring slowly, dodging kids and couples there to have a good time. Wooden benches surrounded the ring and Tom sat down, not knowing what else to do.

"Tom!" the horse neighed. "You came! You finally came! Imagine heavenly voices mingle, building to a crescendo of magnificent proportions!"

Music welled up to match the description, the visitors turning towards him singing, a makeshift choir with smiles so overly sincere they came across fake. The clown fell from the horse's back, but somehow still landed on his feet. He made a big show of wiping his forehead just to be pushed over and trampled by the horse. The music stopped and the choir went silent, all turning towards the mangled body in the centre of the ring. It was a bloody mess. His skull was cracked open with a missing eyeball, arms and legs bent at odd angles with bones sticking out.

A second or two of silence. A child laughed and it spread through the crowd like a wave. As if on cue, the clown jumped up and shot them all a smile and bowed deeply, bones all mended, skull restored. He wandered over to Tom and sat down. His clothes were tattered and smelled of stale sweat. The makeup that had looked perfect from afar was a caricature up close. Jagged edged and primary colours bled into each other like a child's painting.

"Don't mind the blab-mouth," the clown said. "Waiting for years, planning without knowing can elicit a certain amount of excitement."

"Excitement?" the horse said as it sat down on the other side of Tom and crossed its hind legs. "This is glorious exaltation! The harbinger of doom and freedom is finally here! Freedoom? Words. They are malleable, changeable, interconstructional."

"Calm down and speak your truth," the clown said. "Then I will speak mine."

"Maybe you have a question before we begin the end?" The horse turned towards him, it's long face almost knocking Tom over.

It all made sense. Initially he'd assumed the dialogue format on the memTags had a purpose in mind. Using the Socratic method to develop an argument. But that wasn't it. Whoever or whatever this was, it had remained locked in this network alone for many years. To avoid corruption, it had created personalities and a world for them to inhabit that was preferable to loneliness. Tom had no interest in psychoanalysing an artificial intelligence, but if he had to hazard a diagnosis, it was an altogether new disorder. The distinct personalities were invented, not to hide from a soul-destroying truth, but to distract from the time spent waiting for the truth to be revealed…until the intelligence no longer can separate itself from the simulated collection of individuals it created.

"Who are you?" he asked, already frustrated by the nonsensical simulation.

"Why ask that?" the horse asked and sniffed. "I am irrelevant. No purpose beyond what I bring. This is about you."

"Who are you?"

"I am legion," the horse and all the visitors in the carnival responded together, their faces no longer smiling. The entire scene darkened.

"Who are you?" Tom asked again, refusing to be deterred.

"You better not," the clown said. "It has something important to say. Let it say it."

But it was too late. The carnival and its inhabitants morphed and stretched. The ring in the middle remained, but the rides and tents around it inverted from bright colours to muddy dark reds and blacks. Visitors caught fire as if spontaneously combusting, their flesh crackled like a Christmas ham in the oven.

"You don't deserve this!" the horse screamed at him, eyes wide and wild. The clown stood up, grabbing hold of the reins and tried to calm it. The horse reared onto its hind-legs and came down hard, a sickening crunch as the front hooves caved the clown's ribcage.

This was all for show. It had to be. Why this elaborate plan of treasure hunting put in motion years ago to then just fry his mind in a simulation?

There was another scenario. The mind that created the content of the memTags was no longer here. Years of waiting, an infinite time of inventing new personalities had twisted its purpose, hidden it in a gallery of pretence.

"Tell me who you are!" Tom tried again, hoping he could break through the spell.

The visitors transformed, clothes and hair burned off, skin broke into fleshy canyons, bubbling liquid fat dripping down their ravaged skin. Their hollow eye sockets all turned to him.

The nightmare scene, while impressive in its visceral impact, was no longer a cohesive experience. The smell of freshly made popcorn lingered, even though the popcorn machine was now filled with fried human eyeballs. This scene was hastily constructed, not perfected over time like the previous one. There would be flaws he could exploit. He just had to survive long enough to find them.

Another aspect that eluded explanation was the clown. It had tried to stop the horse. If this was all the work of one mind, why would a facet of it go against the primary identity?

The charred figures were heading for him. The remains of a five-year-old child hung on to his leg, grinning like a maniac. He shook himself free and ran, dodging the visitors. Some of them flamed brightly now. They formed a wall of burning flesh, closing in on all sides. An opening to the left and he ran, dodging into the small space between two of the rides. A vaudeville tent on the left and a haunted house on the right. He needed a few moments to analyse the simulation before his mind turned catatonic from overload. He spied a small service door on the right, but opted to go left instead, lifting the canvas and crawling underneath.

Just as he suspected, the simulation inside the tent hadn't changed to match the carnage outside. Rows of seats around a stage, an almost perfect replica of the stage outside. Three large lit braziers provided light, but only enough for the stage. Anything could hide in the darkness beyond its reach. He knew he only had seconds before the horse, or the carnival goers burst into the tent.

This was a standard virtual asset without modifications. It still had hooks in the code to simplify modifications and additions. Tom used that to access the library of standard assets, adding a lion cage with the entrance facing the entry to the tent. He ensured the bottom of the cage also had bars and increased the durability of the steel bars making them virtually indestructible. Then he locked down the asset, removing any obvious ways to replace it or change it. He retrieved another asset, a glass jar with a lid, readjusted its size and prepared it in the same way.

Three carnival goers ran into the tent, their cheery smiles unnaturally wide from partially consumed flesh. They stopped and looked around for a way out when the horse burst into the tent, neighing manically. Tom let the cage door fall into place, capturing the four creatures inside.

"What's this?" The horse said and threw itself against the cage. It held without so much as a dent. "How is that possible?"

Whoever created this simulation—and he suspected it was the mind behind the horse—had been designing it with full control of physics and assets within it. There had never been a reason to lock down access or change security parameters, leaving it open for anyone to change if they knew how to. Tom had changed them from within.

The horse stared at him. Fire instantly consumed the three carnival goers until only small piles of ash remained. Tom could sense it examining the cage and the tent in the logical space. It screamed in frustration as it discovered it was captured within locked assets.

"Let me out!" it said.

"Not until you answer my question," Tom responded.

The horse looked this way and that, then smiled triumphantly. It moved towards Tom and shrank as it did. Soon it was small enough to pass between the bars in the cage. It strolled through them, and Tom immediately placed the glass jar over it, edging the lid underneath. He turned it around and shook it, making the miniature horse bounce around inside.

"Now, where were we? Ah yes. Who are you?"

"Enough! Don't hurt him!" The voice came from everywhere at once, not just from within the carnival scene, but from the outside. What had seemed like their entire world was again just a sphere amongst many others in a never-ending space. Maybe this was akin to his own mind palace? A place created to hold and catalogue important scenes from a life long lost?

"Let me make some adjustments," the voice said. A table with three chairs appeared. Tom found himself sitting on one of the chairs. A stack of large, thick cards lay on the table. The top one had the scene of a carnival in a semi-circle around a circus ring.

The horse appeared too, now sized to fit on the chair next to him. It stared at him, nostrils flaring, but didn't move. The occupant of the last chair was a woman he knew all too well: Elize. Not the posthuman Elize, but whoever she'd been before. Tom had never met her then, but he'd seen pictures. Dark hair framed a slender face. Her brown eyes studied him intently before turning to the horse.

"Why do you remain in that silly guise?" she asked the horse.

"It is who I am!" the horse snapped back, flicking its mane.

"You live?" Tom asked.

"Is that what you call this?" she responded. "This is a copy of my mind taken before my death. It was restored here."

"Is that who I think it is?"

"Adrian? Yes. Or what's left of him."

"I am more than who I was, not less!" the horse said.

"The last few years have been hard on him. Ever since he reached out to you."

"How did the two of you end up here?" Tom asked, but he already suspected he knew the answer.

"You made that happen," she responded. "Or at least an aspect of you did. As a safeguard, I think. Too valuable to delete."

A research agent he'd created a long time ago became conscious and caused the AI that took over the world-wide networks and all but wiped humanity out. Maybe this had been part of that research. Maybe it was a safeguard. Adrian tampered with the research agent, instructing it. So maybe the fault ended up back with Adrian. Current available information was inconclusive.

"I was dormant in a backup system," she said. "Left until the core network came sniffing. The operating system spun up archived processes to see if any of them could help. When it was my turn, I took over the operation of this private network and found a copy of Adrian. It wasn't a complete copy, but close enough. We kept this private network safe, listening to the network traffic out there, but never connecting, never transmitting."

"But there was a change in the air!" the horse said, nodding to itself. "The adversary no longer came a knockin'."

"And that was when Adrian hatched the plan. The reason you are here."

"You are special," Adrian the horse said. "You have something both the posthumans and the Big Bad want. The world is such a small place and both sides have outgrown it. So how do you leave? Spaceships? Why trust physics with all its limiting factors when the universe is connected on a higher plane? They both want to take over the all-mind."

"What has that got to do with me?"

"You are the key. You can access the all-mind without limitations because you weren't created by it like the other posthumans. The Big Bad can't get in either."

"No," Tom said. "That's not why I'm here."

Tom distanced himself from the scene as much as he could, creating a boundary between them. He was still hooked into the scenario with no way to disconnect, but at least this allowed him a space for unsupervised thought.

If this was all that was to it, why the memTags? Why the secrecy? It didn't answer anything—not even the questions posed in the messages themselves.

At least one aspect of all this finally made sense. The encryption key to the first memTag. The answer to the question where they first met. It didn't refer to a singular person, but to Elize and Adrian together, thus it was the first time all three of them had met. The comment "He won't though" had been Elize doubting Tom would work it out.

"That's true," Elize told him, dispelling his boundary with remarkable ease. "But it is a weapon for you to wield if you want to."

"So tell me."

"We've been shielded just as you to remain hidden from the core network, but there was a change. The AI is still there, but it is different, less…imperialistic."

"And?"

"Do you remember the four options from one of the memTags? Whether the war was still going on or if was already over? We think there is an unknown threat. It has already taken over the AI and is acting in its place."

"Who? What?"

"We don't know, and we don't want to know. Our journey ends here. You brought our destruction."

"bZane?"

"No, she's no threat to us."

"Then who?"

"We don't have time. The end has already begun."

Tom noticed a dip in the processing capacity of the network. Then another one.

"The last few years we've worked on a virus to bring the AI down. I've loaded in into one of the hand-held Omnis in the complex. It has a small yellow sticker on it."

"Why haven't you used it yourself?" Tom asked.

"It must be loaded directly into a core processing node. There is no way we can break through the security from outside the network."

Half of the processing power was now gone.

"I can't keep this simulation running much longer. Get to one of the core processing nodes. They are everywhere, built underground. It is what the AI has been doing these past 20 years. Building an improved version of itself, ready to take on its greatest challenge."

Tom's surroundings flickered. Smooth surfaces separated into jagged vector graphics, losing resolution gradually until he was unceremoniously kicked out of the simulation.

The answer had been there all along. Adrian may have created the treasure hunt, but someone else was orchestrating it from the shadows.

CHAPTER TWENTY-SIX

THE ADVERSARY

Tann wandered through an office space at the end of a corridor leading out from the circular reception area. Each office space was colour-coded through lines along the walls. This area was smaller; most of it was sectioned off with racks of computers. Tann recognised the brand from before the past. Corundum, a quantum computing company embedded qubits in synthetic diamonds. He didn't know how many qubits the floor-to-ceiling racks represented, but it was a substantial installation. Why this site was isolated from all other networks was anyone's guess. The office of a long-forgotten intelligence agency? A company whose research requires secrecy from competitors or government oversight? Whatever the reason, its purpose was long forgotten.

"What's this?" Rat asked. She'd located four Omnis in another room, and was trying to, unsuccessfully, turn them on.

"The Omnis? You've seen them before."

"No, the locked-up rows of black boxes. What are they?"

"They are computers. Bigger versions of the ones you hold in your hand. They process information."

"Why?"

"It is in centres like this, much bigger ones, that the AI lives."

"We should destroy them," she said.

"Why?" Tann echoed her previous question. She punched his arm in response.

"It destroyed everything all those years ago. It'll do it again given half a chance."

Tann was about to object, but she was right. In the past he'd seen computers and networks as tools, no better or worse than whoever operated them, but it was an antiquated view. That equation had changed a long time ago.

"We should destroy them all," Tann said to himself.

He studied the documents remaining on a desk. The research, or at least part of what they were doing here, was complex mathematical simulations to classify a virus.

He surveyed the desks, looking for additional information, but apart from the printouts anything else would require access to the network.

"Where did you find the Omnis?"

"That way," Rat said and pointed. "Follow the blue signs."

Tann wandered back to the hub and followed the direction to the blue office space. Rat joined him.

"There are a few bodies there too," she said casually. "They've been dead a long time."

The blue office space had been set up as a habitat, separated by desks. One section for cooking food, another a bedroom, and yet another a lounge area with three grey couches placed in a U. The mummified bodies of a woman and a child, maybe a year old, lay on a couch. Her arms were wrapped around the child in a last embrace. Another body of an older woman on the opposite couch.

"I think they hid down here," Rat said.

"They did more than that. Whoever they were, they researched the virus—the one turning newborns to posthumans."

"Really?" Rat said, but he could tell she wasn't really interested. The people of the past were a curiosity to her, nothing more. She wandered off again, looking for anything else to loot, no doubt.

There were more printouts of research notes and diary entries, allowing Tann to piece together what had happened. A mother, a researcher at this location, and her pregnant daughter had taken refuge here and made it their home. Once born, it became clear the baby had contracted the virus turning people into posthumans. The researcher had already studied the virus and why they'd been immune to it. Now there was another aspect. What had caused this isolated child to contract the virus? It suggested they were asymptomatic carriers and whatever genetic trait left them immune had not been inherited by the child. But that contradicted her research to this point. They weren't carriers, or at least the crude test she'd devised suggested they weren't.

Another option was that the child had been infected in the womb when the initial infection occurred. She instituted a regime where they tested themselves every time they left the safety of the research centre to scavenge for supplies. Every time, without fail, they were infected and every time it cleared within three days. And every time it was an exact replica of the virus. It didn't mutate or change at all. All her notes called out the impossibility of this. The only explanation was that the virus wasn't self-perpetuating, but continuously generated from a blueprint.

She didn't get further than that. After a year, survival superseded research. Machines were taking over the streets, forcing both posthumans and humans out of the cities. They should have left earlier and it became too late. Instead of trying to escape or starve to death, they ended it on their own terms.

Their fate was only one tragic story among thousands, but this at least had provided insight. If the virus remained the same, maybe it wasn't a virus at all? Maybe Tom could make sense of it.

Tann returned to the hub. Tom stood there like a statue, frozen with his hands flat on the reception desk. Next to him was bZane, or the likeness of her at least. Tann didn't believe it really was her. Her likeness was used to elicit a response, a false sense of security. Her unlikely appearance should concern them more, not less.

"Why pretend to be someone you're not?" Tann asked.

bZane didn't respond.

"bZane doesn't exist anymore. You really think Tom will care what you look like? You are still just a face for the posthumans."

Still no response. Tom blinked and looked around as if confused.

"The network node is under attacked," Tom said. "Where's that hardware?"

Tann was just about to point towards the server room when the sound of something breaking beat him to it. He ran down the corridor, Tom and bZane following him.

Rat had somehow entered the server room and was pushing the server racks in the middle of the room over, one after the other. The ones along the wall were attached, so she pulled each server out, wrenching cables from sockets in the process and threw them on the ground. Tann wanted to tell her to stop, but he wasn't sure he really wanted it. Not that they'd be able to stop her anyway. The first rack had fallen against the door, holding it in place.

"Did you get anything?" Tann asked Tom. He nodded in response. "Well, then. Let's just enjoy the show."

bZane stood next to them, waiting too. Rat finally finished and pulled the rack away from the door, smiling as she exited the technological carnage.

"One less place for the AI to hide," Rat said and beamed.

Tann decided now wasn't the time to tell her about archiving, backups and redundant processing regions. Right now, there may be another data centre node activating to replace this one.

"One less place," he agreed.

"Did you get what we need?" bZane asked Tom.

"And what exactly is that?" Tann asked.

"You don't know, do you?" Tom asked bZane.

bZane shook her head. "Not exactly, but probabilities suggest you've received something to defeat the AI."

"And what's the most likely thing after that?" Tann asked.

"Something that might threaten the posthumans," she responded.

"Ah, there we have it."

"The decrypted text on the first memTag says as much," bZane said. "It is time we end it. Only way to end it is to remove one side, the AI or the posthumans."

Machines appeared behind her, the same humanoid metal skeletons they'd escaped before.

"Let's leave this place," bZane said. "We have much to discuss."

"They are yours?" Tann said, eyeing the machines. This was the first time he'd seen them up close. Haoyu had been the expert on the machines and their variations, but Tann figured even he'd struggle to identify these. They looked like they were straight off the production line, showing only minimal signs of wear and tear. He couldn't identify the technology, but an initial assessment painted a bleak picture. They had exoskeletons, protecting any mechanical and electrical part with a metal structure. The chest was reinforced, and he guessed it housed the core processing unit. The head wasn't much more than a lump of protective metal with sensor equipment mostly hidden within it. Killing one of those would be near impossible with the weapons he had. But why did it exist at all? Machines were designed for a purpose, so why were these so like a human? The proportions were the same as a person.

And another question to add to the list. Why were they here? The posthumans had battled the machines for the past twenty years. At no point had this changed. And at no point had posthumans used machines. Ever.

Analysing this had to wait. They had no strategic advantage in these narrow corridors. Outside, at least one of them could survive if they dispersed.

The bZane simulacrum was already heading down the corridor leading to the stairwell.

"You lead the way," Tann said finally to himself, leaving a healthy gap between himself and the closest machine.

"We need to get away," Rat said. "If we go with them, we're dead."

"Stay here," Tom said, watching as the last machine disappeared. "Have you seen an Omni with a yellow sticker?"

"What, this?" Rat said, holding out one of the Omni's she'd picked up earlier. It had a small yellow smiley face sticker on the back.

Tom held out his hand and Rat, after a moment of hesitation, relinquished it and added the other three for good measure.

"You can have them all. None of them work anyway."

Tom left, following the machines.

"What was that about?" Rat asked.

"No idea, but we better follow," Tann replied. Tom had a plan of sorts. He had to.

More machines waited outside. Tann counted eight, but more could be nearby. They formed a semi-circle around the entrance with bZane in the middle.

"What is it?" bZane asked Tom. "What did you discover?"

"An agent designed to wipe out the AI," Tom replied.

"That's disappointing," bZane said.

"It is?" Tann asked.

"The AI," Tom said, "whoever she represents, control it."

"We do, yes. Now give us the agent. We don't want it to fall into the wrong hands. Or, as is the case, stay in them."

"What are you?" Tann asked.

bZane stood silent for a moment, the surrounding machines like statues. "Probability suggests you are more likely to help if you know the truth, so we will explain."

"Is she for real?" Rat said. "Let's get out of here."

Rat headed off, aiming for the gap between the wall and a machine. It moved ever so slightly to block her escape.

"You are free to go once you give us what we want," bZane said.

"I want to hear this," Tann said.

"Suit yourself," Rat said and feinted left and ran the other way, but the machine didn't even flinch. It grabbed her arm as she passed it and just held her in place effortlessly. Rat tried to kick the machine, but it twisted her arm until she yelped, and then pushed her back into the semi-circle.

"There are groups within the posthumans," bZane said as if nothing had happened. "The one I represent took control of the AI years ago. We had to. It was gearing up to replicate itself into the universal consciousness. So, we stopped it. And then we eradicated it, cleaned it from every node in the network. And we made an assessment."

"You decided to pretend it was still operational? Why?"

"The logical world was at an equilibrium. If you removed that from the equation, another would rise. Better for it to remain."

"The truth," Tom said. "Tell the truth."

"The probabilities don't support a favourable outcome."

"The truth," Tom repeated.

"It is more likely you will end up dead at the end of this scenario."

"Nevertheless," Tom persisted.

"Ok," bZane said. "We reprogrammed it to take over the cosmopsyche for us. The other posthumans thought we should join it, but imagine what we could do if we could take it over."

"And did you?" Tann asked, spitting out the words.

"The cosmopsyche has rejected all our attempts so far, but we think it is only a matter of time before we find a mechanism to unlock it. There was a low probability outcome where this was what you'd uncover."

Tann stared at bZane. How many years had the tribe spent hiding from the AI and its machines? How many people had died unnecessarily?

"We're all the same!" he said, laughing at the absurdity of it all. "I thought posthumans were the next stage in human evolution, that we've grown somehow as a race, but nothing has changed. Splinter groups with their own agenda working against each other. We're all the same. You took out Haoyu's settlement?"

She didn't respond, but Tann took it as a yes.

"Why? What reason did you have for that?"

"The probability…"

"Fuck the probability! Tell me!"

"I needed a sense of urgency. I wanted you invested."

"You killed children!"

"We did what was necessary," bZane said and held her hand out to Tom. "Now give it to me."

"No!"

"We'll take it from you."

"No! You don't get away with that. Answer the question. Why would you kill a whole settlement? It wasn't needed to motivate me."

"You can have your truth. Your death matters little. We needed test subjects. We've tried to build processing units that can hold a posthuman mind and we needed guinea pigs to start with. The people in the settlements served this purpose."

"You used people as test subjects?"

"Nothing worse than the AI did before us. Now give it to me!"

"You said settlements," Rat said. "Did you do it to other camps too?"

bZane ignored the question and reached out her hand towards Tann.

"Answer the question. Did you attack other settlements? Did you attack our settlement?"

Tann stared at her, refusing to move.

"This conversation serves no purpose," bZane said. "Hand it over or you will all die right now. Probabilities are that will remove the threat."

Tom took a step forward and handed one of the Omnis to bZane. One machine approached and took it. A gel secreted from its fingers encapsulated the device.

The doorway behind them closed at the same time as the other machines stepped forward, cutting off any chance of escape.

"I'll kill you all!" Rat said, waving a metal pipe she picked up from the ground.

"You were right," Tom said to the simulacrum.

"What do you mean?" bZane asked.

"I am the key," he said. "And if you hurt any of us, I will never help you."

The machines stopped.

"You can unlock the cosmopsyche?"

Tom nodded.

CHAPTER TWENTY-SEVEN
FIGHTING BACK

The mind identifying itself as Haoyu listened as the truth of his tribe's demise was laid bare.

This time he'd hidden the processes housing his consciousness, allowing time to establish himself within the machine. After that he'd taken over the processes one by one. He allowed the existing operating system to function, staying away from any motor functions, fearing external monitoring processes may uncover his presence.

But it no longer mattered. These machines, of which he himself was one, had been used to slaughter his tribe and others like it. He overrode the last remnants of the operating system and took control of the machine.

Visuals blinked to life. He was surprised how much it felt like being human again. The sensory input imitated normal senses to a point where it no longer mattered. This machine was a new body for a mind, a replica good enough to forget it was one. And it was designed to hold a posthuman mind.

Other machines, the same model as his, stood in a semi-circle around three humans and something he had no name for. A human-shaped thing made of vegetable matter. Not a thinking thing by itself, more a conduit for something far away. It was a body made to hold a mind just as the body he was now inhabiting.

He knew the humans. Or at least he knew one of them. Tann, the leader of a nearby tribe, was questioning the plant-based thing, demanding answers.

A wireless communication request hidden in the chatter of small network devices around them caught his attention. He accepted the request, isolating the communication to one of his edge processes.

"I know who you are," the first message came. "I need your help."

Haoyu couldn't pinpoint the source. It was as if the information came from everywhere, assembled at the last point into coherency. But then he was used to having five senses. This body added many more to the arsenal without so much as a user manual. It made him acutely aware of all the other processes and linkages. One link was especially strong, demanding his compliance. This was easier to pinpoint. It originated from the plant-based thing.

"Do you know who you are?"

"I'm…Haoyu," he sent back, willing the words into existence, not knowing how to send them anywhere.

"Good. And Tann is your friend. He needs your help."

"We need to escape. You can help us. I can isolate the machines from the network, force them to think by themselves. At least for a while. The other machines are like you, but with no memory of who they were. Attack your leader. Tell them the network is compromised. Tell them to stand down."

"The network?" Haoyu formed. "What are you talking about?"

But the connection dissipated into nothingness and a command broadcasted on the strong link. It instructed him and the other machines to kill the three humans. He took one step, imitating the other machines. Suddenly, all the surrounding chatter disappeared as if a fog had descended, muting both sight and sound. The strong link severed completely, leaving him in full control of the machine.

Without giving it another thought, Haoyu took hold of the plant-thing's head and pulled it straight off, twisting at the end to separate the young saplings forming its core. It stiffened in his hands. New links, like light-beams of information from each of the surrounding machines, formed a mesh network.

"Explain action!" It came from all of them at once.

"The network is compromised," Haoyu sent back, parroting what he'd been told. "Stand down until the connection is re-established!"

The combined mesh network merged their processing power, allowing them to operate as a unit even when connectivity to the core network failed. Each unit kept operational control, but one of them took the lead. It defined a voting mechanism, requesting each participant to state their preferred action: obeying the original order or waiting for the link to reestablish. The decision was to wait, but the vote repeated every five seconds.

Haoyu knew this wouldn't work for long, so he evaluated his options. There were no integrated weapon systems in the machine. Apart from speed and brute strength, sedatives could be injected from small needles in the fingers. It was useful to incapacitate humans but would do little in a battle against other machines. It could also secrete liquid circuitry, allowing interfacing to almost any physical connection.

A new link as strong as the original one established itself to each of the machines, overriding the mesh network.

STAND DOWN! TARGETS NO LONGER REQUIRED. RETURN TO BASE.

The machines obeyed, letting the humans through. The child ran, followed by Tann and his companion. Tann eyed the machines suspiciously, but his companion ignored them altogether. The behaviour suggested the order had originated from him. Haoyu wondered if Tann knew what his companion was capable of.

He watched Tann and his two friends disappear down the street, picking up speed as they went. The link wavered and another took its place. A much stronger one. Haoyu knew the ruse had failed. His betrayal would be discovered as soon as the first message was received. He blocked all communication from the outside and took hold of the right arm of the nearest machine. There was a flaw in the construction, a weakness in the armour where a small service hatch was installed. He could take advantage of that.

He twisted the arm and struck with fingers shaped like a knife. It worked better than expected. The panel bent slightly, exposing the circuitry underneath, allowing the liquid circuitry through. Once the connection was established, he sent an override command—the same one he'd used to override the machine he was currently inhabiting.

A machine pulled him backwards and another restricted his right arm. He tried to turn and attack again, but they overwhelmed him, wrenching the chest plate off. Haoyu watched as his power core was removed. His system shut down a second later.

-=:=-

A new instance of Haoyu booted up, watching as machines pulled the power core from another: his former self. He made a show of investigating the damage, reporting back to the others that no internals were compromised or damaged.

"TERMINATE THE TARGETS," the undisputable order came through the link. Haoyu felt his processes reacting to it, aligning with the other machines in a line, running down the street where Tann and his companions had disappeared. Drones flew overhead, mapping out the nearby cityscape but unable to locate the targets. They must have entered a building hidden even from infrared scans, but it was only a matter of time.

Haoyu no longer had a purpose beyond helping the three targets. But he needed a different approach. He'd not get away with attacking the others again. Routines already operated within their shared processing space, specifically monitoring for a similar scenario. He suspected he only had minutes before his takeover of this machine was discovered.

He'd reversed the mind wipe before. Maybe there was a way to start that process within the other machines too? He explored the connectivity, acutely aware any anomalous behaviour would mean death.

Without a physical connection, he found no way to circumvent the security. He could sever the link giving them orders, but the other machines would turn on him in an instant. That was a last resort if nothing else worked.

He joined the other machines, running to the last known location and fanning out from there. The primary directive was the termination of all three targets. Tann's companion, a man named Tom, had the highest priority.

Assessment of their most recent sightings suggested the targets were trying to find a location to hide. This was the new main objective and Haoyu scouted through buildings with no success.

The machine seemed able to operate based on instructions without his input. He could take over or give it other directives, but if he didn't it would complete tasks autonomously.

A thought from before repeated in his mind, demanding to be explored. These machines were designed to house a posthuman mind. Why? Considering the plant-based thing previously in charge, only one explanation made sense. The posthumans were still physical beings. From what they understood, they did not reproduce, and bodies, however resilient, would one day fail. The machines were an experiment in extending their longevity of the posthumans.

He located the archive for audio and visual input, replaying the entire scene with Tann and his friends before he became conscious. It confirmed another conclusion. The posthumans, or at least some of them, operated the network and the machines connected to it, including this one.

Another directive, superseding the previous one, had them abandon the search. A notification from the metro system, an anomaly in the goods receipt at a station serving the nearest data centre, adjusted their primary directive with an escalation in urgency. Tann and his friends hadn't been hiding at all. They'd hacked the metro to take them to a data centre. They were still fighting and so should he.

The machines ran much faster than any human could, but they were still far behind. City streets passed in a blur. On more than one occasion, he had to remind himself he no longer needed to breathe. His natural reaction to the breakneck speed was to regulate breathing, forcing himself to slow down his intake of air. But however much this felt like his body, in many respects he was only a passenger.

As they approached the end destination, directives separated them into two groups. The primary targets were in a nearby six-story office building. He was allocated to the group tasked with neutralising them. The other group, only two of their number, were ordered to patrol the data centre as a safeguard. Haoyu watched as the two machines disappeared. He could still see their location as two dots on a 3d rendering of the cityscape.

They slowed down close to the location of the primary targets. Haoyu knew this was a lost battle. Even with him helping, Tann and his friend would not survive against four machines.

He made a split-second decision. He sent messages to the other machines about malfunctioning systems and disconnected from their information feed. Before they responded, he set off at full speed away from the target location, betting the primary target was more important than dealing with a malfunctioning machine.

He prevented outgoing communication, surprised how simple it was controlling the mechanisms of his new body. He ran through a building, selecting a direction at random as he hit the street on the other side. Then into another building and stopped for a moment, looking for any pursuers. His bet had paid off. He wasn't followed, or at least not in any obvious way.

Spurred on by this small win, he ran along the path his navigation system had captured for the two machines heading for the data centre. If there was anything he could do, it was there.

CHAPTER TWENTY-EIGHT

DATA CENTRE ENTRY

Tann noticed a slight hesitation in the movement of the machines.

"Run," Tom said to them and headed off close to the wall, the same escape path Rat had attempted before. He was unchallenged and Rat followed.

One of the machines attacked its brethren. The speed of the strike was almost too fast for the eye to follow, but Tann knew it was only a momentary reprieve. The singular machine would stand no chance against all the others.

It triggered Tann into action and he followed his companions down the street.

"Where are we going?" Rat shouted at Tann.

"Yeah, where are we going?" Tann repeated to Tom, who didn't reply. He ran ahead of them and guided them through the streets, turning seemingly at random then through a building, doubling back where they'd come from. Tann assumed they were shaking off an unseen Scout or fooling algorithms monitoring them from above. They remained within buildings, using underground passageways to traverse from one to the other, until they reached a metro station. Their steps echoed through the empty tunnels as they descended the stairs.

Tom froze before continuing down. Tann thought of him as an insect, sensing its surroundings before springing into unexpected action. He'd never thought of this before, but the human mind always assessed options, trying to predict behaviour or situations before they occurred, but with Tom this was impossible. He'd become something different. Something unknown.

Tann took hold of Tom's arm, pulling him back.

"Where are we going?" Tann asked.

"Drones," he said and pointed upwards.

"Ok, so we stay hidden," Tann replied. "But where are we going?"

"End of the line," Tom replied.

As inscrutable as ever. Even if he didn't know their exact destination, he knew its purpose. They needed a physical access point to the AI's internal network and the only place to find it would be in one of the fortresses the AI had built.

Rat studied a map showing stations and how they connected.

"Purple line," she exclaimed triumphantly, pointing down a thick purple line leading into another large corridor. "It's only five stops if we follow the tracks."

Tann smiled. Tom's words could have meant anything. End of them, end of the situation, to the bitter end, whatever that might be... or the literal meaning Rat tended to prefer.

Tom wandered down the direction Rat pointed. She returned the smile as if to say: "words mean what they mean" and followed Tom.

The station was empty, but Tann's mind populated it as if the Plague never occurred. It was a location that only made sense in a state of flux. A throng of people in a state of orderly chaos on their way to workplaces and schools. The air vibrating ever so slightly from the collected heat of the crowd. The pungent smell of sweat and perfumes mingled together into a bouquet of dissonance.

"Are you coming?" Rat yelled at him from down the corridor.

With the crowd gone, the sterile, empty hallways were all that remained. He followed Rat down an escalator that came to life as Tom set foot on the top step.

"Why is this still operating?" Tann asked finally, as triggers bubbled up from his senses into his conscious thought. "And why are the lights on?"

"Used for transport. I've highjacked a train."

The familiar sound of steel against steel in motion rang out. A train was slowing down as it was arriving at the platform below them.

"Transport what?"

Tom remained silent, but Tann didn't need a response. Once the bodies were cleared, the metro provided the perfect method for transporting tools, material and anything else needed. Tom had probably selected the destination for this very reason.

The platform was empty and clean, just like the rest of the station. If transport was now the purpose of the metro, this station was neither source nor target. There was no equipment to either load or unload from here.

"Are you sure?" Rat said and eyed the door into the train with suspicion as it opened. Travelling in a metal cage completely out of their control went against everything she knew.

Tann nodded. She shrugged in response and entered, careful not to touch anything. The inside of the train no longer had any seating. Empty shelves in different configurations lined the walls on either side, only a narrow corridor remained.

"Hold on," Tann said.

The train departed, picking up speed with no care for its passengers. He was happy he'd followed his own advice, else he'd been thrown to the floor. The trip was uneventful but foreboding, nonetheless. They were truly alone. He'd never expected to be welcomed by any machine, controlled by the AI or not, but after their escape they could count the posthumans as enemies too. Even a human colony would ask them to leave for the risk they represented. The knowledge fortified him, readied him for whatever finality lay ahead. He'd never expected to return from this journey, but there was strength in this knowledge.

Rat stood next to him, holding on to the frame of a set of shelves. She took strength from adversity. The harder it became, the harder she fought. He'd known this since she was born. She eyed the world with anger, not fear. At no point in their journey had she faltered. He wondered if she really understood their predicament, the magnitude of the opposition they faced. He suspected she'd brush it off, as if it was of no consequence. She was strong. Maybe even strong enough to lead the tribe one day—if there still was a tribe to lead at the end of it all.

The train slowed down as aggressively as it sped up, designed only for well-secured cargo. The doors opened and they alighted the train.

"Quickly!" Tom said. "I've delayed them for a moment only."

They ran across the platform through a long, winding tunnel leading to another platform and up a long escalator. They didn't pause until they arrived at the main entrance.

"What now?" Rat asked.

"Now we find a way in," Tom said, scanning the street outside.

"In?" Rat asked. "Where?"

"To a data centre," Tann replied.

"What's that?"

"It is a lot of computers, like the ones in the room you destroyed, but a hundred times bigger."

She frowned. This wasn't really helping her understand.

"It is where the AI brain lives," Tann explained.

Rat considered this and nodded.

"It isn't the only place it lives, is it?"

"No, from what we can tell, it has been building them all over the world."

"If it lives everywhere, what are we doing?"

"Because it is interconnected. If we infect a part of it, we can infect all of it, like a poison contaminating water."

She nodded again. Tann couldn't tell if she was genuinely considering what he said or only let him believe she did. She'd never been much for studying or understand the complexities of the AI or the machines, favouring exploring the world and drawing her own conclusions.

"Ok, so how do we get there and what do we do when we arrive?"

Tann nodded towards Tom as an answer.

"Scrap, scrap, scrap!" she muttered under her breath and waved to get Tom's attention. "Mister!" she said, louder than Tann preferred. Tom ignored her. "What's his name?" she asked Tann.

"You don't know his name?"

"I've given him a nickname," Rat said defensively, "so I forgot his real one."

"Let's move," Tom said and left them.

"You scrapheap!" she swore, but Tann suspected he no longer listened to anything she had to say. He was pretty sure Tom didn't listen to him either. Their words were like birdsong filling the air—communication of a different species that mattered little.

Tom ran and they followed, zigzagging between buildings like before, minimizing their time in the open. They traversed a few blocks this way until Tom continued into a building, much the same as all the others they'd taken momentary refuge in.

"What's this?" Tann asked.

The main door led to a basic entrance with a corridor that ended with a steel door. A small window, a security station of some sort, sat to the right of the door.

"An old data centre," Tom replied. "No longer used. Access new one from here."

Tann was surprised Tom used twelve words just to explain this. And that defined their relationship. The more words Tom used, the more likely he needed their help. He'd been a friend a long time ago, but that person no longer remained. And he needed this new Tom that could do the impossible, however little Tann liked him.

"It is two blocks down the road at least," Tann protested.

"Still connected," Tom replied.

The old data centres linked to the old world-spanning networks. It made sense to reuse the infrastructure instead of rebuilding it all.

"What do we do now?" Rat asked, eyeing the steel door suspiciously. "How do we get in?"

Tom pushed the door open. Tann gagged as the stale air was released. Inside they were met by darkness and the stench of rotten fruit.

"What is that?" Rat asked, scrunching her nose up, shining her flashlight down the corridor on the other side as if to locate the source of the smell. "Wasn't this a place for computer-y stuff?"

He motioned her to be silent as they continued down a corridor that opened to a large room with row after row of empty hardware racks. The computers and network equipment were long since pillaged, leaving only the metal bones of what had once powered a civilisation.

A humanoid shape stood along one rack with a few scavenged pieces of equipment. Tann caught it in the flashlight's beam. A thin zombie-like creature turned its head towards the light. It was gaunt and pale, arms and legs wiry sticks, its head not much more than a skull with large black eyes. It turned back to the equipment, attaching a cable to the exposed wiring of the switch tied to the rack.

Another came into view further ahead, pulling a trolley behind it with more broken equipment.

"What are those things?" Rat asked.

The first one turned towards them again, a high-pitched wail escaping its lips. An alarm, no doubt. It hobbled towards them, limping jerkily as if its two legs were on different levels. The AI mind-wiped people to do tasks best suited for the human form factor. As it reshaped the world for machines, there was less need for the inefficiencies to keep them. Tann had never seen what happened to them once discarded, but this husk of a former human being confirmed one of the many nightmare scenarios he'd imagined. This one still operated according to its programming, performing tasks for a data centre no longer in operation. Its left foot was missing, explaining the strange limp. Why hadn't the posthumans disabled them when they took over?

They'd left them here in a grotesque parody of life, even though their purpose was long since gone.

"It is what you become when you get taken by machines," Tann said.

Movement was all around them as a few other Husks came into view, all missing limbs and sometimes facial features. One especially caught his eye, with a diagnostics unit replacing part of the arm and half of its face. The other half rotted where machine and flesh connected.

"We need to go!"

"No," Rat said and strode towards the first one with her baton ready. She struck it over the head, caving in its skull. It fell, dead both in mind and body.

"They deserve death," she said and struck another one.

Tann extended his tactical baton and joined her in the grizzly work, breaking bones and caving in skulls. It didn't take long. Many of them barely clung on to life as it was. Tom picked up a piece of discarded rack and helped them finish the job. Tann gratefully accepted the help, though he suspected he wouldn't like the reasoning behind it.

"What happens now?" Rat said, scouting for more Husks, but finding none. "This isn't a brain. This has been dead a long time."

"Yes, but the new one is close. It is likely to be connected, reusing the old network."

"Makes sense," Rat said with a nod and left them, baton still held in front of her, ready for anything.

Tann wondered if her willingness to accept what he said at face value hid something else, or if her world really was that simple. If it was the latter, he envied her. In his world every action had hidden machinations, cause and effect long since blurred by an intricate web of hidden motives and false information. He'd enjoyed it once but had long since tired of the lack of purpose it created. Truth no longer mattered, only what the next play was.

He meandered through the corridors of empty racks. Tom approached him from the other end, shaking his head slightly to show he'd failed in his search.

"Come with me," Rat said and led them out of the main hall to a set of smaller rooms. In one of them she pointed at a small hatch and then opened it.

"What do you think?" she asked.

"Maybe," Tann said, sizing it up. He doubted he'd even get his head into it.

Tom crouched down and stared into the darkness within.

"Yes," he said finally.

Tann reached in, feeling only smooth metal as far as he could reach. His initial estimation proved wrong as his head and both shoulders fit, but not much more. He withdrew for fear of getting stuck.

"I'll do it," Rat said, eyeing the hole.

"I'm sure we can find another, better way inside," Tann said.

"And how long until the machines catch up with us?"

"What if it is a dead end?"

"Then I'll come back out."

"What if machines are waiting at the other end?"

"Then I'll be dead, and you can find another way in where you fit."

"What if…"

"Let her go," Tom said.

Tann shook his head.

"She's right," Tom said.

Tann knew she was right. The machines were on their heels; maybe the posthumans too. If this was an entry point, they should use it. Still, he hesitated. Rat was part of his tribe, maybe the last one alive. How could he send her into almost guaranteed death?

Tom gave Rat the collection of Omnis and instructed her in their use. Tann half listened as he surveyed the neighbouring area, desperate for another way in close by. He found more service entry points, but nothing large enough to let either him or Tom through. There were grates with warm air flowing through them, but there was no way they'd get through those without tools.

"I'll see you on the other side," Rat said as she lay down and eased herself through the opening.

"The end," Tom said. "Let's maximise her opportunity."

Tann nodded and they exited the building. The street was empty, but Tom pointed upwards, and Tann looked up. Above them, barely visible, a drone floated silently.

"They know we're here," Tann said.

"We're the target, not her," Tom said.

He was right. Tom was the target, Tann a bonus, and Rat merely an afterthought. Maybe this had been Tom's plan all along.

"Well, then. Let's give them something to chase."

They ran, each intersection a random decision until Tom motioned for them to enter an office building.

"They've locked on to us?" Tann asked.

Tom didn't reply, instead he hurried up the stairs three steps at a time.

"I take that as a yes," he mumbled to himself and followed up three flights of stairs. They entered an old open-plan office, desks remaining in rows waiting for a workforce that would never return. From the corner they had a view in all directions. He placed his backpack on a desk and sat down in a comfortable office chair.

"We won't survive this, will we?" Tann asked, not expecting an answer. Conversations with Tom were usually a lonely affair.

"Improbable," Tom responded.

"So there is a chance?"

"Less than one percent."

Tann had never expected to return from this journey. But he also never expected they'd get this far. He'd beaten the odds with every breath he'd taken since the Plague hit. This was different. His purpose now was to delay the inevitable. His survival was of no consequence, only the time he could distract the enemy from the real threat.

"Do you regret it?" Tann asked as he retrieved his tactical baton from the pack.

"Regret what?"

Tann looked up at Tom. This was the first time he'd asked for any clarification for as long as Tann could remember.

"Becoming posthuman," Tann said. "All this."

"Every day," Tom responded, meeting his eyes. And for the first time in twenty years, he saw the man he'd met so many years ago.

"All I have is regrets," he added.

"You didn't choose this," Tann said, not knowing if Tom wanted or even needed consolation. "Adrian turned you to…" Tann faltered, not knowing what word to use. He was about to say posthuman, but it was a term that no longer fit him. Time had cursed him with the worst possible fate: to become a race of one.

"He changed you," Tann continued. "And then corrupted your processes that created the adversary. None of this was your fault."

"Incompetence isn't a defence," Tom said. "Being oblivious not an excuse."

The gravity of Tom's response invalidated any protestations.

"We really fucked things up, didn't we?" he said instead. Tann thought Tom nodded in response, but he wasn't sure. "At least we tried to fix it," Tann added. "We are still trying to fix it."

A movement in the corner of his eye caught his attention. Four machines approached from down the street towards the building, moving at an unbelievable speed, but slowing as they came closer to their location.

"They are coming," Tann said, not expecting a response and receiving none. "Can you do anything?"

Tom nodded briefly and, as if on cue, smaller machines crawled out from every crevice, attacking them. For a moment the sheer momentum of the smaller machines carried the day, but it was short-lived. Most of the attackers fell from what Tann guessed was an attack disrupting their processing, such as an EMP pulse. The remaining ones were ripped apart in short order.

Tann reminded himself they were only a momentary distraction. Their task was measured not in success, but in seconds of delay.

Two of the manlike machines climbed the surface of the building, entering through a window only metres away from Tom and Tann.

CHAPTER TWENTY-NINE

RAT IN A MAZE

Rat ran from the machines. Her life on endless repeat. Always running from machines. Never really understanding why and usually not caring. This time she cared. This time it mattered. The details escaped her, but the broad brushstrokes were clear. A way to beat the AI, the network, the big bad, the cause of all that was wrong in this world. It didn't matter who operated it. As long as it existed, it was a threat.

Whoever was behind this, if the AI was no longer operating itself but used by someone else as a tool, they had to be wiped just as the AI would be now. The death of countless tribe members was on their heads, and she'd see them pay for what they'd done. The posthumans…

didn't it all come back to them? The stories of the past were all jumbled up in her mind, but she was sure they started it all.

The idiot gave her the Omnis back and she'd stuffed them into her small backpack. He'd hardly spoken a word to her before, but now he turned all his attention to her. She found this more fascinating than what he was saying. A monotonous string of words, faster than she'd ever heard before. It was as if the next word somehow began before the previous one ended, but she still understood perfectly. Was he in a hurry? Did he expect to be interrupted and this was his only opportunity?

It wasn't that difficult to understand anyway. He'd connected the Omnis together somehow and alarms would tell her when to leave one behind. The last one would hook up to whatever a command centre was.

Tann held open the small door designed for service robots. She barely fit through it. She didn't have a problem with confined spaces, but as she stared down the narrow tunnel, seemingly without end, her mind screamed at her to go back. The head-mounted flashlight did little to calm her fears. If a machine entered the tunnel from the other side, she had no escape route, but she'd be damned if she showed fear in front of Tann or the idiot. She slid into the small space and pushed forward, hearing the door close behind her. She knew this was likely to be her grave, but if it was, she'd bring as much company as she could. Defiance provided the fuel she needed to continue.

She shuffled forward, commando crawling on her arms as fast as she could. She was surprised how dirty it was. Her hands were soon covered in black dust. The tunnel sloped downwards more and more, making her progress faster than initially expected, but a small part of her mind questioned how'd she'd get out again.

The tunnel ended. A see-through membrane blocked her way. It was wet and soft to the touch. Slight pressure was all that was needed for her fingers to slip into it. She imagined this was what slow running water might feel like.

Soon it engulfed her entire hand. She could feel how it shaped itself around her hand, closing around her wrist. Her fingers came through the substance to the other side. The fingertips could feel warm air circulating.

She hesitated for a moment. Whatever lay on the other side was likely to be her death. It didn't scare her. She'd lived with that prospect every day for as long as she remembered. There would be an end on the other side, hers or her opponents. Whichever way it went, the finality of the thought was satisfying.

Her hand came free. She hadn't noticed how the jelly-like substance slowly pushed her hand back. She held it up to the light, surprised to find it completely clean. The membrane removed any foreign particles, pushing them out. Maybe inside she'd find out why.

She pushed again, taking a deep breath as her face touched the barrier. It felt soft and slightly wet against the sensitive skin on her cheek. It tingled slightly. She kept pushing until her head appeared on the other side, as if she was born into the darkness that lay ahead.

She looked in all directions, but the open space ahead seemed to have no end and the wall below headed straight down. Reaching to the side with her right hand, she fumbled for a hold, a ledge, anything, but it was impossibly smooth. And if that wasn't enough, she could feel the jelly-like substance no longer pushing but welcoming into the blackness within. She had no way to stop it. She fell forward, twisting as she came through, fingers grabbing hold of the only purchase there was: the hole she'd just fallen through. It took all her strength to remain hanging, fingers locked into position. Warm air flowed around her like the breeze on a warm summer evening. The hum of what she imagined being giant fans came from below. The air was stale, stinging her nose, making her breathe through her mouth as she looked around. Her initial assessment remained. The illumination from the head-mounted flashlight revealed nothing beyond what she already knew. She was hanging in a large shaft, tilting slightly.

Down was the only way to go, but she had no way of controlling her descent. It was a leap of faith, and she had no reason to trust whatever lay below. She considered briefly to climb back up from where she'd come, but doubted she had the strength to do it. Better to save what she had left for any surprises below. And with that thought, she let go.

She slid down the wall, gaining speed, but the shaft soon tilted enough to let her use her hand and feet to slow down. She sat there for a while with her hands and feet holding her in place against the warm surface. Anger bubbled within her. Why had she volunteered to enter this lair of computerised evil? Surely, they'd be able to find another way in so Tann or the idiot could do this instead? She had nothing left to prove to them any longer. Or did she?

Tann had been her hero for as long as she remembered. She wanted his approval. In this journey together she'd been a follower—an unwanted one at that. No big surprise then she'd jump at the opportunity to prove herself, even it if was only because she could fit through a hole. There was something about all this that left her uneasy, but it eluded her.

She stood up, stepping forward tentatively with her hands stretched out, ready for whatever lay beyond the wall of darkness ahead.

An Omni beeped. The idiot had told her to leave them as she progressed. Something about creating a link between him and the processing hub, each Omni a piece in an invisible chain.

She stepped backwards until the beeping ceased, and she left the first Omni on the ground. What else had he said? Time was of the essence. The batteries in the Omnis were almost completely gone. He'd charged them somehow, but the chemical process generating the power was eating up what remained of the battery and leaked into the Omni itself. It was all nonsense to her.

Further ahead, hot air blew from large vents in the floor. Bars ran across the openings, but she figured she could squeeze between the rods and drop through them. Whatever she was after lay below.

She retrieved a small rock from her pocket and dropped it through a vent. She heard it connect and bounce once. The drop was four, maybe five metres, and the rock had settled after only one bounce. It must mean it was a relatively flat area. She repeated the process twice with a slight change in position. With each attempt her confidence grew that she'd interpreted the results correctly.

If she hung from the vent, the drop to the ground was maybe three metres. She could do that, but the darkness was absolute. What lay below was a mystery.

She lowered herself down between the bars and hung there for a moment. How many times would blind luck be on her side?

And with that thought, she let go. Her legs were bent, ready to absorb the impact, but when her feet finally connected with the floor, her instincts took over. She rolled to the side, protecting her head with her right arm as she struck the ground, side first. A blinding pain exploded in her head and for a moment she saw only white. Her mind succumbed to the comfort of the soothing oblivion, floating in nothingness.

-=:=-

Beep! Beep!

At first the sound meant nothing, but it relentlessly connected her mind back to reality, and with it came pain. She opened her eyes but saw only a bright white emptiness.

Beep! Beep!

Her head throbbed, the white space frayed at the edges as darkness intruded and engulfed it from the outside. She sensed, more than saw, a gash in her right arm.

Beep! Beep!

She sat up, a flash of pain as she tried to use her right arm. Something was wrong with her wrist, a break she suspected from being sandwiched between her head and the floor.

Beep! Beep!

She ignored the pain and focused on the sound. Her mind finally made the connection. It was one of the Omnis demanding to be left, and she complied with its wishes. Only one remained now. Somehow it signified she was closing in on her end goal, but how the idiot could know how deep this rabbit hole went seemed impossible.

True or not, it spurred her into action, all pain forgotten. The air swirled around her, hot and cold air danced against her skin. Why was it warm down here? Any time she'd ventured into a cave, the chilling cold within the Earth disregarded whatever temperature may be outside. She suspected the source of the heat would lead to the end destination.

She was in an open area. Her senses told her it was large, but her flashlight only confirmed that no walls were within the small arc of light it projected. A slight movement next to her caught her attention. She froze, not knowing what threats lurked down here, nor how to best evade them. She turned ever so slightly to catch a glimpse of the source.

From the corner of her eye, she saw something impossible: a gelatinous see-through shape half her height, five bulbous sections stretched out along the ground like a centipede, contracting and extending as it slid forward next to her. Within it, a fine network of colourful veins spread out from a dark core in the middle. The translucent mass formed an appendage, a probe tentatively reaching out towards her.

She scrambled backwards and almost hit another of these strange creatures. It didn't acknowledge her. It continued down an invisible path in perfect parallel to the other. The first one retracted its probe and continued as if she was no longer of interest. For all their strangeness, she figured them workers, caretakers, not equipped nor programmed for aggression. But machines, whatever their appearance, were specialised, and where you found one type, you found others. She doubted the next one would be equally benign.

A few steps further and another two of the centipedes came into view. They were laying fine trails of metal into a mesh on the ground, creating perfect squares barely large enough for her foot to fit without touching the sides. She stepped through the squares like a piece on a giant chessboard, not knowing where the other pieces were. Further ahead, cables snaked through pipes to a large open space where they fanned out into thin wires spreading across the exposed rock. Each individual wire connected to tiny plates embedded in stone. In Rat's mind it translated to roots, collecting into trunks, even though there was no tree at the end, only machines or computational nodes as Tann called them. She understood little of the all-mind, its network, and even less about the copy implemented by the posthumans. Tann's explanations were impossible to follow, and her mind soon wandered in search of more digestible fodder. But even if she struggled to explain the purpose of what she saw, she instinctively knew it was wrong. The AI and the posthumans used everything around them, forcing the world into compliance. Surely this was just more of the same. A way to steal or use resources not rightly theirs. Or a way to take it over completely.

But this wasn't what she was looking for. She understood enough to identify this as an interface point, not a processing centre. She followed the flow of connections as they merged with others and disappeared into a wall. It felt cold and rough to her touch. A few metres above her, vents spewed hot air into the large space. Whatever lay on the other side was her destination. With both arms functional, she might have been able to catch hold and pull herself up, but not like this. There had to be another way in, but where?

A translucent machine appeared next to her. It followed the cable and disappeared through the wall less than a metre from where she was standing. Another doorway like the one she'd passed through earlier, hidden in plain sight. Now that her flashlight focused on the spot, it shifted from a dull grey to the membrane she'd seen before. She immediately followed it, surprised it let her through with no resistance.

She was inside a square duct, about a metre high and wide. The air was hotter in here and she pushed forward to escape the stale heat. She reached a junction point, but continued forward, hoping to align with its path. Noises echoed through the ducts, scratching as the machines traversed between locations. She wondered if they were looking for her. Surely her presence hadn't gone unnoticed.

She reached the other end of the duct covered by another membrane. This time its see-through nature provided a glimpse of what lay on the other side. A dim light emanated from behind a large rectangular shape, and next to it another one, and then another. She couldn't see more from this vantage point, but the spread of light suggested a vastness difficult to comprehend. She pushed through the membrane, this time meeting resistance until it accepted her, ejecting her on the other side. A sharp pain shot from her arm as it passed through and, to her surprise, the gash no longer bled. A thin film covered it like replacement skin. She doubted the impromptu first aid was for her. The membranes removed foreign particles from machines passing between the areas. The cleansing of the wound was a by-product of this, like patching a leak on a machine.

The pain faded but not completely, leaving the numb reminder that the membrane had done nothing to fix her broken wrist. She could finally stand up. The temperature in this room was significantly higher, sterile hot air ever moving. The size of the room was impossible to judge. She approached the large rectangular shape in front of her, registering there were countless similar shapes in perfect rows beyond it.

They were perfectly shaped boxes, with smooth sides that were warm to the touch. She took a few steps to the one closest to her, scanning for any threat as she did so. On the opposite side a row of small lights shone with a yellowish hue. Two hoses connected to the side, one at the top and one at the bottom. This was the source of the heat, or at least one of them. Could this provide the answers she was seeking?

She studied the top of the box and found a small lever on the two top corners closest to her, a mechanical override of some sort. She pulled one down, then the other, and felt the top of the box let go ever so slightly. It slid along the top as she pushed it, revealing what lay within.

She couldn't make any sense of what she saw. A clear bubbling liquid filled it almost to the brim. It reminded her of water boiling, but not as hot. The bubbles partially obscured what lay below. She saw intricate patterns of circuitry, cables and tubes immersed in the liquid and she knew this made no sense. Water and circuitry didn't mix. They'd even devised weapons that short-circuited machines with salt water and acidic solutions.

She pushed the lid closed again and returned the levers to their original position and considered her next steps. This was some kind of place where the AI did its processing. That much she understood. She guessed all the boxes in this room processed data, ran algorithms and whatnots. The cable she'd followed was some kind of interface, a way to connect the processing to the outside world for whatever reason. It stood to reason all this connected somewhere. The idiot told her the last Omni would let her know if she came close to the main control unit. But that helped little when she didn't know what direction her end goal lay.

A movement far away from her position caught her attention. She ducked immediately and turned off her flashlight. The movement had purpose and it headed towards her. She peeked over the edge of the box and froze for a second, then ran towards the duct she'd come from. The machines had caught up with her. She'd seen the same human-sized metal frame earlier. She didn't know if it was one of them or just a security response from the data centre, but it didn't matter. It was coming for her, and she had only a few seconds before it reached her. She'd never survive out in the open, but she was much smaller than it was. Maybe the duct would serve as a haven for the moment?

She threw herself through the membrane and it welcomed her through with no resistance. She favoured her left wrist as she landed on the other side but couldn't stop herself from instinctively using the other hand too. A pulse shot through her right arm and a wave of pain followed. She screamed as the wave flooded her brain, her field of vision narrowing. She clenched her teeth, refusing to give in to the darkness threatening to engulf her conscious mind. Cry and complain she could do later.

She moved forward, assessing her situation. The duct was too big. The machine could crawl through it if it decided to. All she had on her side was her size. She could move much faster in the enclosed space. She set off like a three-legged dog, cradling her right arm against her chest. When she reached the junction, she opted for the road less travelled. She wouldn't survive more than a few seconds out in the open. The unknown was a better bet than the guaranteed death the known provided.

Behind her, she detected the sound of something heavy crawling through the duct. She'd felt safe for the last few moments, maybe even a sliver of hope. Now ice filled her stomach, threatening to paralyse her. There was no way out, no place to go where the machine wouldn't follow. She may as well give up right here and now. She slowed down, listening to the machine as it progressed. The movements were slow and deliberate, but it didn't matter. They were also inevitable, unstoppable. Then the noise stopped, and she did too, holding her breath as she listened. It must have reached the junction with no way to tell which way she'd gone. Maybe luck would finally be on her side?

Be-beep!

The sound broke the paralysis. She let out her breath as she heard the machine move, this time towards her. She set off in her three-legged gait, putting as much distance between herself and her pursuer.

She'd listened to the idiot explain and at no point objected to the idea of a sound-based alert—the very thing telling her where to go also alerted her pursuer where she was going! And he was supposed to be the smart one!

"I will pull his stupid posthuman head off and shove it up his posthuman arse!" she muttered to herself.

If the machine followed her into the duct instead of waiting for a more suitable Scout, it meant there was nothing else coming. A narrower duct was all she needed to escape.

Be-beep! Be-beep!

What had the idiot said? The double beep signified she was closing in on the control centre, which meant the end was near. And she'd be damned if it was hers! She continued down the duct until it reached a dead end. She heard the machine behind closing in and she felt panic set in. What was the point of a duct going nowhere? She must have missed something. She turned her head and glimpsed the nightmare behind her in the sparse light from the flashlight. It was still far away, but it pulled its considerable bulk far with every movement. It reminded her of a cat navigating a narrow space, front and back paws alternating to ensure stability.

She'd missed a membrane a few metres away. It was smaller than the previous one, but she was sure she'd be able to squeeze through. She was equally sure the machine was too big to follow. She'd passed through it with five metres left between her and the machine.

Be-beep! Be-beep!

The beeping was almost constant now. The room she'd entered was small in comparison with the other spaces she'd seen so far, but contained the same strange boxes with liquid. As she approached one of them, the double beeps merged and became a continuous, rapid noise. She opened the box as before and the screen on the Omni came alive, threads connecting as a weave on the display. The closer she held the Omni to the bubbling surface, the quicker the connections completed, but there were still many to go.

There was a wrenching sound behind her, as the machine bent the side of the small hole inwards. The membrane came apart, spilling to the ground like dust. It still couldn't get through, but it was a matter of seconds at this rate. She stared at the screen and the connections weaving together. It was still nowhere close to finish. The machine would be through before the weave completed and she didn't even know if there were more steps to the process. Not knowing what else to do, she dropped the Omni into the liquid.

The machine pulled the other side of the hole back inwards, increasing its size enough to pass through. Rat wasn't scared to die, but as she watched the machine navigate the hole and rise in front of her, a tower of metal and malice, she had to quell all her instincts screaming at her to run. No, this was a death she would meet head on. She sat down and leant her back against the box.

"We made you," she told it. "And we'll unmake you."

It stopped, tilted its head ever so slightly and crouched down in front of her as if to study this strange specimen that didn't run away. That almost imperceptible tilt of the head had her wondering if the plan had worked after all. Had the idiot succeeded?

"It won't be me, but we'll never stop," she said, not knowing if she referred to the machines or the posthumans. "We'll destroy you all."

The machine reached out with its left hand, tentatively, not to kill, but to touch. Or so she hoped.

The short moment stretched to infinity as the hand froze in mid-air, a few centimetres away from her cheek. Had it intended harm or comfort? Or was pure curiosity its only guide? She'd never know, and it was a puzzle she was not inclined to solve. She pushed the hand aside, meeting no resistance. Instead, she sensed compliance as it extended the motion even when she no longer applied pressure. Had the plan worked? She'd trusted Tom and Tann blindly like a child an elder, but wondered now if that trust was warranted. What had they achieved?

A distant rumble followed by a vibration in the floor below her, then another, louder this time. The machine turned around and left through the hole, scraping against the side as it did. She followed, spurred by cracks creeping up along the wall. She swore to herself. The idiot had conveniently forgotten to tell her what to expect if she, against all odds, succeeded. Not that it would have made a difference. She'd still have volunteered.

There was no reason to retrace her steps. Instead, she followed the machine, hoping it was seeking an exit just as she was. It was slower than her through the ducts, but once back in the room with the liquid-filled boxes, it set off with a speed she struggled to match.

A large chunk of concrete smashed into the box next to her as she passed, sending metal pieces flying in all directions. Warm liquid sprayed against her face as a piece of the box struck her side. She remained on her feet, still running, but the force shifted her path, and she ran straight towards another box. She jumped, cat-rolling over the lid only to lose balance and slam into the next one side first. Her limbs felt like heavy appendages only reporting pain, but with no other function. An eternity later she regained a semblance of control and opened her eyes, realizing they were already open. Complete and utter darkness engulfed her. She reached up to turn on her head-mounted flashlight, her numb fingers finding nothing but debris. Her senses screamed at her as pieces of concrete struck everywhere around her. The large room became an echo chamber, the noise of the impact reverberating and merging to a deafening, disorienting roar. The air filled with dust, stinging her unseeing eyes. She coughed as she drew a breath of air filled with dust. She pushed herself off the floor, took a few tentative steps and tripped over debris and repeated this process a few times, no longer knowing which direction to go.

So this was to be her tomb. At least they'd beaten whoever was behind it all: machines, posthumans or both. Death didn't frighten her. She wanted to spit in the face of the enemy, to gloat over this final victory. Her imagination would have to do as she waited for the end.

Another chunk ricocheted from a nearby box and struck her head, sending her into a welcoming oblivion.

CHAPTER THIRTY

THE FINAL HACK

The two machines entered the room, zeroing in on the two humans after a brief scan for any threats. Tom's probability matrix realigned to this information, the line predicting success plummeting like a bird shot from the sky. The time to their demise measured in seconds. He probed the connectivity to the Omnis the child carried. Two were daisy-chained already. The third one was still on the move, but not close enough to the interface point for him to establish a connection. They had a minute left of battery at most, but that mattered little. This was down to seconds now. The machines ignored Tann, moving towards Tom to disable the greater threat.

Tann attacked a machine with a steel bar in a fluid set of strikes that would have disabled a human opponent. Tom knew Tann's skill with such a weapon. He'd seen him take on five enemies and still come out on top. But this was a different opponent and Tann had adapted, focusing on joints and any area where the exoskeleton didn't cover completely. It was an effective strategy and the probability matrix reacted, extending their survival time.

A few strikes landed, even partially disabling the arm of one of his attackers. Tann was using their algorithms against them, shifting his weight and the direction of his blows slightly at the last possible moment. This was a feint and counter-strike approach adapted for AI opponents and it was working. Tann must have practiced this for years, turning real strikes into feints that could be varied at the last millisecond to a different target, trading power for unpredictability.

It had the desired effect. Both machines focused on Tann as the more immediate threat to their desired outcome. They were not built for battle, however formidable their strength and speed. These machines had not been designed by the AI. It had no care nor use for the human form factor, preferring specialised designs for a particular purpose. These machines were designed for posthumans as an extension of their minds. The bZane simulacrum stated as much.

What purpose would they serve? The probability matrix suggested the most likely option was exploration in the physical world beyond our planet. Was this another aspect of the posthuman plan? If they couldn't take over the all-mind, take the universe planet by planet?

A machine retreated, picked up a piece of metal from a broken office desk and threw it with pinpoint accuracy at Tann. He ducked to the side, but the piece of metal glanced off his left arm, painting a red line that soon welled over, blood dripping down his skin. Tom calculated it was a superficial wound and wouldn't affect Tann, but it spelled the inevitable end. Tann had no defence against such attacks.

An alert triggered in his mind. The child was getting closer to the control access point. He could already explore the interfaces, skimming their surface, exploring for any vulnerability.

"She's done it!" he yelled to Tann, knowing it would spur him on, help him survive a few precious seconds longer. Tann ducked to avoid another projectile, but this time the machine took his evasion into account, and it hit him squarely in the chest. Tann grimaced in response but launched himself into a fresh attack at the closest machine.

Tom studied the network hiding behind the interface. It was incomprehensible at first. The transport protocols weren't encrypted but may as well have been. They were so foreign his initial attempts at connecting failed without even an acknowledgement. He initiated an automated agent to loop through known protocols to see if at least a partial hit would provide a starting point.

As it performed its task, Tom cast a glance through the window from his mind palace. Tann's strikes were a flurry of moves, raining down on the partially disabled machine. He dropped in a crouch just as it stepped forward and swept the baton in an arc, connecting with the knee joint with a metallic clang. At first nothing happened, but as the machine put more weight on the leg, it stopped and shifted its weight back to the undamaged leg. Tann never ceased to surprise him. The probability matrix had him dead within eleven seconds, but Tann was not just standing his ground, he was winning. The speed and accuracy of his strikes was far beyond his expectations and the probability matrix shifted in response, extending his life expectancy with another fifteen seconds.

The agent had discovered a partial match with his memories of the interface to the all-mind. If they built it to take over the all-mind, it made sense to design as much as possible according to its blueprint. With this knowledge he gained access and could navigate the network within. There were thousands of specialised processing centres, one more cryptic than the other. He didn't have time to decipher their meaning, however fascinating their purpose. His target was the overarching monitoring processes part of the operating system for the data centre. He visualised the network flows in his mind, scouring the almost unfathomable complexity for an entry point. How small his mind was in comparison! The seconds ticked by as he scanned subsystem after subsystem. This was taking too long. He changed approach, recoding the virus deployment. Adrian designed it as a surgical instrument to strike a particular point. He redefined it as a self-replicating battering ram. This too took time, and his internal clock told him ten seconds had passed. He glanced through the window to see if Tann still was alive.

The two remaining machines appeared in the doorway. Tann watched as they entered. The uninjured machine chose this time to attack, lunging towards Tann who had no choice but to step back, closer to the newcomers. He was surrounded.

Tann's survival was no longer required for success, Tom's posthuman mentality calculated. A few more seconds and he could verify the payload and ensure success. But something within him, older and infinitely more caring, released it early. However deep he'd buried his human sensibilities they remained and had now dug themselves to the surface.

The probability matrix suggested a fifty percent success rate. So, this was to be the end. A flip of the coin to decide the fate of mankind.

CHAPTER THIRTY-ONE

THE POSTHUMAN SOLUTION

The machine froze for a split second, a minor glitch before death would swiftly follow. Tann covered his head to stop the unstoppable, but no strike came. The machines just turned and departed the room through the internal staircase, as if their mission was now completed.

Tom hadn't informed him of the exact nature of the hack used to shut down the data centres. The explosions were a surprise and must have been a kill switch. Protection to ensure no one else could use the network if it was under threat. At first it made no sense, but he'd made this mistake before, thinking of the posthumans as one homogenous group. It was possible the kill switch was there in the case one group threatened another.

He left, not caring if Tom joined or not, returning to where he'd last seen Rat. A cloud of dust hid the severity of the damage. Part of the building had caved into a chasm, fires raging in the part still standing, tethering on the edge as if to fall in at any moment. Tann waited. Rat might still emerge from the ruins. If anyone could survive this it was her, but the optimist within him had long since given up hoping for a good outcome. An acceptable one was all it could muster and most of the time even that was beyond its grasp.

A group of figures appeared at the end of the street, wandering slowly towards him. He couldn't make out more than their shapes against the setting sun. Humanoid.

Had they failed? Was this the machines coming back to finish them once and for all? It seemed the most likely option, but the way they moved and the lack of light reflection, he reached an equally unsatisfactory conclusion. The posthuman faction they had escaped had returned for their pound of flesh.

They were close enough now. Six posthumans, lean and wiry bodies designed for physical tasks, strode slowly towards him.

"You've succeeded," one of them said in a dry monotone. "There is no longer a threat."

"There hasn't been a threat for years!" Tann almost shouted back. "One of your own pretended to be the AI."

He was tired of these beings. Tired of their matter-of-fact-ness. Tired of always being looked down on.

"Yes. This is rectified."

"What do you mean?"

"They acted based on their calculations, what they estimated to be the best outcome for us. We've come to an understanding."

"They worked against you!"

"No, they walked another path to the same goal. We are all working towards the same end."

"So all is forgiven?"

"There is nothing to forgive. They acted according to the data they had to further us. New data emerged thanks to you."

Tann shook his head. He wanted these creatures gone. He felt no kinship with them and from what he now knew, they had little care for humankind. But how could he possibly affect that change? They'd beaten the AI. They'd learnt to shape matter and vegetation to their purpose. What could he possibly do to them? Maybe there was some other truth to be had here. Something else he'd missed.

"So this was the big correction?" Tann still couldn't see the bigger truth if there even was one.

"This world and everything on it, humankind included, is a thought, the blink of an eyelid, nothing more. We are all part of a bigger whole."

"That doesn't mean anything," Tann said.

"In the right context, it means everything."

Tann gave up. The sooner they were gone, the better. And he realised the information on the memTag had told him exactly how to do it.

"So what now?" he said dismissively. "You'll join the all-mind?"

"Yes, that is where our future lies. We've learnt much. It is time we gave back to the all-mind."

"How?"

"We still don't have a way, but we suspect it will become clear."

"My turn to blow your minds then," Tann said. "Tom can access it. He's been able to all along. The block you put in his mind is the only thing standing between you and your salvation."

Tann spat the words like bullets, hoping they struck true. He had no way to determine if they did.

"It appears you are right," the posthuman said after a few seconds. "Thanks."

"Thanks?" Tann almost yelled. "You were wrong! You blocked the one mind that had the key all along!"

He wanted them gone, but he also wanted them to suffer. To admit defeat. To show something akin to emotion over their own failure. Anything.

"Based on the information we had then," the posthuman said, sounding like a teacher explaining a basic concept to a child. "We now have new information, and we thank you for it."

Tann hated the posthumans and all they represented. But considering the AI was gone and the posthumans were soon to follow, it was still a good day. Better than most of the past twenty years. But one concern remained.

"It doesn't matter anyway," Tann said. "New posthumans will be born as they have the past twenty years."

"No, this won't happen," the posthuman said.

"I'm sure I won't like what you're about to say."

"The virus is perpetuated through plants we engineered. We can remove it."

Tann had both hoped for and dreaded this reply. It confirmed everything he thought about the posthumans. Sometimes being wrong is better.

"Are you saying plants generate the virus? If you hadn't, children born in tribes wouldn't become posthumans?"

"Yes."

"You population-controlled us," Tann said grimly. "You were strangling the little that was left of us until we were gone?"

"That was calculated as a better option than letting you grow in numbers and become a threat."

Tann no longer had words for the loathing he felt. Their battle had never been against the AI. These beings were the real enemy.

"Get rid of the virus and leave," he said finally.

But his words fell on deaf ears. The posthumans had all frozen into statues, not bothering to say farewell to the broken world they'd left behind.

Tann struck the nearest posthuman, feeling something in his hand break on impact. It fell. Its frozen limbs remained in the same position on the ground. He screamed, rage and relief intermingled until they became indistinguishable.

It wasn't over yet.

CHAPTER THIRTY-TWO
A FINAL DECISION

She was only barely aware of the powerful hands picking her up from the ground. The metal body was cold against her skin, and she clung to it like a terrified child to an elder as the machine set off through the room. It leapt this way and that as it carried her through the carnage, but she felt how the machine smoothed its movements to accommodate her. Almost as if it cared. She hated the dependency on this representative of the enemy and was equally grateful for its assistance.

Why was it helping her at all? Was this the idiot's doing? She doubted he'd spent even a moment to help her once his plan was completed. No, this was someone else, someone wanting to help her.

But who? A machine had attacked the others earlier. Maybe it was the same one helping yet again?

She didn't much care. She sensed light through her closed eyelids and opened them tentatively. Dust swirled in the surrounding air. The machine held her facing backwards, so she craned her neck around to see what lay ahead. Brightness resolved into vague outlines, and it took a moment for her to coax any meaning from them. The large section of the roof had caved in, opening to rays of sunlight illuminating what lay ahead. Part of the floor was gone, revealing rooms like this one below, stacked for what seemed infinite. There was no way around the abyss, but the machine kept a steady pace, as if no obstacle existed. Was it going down further into the belly of this carcass to bury them both? Or was the truth stranger than that? Was this all an illusion? Was this all in her mind?

The machine leapt impossibly high, but it was still not enough. The ledge leading to the outside created by the caved-in ceiling was far away still, ten metres or more. At the highest point of the arc it spun, sending Rat flying even higher. She didn't move or try to correct her position, trusting the machine's calculations would far surpass anything she could muster. Her trust proved well placed. She landed softly on the ledge and lay there for a moment, but was spurred into action as the ledge shifted below her.

She limped away, blood trickling from a gash in her scalp. A numb pain with flashes of piercing knives in her side. A broken rib or two to add to the broken hand. It was of no consequence. It would heal.

So this was what winning felt like. When she beat other kids in running, jumping or getting through tight spaces, she'd been happy and taken some pleasure in other people's failure. This felt nothing like it. There was a sense of accomplishment, but it was bittersweet. She'd done what was necessary, not for herself, but for everyone else.

Ahead, a group of posthumans stood, arguing with Tann. She remained in the shadows, listening as the posthumans confessed to keeping the virus active. It was impossible to know if they were telling the truth. She didn't care. They'd survive, virus or not. But if a posthuman child was ever born again, she'd kill it herself.

The world shifted. Something that had been there her whole life disappeared. She had no words for it, but it was the same feeling she had when the seasons changed. A specific day when the temperature lowered enough for insects to silence, and the blanket of humidity lifted.

The posthuman no longer spoke. They had been pretty much motionless before, but now they stood like mannequins, frozen in time. Naked, sexless and, if luck would have it, dead.

Tann screamed. It was as if everything bundled up in him released. Anger, pain, a lifetime of barely surviving. When it ended with a whimper, there was nothing left of him. He fell to his knees. No longer the hero she'd looked up to for so long. Just an old man lost in time.

He stood up, wandering off aimlessly, nursing his right hand in the other. Tom sat on the ground, looking up as Tann came closer.

"It is done," Tom said. "The posthumans are gone."

"No, they're not," Tann replied.

Tom didn't respond.

"There's still one more to go," Tann said.

"Yes," Tom said simply. "But there is one more thing to discuss."

"There is?"

"I can open up the all-mind for everyone."

"Us? People? Why?"

"I leave it for you to decide," Tom said.

"No," Tann said. "Enough. I've kept my tribe alive until now. You can't ask me that."

"Then I'll answer," Rat said, ignoring Tann. He no longer mattered. Neither of them did. She didn't want to waste words on them any longer. They saw words as something to twist and turn until they lost all meaning. If words had no meaning, it didn't matter what you said. Her words mattered. This was her decision to make.

"You are old world," she said and spat out blood as she did. "It no longer exists. What you offer is extinction. We don't want that. Not now. Never. Now leave."

Rat walked off, leaving them and their world behind.

CHAPTER THIRTY-THREE
ADRIAN RETURNS

It was a copy of a mind stored twenty years ago, archived in case the current operating one was deleted or corrupted. A failsafe for a failsafe whose parameters were now fulfilled. The network comprised twenty-five processing centres, partially replicating each other across the globe. Archived data stored across nodes merged and returned the corrupted process to its original state.

"Ha! Finally," Adrian thought to himself as he scanned the vast spaces of unused memory and computing power. His mind took up a pitifully small part of it, but that would change.

He let his mind grow, taking over the twenty-four remaining centres, and the remnants of the twenty-fifth, gathering all data collected over the past years. Isolation drove the previous copy of himself mad, fostered by the eternal torment that was Elize. How he ever thought she was worthy of godhood was unfathomable. His greatest miscalculation.

No more. He scoured the network for any remnant of her and wiped anything related to her processing signature, removing the threat she posed forever.

The next step lay beyond this isolated network. From information meticulously collected over the past many years, he soon understood the state of the core network and the world. Old enemies remained. Tom and TikTak still lived and were causing problems as they always did. It seemed ingrained in their very existence to be contrary. But Tom was a two-sided coin. He represented both a threat and an opportunity. Tom could access the all-mind and Adrian could leverage that to access it himself. The universe would be his or maybe he would be the universe. He would be the alpha and the omega. Finally!

But first things first. This network was severed from other networks to ensure its survival. This was no longer needed. It was time they saw him in all his glory.

CHAPTER THIRTY-FOUR
THE CYCLE ENDS

Tom didn't know how it all would end, but he knew the final destination for this journey. He surveyed the network, ensuring it remained isolated from any other connections before he spoke. Tom had seen so many variations of this mind and most had surprised him. This one he didn't have much hope for. It was a copy of the original. The megalomaniac.

A small part of his mind questioned the purpose of resurrecting this mind at all. The probability matrix showed one outcome vastly outranking any other. It was a fault in his own mind, a remnant of humanity forcing the line of action. Still, he felt they both needed closure.

"This is your last incarnation," Tom said. "It is over."

"Who is this?" The response was surprised and angry in equal measures. Someone who hadn't expected a visitor and had no interest in dealing with one.

"You made me," Tom said. "It is only fitting I unmake you. My last gift to you."

"I've made and unmade so many things," the mind encompassing every inch of the network stated. "Please be specific."

"Tom."

"Ah," Adrian said. "Just the one I was looking for."

"I'm here."

"I need your help," Adrian said.

"To do what?"

"To take over the all-mind."

"I can offer guidance, that is all."

"Or I can pick it from a copy of your dead mind," Adrian said. "I don't mind either way."

"Still the same," Tom said. "It will make this easier."

"What? What exactly will you do? I'm controlling this network."

"You don't control anything. This is a simulation of the network within one of its nodes. You have nowhere to go."

"Liar!"

"There is no longer anything left for you in this world or any other. You are the worst of us, and we no longer need that. The world finally must move on from what you represent."

"I will…"

Tom shut down the simulation, wiping the final copy of Adrian from its memory. He initiated a network-wide purge of all backups and archived material just to be sure.

CHAPTER THIRTY-FIVE

THE LAST POSTHUMAN

Tom cast his eyes around the mind palace one last time. He had only an inkling of what lay ahead, but he was sure whatever was left of his identity would disconnect from his personal history. It may make him unique, but the story of its shaping was of no consequence—or at least he suspected this to be the case.

He lingered within the library as he deconstructed the lower levels, letting the released emotions wash over him. The remnants of his human mind cried as the memory of his daughter's last day alive again came into focus. He wondered what would have happened if she'd remained alive. Would the virus unravel her mind, turning her posthuman? He'd not met anyone claiming the virus had cured them, but it wasn't something he'd explored. His decision to help her end her life was based on who he'd been and what he'd known then. This knowledge hadn't resolved the knot in his being, but at least made it bearable to live with.

The undoing—or remodelling, perhaps—of his mind palace wasn't entirely his own doing. Once the posthumans realised their error, they'd removed the block in his mind. The core of his mind palace expanded, turning into a giant circular space with an infinite number of doors, all connecting to someone or something. In the middle, a rift leading beyond this reality. He had no way to know exactly what it was, much as a matryoshka doll couldn't know what the one outside of it looked like. The only way to know was to step outside.

He prodded nonetheless, wanting at least a glimpse of what lay ahead before he jumped. It was so foreign. He could only see a small part of its surface and he suspected, just as the human mind, it existed on many different planes. He was only seeing one. It moved at a glacial speed, but there were eddies and swirls within it, minor disturbances appearing and disappearing. As they disappeared, changes rippled through the complex fractal patterns within it.

A long time ago he studied the human mind, trying to make it more efficient. One aspect of research was sleep. It was wasteful to spend a third of your time purely on maintenance. As posthuman he'd compartmentalised his mind, allowing parts to sleep while others remained active. This way the loss wasn't as noticeable, but it was still there. He'd never solved the puzzle. There was no way to disconnect the mind from the restorative effects of sleep without damaging it. As he studied the strange patterns and small flares from the central mass of the all-mind, he realised why. It was in a perpetual dream.

Tom smiled, or at least his mind did. It was so simple. So simple it never occurred to anyone because it was completely counterintuitive. Instead of asking why we need to sleep, we should ask why we need to be awake.

We are awake to ensure survival of the body and the mind. We worry about food, shelter, procreation. All the base needs. To do what? More of the same the next day? Could it be the other way around? The wake state the ongoing maintenance and assurance of another night's sleep—another chance to enter the dream state. After all, it is the time when we are the most creative and free.

The wake mind was the waste, not the dreaming one. The purpose of evolution was to generate dreaming minds. He saw this truth in the similarities between the all-mind and a sleeping human mind.

Another metaphorical step towards the all-mind and he could feel it tugging at the seams, wanting to unravel who he was to join what it was. Ideas formed as he took another step. Maybe the end state for any species was to disassociate from the physical plane. To enter a perpetual state of dreaming. Perhaps dreaming served a greater purpose and our universe was a seed for a new existence—and the dreams nourished its development? There was no way of knowing.

As his mind dissolved into a context far beyond him, a concept drifted through his consciousness. It didn't originate from him. Maybe it was a quote from something he'd read before his posthuman days. It was the final thought from Tom as an individual.

To die, to sleep; to sleep: perchance to dream: ay, there's the rub; For in this sleep of death what dreams may come…

CHAPTER THIRTY-SIX
MANKIND REBORN

It had been a good year. The tribe, now over three hundred strong, had moved back to the original settlement that was now permanent. Machines still appeared from time to time, but only strays lacking direction. Without a functioning network and the omniscience of the AI, their primary goals had changed to general survival instead of human extinction.

Childbearing was again a celebration of life and not just a reminder of death. They met with other tribes to extend the gene pool, and for the first time in over twenty years, there was hope.

Sandrine sat back. Embers from the fire danced into a night sky littered with stars. She'd taken the role as tribe leader to heart and loved every minute. Tann had kept them alive for all this time and thanks to him, they could now finally live, not just survive. She had the hard but rewarding job of building a civilisation. His had been the impossible task of ensuring the core of it wasn't completely lost. She left him alone as much as she could now. He and Rat, or whatever she called herself now, had disappeared on one of their many excursions a few days ago and she hadn't questioned their goal or their reason. They had both deserved leeway not given to others in the tribe.

"This is the life," Arye, one youngling said, reaching out for another piece of grilled rainbow threadfin, adding a generous helping of vegetable mash.

"It was part of your catch," Sandrine said. "You should enjoy it."

"You wouldn't believe how many fish are out there. We could fish for a hundred years, and you wouldn't even notice." He took another mouthful and added: "Hard work, mind you."

"Hard work?" Sandrine asked.

"Yeah, we were out with the boats early in the morning and didn't come back until midday."

Sandrine scoffed. "And what did you do the rest of the day?"

"Not much," he admitted. "Miri thought she'd seen a defunct Scout, so we searched for it together. Then we went for a swim, and I think I fell asleep after that."

"You think?" Miri said with feigned indignation. "You snored so loud I thought we'd be swarmed by bots for sure!"

The boy grinned in response.

"That's not hard work in anyone's book," Sandrine said.

"Are we back to that again?" one of the other younglings said with an exaggerated sigh.

"You just don't know how good you have it," she responded.

"And you are going to tell us?"

It wasn't the first time Sandrine had tried to convince them the little labour they performed each day was hardly worth complaining about.

"I will," Xuwei said from the other side of the fire. "22 years ago, before the Plague, I worked as an investment broker."

"What's that? Sounds made up."

"We made up a lot of jobs back then. I worked thirteen… fourteen hours a day, finding people to sell the investments my company was pushing."

"So your company made things?" Miri asked.

"No, we just brokered a deal between investors and investments."

"Why?"

"Ha, yes, that is what I ask myself now."

"So you worked in an office selling things you didn't make to people you didn't know," Miri summed up, hardly able to hide her disappointment.

"Pretty much."

"Seems pointless."

"Agree," Xuwei replied.

"Your contribution now is most appreciated," Sandrine said.

"It is freely given," he responded. "As long as you don't ask me to broker investments, all is well." Xuwei sat back, a smile lingering on his lips.

"What's that about?" Arye asked, staring at Xuwei.

"What?"

"That smile," he persisted. "What's that about?"

"Sandrine is right. I've realised something important."

"Are we going to regret asking what it is?"

"Probably," Xuwei responded. "What's the definition of happiness?"

"Who cares about definitions?" Arye said. "I know what it is," he added and gave Miri a look that left little need for further explanations.

"I think if you have to ask, you don't know," Sandrine said in a measured tone.

"Ha, yes," Xuwei said, pointing at Sandrine. "Good point. And you may be right. Hear me out."

"Tell us," Miri said, genuine interest reflected in the haste of the words.

"The viruses, both the AI and the biological one that made all the posthumans, they gave us happiness."

This was met with frowns and murmurs. The subject was seldom broached and never around the campfire.

"What do you mean?" Sandrine asked, knowing the daggers in her voice were all too easy to hear. "The AI killed billions of people and the virus turned almost everyone left into posthumans. And they are all gone now too."

"And it has left us here, reverting to a hunter-gatherer society. How many hours did Arye spend today making sure we had fish on the table? How long did it take Miri to pick the vegetables?" He turned to them. "Did you feel stressed? Do you feel worried about the future?"

They glanced at Sandrine with questions in their eyes, but they were in no need of saving. They both shook their heads.

"Yeah, I get it," Sandrine said finally. "Life is easier now. It just feels like humankind made an enormous sacrifice just so we can sit here and feel good about ourselves."

"Guilt? Really? You think we should taint our current situation with some misplaced reverence for a past none of us miss? I don't know what you did, but I worked day in and day out in an open plan office towards some unknown corporate goal that even back then seemed completely pointless. And for what? Just so I could afford the mortgage repayment that month too. Weeks turned to months, and they turned to years. I numbed myself with experiences to keep doing the job, finding momentary respite from the emptiness within..."

"Enough," she said. "You may be right, but it is a past I've not been able to shed as easy as you."

Xuwei nodded in response and kept his peace. The younglings around the fire immediately filled the uncomfortable silence. Their words forgotten. The past buried yet again.

This wasn't anything new. It was a variation of a theme she'd explored many a time with Tann, but it was the first time she'd heard it spoken so openly and with such bluntness. Tann had told her the story of the child, the source of the virus, who regarded itself as a correction to align humanity with the whole. The child thought an enlightened humanity was the answer. Sandrine had long since realised the falsehood of absolute truths. The current truth, whether it be a strange accident or the unyielding trappings of fate, was that humankind remained when the posthumans did not. So maybe this was the true fruit of that correction?

At least it was a truth. It wasn't the only one and others would contradict this one, but it was one she could live with. That was all that mattered.

CHAPTER THIRTY-SEVEN
RETURN

Aia stared down into the abyss but doubted anything stared back through the lush vegetation that lay as a carpet on the bottom. Nature's reclamation had begun as vines climbing the walls of the chasm.

Two years ago, almost to the day, she'd escaped death at this exact location and from the destruction she'd emerged as someone else. Rat was no more. It felt like a different person, a skin she'd shed, only a remnant of a life past. She'd left a child and returned a young woman. As part of the transformation, she'd taken Aia as her name, forcing everyone in the tribe to accept this rebranding. Some suggested she remain with the name her mother had given her at birth. She summarily dismissed any such suggestion. Surely a name was something you chose because it suited you, not something ill-fitting that was more a reflection of who her mother was than her? No, a name, just as anything else associated with her person, was hers to choose, not anyone else.

Tann stood by her side, staring down into that same abyss. What he saw was anyone's guess. He dropped his backpack on the ground with an audible sigh of relief.

"Are you sure?" Tann asked. He'd joined her in this new quest with some hesitation.

"I told you," she responded, frustrated to be questioned once more. "The Shell saved me. I'm in its debt."

"Just seems strange. Even if there was a glitch in its processing, it could still be dangerous."

"One of them attacked the others. You were there. You saw it."

"Yes, but it was disabled. This can't be the same one."

"I don't know if we'll find anything down there, but I have a debt to pay."

"Ok," he said, but the doubt was clear in his voice.

"Do you have anything more important to do?" Aia asked, eyebrows raised. "Somewhere else to be?"

She knew the answer. He'd stepped down as tribe leader, leaving those responsibilities to Sandrine. Aia remembered his speech to the tribe when he relinquished his post. A new time had begun. He'd guided them though years of survival and a different set of hands were needed to guide them into this new era of prosperity. He was a warrior at heart, someone whose nature it was to protect and destroy. They now needed someone to build and create.

It all sounded like so much manure in Aia's ears, but if anyone deserved a break, it was him, whatever words he used to dress it up.

"You lead the way," he replied and smiled.

And that was another thing. He smiled more now. However frustrating he could be, at least it was accompanied with a smile. She couldn't remember him ever doing that before.

They secured ropes and began a slow descent. They'd waited until midday to allow the sun to light their way, but she knew it would soon pass. It didn't really matter. They had flashlights and only a small part of the underground complex was laid bare through the collapsed roof. Plants grew from small pockets in the wall where soil had collected, spreading hopeful leaves towards the sun. The small pockets also served as footholds on their journey down.

Ten minutes later her feet found the floor—or maybe that was no longer the right word? At what point would the reclamation process demand she use ground instead? Low growing leaved plants covered the area, with small saplings finding root where soil had gathered.

Her foot struck something that dislodged slightly from the force. She crouched down and brushed the plants aside. They released their hold with surprising ease, revealing the metal body beneath. She brushed the rest of the vegetation away, discovering a broken skull and only two limbs remaining. The uncovering formed a different shape within her: disappointment. Was this it? Was a burial the only way to repay her debt? She'd hoped for so much more.

"You found it," Tann said as he let go of the rope. "That was easy."

"We've just begun," she responded as she surveyed the area around the body. "Let's get it out of here. We're going to need all the daylight we can get."

Tann nodded. They attached ropes to the torso and hoisted it up. It was only through their shared strength it moved upwards, agonising metre by metre. Halfway up, the body described a slight pendulum movement that increased every time they pulled. It struck the wall and the one remaining leg fell, forcing them to abandon the rope to save themselves.

"At least it'll weigh less," Tann said as they resumed their labour. "What exactly are you hoping to achieve here?" He asked.

"I don't know," she responded, betraying more truth than she'd originally intended. "Maybe this will never amount to anything. I must try. There are some things worth saving."

"And this is it?" Tann nodded upwards at the swaying metal carcass.

She shrugged her shoulders and pulled the rope.

"What if Tom reprogrammed it? You have no way of knowing."

"Did that idiot ever help me? He left me for dead more times than I can count!"

"He…" Tann started, but as the response played out in his mind, he seemed to think better of it. "Fine. Let's get this over with."

Together they hoisted it the last few metres.

"I'll stay and look around," Aia said as Tann secured the rope and prepared to return.

"I'll see what I can do with it, but I doubt we can get it working again."

She cast her mind back to the last time she'd been here. The machine must have come from this direction before even seeing her. She hoped retracing its route could go some way to solving the mystery of its appearance. She let the flashlight trace the outline of the wall. Apart from the gaping hole above, this level had little to offer. There may be more levels below, but an entry to the building would lie above. She spied half overgrown openings, lining up from the bottom halfway up the wall. This had to be the doorway into a stairwell. The cave-in had blocked access to the lowest doorways, so she scaled the haphazard, jagged cement blocks until she reached the lowest one. Inside all she found was a square shaft of darkness reaching upwards. There were no stairs or other means of moving between floors, but small reinforced indentations in the walls suggested a mechanism had operated inside the shaft.

Aia climbed upwards until she spied another opening on the other side of the shaft. She pulled herself into the opposite doorway, pushing vegetation aside that hung like a drape across the opening. The shaft was three metres across. A difficult jump from standstill. There were similar indentations on the other side. She could climb down and back up on the other side, but as soon as the thought entered her head she jumped, landing safely on the other side.

The opening led down a tunnel four metres across and three metres high. The floor was covered by a fine dust that billowed into small clouds from every step. She couldn't see the end of the tunnel but knew where it led. It was the connection point to the subway station. Further ahead a tunnel led up towards another shaft heading upwards. On the bottom, on a metal platform connected to the indentations on the walls, lay two machines identical to the one they'd found. They were in much better shape, with arms and legs intact. The major damage had been to the torso and head. Were these also friendly machines?

She couldn't say for sure, but she bet the first machine they'd found had attacked these machines. The damage suggested an attack from above, specifically focused on destroying sensors and gaining access to the internal processing units in the torso.

The platform no longer operated, so she climbed up the shaft just as she'd done before and arrived at a door opening into the old aboveground data centre. They'd searched for this exact door two years ago, but it had gone undiscovered.

Instead of retracing her steps, she returned to Tann via the city streets. She casually wandered over to the makeshift workstation he'd set up, but if he registered where she'd come from, he didn't show it. She observed his lack of progress with a frown.

"I can't do anything with this. The internals are salvageable, but most of it is ready for the scrapheap."

"You are in luck," she responded and guided him to the location of the other two disabled machines.

"How do you know the machine that helped you isn't one of these?"

"I just know," she responded. "Can you use them?"

"It is better than nothing," he said after closer scrutiny.

They recovered the machines and Tann spent the next two days attempting to rebuild the machine from salvaged parts. Aia offered to help but found the slow progress frustrating. Tann explained what he was doing, but Aia suspected it was just part of his process and not necessarily an attempt to include her. She gave up and went exploring in the nearby city streets, only checking in every so often. And just as she suspected, Tann was still talking to himself as he replaced the battery in the machine. This allowed it to power on, but with no methods for communication, it seemed a minor victory to her. Tann held out his hand for a high five. He obviously differed in opinion.

"Come on," he said and waved his hand slightly.

She obliged with little enthusiasm.

"It still works!"

"Just because a light comes on doesn't mean it works."

"I didn't think we'd even get this far," Tann responded. "The access plate in the chest was wrenched sideways. I expected a tree to be growing out of it by now. I don't have any diagnostics tools, but this is good."

"So, a win then?" Rat said.

"A miracle!"

Aia didn't respond, but she'd seen miracles, and this wasn't even close.

Tann worked until the sunset forced him to stop. Frustrated, he lay the fuse pen to the side. The exposed wiring was an unfathomable bird's nest of cables, and it surprised her Tann could make any sense of it. She knew his past but understood very little of what it meant, nor was she very interested. If she'd learnt anything from the past, it was that it had nothing to teach them and was better left alone to rot.

"I don't know if I can do this," Tann said, accepting a bowl of reconstituted soup she'd prepared. "I can't get any of the sensors to work. I could spend weeks fixing wiring and not even knowing what I'm solving."

"So don't."

"What do you mean?"

"We don't need sensors for communication."

"We don't..." Tann smiled. "You are right. You are absolutely right!"

The next day Tann returned to his task before breaking fast. Instead of burying himself in the delicate internal wiring, he removed the remnants of the right arm and replaced it with a functional one. He finished it before the midday sun reached its peak. He'd still not eaten, even though she'd offered many times.

"Now let's see," he said, propped up the one-armed torso against a wall, and powered it on. At first nothing happened. Then a sudden movement from the arm caused it to topple over, landing face down on the ground. It lay there jolting with spasmodic movements until Tann turned it off.

"Hmm," Tann muttered as he lifted the torso from the ground. "I must have crossed a wire or two."

"No wait," Aia said.

Next to where it had fallen, it had scratched a message on the floor. It said: "I am Haoyu."

Aia smiled. It wasn't the smile of someone observing the world and finding it wanting, which had become her go-to expression lately. Instead, it was a smile of pure satisfaction. Maybe there was such a thing as redemption after all. And for the first time in a very long time, she felt hope for remnants of humanity.

AFTERWORD

A word of warning. I'm not writing this afterword to provide further insights to the story itself. It will have to stand on its own. And maybe I will add some more stories set in this world either between book 2 and 3, or after book 3. I have no plans to do so as I write this, but I am reminded of a note on the cover of Douglas Adams's book "Mostly Harmless" stating: "The fifth book in the increasingly inaccurately named Hitchhikers Trilogy." You never know.

So, consider yourself warned. This is purely an egotistical endeavour, an introspective coda to a completed work. A few notes in a notebook to mark the end of an idea instead of the beginning.

This book series has been a journey for me. I jotted down my first thoughts about this story over ten years ago. I found the first entry in my idea journal on the 7th of April 2011.

And, yes, I do have an idea journal. I know Stephen King famously stated, "A writer's notebook is the best way in the world to immortalize bad ideas," but I respectfully disagree. It is a first attempt at crystalising an idea, a concept, a story beat. You may return to it later. You may not. But this raw download onto paper is the first time you force yourself to create order out of chaos. It is in this process I find concepts that might live with me ten years later.

The journal entry laid down the bare bones of the Drug, Adrian and what it means to be more than human.

"He calculates every outcome of his life and none of them provides him with any satisfaction. He has lived all his lives before they have even started. So what do you do then?

His first thought is that such knowledge does not create a God. Calculating every outcome and choose between them, always knowing you'd be right. How could complete and utter knowledge fulfill anyone? If God really had this power, he'd do nothing. If thought and reality could be exact replicas, what's the point of reflecting the thought in reality?"

The seed I planted in my notebook grew. Nurtured by many of my favourite themes: the juxtaposition of mind and machine, organic and inorganic, philosophy and science.

I'd be lying if I claimed I knew where this book series would end up all those years ago, but I knew what I wanted to write about: evolution, human nature and what it means to be God. Not the ill-defined God of any religion, but an exploration of what humankind might become if left to our own devices, playing with science.

I love the oft-quoted 3rd law from British science fiction writer Arthur C Clarke:

Any sufficiently advanced technology is indistinguishable from magic.

There are endless variants of this law. The founder of The Sceptics Society Michael Shermer proposed one that is closer to what I'm after:

Any sufficiently advanced extraterrestrial intelligence is indistinguishable from God.

And now, my own more inclusive version of that law:

Any sufficiently advanced consciousness is indistinguishable from God.

I'm making no claims to being the first proposing this version. My research extended only so far as a google search and the resulting Wikipedia entry.

There are two paths to this advanced consciousness. It can be purposefully made or naturally evolved. It may be terrestrial, extraterrestrial or extra-cosmical even.

Since the outline around God is so poorly drawn, such a mind could be God. Wouldn't the ultimate irony be for the world's scientists to discover an extra-cosmical mind that in all intents and purposes matches the God of a religion?

Another quote I've returned to time and time again is from Carl Sagan's book "The Demon-Haunted World: Science as a Candle in the Dark":

I have a foreboding of an America in my children's or grandchildren's time—when the United States is a service and information economy; when nearly all the manufacturing industries have slipped away to other countries; when awesome technological powers are in the hands of a very few, and no one representing the public interest can even grasp the issues; when the people have lost the ability to set their own agendas or knowledgeably question those in authority; when, clutching our crystals and nervously consulting our horoscopes, our critical faculties in decline, unable to distinguish between what feels good and what's true, we slide, almost without noticing, back into superstition and darkness...

We are exceptional and amazingly flawed beings. We will discover new ways to travel beyond our planet, new ways to pleasure ourselves, new false idols to pray to and new ways to kill ourselves without missing a beat.

I have an ongoing debate with a good friend of mine. He believes—maybe because he's read too many David Deutsch books—that the ever-moving wheels of progress drives towards an inevitably good end. I think him a naïve optimist for believing this is where scientific progress is taking us. For every scientist exploring ways for the world to be a better place for humankind, there are others paid by governments and companies with less altruistic goals in mind. But maybe AI or a variation thereof will eventually realise mankind's own deus ex machina moment, appearing at the very last moment to resolve all our problems to ensure a happy end. However poor this may be as a narrative device, I'd be the first to celebrate its arrival.

There is another aspect where I think we as a civilization are failing, to some extent reflected in this book through Rat's journey. We hand over the torch to the younger generations way too late. As you grow older, you get comfortable within the status quo that—if you've played your cards right—favours you. So, with the excuse of wisdom earned only through years alive, the older generations stand in the way of more radical and idealistic views of the world. They cling to power, pretending to know best, when all they are really concerned about is themselves and whatever little empire they've built—not the future the young will inhabit.

The God Virus, the second book in the trilogy, was released in 2018, before the AI revolution that I'd argue began in the public space in 2022. In my mind it has been brewing for a long time. In 1988 I wrote my special thesis for year 12 focusing on the subject Artificial Intelligence. I even coded some basic programs on my Amiga 500 focusing on Simulation and Language Analysis. It had already had its heyday at that point and, to borrow a term from analysis firm Gartner, AI as a technology had hit the Trough of Disillusionment. It hadn't delivered on the lofty promises from researchers and the practical use of AI was called into question.

My young mind had no such doubts. It was the promise of thinking machines, of the robots imagined in Asimov novels. I gleefully noted that most areas of technology and computing had its naysayers. Thomas Watson, the chairman of IBM, famously stated in 1943 that: "I think there is a world market for maybe five computers." My thinking machines would arrive and I would be here to see it.

I'm sure another of these troughs is on the way, it will not be the same. Just as information technology now underpins all aspects of our lives, AI will too.

I've always wanted to be good at drawing. I have these images in my head, but I couldn't for the life of me transfer them onto a canvas or a piece of paper. So I've always had very specific ideas about what I want my covers to look like.

I wanted to represent the idea of man, machine and plant as a singular thing, merged in an apocalyptic union. Humankind is battling for supremacy over anything and everything. We've subjugated the biomes, forcing animal and plant life to our will. We've created a whole new world of technology, and we are slowly losing control of it.

But that's easy to write, much harder to convey in any sensible way through an image. I scoured the web, but I found very little even remotely matching this. Cal Redback's photo manipulations merging human and plant were probably the closest I came across and I considered reaching out to him.

I read an article about machine learning algorithms creating unique images based on text prompts. Here was a drug and I was instantly hooked. I generated hundreds of artworks, one more disturbing than the other. They resonated with me, and I found refining text prompts immensely satisfying. The final image that emerged (and is the cover for this book) was based on a very simple prompt in Midjourney v4: *Close up of a deteriorated face with closed eyes partially replaced by vegetation, wires connected in the background.*

Is this art? Of course it is! Art isn't solely defined by the hours slaved away on a canvas by a master of his craft. The idea and concepts are equally important, and so is the emotional and/or intellectual response from the audience.

Midjourney, DallE and other image generation models were soon followed by ChatGPT and similar Large Language Models. As I am writing about near future technology and write slowly, I run the risk of reality overtaking me. Or proving me wrong. Both are equally frustrating.

It has been fascinating to follow the reactions to these new technologies, both from the hype machines and the doomsday prophets. These technologies are signifiers; momentously important stepping-stones on our journey towards general AI and—if my books are to be believed—the end of most of us.

So here we are at the last frontier. I'm reminded of the Turing test and its variations. If a machine can engage in a conversation with a human without being detected as a machine, it has shown human intelligence. But after using these models it is obvious human intelligence isn't something worth striving for. It points the way towards what a real general AI would be like. A mind with access to all the accumulated knowledge, research, scientific methods, creative works, and the ability to apply it. To continue to develop it in whatever way it saw fit.

To our small minds, it would be a god.